DOWNSIZED

With Extreme Prejudice

David G. Hanrahan Esq.

Copyright All Rights Reserved January 1, 2016 by
David G. Hanrahan, Esq. Thank you for purchasing an
authorized addition of this book and for complying with
copyright laws by not re-producing, scanning, or distributing any
part of it in any form without permission.

Downsized is a work of fiction. Names, characters, businesses,
places, events and incidents are either the products of the
authors imagination or used in a ficticious manner. Any
resemblance to actual persons, living or dead, or actual events is
purely coincidental.

ISBN: 1541004698
ISBN 13: 9781541004696

<u>Boston, February 14.</u>
Sam Johnston looked anxiously at the imposing antique grandfather clock on the far wall of his spacious office. The recessed fluorescent ceiling lights were dark. An elegant bronze swan lamp with an emerald green shade decorated the front left corner of his desk and provided the only source of illumination. Sam leaned forward and slowly tilted the lampshade. He watched the light race across the room and climb the wall until he could see the polished brass numerals on the Tiffany clock face. It was precisely five minutes before nine p.m., plus or minus a second or two. Time was only one of the many details of life over which he had to have complete control.

David G. Hanrahan Esq.

Sam lowered the lampshade and licked his lips nervously. He quickly spread a stack of financial documents until they covered the entire desk. When he was finished, he looked down at his handiwork and smiled a contented smile. Tonight, his job as chief financial officer of Amalgamated Worldwide Enterprises was not on his mind. Sex. Rough, tempestuous and uninhibited sex consumed the brain of AWE's financial wizard.

It started only a month ago. Since then, Ailida, the 23-year old cleaning woman from Cartegena, Colombia, had given up vacuuming the rug in Sam's office on Monday nights. Instead, she and Sam spent those evenings rolling around on the rug, locked in a sexual embrace. For a man who seldom had sex -- and when he did, it was usually in the dark and under the covers with the same woman for 30 years -- those stolen moments with Ailida were exhilarating.

He pushed his chair back to better visualize his fantasy. Uncharacteristically, he laughed at the thought of it. How many times had he been accused by his auditors of screwing around with the numbers? Well, tonight he would screw around on them. His wild thoughts were interrupted by the slight *crrrank* of the large bronze door handle turning, disengaging the latch. The door opened slowly. The big clock began tolling the hour of nine in deep, resonant tones. Sam smiled. "Right on time," he said softly to himself. "Good girl." He removed his brightly polished shoes and placed them neatly, side by side, under the desk. "Ailida, *mi amor*. Don't keep me waiting," Sam whispered as he stood up and stepped out of his trousers quickly.

No response.

The visitor turned briefly, plugged a vacuum cleaner into a nearby outlet, flicked on the switch and locked the door. This had been Ailida's clever idea. The constant whine of the motor created the illusion of work in progress. It was also great camouflage for the variety of wild sounds that accompanied their lovemaking. Sam stared into the shadows, trying to glimpse Ailida's beautiful face. As his guest came closer to the light, he realized she was wearing a veil that covered head, shoulders and arms.

"What the devil are you wearing?" he asked.

No response.

"Linda mia, you have a surprise for me tonight? Good! *Bueno, Bueno!*"

Sam walked around to the front of the desk and quickly removed his underwear. "What game do we play tonight?"

No response.

Sam could not wait to lift the veil revealing Ailida's beautiful Latina face. He anticipated the surge of sexual power as he caressed her firm young breasts. The veiled figure approached steadily toward Sam, now half-naked and not hiding his enthusiasm for what was about to happen. "Ailida, Ailida, *te amo*. Come to me, come to me," Sam implored as he unbuttoned his shirt in a clumsy rush and let it fall to the floor. He could no longer wait to feel the pleasure of her warm, moist lips on his body. "Take the veil off, linda m*ia*. I can't stand it anymore!"

The last gong from the old clock sounded as Sam lifted the fabric hiding his sexual prize. He glimpsed a flash of steel briefly as a knife blade was thrust upward into his chest. The first three-and-a-half inches of a six-inch hunting knife had already entered his heart when Sam realized what was happening. He grabbed at the hand holding the knife and, reflexively, rose up on his toes. His body trembled briefly and, with a long, hissing gasp, Sam fell back across the desk upon which he had for so long guided the financial destiny of his giant company. Death came quickly, but not quickly enough. The killer watched without emotion, savoring the last moments of Sam's torment as he writhed in agony, gurgled briefly, and died. It was precisely one minute past nine, give or take a second or two.

Downsized

It was ten past midnight when Gus Warner, Boston's young, ambitious district attorney, received the message in his Harbor Towers apartment. "Jesus Christ," Warner yelled into the phone when he finished listening to the macabre details of Sam Johnston's murder. "I'll be right over."

Warner lived several blocks away from AWE's headquarters. In fact, he could see the sparkling blue glass building from his window on the twenty-second floor of Boston's Harbor Towers condominium complex. The elevator ride to the lobby was longer than his drive to the murder scene. As he turned onto Congress Street, the AWE headquarters building entrance was ablaze with flashing red lights and blocked by a tangle of fire hoses. A full complement of fire apparatus was on the scene: Two ladders, three engines and a command post. Fire and murder were frequent companions, but why tonight, Warner wondered, and why at Amalgamated headquarters? Helmeted firemen with oxygen tanks strapped to their backs scurried in and out of the building. Warner ducked into the lobby before the press corps noticed him. Fire Captain Jim Donahue stepped out of an elevator and spotted Warner. "Going up?" he asked.

"What the hell's going on?"

"You'll see," said Donahue. "You won't believe your eyes."

David G. Hanrahan Esq.

The door started to close. "What floor?" yelled Warner.

"Ten..."

The door slid shut noiselessly. Warner paced back and forth in the richly-decorated box, his progress recorded by the blinking lights above the door. Finally, the door opened and Warner stepped out onto a soggy wall-to-wall carpet in Johnston's luxurious reception area. He sloshed his way toward a huge mahogany door. The sign attached to it read,"Samuel Johnston, CFO." As Warner entered Johnston's office, he was not ready for the bizarre scene that greeted him. Except for executive length socks, Johnston was naked and draped over a large desk. The handle of a knife was clearly visible, grotesquely protruding from his chest. Blood mixed with water spilled over the desk and dripped down onto a cream-colored rug. Warner did not look long at Johnston's face. No matter how many murders he had investigated, he could not tolerate looking at the frozen, lifeless stare of a corpse.

"Gus! Glad you're here," said Boston police Lieutenant Patrick Walsh. He was a big man and looked every bit an Irishman. Walsh was an eighteen year man and unhappy that he did not make captain. He enjoyed working with Warner, but was disappointed when a young state trooper joined the team, frequently upstaging him. His relationship with state police Detective Sergeant John Neiberg was rather tenuous, but Neiberg did show Walsh the respect his experience and position deserved.

"Well, what do we know?" Warner asked, hoping for a reassuring answer.

Walsh shrugged. "Not much. Cleaning woman's the only person who had any contact with the killer." Walsh paused, pointing at Johnston, "Except for him," he added with a smile at his macabre joke.

"Can she I.D. the killer?"

"No. Someone came up from behind and threw a bag over her head. Next thing she knew, she woke up in a utility closet, bound and gagged." Walsh gestured to the young man in the far corner of the room, neatly dressed in slacks, white shirt, tie and sport jacket. "Neiberg interviewed her. She don't speak English that well, but Officer Ramirez did the honors."

Neiberg was deep in thought. Walsh had to call out to him twice. Neiberg finally looked up from a large black and white composition notebook and saw Warner staring at him. Neiberg pointed at the book. "Can't stand those little notepads," he explained. "Have to squeeze things in." He held it up for emphasis. "This is much better."

"OK," Warner said. "What's in it so far?"

"Not much," Neiberg answered with a shrug. "What we know for sure is that Johnston was sitting at his desk, started taking off his clothes and willingly met his killer in front of the desk. So he either knew his assailant, or thought he knew him." Neiberg paused, looked over at the vacuum cleaner and added, "or maybe he thought he knew her."

Warner smiled. He liked Neiberg's style. Humble but smart, with great deductive instincts. "I'm glad you use a big notebook. Continue."

"Well, this Ailida, Ailida Estrella, the cleaning lady, she was about to clean Johnston's office." Neiberg paused to check his notebook. "She vacuumed the rug every Monday night, usually around 9 p.m." Neiberg took long squishy steps over to the vacuum cleaner. He pointed. "Look, it's plugged in. But Ailida said she didn't bring it into the office."

"Right, so the killer did. Why is that so important?" Walsh asked impatiently.

"Our assassin knew exactly when Ailida was going to vacuum Johnston's office. Apparently, so did Johnston." Neiberg sloshed over to the desk, trying not to step in Johnston's blood. He pointed to the cheesecloth lying near the dead man's feet. "That's how the perp got close enough to stick him. I figure we're looking for someone not much taller than Ailida. Johnston was no dummy. Hell, he went to Yale and then got himself a Harvard M.B.A. He would've noticed if his killer was bigger than Ailida."

"You telling us Johnston was doing a strip tease for Ailida when he got snuffed?" Walsh asked incredulously.

"Precisely. That's where the cheesecloth comes in. The killer must have had it covering his face." Neiberg paused before adding, "or her face."

"Waddaya know! Johnston was porking the cleaning lady!" Walsh laughed. "It all makes sense."

"So where do we go from here?" Warner asked.

"Dead end," Neiberg said, not hiding his disappointment. "Ailida is still unwilling to admit the sex routine. But I'm sure she will in the face of all the evidence. So we know what happened, but we haven't got any obvious suspects."

Warner looked around at the wet mess that was once Johnston's office, "One last thing. What's the story with all this water and the fire department showing up for a murder?"

"Our killer is also skilled at making incendiary devices," Neiberg said as he walked over to a badly charred wastebasket in the middle of the room. It was filled with a dirty mix of ashes and water. "Forensics has the little bugger that started the fire," he continued. "Would you believe that a little cheap watch face attached to four double a batteries, a blasting cap and an accelerant created this mess?"

"Why the hell go to all this trouble just to make it rain?" Walsh asked, gesturing toward Johnston's body sprawled across his desk.

Neiberg paused for a moment, deep in thought, as he walked over to the grandfather clock. "We know that the fire department arrived at 11:30 p.m. But look at this." Neiberg opened the wooden door of the clock's cabinet. "The pendulum stopped at precisely 9:01 p.m. But the weights are not all the way down. We've got several more days, at least, on a seven day clock. I figure the killer wanted us to know the time of death."

Walsh laughed.

"What's so funny," said Warner.

"If every wacko who killed somebody did that," Walsh said with a grin, "the medical examiner's office would be outta business." Warner shot another disapproving glance at Walsh.

"For chrissake, Gus, the damn clock could be just a coincidence. Besides, the clock shit doesn't explain the deluge, unless boy genius over there," a stab with his right index finger in Neiberg's direction, "can look into a crystal ball for us."

Warner frowned.

"O.K Neiberg," Walsh said apologetically, "if you've got more on this water theory, let's get it over with."

"Well," Neiberg continued. "The killer went to a lot of trouble to delay the start of the fire. We know from the fire department that the first man arrived about 11:30. But all the killer had to do to destroy evidence was light the fire with a match. Setting a time fuse for over two hours had to be for two possible reasons. It would allow time to escape before the murder was detected. But 10 or 20 minutes would be enough for that. Two hours looks like maybe Ailida's replacement wanted the time period from 9:01 to 11:30 to fit into some alibi scheme."

"But there's a flaw in that logic," Warner said. "Someone could have come in looking for the cleaning lady. Two hours is a helluva long time."

"Apparently, our killer is willing to take big chances, make a game out of a well-planned murder but leave an important part of the scheme purely to lady luck."

"Well," said Warner, "let's hope his luck runs out. Until then, who should we suspect?"

"Unfortunately, at this point we need to cast a wide net. It could be Ailida's jealous boyfriend or anyone who ever crossed paths with Johnston."

"Not good, not good," Warner groaned. Gazing heavenward he added, "Please, God, let it be the jealous boyfriend."

"Not on your life, Gus," Walsh said emphatically. "The boyfriend would have slashed Johnston to pieces in a jealous rage. The medical examiner would be up all night counting puncture wounds. Nope," Walsh pointed at the knife still protruding from Johnston's bloody chest for emphasis. "You're lookin' at an execution."

<u>San Francisco, 8:45 p.m. Pacific Time</u>.
The white Rolls Royce climbed effortlessly up Powell Street, turned left onto California, and continued to Mason at the top of Knob Hill. Vanity plates front and rear were emblazoned with three large gold letters on a navy blue background: *AWE*. Tinted windows hid the lone passenger in the rear seat. However, every doorman at every top hotel in every major city in North America and Europe knew who was arriving when the big white Rolls pulled up to the entrance. He was no stranger at the Fairmont Hotel.

"Good evening, Mr. Baxton," the doorman said as he opened the right rear door. Bradford Baxton,III was Chairman and CEO of Amalgamated Worldwide Enterprises, a self-made billionaire whose immense wealth was legendary. Wherever he travelled in the civilized world, it was imperative that a white Rolls Royce be at his disposal. This idiosyncrasy was not just because Baxton wanted to project a wealthy image. He was consumed by an unquenchable thirst for power.

Downsized

Money was only one part of his personal formula for dominance. In the world according to Baxton, the quintessence of power is the ability to instill fear in others. "A man's true power in the business world," he often said to a captive audience of his top executives, "is directly proportional to how many people break out in a cold sweat when they have to confront him." For good measure, he would add, "Compassion is a major roadblock on the path to power."

On that basis, Baxton was a big league power player. A short man, only five feet five inches, his face was carefully set in a perpetual scowl. He was lean and muscular with a year-round tan that complemented his somber personality. Jet black hair combed straight back and bushy eyebrows accented his forbidding appearance.

"May I take your bags, sir?" the doorman offered, extending a hand toward one of the two attaché cases held by Baxton.

"No," Baxton barked as he walked quickly into the lobby, clutching the smaller of the two cases tightly under his right arm. As soon as Baxton disappeared into the cavernous lobby, the doorman strode directly to the house phone adjacent to the front entrance and dialed the penthouse suite. It was a ritual for which he was handsomely rewarded. He waited briefly before he spoke softly. "He's on his way and in a big hurry . . . a bit grouchy, too."

Howard Van der Meer, senior vice president and chief of AWE's North American operations, hung up and yelled a warning. "The ballbuster's coming up and he's in one of his moods."

Van der Meer and the vice president of Aero Space products, Sid Fulton, quickly erased all signs of their billiard game. Baxton's General Counsel, Glenn Franklin, in the library deep in research put down his pen in mid-sentence. They all quickly buttoned collars, straightened ties and put on jackets as a loud bang on the door announced Baxton's arrival. A second kick emphasized his impatience. Van der Meer ran to the door, took a deep breath and opened it. "Good evening, Bradford," he said politely. Van der Meer and Johnston were the only executives privileged to refer to him by his first name, but it was never just Brad. "Have a nice flight?"

Baxton brushed past him, turned sharply to the right and went directly into the main parlor, crowded with charts and graphs displayed on three easels.

"No," he answered matter-of-factly as he placed the smaller attaché case on the highly polished mahogany coffee table. Fumbling with the combination lock, he pressed the latch and opened the lid reverently. He removed a solitary blue folder

Downsized

and, without turning to face Van der Meer, held it in his left hand, waving it at arm's length. "Well, damn it, are you going to look at it or not?"

"Sorry. Of course," Van der Meer said apologetically as he reached for the document. He opened the folder and immediately recognized the Jet Age Aircraft acquisition agreement. He glanced at the middle of the page and noticed the sum of $1.2 billion was crossed out and the number $950 million was written in ink above it. There were no initials next to the change. Van der Meer went directly to the last of nine pages. It contained only one signature in bright turquoise ink: Arthur Greer, President, Jet Age Aircraft Co., Inc. Van der Meer looked perplexed.

Baxton turned to face him. "Well, what do you think? How does that 950 million dollars look to you?"

"Greer hasn't initialed the change," Van der Meer noted cautiously. "Does he agree with it?"

"Hell no," Baxton exclaimed. "He doesn't even know about it yet. I redid the numbers on the way out here. You'll be the first to tell him."

"I don't understand. Johnston called yesterday about noon our time and said you and Greer struck a deal. Signed, sealed and delivered."

"He spoke out of turn," Baxton said, frowning as he walked around the coffee table and sat down. He stretched out both legs, leaned back and loosened his tie. "Look," he added firmly. "Greer is in debt up to his ass. Johnston figures he owes at least 750 million and he's on his last legs, economically speaking. He's had nothing but tunnel vision since he went for his dream to develop the first corporate jet to fly mach 3 at 110,000 feet. He didn't pay attention to business. Now he's about to lose everything and I'm in the pilot's seat, pun intended."

Glenn Franklin spoke softly, almost apologetically. "But Mr. Baxton, he can file for Chapter 11, restructure the debt and thwart your plan quite easily."

Baxton sat up straight and leaned forward. Neither his expression nor tone of voice changed, but it was clear he did not like what he just heard. "Bullshit. That's pure bullshit." He looked at Van der Meer and Fulton as he pointed at Franklin. "What the hell am I paying this guy for?" Baxton banged his fist on the coffee table. "Damn it, Franklin, I'm Greer's biggest creditor. I'll control the creditor's committee and crush him. Even *he* knows that, and he never went to law school."

"But,--" Franklin began softly, nervously.

"But hell!" Baxton stood up and paced around the room, gesturing as he spoke. "Greer is 80 or 81 years old. He's got his Korean War hero fly boy medals. He's proud, but he's tired. In exchange for the cut in price, we give him a 10-year employment contract. He'll be lucky to live through five of them. At $250,000 per year, he'll be thrilled. He'll assume he'll be president of Jet Age Aircraft Co. when the plane takes its first flight." Baxton stopped pacing and looked directly at Franklin. "And this is where you come in. We have an airtight blow-out clause so I can dump him quickly. He's out when I say."

"Yes, sir," Franklin said quietly, hiding the sickness he felt in the pit of his stomach. "I'll do my best."

"Wrong," Baxton shot back. "You'll just damn well do it." Turning to Fulton, Baxton pointed to one of the easels. "OK, Sidney, let's hear the good news. How much is all this stratosphere cruising gonna be worth to us."

Fulton's presentation was interrupted by the phone. "Good God Almighty!" cried Van der Meer. He looked at Baxton with a terrified expression.

"What the hell is it?" Baxton asked, frowning.

"Johnston. He's dead. He was murdered."

"Give me that damn phone," Baxton said, pushing Van der Meer out of his way. "Who is this?"

"Joe McGillicuddy, chief of security in Boston."

"When did it happen?"

"Nine p.m. our time."

Baxton looked at his watch, still set on Boston time. "Why the hell weren't we notified sooner?"

"Just found out."

"McGillicuddy, listen carefully. Johnston had important papers on his desk. I want you to get them."

"I Can't. Johnston was killed on his desk, the sprinkler system came on and everything is a mess. There's water and blood all over everything. It's awful."

"The backup would most likely be on Johnston's computer. Secure the computer."

"It's too late. The police took it. They've taken control of everything in Johnston's office."

Baxton slammed the phone onto the cradle in a rare show of emotion. "Fucking imbecile!" He shoved the Jet Age acquisition papers into Franklin's hands. "We'll go over this deal later, after I find out what the hell really happened to Johnston."

"Bradford," Van der Meer interrupted. "What about Sally?"

Baxton looked puzzled.

"You know," Van der Meer said patiently, "Johnston's wife."

"What about her?"

"Shouldn't you call or something?"

"You do it. I don't have time to waste."

Baxton left as quickly as he came. As usual, the unpleasant task of expressing AWE's condolences regardless whom in the company had died was left for Van der Meer.

<hr />

<u>Allston, Massachusetts. February 15, 7:00 a.m.</u>
Bill Coine adjusted to retirement from the state police with very little difficulty. One day he was up to his armpits in murder, mayhem, bad guys and petty politics; the next he woke up late, yawned, punched up his pillow, turned onto his right side and went back to sleep. For Coine, one of the true pleasures of retirement was resetting his biological clock and shutting off his internal alarm. So when a ringing phone yanked him out of a sound sleep at seven in the morning, he was not happy. He was even less pleased when his wife Jeanie walked into the bedroom with a cup of tea in one hand, a cordless telephone in the other and a big smile on her face. "Bill, guess who's calling?" Coine pulled the covers over his head and mumbled his best guess from hiding. "Hillary Clinton?" Jeanie pulled at the blankets until Coine reluctantly loosened his grip. She placed the phone on the pillow next to his right ear. "No silly. It's John Neiberg."

David G. Hanrahan Esq.

The news took a few moments to sink in. It was a combination of deja vu and a bad dream. When he was Detective Lieutenant Bill Coine, an early morning call from Neiberg usually meant no breakfast and a visit to some gruesome murder scene. Coine was Neiberg's mentor for several years before retirement. However, he had now been retired for two years and only saw Neiberg once for dinner with Jeanie and a second time at Neiberg's promotion party. Without lifting his head from the pillow, Coine took the phone. "John, what's the matter? Are you in trouble or something?"

"No. I'm on my first really complicated murder case and I'm at a loss where the heck I should start."

Coine shook his head. "John, listen carefully. Have you been to the murder scene?"

"Yes."

"Wonderful," said Coine sarcastically. "Then, believe it or not, you've really started at the right place."

An awkward silence followed.

"I guess I should have waited 'til later to call you?"

"That would have been nice."

Jeanie was not pleased with the way Coine was treating Neiberg. She shot him one of her looks.

"Well," Neiberg said apologetically. "I'm meeting with the D.A. in an hour and, frankly, the case looks impossible."

Coine finally sat up. "Dammit, John, didn't I teach you anything?" Another look of disapproval from Jeanie. Coine closed his eyes tightly as Jeanie grabbed a pillow and slammed it over his head. "Look, John," Coine said, realizing he had better deal with the situation pleasantly or risk another pillow to the head. "You know no case is impossible. Some are just harder than others. Just keep your mind open, do your homework, sweat the details and follow your instincts. No detail is ever too small to ignore." There, thought Coine. I've given him some words of wisdom. He smirked at Jeanie as she put the pillow down. "By the way, who's the victim?"

"Samuel Johnston, C.F.O. at Amalgamated Worldwide Enterprises. He was stark naked when they found him except for his socks."

Silence.

"Bill, what's wrong?"

"Nothing. I'm thinking. Where was he killed?"

"In his office. Actually, he died right on his desk on top of a whole pile of financial documents." Neiberg paused. "It looks like he was waiting for the cleaning lady to arrive. It seems like she was doing more than your average cleaning."

"John, that building is loaded with security. What about the surveillance video tapes? The murderer had to come and go past a dozen cameras. There must be something."

David G. Hanrahan Esq.

"Nothing yet," Neiberg sighed. "We're really stymied."

Coine suddenly realized he was actually getting too interested. He quickly shook it off. "John, I'm sorry, but I really can't be too much help to you. My sleuthing days are over. Don't worry, you'll be fine."

"Can I call you from time to time?"

"Sure John, but after 9 a.m." Coine lied. He was fully retired and really wanted to stay that way. "But, look," he added quickly. "You'll catch whoever did this thing. Be patient. Just be patient, O.K.?"

Neiberg was not certain he could remain patient, but he realized he was imposing on his old mentor. "Thanks, Bill. I'll keep you posted."

Coine reached for the TV remote. After several minutes, the local news came on leading with the Johnston murder. There's nothing about the victim being in his birthday suit. *Good*, Coine thought. He shut off the TV and tried to get back to sleep.

"Bill?" Jeanie asked. "Is the Johnston murder the reason Neiberg called?"

"Yes."

"Are you getting involved?"

"Nope."

"Good."

<u>Boston, Suffolk County District Attorney's Office. 8:00 a.m.</u>

Warner stared at the headline plastered on the front page of the *Boston Herald*. *St. Valentine's Day Murder*. Great, he thought. Now Johnston's murder is equated with the infamous days of Al Capone and Chicago lawlessness. Warner realized the case was a genuine good news, bad news situation. Warner was about to become a household word with all the visibility his political aspirations demanded. That was good. But given the circumstances of Johnston's murder, and despite Neiberg's demonstrated aptitude, a quick solution did not seem to be in the cards. *That* was bad. However, it was an opportunity he gladly embraced. His thoughts were interrupted by the intercom.

"Mr. Warner, Sergeant Neiberg and Attorney Jones are here."

He looked at his watch. Eight sharp.

"Good, send them in."

Warner greeted Neiberg and Jones with a friendly handshake as he ushered them to a conference area furnished with a leather couch, a leather reclining chair and three uncomfortable but impressive Harvard Law School captain's chairs. "Sergeant Neiberg, have you met my new chief of homicide?"

David G. Hanrahan Esq.

Neiberg tried not to look surprised. Sandra Jones was a stunningly beautiful African-American who looked too young to be a chief of anything, let alone homicide. "Not officially," he said, sending a polite smile Jones' way. Warner knew precisely what Neiberg was thinking. Jones' promotion had stunned the office. The job of homicide chief invariably went to a tough, hard-boiled 20-year man.

"Don't let her youthful appearance fool you," Warner said. With a knowing smile he added, "She's older than she looks, but that's her secret. And she's damn good at getting convictions. You guys are gonna get along great." Warner sat back in his chair looking approvingly at two-thirds of his Johnston murder team. He glanced down at his watch impatiently. "Has anyone seen Walsh?"

"No, sir," said Neiberg.

"He'll be late for his own funeral. And call me Gus." Warner held up the *Herald* headline. "Seen this yet?"

"Yes," said Jones. "Clever as usual."

"I don't like it," replied Warner. "Has the ghost of Al Capone all over it."

"What about Al Capone?" Lieutenant Walsh asked as he entered the office with a box of donuts and four cups of coffee. Warner pulled a cup out of the box, selected a glazed donut, and continued. "*Herald*'s calling this case the St. Valentine's Day murder."

"Big deal," replied Walsh. "That was a whole bunch of guys and machine guns. We've only got one victim and a big knife. Don't worry about it."

"Who the hell's worried? It's just that the damn thing has a ring to it. People will remember it longer." Warner leaned forward, holding his coffee cup at the rim by the thumb and forefinger of both hands. "We go straight to hell if we don't come up with something soon. We're sitting on a time bomb. This guy Johnston is a VIP. His boss, Bradford Baxton, is a real high-wire act. He's plugged into Beacon Hill, Washington, and everywhere in between. He'll be on our ass to solve this case and so will the governor and the mayor."

Walsh bit into a jelly donut and wiped his chin. "Since when have you been concerned about pressure from upstairs?"

"Since last night when it became clear that we're up against a highly skilled, experienced professional."

Neiberg started to speak, but decided against it. Warner noticed the hesitation.

"Speak up John, don't be bashful," urged Warner.

"Well, I agree our killer is a professional, but *experienced*?" Neiberg shook his head. "I disagree."

"Are you crystal ball gazin' again?" Walsh asked sarcastically.

"No. I couldn't sleep last night, so I went to State Police headquarters and checked out a long list of recent, unsolved murders nationwide. What happened last night doesn't fit any prior M.O. My guess is we're looking at someone's premier performance."

"Jesus, Neiberg," said Warner, almost choking on his coffee, "if last night was somebody's debut on the murder scene, I sure as hell hope it was a one-night stand."

"If it isn't," Jones said, "then we better get the bastard before the next show."

"From your lips to God's ears," said Warner, "which brings me to my theory." Warner sipped from the coffee cup before he continued. "Whoever did this has to have been around awhile, had to know that building and Johnston's habits intimately. Anyway, point is, we may be looking at an inside job. Like Neiberg said last night, we cast a wide net. We don't rule out any possibility. Not even Brad Baxton himself." Warner paused, looking for any reaction from Jones, Walsh and Neiberg. None. "Good," he said. "We're on the same wavelength."

"Hey," said Walsh, "it could even be Johnston's wife. You know, finds out about the cleaning lady, hires a killer, and lives the life of the rich widow."

"Point well taken," said Warner. The phone rang. Warner walked over to his desk and picked it up, listened and mouthed: "One of Baxton's in-house lawyers." Warner listened for a moment and frowned.

"Wait a moment," he said, pushing the hold button so he could speak in confidence. "What does anyone know about Johnston's computer?"

"I had it removed and we are holding it for protective custody," said Neiberg.

"Why?"

"It seemed like the right thing to do. Once we left Johnston's office, if there were any clues on his computer hard drive they could be lost forever."

Warner smiled. "Good job, Neiberg. We keep it." He returned to the caller. "Yes, we have it. No, we will not return it without a court order. Be my guest." Warner slammed the phone down onto its cradle. "Sandy, be ready to oppose Baxton's motion to return Johnston's computer. They're gonna argue their proprietary interests outweigh any investigative purposes. We'll have to articulate some reasonable basis beyond Neiberg's instincts." Warner looked at his watch. "Damn, only one hour until a press conference." He turned to Walsh and Neiberg, arms outstretched, "Please, guys, get me some good stuff on this case, and soon."

Boston, AWE Headquarters. 8:55 a.m.
Angela Frechetti was a single mom happy to be a small cog in a gigantic wheel. She had been an

assistant to the director of AWE's worldwide communications office for three years. She sipped her coffee as she thumbed through the pile of messages to be disseminated around the world on AWE's e-mail network. One document caught Angela's attention; a plain large envelope addressed to Van der Meer, Fulton and Baxton stamped "for immediate transmission." She could feel it contained a disk. She knew these men were at the Fairmont Hotel penthouse in San Francisco, three hours earlier, California time. It was now almost 9 a.m. in Boston. It would keep for awhile, she thought. She moved the envelope aside as she rummaged through the rest of her messages, making a mental note to fax the document to San Francisco before 10 a.m. At 9:20 a.m., her phone rang. It was bad news from the school nurse. Her 12-year-old son was having an acute asthma attack.

Angela grabbed her pocketbook and, as she turned to leave, accidentally brushed it across the envelope containing the computer disk. It slipped silently to the floor and partly under the desk, where it lay barely visible. As she left, her supervisor gathered the remaining documents and handed them to a co-worker. Today, over a thousand e-mail messages and several hundred faxes would leave AWE's communications command center at the speed of light and arrive at their respective destinations within seconds, except for one envelope lying unnoticed on the floor by Angela's desk.

<u>Allston, 11:30 a.m.</u>
Bill Coine spent the better part of the morning gathering all the news he could find about the Johnston murder. After reading articles in the *Herald,* the *Globe* and *Wall Street Journal,* he was still not satisfied he knew enough about what really happened. In particular, he knew very little about Amalgamated Worldwide Enterprises and even less about Samuel Adams Johnston. He walked into the kitchen where Jeanie was making sandwiches for lunch. He held up his smart phone and quietly said, "Google, I want information on Samuel Adams Johnston and Amalgamated Worldwide Enterprises."

Jeanie had lived with Bill for 32 years. She thought she had finally figured him out. She was wrong. Jeanie stopped making the sandwiches and looked directly at Coine. "Bill, if you are not getting involved, why in heaven's name do you need information about this Johnston fellow?"

"Ever since Neiberg called, my curiosity has been eatin' at me. We've had corporate executives whacked before, but by crazed ex-employees who run in, shoot 'em up and get caught red-handed."

Jeanie did not like the term whacked and winced noticeably.

"This guy Johnston," Coine continued, "was executed quickly and cleanly. Not a clue. And he was stark naked at the time."

Jeanie looked surprised. "I didn't read anything about that."

"It's still a secret. Neiberg told me. It's good they're keeping it quiet. In a case like this, you should always have something that only the killer knows."

"Not to mention the embarrassment to his poor family. But you are avoiding my question. Why the sudden interest in a murder case if you are not going to get involved?"

"I'd like to know more about this Johnston guy and his company. It's that simple."

"What the devil for? Seems like a big waste of time unless you're planning on getting involved." Jeanie cut the sandwiches neatly in half. "Please don't tell me you're going to get involved." She handed him a plate containing a sandwich, several sliced tomatoes and a pickle. "Want some hot chocolate?"

"No," he answered.

"Well, what do you want to drink, then?"

"I mean no, I'm not gonna get involved. Yes, I want some hot chocolate."

"Bill, for a top-notch detective, do you realize that sometimes you don't have a clue about what's going on?"

Coine knew when he was not going to win one of Jeanie's arguments. "Yes, honey, I know."

"Don't patronize me, Bill Coine." Jeanie remembered the many sleepless nights when Coine was involved in tracking vicious killers. "I want you to promise me this is just a hobby and you are *not* going to get involved."

Coine took a big bite out of the sandwich and with his mouth still full, held up two fingers of his right hand and said, "Scout's honor."

"Bill Coine, you were never a boy scout. Just say 'I promise'."

"OK, already! I promise."

"What?"

"I promise that I will not get involved in the Johnston murder case. OK?"

"OK."

<u>San Francisco, February 16, 11:00 a.m., Pacific Time</u>

Arthur Greer's full head of thick white hair and his signature bow tie pegged him as a man in his eighties but he hid his age well. He stared at the first page of his agreement with Brad Baxton, focusing on the purchase price. He was not happy with the $1.2 billion for his brainchild, but it would get him out of debt and give him something on which to retire. Meanwhile, Baxton's unlimited resources would insure success for his life long dream of being the first to launch a truly supersonic commercial plane. Designed to be faster and fly higher than the Concorde, it would travel at 1,500 miles per hour at 70,000 feet and go from New York to London in a little less than three hours.

Greer's thoughts were interrupted when his secretary ran into his office, waving an envelope. "It's here," she said excitedly. It was from the Federal Aviation Administration.

It was not good news. "Dammit to hell!" he yelled, slamming the document onto his desk. "The feds say they will not recommend approval of my bird." Greer was crushed by the news. It could not have come at a worse time. Howard Van der Meer and Sid Fulton were expected shortly to deliver the executed acquisition agreement and start the process of absorbing Jet Age Aircraft operations into AWE's Aero Space products division. "Carol, this could be it for the project," Greer groaned, sinking back into his chair. He reached for the phone and dialed the number for the Fairmont Hotel. He was too late. Van der Meer and Fulton were already on the way. So was Greer's attorney. *Oh, well,* he thought. *It will be a short meeting.*

<u>Boston, AWE Headquarters. 3:30 p.m.</u>
Bradford Baxton's office projected his personal and business style perfectly. His "power wall" was

covered with pictures of hundreds of influential statesmen, ambassadors and world leaders, all posing with Baxton. Each was autographed with a personal message, evidence of the huge sums of money Baxton contributed personally as well as through his many business entities. Nothing was ever left to chance. Important votes in Congress, a decision by a critical federal department, state governors and legislators, foreign governments and leaders, Baxton played them all like a violin.

Knowledge was also a key component for getting and keeping power. Facing Baxton's power wall was an array of built-in TV consoles that put him in touch with all of his 50 business entities and their executives around the world, 24 hours a day. In addition, a continuous stream of up-to-the-minute stock market prices lit up the top of the wall. Baxton's desk was a solid block of Italian marble, stark and shining in the center of the room. Behind the desk was a glass wall, framing a panoramic view of Boston Harbor and Logan Airport. His present guests were not enjoying the view.

"I don't like what you're telling me," Baxton said with his usual scowl. "How in hell can you lose a simple goddamn motion?"

John Hogan, in-house counsel and chief of the litigation section, shifted nervously in his chair. "Sir, the D.A. is claiming that his interest in

Johnston's computer outweighs any business interest that AWE may have. Frankly . . ."

Baxton cut him off before he could finish. "Frankly, hell!" he shouted. "You went in unprepared and *that's* what the hell happened."

Hogan's face reddened. He could feel the blood pounding in his ears. He coughed nervously. "We ...."

"*You*, not we" Baxton shot back. "*You* didn't see fit to consult me before you went to court. *You* didn't have enough facts to convince the judge. And you, dammit, didn't give me an opportunity to use my influence at City Hall."

Hogan did not have any defense to Baxton's verbal onslaught. Besides, the whole truth about what happened in court the day before had not yet been disclosed. He had no idea how to break the news and not get fired. "Sir," he began tentatively.

"Don't 'sir' me. Name's Baxton."

"Yes sir, Mr. Baxton. The whole situation is extremely unusual and the judge is inexperienced."

Baxton slammed his hand hard on the desk. "Then you should have won, dammit!"

"Mr. Baxton, I'm not going to make excuses. But we . . . I was told that everything on Johnston's computer that was of any concern of ours was irretrievable without his password, and only Van der Meer knows it."

Downsized

"Great! You never heard of hackers? Somebody can crack that problem given enough time and motivation. That computer is my property and I want it back immediately."

Hogan coughed again. "It won't be soon, Mr. Baxton. In fact, the court issued an order that the company supply the D.A.'s office with the password no later than close of business Monday."

Baxton jumped to his feet, his face purple with rage.

"Outrageous!" he shouted. "It's a goddamn outrage."

Hogan spoke up quickly. "We've appealed. It's not over yet. Meanwhile, we had the presence of mind to have the court order the D.A. to let us download the information onto a disk pending the appeal."

The phone rang. "Yes?" Baxton barked as he answered the phone with the same anger that characterized his dialogue with Hogan.

"It's McGillicuddy, chief of security. I've got some startling news. I've got to talk to you right away."

"Tell me over the phone."

"I would rather not, sir. It's very serious."

Baxton turned to Hogan and his young assistant.

"We'll talk later. Meanwhile, I want information from you minute by minute . . . no more losses. Understand?"

"Yes, Mr. Baxton," Hogan said, relieved to be momentarily off the hook by something more urgent.

<u>San Francisco, 12:30 p.m. Pacific Time.</u>
Howard Van der Meer and Sid Fulton sat in Greer's conference room behind a stack of papers. Greer and his attorney, Aaron Spellman, walked in as Van der Meer stood up, extending his hand.

"No need to get up, gentlemen," Greer said. "I don't think the meeting will last long."

Van der Meer looked at Fulton with raised eyebrows. Did Greer get wind of Baxton's price reduction?

"What's wrong?" Van der Meer asked cautiously.

"A lot," said Greer matter-of-factly, handing Van der Meer and Fulton a copy of the FAA decision.

"This is bad," said Van der Meer. "But is it final?"

"I'd say so," said Greer. "Problem is we've thrown everything into satisfying all of the FAA's objections. We're just plumb out of ideas."

Van der Meer shook his head. "I don't know what to say. I'm shocked. I'd better call Baxton."

"Yes, you do that," Greer said, resigned to his fate. "You can use the phone in my office for privacy."

Greer walked Van der Meer down the hall, only part way. Van der Meer walked the last 30 feet and entered Greer's office, closing the door tightly behind him.

<u>Boston, AWE Headquarters. 3:40 p.m.</u>
Baxton stared at the document McGillicuddy had handed him just a few minutes earlier. It was sensitive information that could damage vital business interests if it became public knowledge. Now Van der Meer was calling about the Greer deal which was no longer Baxton's main concern. "So, what's the big problem you can't handle by yourself?" he barked.

"Bradford, I have bad news. The FAA has deep-sixed the stratocruiser project."

"Good," said Baxton.

"I'm not sure I heard you," answered a bewildered Van der Meer. "Did you say good?"

"Yes dammit. Has Greer seen the reduction in price yet?"

"No."

"Great. Blame it on the feds and get the deal signed."

"Bradford, are you . . ." Van der Meer hesitated.

Baxton added the missing adjective. "Nuts? No, Howard, just an opportunist. The FAA is politics. That's my forte, so don't worry. Get me that stratocruiser." Baxton returned the phone to its cradle and picked up the paper that now deserved his full attention. He waived it in front of McGillicuddy. "Well, what do you make of this?"

"If you ask me, you should have told Van der Meer about it."

"We tell nobody; is that clear?"

"Well, I think it's a matter for the police."

Baxton frowned. "Under no circumstances do we give this to the police."

"Yes, sir," McGillicuddy said, not hiding his disappointment.

"One last thing. Who was responsible for misplacing this document?"

"Angela Frechetti. She works down in communications. It was an accident."

Baxton did not tolerate mistakes or excuses. "I want her fired."

Baxton took one last look at the offending document. "Shit," he muttered to himself as he threw it into the top middle drawer of his desk, slammed it shut and locked it.

San Francisco, 12:45 p.m. Pacific Time.

When Van der Meer returned to the conference room, Greer was entertaining Spellman and Fulton with another lecture on his favorite subject-- the stratocruiser. Greer stopped in mid-sentence when he saw Van der Meer. "Well," he said cheerfully, "what sayeth the great Brad Baxton?"

Downsized

Van der Meer stood quietly for several seconds. "Let me get to the point." He handed Greer and Spellman copies of the revised acquisition agreement. Van der Meer continued, making certain to keep eye contact with Greer. "Baxton is a born gambler. He views the FAA's decision as just another one of life's challenges." He looked at Greer and Spellman, searching for any sign of trouble evident in their facial expressions. Spellman was busy scanning the document. So far so good, Van der Meer thought. He continued. "The terms, I'm sorry to say, are not negotiable."

Spellman interrupted angrily. "Arthur, these non-negotiable terms include a major reduction in the purchase price."

Greer held his hand up, signaling a time out. "Aaron," he said, "the FAA just kicked me in the ass . . . hard. I'm lucky to still have a deal."

Van der Meer seized the opportunity presented by Greer's fatalistic approach to Baxton's new deal. "Arthur," he said with a salesman's sincerity, "consider the upside. You'll be out of debt and gainfully employed." He held up all five fingers of each hand for emphasis. "For 10 years," he added, "if this project ever gets off the ground, you'll have hands-on control. It'll still be your baby."

Spellman shot a nasty look in Van der Meer's direction, turned to Greer, and in his best this-is-your-lawyer-speaking tone said, "Arty, I'd like to talk to you . . . alone."

"What for Aaron? I've got no secrets at this point. Right now I'm dead . . . in debt up to and beyond my ass. Baxton's just thrown me a life jacket."

But . . .," said Spellman.

"No," said Greer. "You want to protect me. I appreciate that. Let's get on with it."

At approximately 1 p.m. pacific time, Bradford Baxton added Jet Age Aircraft Co., Inc. to his long list of acquisitions and tightened further his grip on the aerospace industry, consolidating a power base that would launch him profitably well into the twenty-first century. On the way to the airport Fulton broke a long silence. "Howard, did Baxton buy the FAA?"

"Please, let's not go there. I have enough on my conscience."

<u>Allston, 7:30 p.m.</u>
In a very short time, Coine was finding a lot of dirt, not only on Johnston, but also on Baxton himself. Thanks to Brad Baxton's propensity for cutting throats in the business world and making billions in the process, AWE and its notorious CEO attracted a great deal of ink. Depending on the writer's philosophical bent, Baxton was either the devil incarnate or the second coming of God. Either

way, Coine was in researcher's heaven for the first time since his retirement. His harvest of information was now strewn all over the couch, the coffee table and the usually neat living room floor. Jeanie was not happy. However, the mess was not fueling her discontent. Rather, Coine's intense research efforts hinted at more than just a passing interest in a local murder case.

"Excuse me," said Jeanie with a touch of annoyance in her voice. It was tea time, an activity to which Jeanie looked forward each evening ever since Coine's retirement eased him into a nightly routine of tea, cookies and the O'Reilly Factor. She searched for a clear space on which to place the tray she was carrying. There was none. Experience taught her that when the great detective was deep in thought, more was needed to get his attention than a simple "excuse me."

Coine leaned back on the couch, legs outstretched, stocking feet on the coffee table. Reading glasses were perched precariously on the end of his nose as he devoured one of the newspaper articles. Jeanie stood in front of him, held the tray about six inches above the cluttered table, made sure it was level and dropped it just to the right of his feet. The loud bang and rattle of spoons on tea cups nocked Coine's glasses off his nose and jolted him out of his trance-like state.

"What the hell?"

"It's tea time!" Jeanie said cheerfully.

"Tea time? Is that any reason to give me a heart attack?"

Jeanie poured tea into one of the cups, added two sugars and handed it to Coine. "Your heart is as strong as an ox," she said matter-of-factly. "I'm worried about your eyes. You've been sitting there reading for more than two hours."

Coine removed his feet from the coffee table, leaned forward and stirred his tea as he spoke. "Well, it certainly didn't seem that long to me." He sipped from the cup. "Next time, try switching the lights on and off."

"Good idea." She poured a cup for herself. "Meanwhile, what the devil is so interesting that you've been unable to come up for air?"

Coine pawed through the piles of paper until he unearthed a copy of a *Time* magazine cover, and handed it to Jeanie.

"My," said Jeanie, as she studied the stark features in the photo. "He sure looks mean enough. Who is he?"

"Bradford Baxton."

Jeanie shrugged. "So?"

"He is one of the richest men in the world."

Jeanie still looked puzzled. "So what does he have to do with the Johnston murder?" "Don't know," Coine admitted. "But this Baxton fellow is . . . was . . . Johnston's boss."

Jeanie took a small bite out of a homemade chocolate chip cookie. "I must be a little dense," she said apologetically. "Why is that important? Do you think Baxton did it?"

Coine smiled. He always enjoyed Jeanie's penchant for jumping to conclusions with hardly any facts to support them. He also knew how many times her intuitive guesses were right on the money.

"Just a minute," he said as he rummaged through the mess of papers. "Here's the cover story *Time* ran with that picture." Coine handed several pages to Jeanie.

"Hmm," she said, as she turned the pages. "*Time* calls him the king of downsizing."

"That's probably an understatement. This guy Baxton uses downsizing purely for personal gain. He's a ruthless bastard when it comes to building his business empire."

Jeanie continued to read the *Time* article and it did not take long before she was quite upset. "Oh my goodness, it says here that he shut down a company in northern Maine two weeks before Christmas . . . wiped out a whole town in the process." Jeanie looked at the top of the page for some clue as to when the article was written. Coine answered instinctively. "That was almost five years ago," he told her. "Turn to the next page," he instructed. Jeanie obliged. "Just one month after he decimated that town in Maine, some local Chicago business group gave him their man-of-the-year award." She shook her head. "Were they all recent graduates from a mental institution?"

Coine smiled. "No self-respecting schizophrenic would've given Baxton the time of day. They were just a bunch of guys who obviously had some reason to kiss Baxton's ass."

Jeanie raised an eyebrow.

"Sorry," Coine said defensively. "It happens to be the truth."

Jeanie turned to the last page. There were several pictures of demonstrators picketing Baxton's award dinner. She took delight in reading the picket signs out loud. "Baxton is Bastard of the Year." She put the page down on the coffee table and turned it so Coine could read with her. She chuckled at the next sign. "Choke on your chicken, Baxton," she shouted, as if to get into the mood of the demonstrators.

"I like this one," said Coine, pointing to a young woman with a pretty face holding a sign that read: "Baxton Should Be Tarred and Feathered -- Not Feted."

"She seems awfully young compared to everyone else in the picture," said Jeanie. "I wonder what her story is.?"

Downsized

"They all have a story, and I'm sure it ain't pleasant." Coine placed the *Time* article in an envelope for safekeeping. "Trouble with downsizing," he added sympathetically, "is it cuts you down in your prime and leaves you looking for a comparable job at a time when jobs like the one you had are going over seas."

"How many people has this Baxton fired?"

"Laid off," corrected Coine. "They're told they're laid off. Fifteen thousand."

"Ouch," Jeanie said.

"And that was as of three years ago. By now, there's bound to be more."

"Baxton doesn't sound like a very nice man."

"Nice doesn't always count in the business world. Power does and Baxton has the juice. He's president, CEO, and chairman of Amalgamated Worldwide Enterprises. He has been buying up companies left and right. Seems he's widening his influence in aerospace, artificial intelligence and global positioning systems. His trademark is to acquire some company that fits into his global planning, absorb it into his corporate structure, decimate the staff, pocket the profits and move on to the next conquest. One minute you're a senior executive in a company where you've slaved for 20 years and the next you're on the street."

"Sounds like a man with a lot of enemies."

"Exactly," said Coine emphatically. "I figure at least one hundred thousand roaming around out there with a reason to get even."

"But why kill Johnston?"

"Good question."

Jeanie smiled. That was two so far.

"Not much has been written about Johnston. He was the financial brains behind Baxton's moves but he's managed to stay clear of the limelight. But suppose," said Coine, now standing up and walking back and forth, forcing Jeanie to follow him with her gaze, like a spectator at a tennis match, "just suppose I've got this big grievance against Baxton."

"Is just a grievance enough reason to murder someone?" Jeanie asked incredulously.

"Well, a big enough one to want to hurt Baxton where he could really feel it . . . see it, know it was happening."

"I get it," said Jeanie excitedly. "Killing Baxton would not be enough, he'd be dead, so what?"

Coine stopped pacing. He pointed at Jeanie.

"So who would you kill to get at Baxton?"

"I wouldn't kill anyone," said a surprised Jeanie.

"But if you were my hypothetical grievant, Johnston wouldn't be a bad pick. You know, knock off Baxton's financial wizard. That would make Baxton squirm. Besides, he'd have to start lookin' over his own shoulder. That would be a very painful situation. Lose your financial brain and have your private life turned upside down with one well placed thrust of a knife." Coine sat down, drained his tea cup and held it out for more. Jeanie poured. He held the cup in the palms of both hands and stared into the golden tan liquid. "My theory scares me, Jeanie," he said, not looking up, gazing into the cup as it if might show him the future. "What if I wanted to hurt him even more? Maybe I'd kill again . . . work my way around to Baxton."

Jeanie shuddered at the thought. "But what kind of person would do that just because he's been . . . laid off?"

"A very special person," said Coine pensively, "Certainly a skilled person with a bigger grievance than just being laid off."

"Bill, have you told any of this to Neiberg?"

"No."

"Shouldn't you?"

"If he calls, I will, but only if he calls. Hey," Coine said abruptly, as if he just thought of something. "In case you're wondering why I'm so damn interested in this case, it's your fault."

Jeanie looked totally surprised. "How so?"

"Well, you made me feel guilty about not being nice to Neiberg yesterday. So I figured next time he called I'd be ready to give him help. I guess I just don't know how to go in easy." Coine looked around at the mess he created. "I need all these articles on Baxton like I need a hole in the head."

"My sentiments exactly, but Neiberg will be appreciative. I hope he calls again."

"He will," said Coine confidently, "you can bet on it."

Jeanie looked at her watch and picked up the TV remote. "Still some time for Bill O'Reilly."

It was reassuring to Jeanie that her Bill was back to tea, cookies and the no spin zone. He was just engaging in a hobby after all. Neiberg will certainly be happy, Jeanie thought as she snuggled next to Bill and turned on the TV.

San Francisco, 9 p.m. Pacific Time.

Van der Meer took one final look around his luxurious bedroom in the penthouse suite. Certain nothing else remained to be packed for his return trip to Boston, he zippered his leather clothing bag and folded it in half. For 22 years, he had been point man in Bradford Baxton's war on corporate America. As soon as Baxton set his sights on a likely target, Van der Meer was launched like a guided nuclear missile.

However, the Greer deal bothered Van der Meer more than any other acquisition. Baxton was not just buying a faceless corporation. He was stealing a man's dream. Greer deserved better. Baxton was unnecessarily vicious. Van der Meer had given some thought to Fulton's idle speculation that Baxton had been responsible for the FAA's rejection of Greer's design, and he knew anything was possible for a man like Baxton. He was grateful that Baxton never took him into his confidence when it came to the dirty side of the business. Johnston, on the other hand, was Baxton's willing accomplice in every underhanded scheme. Now that he was dead, who would be heir to Johnston's place of dishonor as Baxton's right hand man? The answer to that question had been plaguing Van der Meer since Johnston's murder. The answer was too obvious. Who else besides Van der Meer, faithful hatchet man? That fact was the catalyst for a decision Van der Meer had been contemplating for a long time. He picked up the phone next to his bed and dialed, slowly, deliberately. "Hello, honey. Did I wake you?"

"No," answered Mary Van der Meer. "You know how it is when you're away. I stay up late and read a lot. Is something wrong?"

"No, sweetheart, not really. But I have something very important to tell you. Need your thinking on it."

Mary was unaccustomed to Howard calling late in the evening for her opinion. An uneasy feeling settled over her. "It must be important," she said, trying to camouflage her anxiety. "You sound very serious. It's certainly not like you." She paused, briefly scanning the variables in her mind and took an educated guess. "Has Baxton finally gotten around to laying you off?" It wasn't a bad guess for someone who watched the parade of suddenly unemployed Amalgamated executives grow steadily at the whim of Bradford Baxton.

"No, nothing like that," Van der Meer said reassuringly.

That left Mary with fewer possibilities. She made a wild guess in jest. "You've found someone else in San Francisco?"

Van der Meer laughed. "No. Too busy..."

"Oh," said Mary, "so you've just been too busy to find someone."

"...and I *ain't* been lookin', either," he said quickly.

"That's good. So what is it now that you've got me on the edge of the bed?"

"I'm thinking of resigning . . . calling it quits."

Silence.

"Did you hear me, Mary?"

Mary placed her left hand on her chest, just below her neck and took a deep breath. "Yes. I'm shocked. I don't know what to say. Have you thought about what you'll do? Where will you go? Do you know how rough it is out there?"

"No, honey I just made the decision. I have no plans. It's gonna be close my eyes, hold my nose and jump."

Mary did not like that picture. Van der Meer always made plans. "Will it keep until you get home next week? We can talk to my brother Tom. He's a head hunter. His input would be helpful."

"Actually, I'm returning tomorrow. I was planning on telling Baxton as soon as I see him. Mary, I know you're not happy to hear this, but I can't stand what I'm doing anymore. Baxton is a bastard. People are just commodities to him, all expendable, useable until they're exhausted, then thrown into the trash pile."

"But . . ."

"I know the thought frightens you, but don't worry. We've saved enough to hold out for awhile. Plus, my skills are portable. Hey . . . maybe I'll start my own consulting business. So keep your chin up, OK? I need your love and support."

"Of course you've got that. I'm a little nervous about the idea of change, that's all."

"I remember a young woman who married a guy who was still wet behind the ears. You took a big gamble when you married young, inexperienced Howard Van der Meer, weird name and all. Well, just one last roll of the dice . . . and this is more of a sure thing. There's life after Amalgamated, you'll see."

David G. Hanrahan Esq.

Van der Meer sounded confident. It eased Mary's tension.

"Howard?"

"Yes."

"Are our club dues paid up for the rest of this year?"

Van der Meer laughed.

"Yes."

"Good," said Mary with a smile Van der Meer couldn't see but knew was there. "Then everything will be fine," she said reassuringly. "No sweat. When do I see you?"

"About noon tomorrow. I'm catching the red eye. I'll be meeting with Baxton about 9:30 in the morning. I should be emptying my desk shortly thereafter."

"What about two weeks notice?"

"Not Baxton's style. He'll call me a traitor, remind me he'll sue my ass if I ever divulge trade secrets and order security to usher me out of the building . . . down the freight elevator."

"Sounds awfully embarrassing for a man of your stature," said Mary indignantly.

"Actually, I'm looking forward to it."

"Can I pick you up at the airport?"

"No. Baxton's sending his Rolls. I'll take one last ride in the ballbuster's precious luxury car. It'll burn his ass that I used his limo and chauffeur to come tell him I've quit."

"Wish I could see it," said Mary.

"I'll tell you all about it. Good night, honey. See you for lunch."

"Good night, Howard . . ." Mary paused, wanting to keep talking, but it was very late. "Love you," she said warmly.

"I love you, Mary. See you soon. Sweet dreams."

Mary looked at the clock on her night stand. It was five minutes past midnight. She shut off the light, said a brief prayer, and tried to sleep. She knew it was going to be a long day.

Boston, AWE Headquarters. February 17, 8:30 a.m.

Joe McGillicuddy sat in his office staring out the window at nothing in particular. His title sounded important enough. But Chief of Security wasn't as lofty as Boston Police Deputy Superintendent, the job he had held for seven years prior to his retirement. He was at a low point in his life and the immediate future seemed bleak. Somewhere out there was someone who could move invisibly through the multi-million dollar network that was AWE's space age, electronic security blanket, stick a knife in Sam Johnston's chest, and disappear without leaving a trace. That was bad enough. Baxton's decision to keep secret the information contained in the envelope McGillicuddy delivered to him the day before put both men in serious legal jeopardy.

David G. Hanrahan Esq.

Three times since 8 a.m. he picked up his phone, and three times his finger froze in place an inch above it. At 20 minutes to nine, on his fourth try, McGillicuddy slammed the phone down. "To hell with the phone," he muttered as he headed for the door. "He'll just hang up. He'll never listen." He paused before entering the hallway and gave himself one more instruction. "Just go to the man," he said as if he were motivating someone else. "Look him in the eye and just tell 'im."

Howard Van der Meer looked at his watch still set on California time. He advanced it three full hours and felt a bit cheated in the process. In an instant he was three hours older and soon to be a lot colder on Boston time. It was a quarter to nine. He adjusted his seat belt, leaned his head back and glanced out his portside window. Somewhere beneath the leading edge of the wing was Route 3 clogged with thousands of commuters struggling north into Boston. It didn't take long to find. A line of red brake lights clearly visible from 6,000 feet snaked its way north, blinking randomly like a string of Christmas tree lights. Was he looking at Hanover, Rockland or Weymouth? It was hard to tell. The sound of a microphone redirected his glance toward the front of the plane.

"This is Captain Harley," said the voice with a slight Southwestern accent. "All of us on flight 180 wanna welcome y'all to Boston and thank you for flyin' Delta. As y'all can see, the weather is great . . . if you like it cold. Twenty degrees . . . but no snow." Van der Meer winced. He had opted to keep his topcoat in the clothing bag for convenience when he changed planes in Cincinnati. No problem, he thought. Alfredo will be waiting with the Rolls. He relaxed. The calm voice continued. "We've been enjoyin' a good tail wind since we left Cincinnati so we're a bit ahead of schedule. Logan's given us clearance to land on Runway 22R and we expect to be sittin' at the ramp . . . oh . . . about five minutes to nine. Ya'll come fly with us again. Meanwhile, enjoy your stay."

As the plane descended, Van der Meer watched the tip of Hull slide under the wing, glimpsed the JFK Museum glistening on the water's edge in the distance, and straightened his legs. It was a habit born of a belief that he should be in a good sitting position if the plane crash-landed. He nervously wrapped both hands around the ends of the arm rests and waited for the sound of tires on runway.

"Damn it, McGillicuddy," yelled Baxton. "What in hell is your problem?"

McGillicuddy was doing a good job of controlling his own anger. "Mr. Baxton, let me explain it one last time," he said, pausing briefly to take a deep breath. "It's your problem . . . and it'll be our problem if you don't listen to me." McGillicuddy knew he was bordering on insubordination, but it was too late to turn back. "If you don't believe me, ask your general counsel," he added.

"I don't need a lawyer to tell me how to handle a business problem."

"When's the last time you dealt with a business problem that would land your ass in jail?"

Baxton's face reddened. He stared at McGillicuddy long and hard, and then punched his intercom button. "Jane, is Glenn in?"

"Yes, Mr. Baxton, he's in a meeting with John Hogan. He said not to disturb him. It must be important."

"Well, this is more important. Tell him to get in here right away."

⇒+⇐

Van der Meer felt the chill as he stepped from the plane. He glanced at his watch. 9 a.m. Right on time, he thought as he reached into his jacket pocket to retrieve a small cellular phone. He always called Mary as soon as he landed. His home phone rang only once and was interrupted by an answering machine. He waited for his wife's voice to finish the friendly greeting.

"Honey, it's me. Back safe. A bit nervous about my meeting with Baxton, but I'm ready. I'll call you . . ." Several loud beeps interrupted his message. He held the tiny phone at arm's length in order to read the blinking letters without glasses. *Battery Discharged.* "Damn," he muttered. "Well, at least she'll know I've landed safely."

General Counsel Glenn Franklin started to read the document Baxton handed to him. He didn't get far.

"Jesus Christ Almighty," he yelled. "When the hell did we get this?"

"Last night," Baxton said softly, "late in the day. But it sat around here since Tuesday morning," voice rising in volume. "Some incompetent person in communications misplaced the damn thing. I fired her."

Franklin, his face drained of color, finished reading the one-page document and turned to McGillicuddy, "What do the police say about this?" he asked. McGillicuddy glanced at Baxton.

"They don't know yet," Baxton said. "I wanted to wait until Van der Meer got here." He looked at his watch. "Shit, he'll be here in just 15 or 20 goddamn minutes."

Franklin walked over to Baxton's desk, reached for the phone and started dialing. Baxton slammed his opened hand on Franklin's. "Stop!" he yelled, then abruptly switched gears. "Let's discuss this intelligently," he added softly.

"Bradford," Franklin said evenly, taking the liberty of first-name familiarity to signal the importance of his advice. "If this document is authentic, it's a message from Sam's killer."

"It could be some sick bastard's idea of a joke," said Baxton. "If this is a hoax, it could have a devastating impact on our operations."

"Bradford, I've made a career out of bending over backwards to manipulate the law to achieve your business objectives," Franklin said calmly. "I know goddamn well how to walk the fine line between an honest profit and pure bullshit. But this is murder -- no, an execution -- of our chief financial officer. And the bastard who did it is telling us that Johnston's murder is part of some macabre downsizing scheme. If you keep this from the police one second longer, you'll be guilty of obstruction of justice." Franklin looked over at McGillicuddy for support.

Downsized

"That's what *I've* been tellin' him," McGillicuddy said.

"For Christ sake, Bradford, we'll all be guilty now!" Franklin yelled.

"What's the penalty?" Baxton asked, still hoping to balance the risks in his search for a way out. "What'll they do to us?"

Franklin, the consummate corporate lawyer, deferred to McGillicuddy's police experience.

"Judge can give you up to five years in the state pen."

Baxton noted McGillicuddy's use of the word "you" instead of "us."

"OK," Baxton said, resolutely, "Do it," handing the phone to McGillicuddy. "Let's not make a big deal over this short delay." Remember, it was . . . what's her name's fault," Baxton said.

"Angela," answered McGillicuddy.

"Yeah," Baxton replied, "it was Angela who screwed this up."

⇌

It was five minutes past nine when Sandra Jones took McGillicuddy's call. "Hello, deputy, how are you?" she asked cheerfully.

"Sandra, something's come up that puts the Johnston case in a whole new light."

"Any light will be better than the dark I've been operating in," she said, relieved that there was incoming. "What is it?"

"Well, this thing sat around here for awhile because one of our employees misplaced the envelope it was in."

"What's this thing you're talking about?"

"It's a memo. No," he added after a brief hesitation, "more like a press release."

Jones felt a rush of excitement. "Go ahead," she said impatiently, "tell me what it says."

"I'll read it to you. By the way," he added, "it's written like one of our company press releases when we announce layoffs: Amalgamated Worldwide Enterprises regrets to announce that due to business exigencies beyond our control, it has become necessary to reduce the size of our staff. Accordingly, effective 9:01 p.m. last night, February 14, Samuel Johnston, our loyal and trusted chief financial officer, was terminated in a downsizing program that will enhance the profitability of our operations." McGillicuddy stopped reading for a second. "Here's where it really gets sick," he added before continuing. "Fortunately, Mr. Johnston was spared the pain of an exit interview and the endless negotiation over the appropriate severance package and other termination benefits."

Sandra interrupted. "Joe, get that thing over here immediately," she said, unable to hide her impatience. "Have you preserved the integrity of that document to isolate the fingerprints of whoever wrote that thing?"

"No, it was printed in-house. The damn thing came to us on a disk. I've preserved that . . . and the envelope it came in. But, I'm not finished!"

"There's more?"

"One damn frightening sentence: Amalgamated wishes to assure everyone concerned that great care will be taken in this continuing downsizing program so that no one will be eliminated needlessly."

"My God," Sandra gasped. "If this thing is legit, we've got a vicious killer on our hands and Johnston will not be the last victim."

"I know."

"Was this disk addressed to anyone in particular?"

"Unfortunately, yes. The envelop it came in was addressed to Van der Meer, Fulton and Baxton, in that order."

"We need protection for these guys immediately. Do we know where everyone is?"

"Yeah, Baxton's here. We'll notify Fulton in San Francisco. Van der Meer should be arriving at Logan Airport right about now."

"Does he know about the memo?"

"No.

Jones looked at her watch. 9:08. "Can you get the word to Van der Meer that until we come to grips with this thing, he may be in danger?"

"Sure. We'll get on it right away."

"Call me as soon as you've made contact with Van der Meer. Neiberg's on his way to your office. Tell him to call me as soon as he gets there."

"Will do."

McGillicuddy looked at Baxton with a sense of relief etched on his face. "We've done the right thing. Sandra Jones wants us to alert Van der Meer that he may be in danger. Does he have a cell phone?"

"Call Alfredo in the limo," said Baxton.

McGillicuddy dialed the cell phone number he knew so well. "Damn! He's not answering. We're getting the message that he's left the car."

"Bullshit," said Baxton. "Alfredo would never leave that car unattended and he always has the cell phone on."

"What's Van der Meer's cell phone number?" asked a worried Franklin.

"No luck with Van der Meer's cell phone either," said McGillicuddy.

"For Christ sake, we're in the worldwide communications business. Can't we make a fuckin' call to Logan?" Baxton shouted angrily.

Downsized

Baxton's door opened with a loud bang as it slammed into the door stop on the adjacent wall. Jane Tierney, Baxton's executive secretary ran into the office. "Mr. Baxton," she said sobbing, "They just found Alfredo bound and gagged in one of the air intake vents in the garage. He was supposed to get Van der Meer at the airport. Oh, my God, what does this mean?"

"Quick," said McGillicuddy. "He has a beeper, what's the number? Glenn, call Delta, see if Van der Meer's flight landed and when. Jane, get control of yourself and call the state police barracks at Logan. Tell them to grab Baxton's white Rolls Royce. Tell'em the driver may be armed and dangerous."

McGillicuddy then dialed Van der Meer's pager number, waited impatiently for the interminable instructions to end and keyed in the following message: "Howard. *Don't get in the Rolls.* Your life is in danger. Find state police immediately."

Howard Van der Meer stepped out of the main Delta terminal on the arrival level at 9:10. He quickly lowered his bag to the ground and raised his jacket collar against the wind. He picked up his bag and closed both lapels tightly against his chest with his right hand in a feeble attempt to block the bone-numbing cold. Buses, large and small, jockeyed for a place to pick up and disgorge passengers. Impatient cab drivers honked horns at double-parked cars clogging the narrow road. A large MBTA bus discharged a plume of black soot as it pulled away from the curb. Finally, Van der Meer could see the majestic white Rolls across the roadway, a welcome and inviting refuge from the hustle and bustle surrounding him. A state trooper waved his arms repeatedly, urging the recalcitrant double parkers to move. The Rolls occupied a space clearly marked "no standing," and the trooper looked sternly in the direction of the big white car and gestured menacingly. Van der Meer took a deep breath before running through the dirty exhaust toward his ride. In the din he vaguely heard the beep, beep, beep of his pager. It was buried somewhere in his suitcase. Damn! He thought. Just got back and someone can't wait to beep me.

Mindful of the trooper's impatience, he quickly opened the right rear door, threw his bag to the far side of the large seat and jumped in. The car pulled away quickly, quietly as Van der Meer slammed the big door shut and fell backward into his seat. The car accelerated as both door locks slammed into place. Van der Meer smiled. Alfredo was always security conscious. The mahogany veneer privacy screen was up, blocking Van der Meer's forward view. He was not happy about that. Leaning forward he made a fist and started to knock on the panel. However, the pager's insistent beeping reminded him of the message waiting to be read. He opened several compartments in his bag before he found it. Van der Meer settled back and retrieved the message. The words hit him in the pit of his stomach, like the feeling he got as a child each time the giant roller coaster at Nantasket Beach hurtled down that first, scream-inducing drop.

"Howard. Don't get in the Rolls."

He breathed deeply, slowly, desperately trying to stay calm. Fuck it, he thought, my timing sucks. Always has.

"Your life is in danger."

Oh God, I'm next, he thought. First Sam, now me. That's why the screen is up. That's why Alfredo didn't open the door. It isn't Alfredo. Van der Meer analyzed his predicament. Believing the driver did not know about the message and realizing he had to act quickly, he reached for the lock release on the right door and pushed it slowly. It opened with a loud click. "Shit," he muttered softly. He grabbed the handle and, in one powerful move, shoved his full weight against the door, steeling himself for a painful fall to the pavement at 30 miles an hour. Nothing! The handle was useless. The door was disabled. He was trapped. His mind churned. *Have to think. Have to think. Have to think. The tunnel! I'll attract attention at the toll booths. Oh, no. What if the bastard heads north? Plenty of cars. I'll be in plain view. Shit! The tinted glass is too dark.*

With no ideas for a quick escape he banged on the wooden panel.

"Hey! Who the hell are you? Whaddaya want, dammit?"

The panel moved silently. *Good*, Van der Meer thought. *He wants to talk.* It stopped after dropping only two inches. He strained to see through the tiny space. All he saw was sunglasses in a rear-view mirror, a dark jacket turned up at the collar and a chauffeur's hat. No clues. Suddenly, a gloved hand flashed toward him holding objects. One by one, two hand grip exercisers attached to wires were shoved through the space. The wires were just long enough for the grips to drop a few inches below the opening. Puzzled, Van der Meer peered through the tiny space hoping to get some idea about what was in store for him. The driver's right gloved hand twirled a small ballerina on top of a music box mounted on a board which was attached to the dashboard. Through the small opening he could see wires attaching a battery to the small ballerina and from there to the hand grips dangling on his side of the panel. "What's going on?" he asked angrily. "For Christ sake will you talk to me."

Music. Music-box music began playing. Van der Meer recognized the haunting tune, but couldn't place it. "Look, if you just tell me what you want, or need, maybe I can help."

The gloved hand maneuvered a folded piece of paper into the slot and pushed it through. Van der Meer caught it in mid-air and hastily unfolded it. Carefully crafted block letters in red ink told him all that he needed to know about his driver from hell.

> WHEN THE SONG ENDS YOU WILL DIE. THAT SIMPLE! SQUEEZE THE GRIPS TOGETHER AND THE MUSIC WILL STOP. IF YOU CAN HOLD THEM LONG ENOUGH, MAYBE YOU WON'T DIE. DID YOU EVER THINK ABOUT WHAT IT FEELS LIKE FOR A LOYAL EMPLOYEE TO WONDER IF HE/SHE WOULD BE DOWNSIZED? MAYBE NOW YOU'LL KNOW.

Van der Meer grabbed the handles. He squeezed, hard. The music stopped. But the grips were heavy gauge steel. It required all of his strength to keep the grips closed enough to stop the music. He could feel the pressure building in his forearms. An overhead sign briefly visible gave a clue as to where they were heading. *Good,* he thought. *We're heading toward the Callahan Tunnel.* Van der Meer strained to see as much as possible through his tiny window. The hand grips were above his shoulders, and the weight of his arms added to the torment. He wanted to scream in agony. *No,* he willed himself. *Don't give the bastard satisfaction.* A car rental return sign came into view, and the Rolls swung to the left.

Oh, no! We're not going through the tunnel, Van der Meer thought. Buses appeared on the right. People were walking toward the subway. Van der Meer dropped the hand grips, pressed his face against the tinted glass and banged furiously on the bullet-proof glass with both fists. He might as well have been invisible.

The music played on. Now he recognized it. It was the theme song from the movie, *Dr. Zhivago.* Why *Dr. Zhivago?* He listened, wondering what connection that song had to this madman and to him. *Damn,* he thought as he grabbed the grips and squeezed. The music stopped. But now, it was much harder to hold them shut.

"How long do I have?" he asked his driver. "That's the least you can do. Come on, at least tell me that." Van der Meer paused briefly and changed his tactics. *Take control*, he told himself. "Tell you what," he said confidently. "I don't think I'll play your game." He waited for a reaction. There was none. "See, I'm gonna just let go of these suckers and let the music play out. We'll go together. How's that grab ya?"

Van der Meer dropped the handgrips. The music played again. Was it slowing down? Yes. Still no word from the mystery driver. The car stopped and then slowly turned right. Van der Meer saw the street sign out his passenger window. "Harborside Drive." That was a big clue. They weren't leaving the airport. *But where?* thought Van der Meer wildly. His bluff didn't work; there was no reaction from the driver. Van der Meer grabbed the diabolical grips and squeezed. A pain shot down his left forearm. He bit his lip and moaned softly.

Trooper Verriel slammed his open hand twice, hard, on the left rear quarter panel of a grimy cab and barked an order. "Move it!."

His lapel radio diverted his attention. "F nineteen, F nineteen . . . this is a code 8, a code 8."

"F nineteen here," the trooper responded routinely.

"Be on the lookout for a white Rolls Royce, front vanity plate has letters spelling Alpha, Whiskey, Echo. Driver is reported to be armed and dangerous."

"This is F nineteen. Suspect vehicle was already here, picked up a white male and left . . ." Verriel checked his watch ". . . about three, maybe three and a half minutes ago."

The dispatcher switched gears immediately. "Attention all units. White Rolls is three minutes out of Delta terminal. Driver is presumed armed and dangerous. Do not approach. Report the suspect vehicle's location immediately."

Sergeant Ben Klein, F Troop shift commander at the airport, knew he had a hundred eyes out there with scanners. Shuttle drivers and cabbies were listening.

"Come on, somebody. Call in. I know you've seen the damn thing. Do it," Klein whispered urgently. "Just do it."

Van der Meer now knew it was useless to communicate with his executioner. With the inexorable, deliberate, unswerving determination of a great white shark homing in on its prey, the person driving Baxton's Rolls Royce could not be diverted from his deadly course. Van der Meer tried to conserve energy. He was able to get enough slack in the wires to lift the hand grips a bit higher, allowing him the luxury of resting his elbows on the padding below the privacy screen. But this meant he had to lean forward, barely sitting on the seat, making it impossible to hold onto the grips when the Rolls turned. There were three turns thus far. Twice Van der Meer had to release the grips to ease cramps in his forearms. Each time the haunting theme plinked ever more slowly.

The big car suddenly lurched to the right, and Van der Meer fell against the left rear door, hard. He welcomed the brief release of the grips. Both arms now ached beyond his endurance, and hung limply, trembling out of control. Although Van der Meer could see out of the car, the tinted glass hid him from view. Several times, people who stared at the handsome car looked directly into his eyes, but his shouts never carried more than a few feet past the heavily sound-proofed doors and bullet-proof glass. Now the limo was headed directly toward the Harborside Hyatt Conference Center, strategically located at Logan with a magnificent view of Boston Harbor and the downtown skyline.

"Hey," Van der Meer said to the driver, rubbing his arms, listening to the music getting slower. "They've got a great breakfast buffet in there. I'm buying. We can talk things over." The car turned hard right again and accelerated. This time, Van der Meer fell back into the seat. Only the *plinkety plink* of the tiny music box broke the frustrating silence. "You know what?" Van der Meer said. "Buy your own goddamn breakfast." He picked up the hand grips, gritted his teeth, and squeezed "and go fuck your self," he hissed.

The big car turned hard to the left throwing Van der Meer into the right rear window. He sat up and peered out the front window as the driver nosed into a very tight parking space. The car on the left, an old, grey Buick Le Sabre, was strategically parked so that the right wheels encroached into the adjacent space. No one would be able to squeeze in once another car parked to its right. The right side of the Rolls scraped against the adjacent car and stopped. Van der Meer watched the driver calmly exit the limo, slip out of the tight space and get into the Buick. The engine turned over but didn't start immediately. "Don't start," pleaded Van der Meer through gritted teeth. "Don't start, please don't start." It started and the LeSabre quickly pulled away. He strained to see the face of his persecutor but he could not. The Buick left the parking lot, turned left and headed back toward the airport. Van der Meer was now alone. Ironically, his narrow view of the downtown

Downsized

Boston skyline across Boston Harbor included the AWE headquarters building, its blue glass glistening in the early morning sun.

"Damn you, Baxton," he yelled. "Damn you." Van der Meer, exercise grips closed tightly, rested his forehead on the security screen and pressed the knuckles of his two hands hard against his cheeks. It helped to keep his fists tightly closed and ease the pain in his arms.

He prayed.

Xavier Munoz had only seen a Rolls Royce up close once in his life. That was 10 years ago in Puerto Vallarta and he never forgot that special look of elegance. He knew that only the truly rich people in the world could own one -- *los ricos*. He'd never bothered to fantasize about owning such a car. Now he saw his second Rolls in the rearview mirror of his Hyatt mini-van. He watched in amazement as it turned into employee parking lot B, next to the hotel.

A strange place for a Rolls Royce, he thought. Xavier noticed where it parked, facing the harbor. His curiosity got the better of him. One glance at his watch told him it was time for another run. He radioed the desk. "Is anybody going to the terminal area?" "No," was the terse reply. "Got a group waiting at American."

Xavier didn't want to miss this opportunity -- only a few minutes out of an otherwise boring day. He didn't pay particular attention to the Buick that passed him on the way out of the lot. He pulled directly behind the limo, got out and slowly walked to the right side.

"Jesu Christo!" he exclaimed when he saw the expensive Rolls jammed against the adjacent car. He ran around to the left side, pressed his face against the tinted glass, cupped his hands around his eyes and peered in. Van der Meer dropped the grips and lunged toward the window. Xavier jumped back when a face suddenly appeared.

"Help," yelled Van der Meer. "Can you hear me?"

"Yes," answered a surprised Xavier.

"Get the police. Please hurry. No time to waste. There's a bomb in here. A bomb," Do you understand?"

"Yes," said Xavier. "En el nombre de dios," he muttered as he ran back to the hotel in a panic, leaving his mini-van behind the Rolls, engine running.

Van der Meer listened to the music slow down to the point where each note followed the next painfully, the tune unrecognizable. "Why didn't he take the van?" he thought. "Damn, it's 80 yards

Downsized

to the hotel." Van der Meer watched as several people disembarked from the water shuttle bus merely yards from him. His eyes focused on the bright flashes of colored light splashing off the mobile sculpture next to the hotel. It reminded him of sparklers he played with as a child on the fourth of July. Help was on the way. He wondered if it would arrive in time.

Baxton reached for the ringing phone on his desk, but McGillicuddy beat him to it. Baxton frowned. "McGillicuddy here, what's happening?" Neiberg, Baxton, Franklin and Ms. Tierney stared at him. He raised his right hand exuberantly in a thumbs-up signal. "They've found the Rolls! Van der Meer's alive!" Ms. Tierney made the sign of the cross.

"Oh, no," McGillicuddy said, raising his hand to stop the brief celebration that had erupted spontaneously. He looked over at Neiberg. "There's a bomb in the car."

"Where's the Rolls?" Neiberg asked.

McGillicuddy hung up the phone and walked over to the window. "For Christ's sake," McGillicuddy said, pointing across the harbor. "He's sitting right over there, to the left of the Hyatt Hotel, in a goddamn parking lot, in full view of everyone." He made a fist with both hands and pressed them against the window, "and I can't do a damn thing to help him."

Van der Meer was not encouraged by the sound of emergency vehicles rushing toward him. He looked at his watch -- 9:17. His ordeal had only lasted seven minutes and he was exhausted. First, the left hand gave out. He willed his hand to close. It would not. He cursed whoever wrote the theme for Dr. Zhivago. There was not much time left. Seconds? Maybe.

Baxton's glass wall was strategically placed for the drama unfolding at Logan. Tiny white caps dotted the harbor's surface, signaling a strong northeast breeze. Franklin, McGillicuddy, Ms. Tierney and Neiberg all stood quietly in front of the huge window overlooking Boston Harbor and the airport. Baxton remained seated, chair swiveled around to face the harbor. He looked down at the envelope in which the ominous downsizing memo had been delivered. "Van der Meer, Fulton and Baxton," he read.

Downsized

The inference was inescapable and not lost on Baxton. Johnston was already dead. Van der Meer's life now hung on a thread. Two names remained -- Fulton and Baxton. Was this really the list of persons to be brutally murdered? That thought sent a chill through Baxton. McGillicuddy ran to the communications wall, played with a dial and adjusted the volume. A crisp, clear radio transmissions broke the silence.

". . .we are approaching lot Bravo."

"This is F 19, turning onto Harborside Drive."

"F 12 Here. Subject vehicle in sight . . . Damn, we've got a hotel minivan sittin' right behind it."

Neiberg saw the blue flashing lights of F 12's cruiser moving through the parking lot. His eyes followed. The lights stopped. "There it is!" yelled Neiberg, pointing. "I can see the minivan. It's red. That must be Van der Meer right in front of it, up against the fence."

Van der Meer breathed heavily. Sirens and flashing blue lights signaled that help was just moments away. He should be excited, he thought. But the little music box kept him from celebrating prematurely. He knew that time had run out. He quickly folded the handwritten instructions given to him by the person intent on killing him. In one brief respite from squeezing the handgrips, he wrote a very short message to Mary on the back of it. He placed the document into his wallet and shoved it deep within his leather clothing bag. He hoped it would survive whatever happened if the bomb actually exploded. There were moments when Van der Meer considered the possibility that there was no bomb; that his ordeal was someone's idea of a sick joke. He took one last look at the handgrips, looked down at his now useless hands and laughed. The irony of his predicament was not lost on him. Even in the face of death, he was buoyed by his good sense of humor.

"I couldn't squeeze you suckers again . . . even if my life depended on it," he said, settling back on the luxurious leather upholstery of Baxton's limo.

Baxton, Franklin, Neiberg, McGillicuddy and Ms. Tierney remained hushed at the window, watching the gathering of blue flashing lights in the distant parking lot. They waited breathlessly for the radio transmission that would announce Van der Meer's rescue.

"Oh, my God, oh, my God, oh, my God," cried Ms. Tierney, blessing herself repeatedly as a jet black plume of smoke rose high into the air above the spot where Van der Meer was trapped. It climbed upward, silently, ominously, slowly revealing an orange fire ball deep within the belly of the black cloud. The police radio chronicled the obvious.

"This is F 19! She's blown. Repeat -- subject vehicle is blown."

Neiberg's shoulders slumped. He felt a deep sense of responsibility for the failure to save Van der Meer. Someone had now killed two men and he still didn't have a clue. He turned from the window, picked up the downsizing memo on Baxton's desk and quietly left the office.

Baxton broke his long silence and pointed at McGillicuddy as he spoke. "Alert all of our security personnel at every location…Van der Meer will be the last victim. Not one more man dies. Do you understand me?"

"Yes." McGillicuddy said, but he had no idea how to stop someone who moved as freely and invisibly as the air he breathed.

<u>San Francisco, 6:25 a.m. Pacific Time</u>.
Sid Fulton intended to sleep late on this first full day of the Jet Age Aircraft acquisition. Around-the-clock meetings were scheduled with Greer's production and design managers. The first was

at 10 a.m. in Greer's office; the rest would be at the penthouse suite with sumptuous luncheons and suppers augmenting the business discussions. A call so early in the morning annoyed him. He reached for the phone and didn't hide his displeasure. "I did not ask for a wake-up call," he said sternly, squinting at the fuzzy red numbers on the radio clock across the room.

"Fulton, is that you?" asked a very familiar voice.

"Yes Mr. Baxton, it's me." Fulton sat up, switching gears instantly. "Is there something wrong?"

"Yes. You'll be hearing about it soon on the news. Van der Meer's dead."

The words made no sense to Fulton. He had a late supper with Van der Meer at La Contadina's. They shared a bottle of wine and a few laughs about old times. He saw Van der Meer jump into a cab and give him a cheery- thumbs- up just nine or ten hours earlier. He could still see the big grin on his face. For some reason unknown to Fulton, Van der Meer was particularly happy, looking forward to returning to Boston. "Jesus, did his plane crash?" Fulton asked nervously. "Good God Almighty, what happened?"

"No. It wasn't a plane crash. The details aren't important. He was murdered." Baxton's tone was unemotional. He might as well have been talking about last quarter's sales figures. The message carried its own emotional impact.

"When the hell was he killed?" Fulton asked. "Where did it happen?" he added, unable to control his emotions. "Jesus, what's goin' on back there? What the fuck's goin' on?"

"Stay calm," said Baxton sternly. "You'll learn all about it soon enough. For now, I want you to know you'll have two bodyguards with you 24 hours a day."

That comment hit Fulton hard. Until now, it was somebody else's problem. Johnston dies -- that's terrible, but it's Johnston. Van der Meer dies. That's horrible, too. But it's still not personal. Not really. News of personal bodyguards brings it close to home. Fulton was suddenly speechless.

"Did you hear me?" said Baxton.

"Yeah . . ., yes. But I don't understand. Am I in danger? Is that what you're tryin' to tell me? I'm in danger?"

Baxton thought about that question carefully. In business, honesty was not always the best policy, particularly for Baxton. "No, damn it. It's just a precaution and I don't want attention drawn to those bodyguards. They'll be dressed like businessmen. Introduce them as your assistants. You got that?"

"Yes. Yes."

"Fulton, I'm announcing your promotion," Baxton hesitated briefly, "to acting V.P. of Operations." He emphasized "acting."

"Yes. Yes." Fulton was now repeating himself nervously. *Damn!* He thought, Baxton could smell weakness from a mile away. The conversation ended as abruptly as it began, leaving Fulton to ponder an uncertain future. Acting V.P. of National Operations, he thought. Why acting? He made certain all entrances to the penthouse suite were secure and headed toward the bathroom and a hot shower.

Fayetteville, N.C. February 18, 0630 hours

Kimberly Hale stood at attention in the living room of her modest one bedroom apartment. She stared intently into the free standing full length mirror strategically placed to the right of the front door to permit a final inspection before leaving. A first lieutenant stared back, dressed in camouflage combat fatigues bearing the arrowhead, broadsword and lightning bolt insignia of the United States Army Special Forces Command, Airborne. The uniform was well starched, creases dead center and sharp as a razor. Each trouser leg was bloused evenly just below the tops of spit-shined jump boots. A tailored shirt was tucked in tightly at the waist but cut to minimize her distinctly feminine bust line.

She carefully placed a helmet on her head, leveled it and tightened the chin strap until it squeezed the flesh on her cheeks, giving her lips the appearance of pouting. It was a necessary accommodation for a head too small to keep a helmet in place during a jump from a C-130 Hercules traveling at more than 120 miles per hour. A quick tug on the chin strap release returned her face to normal. Kimberly's face was very pretty, with penetrating light blue eyes framed by natural blond hair cut short for a more military appearance. Actually, that face seemed out of place in combat garb. But the Special Forces Command Public Affairs Office at Fort Bragg was precisely where Kimberly Hale wanted to be, at least for now.

A single loud bang on her apartment door signaled the arrival of Captain Andrew "Andy" Grissom, an A-Team leader in the 7th Special Forces Group. "Hey, Hale! Y'all in there?" he shouted. Andy spoke with an easy on the ears Texas drawl.

"No, sir," she responded playfully. "This is a recording."

"Well, y'all better push the fast forward button if you're gonna ride with me."

Kimberly smiled. Andy was quick witted. He always found a way to make her laugh. She liked that. Andy did not hide his feelings toward "the prettiest lieutenant in this here United States Army," as he frequently referred to her. However, Kimberly was not ready for any romantic entanglements. She kept their relationship at a comfortable arms length -- a feat made more difficult because of Andy's persistence. She removed the helmet, shook her head from side to side several times to smooth out slightly matted hair, took one last look in the mirror and turned to leave. "Coming," she said as she opened the door. "What's your hurr ..." She stopped in mid-sentence at the sight of a six foot, three inch man in combat gear wearing a foot wide banner that went from helmet to waist. "Welcome Home Lt. Hale," it read in large block letters. Kimberly laughed. "Well Andy, thanks," she said, her face briefly flushing with embarrassment.

"Thanks?" Andy replied in mock disappointment. "Ah was hopin' for a kiss too."

Kimberly pushed Andy aside, giving him a light nudge to the stomach with her helmet. The banner fell to the floor. "You know lieutenants don't kiss captains in uniform," she said in an instructional tone as she headed toward the rear door leading to the parking lot.

"Good," Andy yelled as he rolled up the welcome home sign. "Ah'll get naked then."

Kimberly looked back toward Andy just before opening the door. "Captain, haven't you been reading the papers? That sounds like sexual harassment to me."

Andy opened a button just below his name tag and shoved the rolled sign into his fatigue shirt. "Hell, lieutenant, no such thing. For your information," he added taking giant strides in an effort to hold the door for her, "What Ah'm doin' is good ole fashioned Texas-style flirtin'. And besides," he shouted to the back of Kimberly's head as she walked quickly toward his car. He softened his voice, "Ah'm not your commanding officer. Ah'm just your friendly next door neighbor."

Kimberly smiled again but did not let Andy see it. Behind the wheel, Andy changed the subject. "How was Boston?"

"Boring."

Andy drove out of the parking area and turned right. "What did y'all do for thirty days?"

"Nothing much. Saw a few bad movies, read a few good books and . . ."

"Damn. Sounds like a complete waste of thirty days' leave."

"That's your opinion," she replied tersely. "I needed the rest."

"Well, neighbor, my mission is gonna be to bring back the excitement in your life." Andy reached into his top left pocket and retrieved four tickets. "We're gonna start off with the Fayetteville

Symphony Orchestra tonight and on Sunday we're goin' to the NASCAR races in Rockin'ham."

Kimberly hit Andy on his right shoulder with the top of her helmet.

"Ouch!" he yelled.

"Do you ever ask ladies for a date or do you always just tell them they're going?"

"Hell, mostly, they ask me," he said with a big grin on his face. "Only kidding," he quickly added. "Really, Ah thought you'd enjoy the symphony. Ah'm just hopin' you'll go to the races."

"I'll think about it."

"Good."

Andy drove slowly past the "Welcome to Fort Bragg" sign, leaned forward to look at the sky through the windshield. It was one of those cloudless, blue, infinitely high skies.

"Great day for a jump, ain't it," he said.

"Every day's a great day for a jump."

Andy pulled into a parking space marked "Capt. Grissom, 7th SFG". He turned to Kimberly and gave her left knee a gentle slap with his right hand.

"Well, let's go do it," he said. "Let's go do it."

<u>Boston, District Attorney's Office. 7:30 a.m.</u>
Gus Warner held up the *Herald*: A one-word banner headline filled the top third of page one: <u>**DOWNSIZED**</u>! A picture of the bombed-out hulk

of Baxton's limo filled the rest of the page. The killer's press release was featured on page two. "Another goddamn catchy headline and we still don't have a clue."

"I like it," Sandra Jones said. "It puts the whole case in perspective."

"What the heck do you mean by that?" Gus asked incredulously.

"Hey, if we don't find the killer soon we'll all be outta here, or should I say downsized." Sandra replied, drawing her right index finger across her throat.

"Very funny," Warner said. "Just remember, I'm an elected official. Two years 'til next election. Meanwhile, you'll make a great scapegoat if things get rough."

"Somebody remind me not to joke with the elected official so early in the morning!"

A ringing phone ended the idle chatter. "Warner here." He held his hand over the mouthpiece and whispered: "The Mayor." "I know," he continued, "the bombing was dreadful. Sure. See you there." Warner banged the phone down hard. "Damn. We're having a press conference this morning. The bombing's focused national attention on the case. Governor called for a media show."

Warner glanced at Jones. "Sandra, can we be ready?"

"Don't worry about it," she said confidently. "We'll knock their socks off."

"Hey, I don't know from socks," Walsh said, "But if you play your cards right Gus, you'll be the next governor."

"Who's got cards?" Warner lamented. "Who the hell has cards?"

<u>San Francisco, 4:45 a.m. Pacific Time.</u>
Sid Fulton could not sleep. Each time he looked at the glowing red numerals on the digital clock by his bed stand they had only advanced 10 or 15 minutes from when he last closed his eyes. The two bodyguards who arrived the evening before did not relieve his anxiety. Johnston and Van der Meer were dispatched by a magician, a ninja-like assassin who struck without warning. Fulton kicked back the covers, jumped to his feet, turned on the light and began shoving clothing into a suitcase. He stopped abruptly and walked out into the hall, putting on lights as he went. "Wake up," he yelled opening the door to the large bedroom next to his, turning on the lights and clapping his hands. "Up and at 'em."

"What the heck you doin'?" said the sleepy voice from a pile of blankets. He looked at the clock. "For Chrissake, it's not even five yet."

"We're leaving," Fulton yelled. "Don't even brush your teeth."

The second bodyguard appeared outside his bedroom door. "You know somethin' we don't?" he said, rubbing his eyes.

"Yeah," replied Fulton. "We're outta here."

"Slow down," said the first guard. "We're not going anywhere without orders from Boston."

"Suit your self," yelled Fulton. "But I'm leaving in 10 minutes." Both bodyguards followed him back to his bedroom. The first guard spoke firmly. "Hey, you're not goin' anywhere unless we say so. And we say you stay put until we get approval from Boston."

Fulton took a good look at the muscular man giving orders. If he meant what he said, Fulton would never get past him. "Look," said Fulton. "You guys are here to keep me alive, right?"

"Yeah.".

"What's your name again?"

"Tony. Tony Vee, that's V-E-E."

"Look, Tony. Lyin' awake all night in the dark made me see something plain as day."

"What?"

"Whoever killed Johnston and Van der Meer had to know every move those guys were gonna make. Shit, nobody knew Van der Meer was heading home except his wife, me and Baxton . . . and Mrs. Tierney, Baxton's secretary. She made the travel arrangements on the company computer.

David G. Hanrahan Esq.

She pressed a button and Van der Meer's itinerary was immediately e-mailed around the world on the AWE net. The killer was given blueprints for setting up the kill. Well, starting in," Fulton checked his watch, "five minutes, I'm off the system. The son of a bitch is gonna have to kill me the old fashioned way . . . find me first!"

"What ya say makes sense, but we don't even know for sure if you're a target."

"Don't care. We act like I am."

"OK, OK. I agree. But shouldn't we tell the cops about what you figured out?"

"God help us all if they have to be told something that basic. But you're right. I'll send Boston a fax and then we leave."

A few minutes later, the three men, unshaven, stood in the foyer facing the lone elevator that serviced the penthouse. Tony reached for the button. Fulton grabbed his wrist. "No," he said firmly, "we take the stairs."

"Shit, it's a long fuckin' way down."

"But we're a hell of a lot safer. Wait a minute," he added, turning and heading back into the penthouse. "I almost forgot my laptop."

The trio left the hotel and walked down California Avenue, the eastern sky brightening with early morning light. Fulton breathed easier as he walked past Chinatown, heading toward the

Embarcadero. A fax arrived for Baxton at AWE headquarters logged in at 7:55 a.m.:

> KILLER HAS PICKED OUR NET CLEAN. KNOWS OUR EVERY MOVE. TELL POLICE. I'VE VACATED PENTHOUSE. WILL KEEP MY LOCATION A SECRET. BODYGUARDS NOT ENOUGH - BUT I FEEL SAFER WITH THEM. THANX.

<u>Allston, 7:50 a.m.</u>
Jeanie stared at a montage of papers and string taped to her bedroom wall. "William Coine! What in heaven's name are you doing?"

"The beginning of a wall chart," Coine said without turning around. He was sitting on the edge of the bed, contemplating his creation. Jeanie had been to her husband's office when he was on the force and saw his infamous method of compiling evidence in a case. She never expected to see it decorating her bedroom wall.

"OK. First you tell me it's only a hobby. Now there's a wall chart. Is this still a matter of passing interest or," Jeanie paused and folded her arms, "well, suppose you tell me."

"I confess I'm intrigued. But it's still only a hobby thing." He hesitated briefly and smiled. "Would you rather I collect stamps?"

David G. Hanrahan Esq.

"Good heavens, not if you stick 'em on the wall." She sat down on the bed next to Coine. "Don't you need more information . . . you know, like inside stuff that doesn't appear in the papers?"

"Oh, sure I do. But that's if I was working on the case. All I'm interested in is developing an understanding of what's really going on here."

"Gee, you're slipping. There's a murder going on here . . . looks like maybe a serial killer with a sick sense of humor."

"Smart alec," Coine said. "We can't really be sure if we're dealing with a classic serial killer profile yet. We've got two different methods . . . knife and bomb. We also have two executives in the same company. The serial killer compulsively selects victims in the same general class, but randomly."

Jeanie pointed to the names of Fulton and Franklin on Coine's chart. "Are you making a prediction here?" The morning papers and local TV news had headlined the killer's downsizing memo but there was no mention of the envelope in which it arrived.

Coine laughed. "Hell, no. I'd join a carnival if I could do that. No prediction. It's just a wild guess."

"Detective's guess do they?"

"All the time. Look," he said, tapping his finger on Baxton's picture. "This guy hand picked his top

Downsized

four executives. Johnston, Van der Meer, Fulton and Franklin were numbers 1, 2, 3 and 4 in the company chain of command under Baxton. 1 and 2 are gone. That seems to have been deliberate. 3 and 4 must be having a hard time sleeping. I've put them on the chart because it's logical. Now, if Fulton ends up dead, I'll put money on Franklin's being next."

"You'd think they'd give those poor men around-the-clock protection."

"I'm sure they will. Hell, if I were those guys, I'd trade my Mercedes in for an Abrams tank."

"And the serial killer issue?" Jeanie asked.

"Killing the top executives in the same company smacks of a vendetta, not the work of your typical serial killer. A knife to the chest is the mark of an assassin. On the other hand, a bomber who goes to great lengths to eliminate one man is most likely a person with a mighty grudge. Soon as we find a person with a motive to kill Johnston and Van der Meer for personal reasons and/or a grudge against the Company, and an opportunity, we'll have our killer."

Jeanie noticed the "we" and it was some cause for concern.

"So when does it end?" she asked.

"Who knows? Not until they catch the killer or the bugger's appetite for murder is satisfied."

David G. Hanrahan Esq.

"No, not the killings," said Jeanie, smiling. "The wall chart papering our bedroom. How long do we have to look at it?"

"It really bothers you?"

"Well, it sure gives the bedroom a messy appearance and I'm not thrilled with Baxton's brooding face staring at me."

Coine took Baxton's picture, lifted it carefully, replaced the scotch tape and returned it to the wall face down. "There. Is that better?"

"Yes. Let's have some breakfast," Jeanie said, giving Coine a hug.

"Sold."

Coine took one last look at his handiwork before heading for the kitchen.

"What if . . .," he said, pausing in the doorway.

"What if what?"

"What if the wall's not big enough?"

Jeanie grabbed his left ear lobe and led him out of the bedroom. "Bill Coine, don't you dare wallpaper this house with your hobby . . . one wall! That's the limit!"

"OK already, just kidding."

The phone rang. Jeanie winced. A wall chart and a ringing phone spelled trouble.

"Hello," Coine heard her say. "Is this some kind of joke?" She hung up suddenly.

"What was that all about?"

Downsized

"Some clown said he was Bradford Baxton."

"Hell, nobody but Neiberg even knows I know who the hell Baxton is or that I'm the slightest bit interested in this case."

"It's a stupid joke," said Jeanie, as the phone rang again. Coine picked it up and said nothing. He listened with an educated ear -- background noises, breathing pattern -- all could be important.

"Hello," said the voice. "Is anyone there?" It was a firm voice. Not the least bit suggestive of a prankster.

"Yes. Who are you looking for?" Coine asked warily.

"Retired detective William Coine."

"Who wants him?"

"This is Bradford Baxton and . . ."

Coine cut him off immediately. "Where are you?" he demanded.

"My office in Boston."

Coine pressed the disconnect button then lifted it, waited for a dial tone and dialed 411. Armed with Baxton's office number, he dialed it quickly.

"Good morning, Amalgamated," said a friendly female voice. "How may I help you?"

"Bradford Baxton."

"Whom shall I say is calling?"

"Bill Coine."

"One moment please."

After a long pause, "Well, at least you're not a fool," said a now-familiar voice.

"I wouldn't care if I was. Even fools enjoy retirement," said Coine. He held his hand over the speaker. "It is Baxton."

Jeanie's jaw dropped. "Dear mother of God. Why?"

Coine put his index finger over his mouth signalling her to be quiet.

"You must be wondering why I've called you . . . by the way, I hope I'm not calling too early."

"No, it's not too early and you're no fool either. Why are you calling me?"

"Touché. I called on the recommendation of Joe . . . Joseph McGillicuddy. He's chief of our security."

"Is that retired Deputy Police Superintendent McGillicuddy?"

"Yes. You remember him?"

"Of course. But I'm not looking for any security job and something tells me you're not in charge of the personnel department."

Jeanie frowned. Coine was being typically rude. Coine frowned back.

"So what is it . . . what do you really want?"

"Good," said Baxton. "I like a man who gets to the point. I want to retain you as a private detective to . . ."

Downsized

"Hold on! Who in blazes told you I was a private detective?"

"No one told me that."

"Good. Then you know the answer is no."

"But I haven't asked you the question yet," said Baxton, now trying to restrain his own temper.

"Well, unless I heard wrong . . . and I didn't . . . you said you wanted to retain me as a private detective."

"But you did not let me finish why."

"Why's not important. Answer's no."

Baxton had never been treated like this by anyone. He could feel his face turning red as he tried desperately not to let his anger interfere with his mission. "Well," Baxton finally said apologetically. "I misspoke. I need someone to consult with concerning the deaths of my two officers . . . Johnston and Van der Meer. What I have in mind is a wide range of services including . . ."

Coine interrupted again. "Mr. Baxton. I'm retired . . . happily. And my wife doesn't want me working 24-hour days anymore." Coine walked over toward Jeanie. "Here, let her tell you herself. Honey, do you want me to be a consultant for Baxton to help solve the Johnston and Van der Meer murders?"

Jeanie's face reddened with embarrassment as Coine handed her the phone. "I'm sorry, Mr.

Baxton. Bill gets like this when he's trying to make a point. I would never interfere in his life . . . honest."

Baxton sat stunned, knocked completely off balance by Coine's style. "Well, Mrs. Coine . . ."

"Call me Jeanie."

"Well, Jeanie. I'm sure your husband gives your feelings and judgments a great deal of weight. Ask him to think about it, will you? We need his experience. He comes highly recommended. Thank you."

The phone went dead before Jeanie could answer. She turned to Coine. "Darn you, that was embarrassing."

Coine laughed. "Well, if you want me to go to work, say the word."

"You know I don't."

"Well, you should have been honest with him."

"I was. If it is really important to you, you know I'd give in."

"Tell me another one," said Coine, still smiling. He took the phone from Jeanie before she decided to throw it at him.

"Thanks for saying no," Jeanie said. "Come over here. Let me give you a big kiss." Coine obliged.

"Waddaya know, a call from Baxton himself," Coine said, unable to process what just transpired.

"Hey, it's only fitting," said Jeanie smugly.

Downsized

"How so?"

"The King of Downsizing wants the King of Detectives."

"Good point, but I'm the ex-King of Detectives. Hey, let's go for a walk. After that close call with a job, I could use some fresh air."

<u>Boston, AWE Headquarters. 8:15 a.m.</u>
Baxton hung up his phone and exploded in rage. "Are you crazy?" he shouted at McGillicuddy. "Do you think a . . ." Baxton searched for the right word, ". . . an insolent buffoon like this Coine could ever work for me? He was contemptuous of me. Damn it all, McGillicuddy, you should have warned me I'd be dealing with an eccentric."

McGillicuddy sat quietly in one of the two chairs in front of Baxton's desk.

"Well, say something, dammit," Baxton demanded.

"Mr. Baxton, you wanted my recommendation for the best detective. That's Coine. But don't take my word for it."

"I won't," said Baxton, pushing his intercom button.

"Jane, tell Franklin to get me all the info he can on William Coine, retired Massachusetts state police lieutenant detective."

"Detective Lieutenant," McGillicuddy corrected.

"Detective Lieutenant William Coine, retired. I need it as soon as possible."

McGillicuddy leaned forward. "You know, Mr. Baxton, I did tell you to let me talk to him first."

"Next time, suppose you tell me why! Meanwhile, find me that damn fool, Fulton."

San Francisco, 6:00 a.m. Pacific Time.

Tony stood at the bottom of what appeared to be a stairway to the sky. He bent his neck to the limit, leaned over backwards until it hurt, and still he couldn't see where it ended. "No fuckin' way I'm goin' up all those stairs," he protested. The three disheveled men had travelled the length of California Street from the Fairmount, turned left onto Drumm, walked along the Embarcadero and were now standing at the foot of Telegraph Hill.

"Look," said Fulton apologetically, "I'm sorry, but we're almost there."

"Where?" said an exasperated Tony.

"There are a few rooming houses off of Washington Square, just below the Coit Monument. There are bound to be some vacancies this time of year."

"Shit," said Tony, looking up the viciously steep hill and the endless steps. "I figured the worst that could happen to me in this job was to get shot at." He removed his jacket and swung it over his right shoulder. "I ain't gettin' paid enough to have a fuckin' heart attack walkin' up all them stairs."

"Come on," Fulton cajoled. "We'll take it nice and easy . . . stop and rest whenever you say."

"We don't even have our runnin' shoes on," complained the second bodyguard, who usually said very little, leaving most of the talking to Tony.

"I promise," said Fulton. "We get rooms, grab a hot shower and . . ."

"Get me some oxygen," said Tony.

"No, but we'll take the rest of the day off."

"O.K.," said Tony, shaking his head slowly from side to side. He pointed his left index finger at Fulton and shook it in scolding fashion. "But if I get a fuckin' heart attack, I'm gonna kill you myself."

"It's a deal," said Fulton, smiling.

The three men slowly climbed, Fulton in the lead, followed closely by his two unhappy bodyguards. "Look at the bright side," Fulton said, already noticeably out of breath after only a few minutes, "your job just got a lot easier."

"Oh, yeah, how you figure?" asked Tony.

"*We* don't even know where we are," said Fulton. "The killer will never find us."

"Oh, yeah," Tony shot back, wheezing slightly. "Fucker's probably trackin' you with a satellite." The second bodyguard laughed. So did Tony.

"Very funny," said Fulton.

"Hey," yelled the second bodyguard. "You see that sign?"

"Fulton stopped and turned.

"Over there," pointing. "In the window . . . that brown house behind the trees."

The sign was barely visible; Fulton had passed it by.

ROOMS FOR RENT
WEEKLY-MONTHLY
MEALS

The house was one of many dotting the steep hillside on both sides of the stairs. Built precariously in the side of Telegraph Hill, it appeared to defy gravity. Redwood stain, dulled by time and weather, blended nicely into the tree-covered terrain. Fulton was delighted by the complete isolation and perfect camouflage. He jogged down a path leading to an unlocked gate. Lights were on in several areas of the tri-level building. The smell of freshly brewed coffee and muffins baking was irresistible.

"Men, if the three of us can be accommodated," said Fulton with a broad grin, "we're home, sweet home."

"Shit," replied Tony, unsmiling. "There's no fuckin' elevator up here."

Fulton rang the door bell.

"Come in," called a friendly female voice. "Door's open."

As he opened the door, Fulton breathed in the delicious aroma, and felt a sense of peace for the first time since news of Van der Meer's tragic death.

Allston, 10:00 a.m.
"Bill, get in here . . . quickly."

"What is it?" he yelled from the bedroom, preoccupied with his wall chart.

"If you don't move it, you'll miss it!"

"What? I'll miss what?"

"The press conference about the Johnston and Van der Meer murders."

Coine walked into the living room. "Why didn't you just say so?"

"Be quiet and listen," Jeanie commanded.

"Yes, dear."

Boston, AWE Headquarters. 10:00 a.m.
Baxton, Mrs. Tierney, Franklin and McGillicuddy sat in front of Baxton's TV wall. A very large flat screen showed Sandra Jones standing behind a podium, flanked by several men. Warner was one of them. Sandra surveyed the assembled press corps, squinted slightly under bright lights and waited for the group to settle down. She spoke confidently, no hint of nervousness.

"Good morning, ladies and gentlemen. I'm Sandra Jones, First Assistant District Attorney and Chief of Homicide. As you know, two prominent executives at Amalgamated Worldwide Enterprises have been murdered. You also know that the killer . . . or killers . . ." Sandra's use of the plural sent a murmur through the crowd. It especially angered Baxton. Sandra continued. ". . . issued a press release suggesting that the murders were part of a macabre downsizing scheme."

"Damn it all," shouted a red-faced Baxton, "that's irresponsible. One goddamn killer is bad enough. Now she's suggesting there may be a terrorist squad." Baxton grabbed McGillicuddy by his arm. "I want that b...." he stopped, remembering Mrs. Tierney was sitting quietly nearby, "sorry excuse for a District Attorney squelched. Get me the mayor as soon as this preposterous conference is over."

Across town in the Coine apartment, Jeanie was surprised. "Have you considered the possibility of more than one killer?"

"No. It's too soon for that kind of speculation. Suggesting multiple assassins in a press conference could come back to haunt the D.A."

"Why?"

"Not now, honey. Don't wanna miss anything."

". . . and so," Sandra continued, "Because of security concerns, we decided earlier to withhold one piece of information related to the press release. However, we believe it is important to divulge it now."

Coine leaned forward in anticipation.

"Now what is she going to do to sabotage us?" Baxton yelled, slapping his hand loudly on his knee. "This woman is single-handedly going to destroy my company."

Sandra picked up an envelop and displayed it for the audience. "The note was received at Amalgamated's headquarters in an envelope addressed to three named individuals."

"Oh, no, don't do it," yelled Baxton. "Jesus Christ Almighty, *don't do it.*"

"It contained the names of Van der Meer, Fulton and Baxton in that order."

"Bingo," yelled Coine. Jeanie jumped.

"What?"

"I was right," he said. "This is a vendetta of some kind and Fulton's next."

"The poor man," Jeanie said sympathetically."I wonder if he's watching the press conference?"

Coine could not contain himself. "I've got to get in touch with Neiberg right away."

"But he's standing behind Sandra Jones."

"I wish Neiberg told me about that envelope," Coine muttered as he walked over to a phone.

". . . if the killer intended that to be a list of victims, we feel . . ." Sandra was about to say "confident," but she dropped it. "There is a good chance the killing will stop with Van der Meer's death. It would be folly to make any more attempts now in the face of stepped-up security measures."

"Bullshit," said Baxton, still red-faced with anger. "McGillicuddy, what have you done to locate Fulton?" he added.

"Got our security people lookin' for a needle in a haystack in the streets of San Francisco."

"That's useless," Baxton shot back.

"Listen," said McGillicuddy, "Fulton's scheduled to meet with Greer in Greer's office at 10 a.m. his time. That's three hours from now. When he does, we'll grab him."

". . . so with Boston p.d., the state police and F.B.I. now coordinating efforts, we expect to have some meaningful answers soon. In the meantime, District Attorney Gus Warner is here to answer as many questions as he can . . . keeping in mind the need for some security."

Jeanie watched Coine punching numbers on the phone rapidly.

"You're going to miss the D.A.," she said.

Coine waived her off. "Hello. I need to speak with Joe McGillicuddy. This is an emergency." Coine paced back and forth. "No, dammit, it can't wait. Get him now." Coine covered the phone. "He must be in Baxton's office watching the press conference."

Downsized

"You should be doing the same thing," Jeanie said, annoyed at the interruption, "not with Baxton; I mean here," she added.

A reporter stood up when Warner pointed to him. "Sir, it's no secret Amalgamated has been a leader over the years in downsizing. Are the chickens coming home to roost, so to speak . . . I mean, are these murders related to the company's history of laying people off by the thousands?"

The phone in Baxton's office rang. "Who the hell is that?" Baxton shouted. "I said no interruptions. Mrs. Tierney, tell whoever the hell that is to call back later . . . much later, and cut off all calls."

"One moment, please," Mrs. Tierney whispered to the insistent caller. She walked over to McGillicuddy, cupped her hands over his ears and whispered, "Joe. It's for you. He wouldn't give his name. He said it was a matter of life and death."

". . . and because of that, it is much too early to focus on any single motive. At this point, we're keeping all options open and casting a wide net," Warner said, feeling the heat from television lights and wondering if his rise in blood pressure was making him break out in a sweat. He was not happy as he pointed to the next interrogator.

"Who the hell is this?" asked an annoyed McGillicuddy.

Coine could hear Baxton shouting in the background. "Bill Coine, and please don't announce me to Baxton."

"For Chrissake, Bill, Baxton's on my ass for answering the phone. What's this life and death shit?"

"I had to get you to the phone . . . besides, it is critical info."

"Dammit, I don't have time right now."

"Later could be too late. Now just give me a minute."

McGillicuddy looked at one of the TV screens. He struggled to listen to Coine and Warner at the same time.

". . . good question," Warner said. "I'll try my best to answer it. Remember, we're in an ongoing investigation, things are fluid and can change as we piece things together."

". . . in other words," Coine said, trying to impress McGillicuddy with the importance of his hunch, "the killer now knows for sure the heat is on. I figure there'll be no more in-your-face open attacks. We know the bastard spent a helluva lot of time in and around company headquarters planning the Johnston hit. There was plenty of time and opportunity to booby trap Fulton's and Baxton's offices either before or on the night of Johnston's murder."

"We're convinced," said Warner, "that the perpetrator spent a great deal of time in and around Amalgamated's headquarters building, planning Johnston's murder."

McGillicuddy was shocked. Except for the booby trap idea, Coine and Warner were on the same page.

Baxton could no longer restrain himself. "Goddammit, Joe, you need to hear this more than me," he yelled. "Get the hell over here."

"I'll be right over, Mr. Baxton." McGillicuddy turned away from Baxton and whispered, "Coine, you gotta be nuts. What kind of booby trap?"

"Who the hell knows?" Coine yelled.

". . . so we know how the bomb used to kill Van der Meer was constructed, and that's extremely helpful," Warner said confidently. "We also know how the perpetrator ambushed Baxton's limo driver . . ."

"Point is," insisted Coine, "our killer went to a lot of trouble to kill Johnston and Van der Meer. He means business. If he listed victims, he's gonna give us victims. Now he'll be forced to kill via long distance. You know, with high powered rifles, some kind of timed device or booby trap. Damn it man, I'm right."

Now McGillicuddy was being yelled at on both ends of the phone. "What the hell should I do?

Baxton's gonna think I'm nuts suggesting booby traps."

"Will you get off the damn phone and get over here?" Baxton commanded.

"Bill, I gotta go."

Coine ran out of patience.

"Damn it, Joe, you've been around the block. To hell with Baxton, just take charge and do something. Just don't stand around with your finger up your ass." Coine slammed the phone in disgust.

"Bill Coine, who are you talking to like that?"

"McGillicuddy . . . I'm sorry." He sat down next to Jeanie, shaking his head. "I just can't believe that McGillicudy went from being a top notch cop to a befuddled corporate flunky."

"Will you try to contain your self. Listen to the D.A. Maybe you'll learn something else that's important."

". . . Baxton's Rolls Royce was equipped with bullet-proof material installed between the trunk and rear seat. The killer apparently gained access to the car during the early morning hours of the seventeenth while it was garaged at the Baxton residence. With simple tools and a great deal of patience, the killer prepared an entrance from the trunk into the passenger compartment. We think the killer remained in the trunk and went along for the ride from Baxton's home to the company underground parking garage. The big car blocked a security camera's view of the adjacent air exhaust vent cover, tinted glass shielded any activity in the car . . . and the rest you can imagine."

"McGillicuddy, I'm a goddamn laughing stock now," Baxton yelled, his face now contorted with rage. "Do you hear what they're saying? I drove the killer to work. Jesus, I've paid millions for security. How the fuck did you let this happen?"

A stinging rebuttal flashed through McGillicuddy's mind regarding Baxton's crucial delay in reporting the killer's press release. He bit his tongue. Suddenly, Baxton's attention was jolted back to the TV screen.

". . . and on that point, the Appeals Court just announced its decision confirming our right to keep Samuel Johnston's computer. But that's all I'm going to say on the subject."

Baxton jumped to his feet, now completely enraged. Mrs. Tierney quietly left the room.

"I'm surrounded by incompetents! And, Franklin, you're one of them. Why the fuck do I have to get an important court decision from the goddamn D.A. on television?"

"He must have received it just before the press conference," Franklin said nervously. "I'm as surprised as you."

"Your job is to not be surprised and to be goddamn certain I'm not surprised."

"But . . ."

"But hell! I want that computer back. Your job is on the line. You don't get it back soon, you're outta here. Do you understand me? Well, do you?"

"Yes," said Franklin, shocked at Baxton's irrational fixation on the return of Johnston's computer. "But . . ." He knew there was nothing further to say, so he wisely said nothing.

McGillicuddy took the opportunity to take the heat off Franklin. "While we're speaking about surprises, that call I took was from Bill Coine."

Baxton registered surprise. "What in hell did he want?"

"Nothing. He warned me that you and Fulton are in danger."

"Brilliant," Baxton said sarcastically. "The man's brilliant. Who in hell doesn't know that by now? And you wanted me to hire that jerk?"

"He was specific. He thinks your office -- or Fulton's -- may have been booby trapped. Says the killer had time to do just that either before or after Johnston's murder. I say Coine's hunch is a good one. I say we listen to him."

"And do what?" said Baxton, his voice deadly calm.

"We call in experts and have them tear the place apart. There are ways to determine if any electronic devices have been planted."

"Great. That'll look good in the press."

"We don't let on. We keep it a secret."

"What else?"

"You have to stay out of sight. Coine says the next attempt could be a sniper from long range."

"Coine says, Coine thinks . . . I say Coine knows shit. I'll be damned if I'm going into hiding. This company needs active and visible leadership now . . . not later when it's safe. You get the experts up here. Meanwhile, you just make sure I stay alive. No more fuck ups. If anyone leaks this booby trap shit to the press, you'll be on the street with Franklin."

<u>San Francisco, 7:30 a.m. Pacific Time.</u>

Tony opened Fulton's door without knocking. Fulton was almost asleep, suspended somewhere between semi-consciousness and a deep coma. A stomach sleeper, he was sprawled across the mattress, fully clothed, the right side of his face buried in a soft down pillow.

"I don't approve of this," Tony said emphatically. "You're makin' a big mistake and my ass is on the line."

"I'll take full responsibility," Fulton mumbled sleepily.

"You bet you will," Tony said in a tone bordering on insubordination. "I've put my objections in writing . . . it'll be on your dresser when you wake up." He turned to leave. "And I've got a copy," he added.

With a herculean effort, Fulton gathered his arms and legs, rolled over, sat up and rubbed his eyes. "Wait a minute . . . just wait a minute," he said. "I thought we agreed we'd stay here for a few days."

"Yeah, we did. But I never agreed to lyin' to the landlady." Tony paused. "Besides, the names you picked are stupid. How many people come walkin' up all those fuckin' stairs practically in the middle of the night named Brown, Jones and Smith?"

Fulton laughed.

"It ain't funny," said Tony. "I can't believe she bought it. . . maybe she didn't. If she's smart, she's probably callin' the cops right now."

"So big deal. Then your worries are over." Fulton swung his legs over the edge of the bed and brushed his hair back with both hands.

"Look, you let me sleep for . . ." Fulton looked at his watch, "for a measly hour and a half. I've gotta call Mr. Greer at 9 a.m. to reschedule a production meeting. Then I'll do whatever you want. Well, within reason," he added. "But whatever it is, I'd like to stay out of the AWE communications network."

"O.K. Gimme the note."

"You want to tear it up?"

"Hell, no, I wanna add something."

Tony leaned on the dresser and wrote briefly on the note paper. He picked it up and read it to Fulton.

"P.S. I'm staying on the job because Fulton has agreed to listen to me."

Fulton smiled. "Good." He rolled over, fluffed the pillow, and was soon breathing deeply.

Fort Bragg, N.C. 1100 hours.
Captain Andy Grissom did not bother to knock on Kimberly Hale's office door. He liked surprises -- mostly when he surprised others. Kimberly jumped at his sudden appearance when the door swung open and Andy jumped in.

"Hey," said Andy. "Soldiers are supposed to have nerves of steel. What are y'all doin'?"

Kimberly was in the process of shading in red ink the number 18 space on a large desk calendar. "What does it look like I'm doing?"

"Colorin' today's date on your calendar." He walked over to get a closer look. "Hey, y'all doin' that because our date tonight is gonna be somethin' special," he added with one of his big Texas grins.

"Don't be planning on it," she said with a smirk on her face.

David G. Hanrahan Esq.

"Well, why is today so important?"

"Do you have to know everything about me? Don't you think a little mystery would make me more interesting?"

"Honey..." Kimberly shot a mean look his way. "Ah mean, Lieutenant Hale, ma'am, one, I wanna know everythin' about you and two, Ah like you fine just the way you are."

"Good, then you'll appreciate my not wanting to share everything with you."

"Well, don't reckon Ah like that idea... but you do have the right to some privacy."

"Well, thank you, Captain Grissom," she said with a bow in his direction and a wave of her hand.

"No kiddin', y'all don't have to tell me, but Ah'd sure like to know why today's so dern important."

Kimberly shook her head, wondering if he was this persistent with every woman on the base. "If it's so important, I'll tell you."

"Ah'm all ears."

Kimberly laughed. "You've got <u>that</u> right. Your ears are pretty big."

Andy smiled.

"I've made up my mind today about something important to my future."

"Sweetheart, Ah ain't even asked ya yet."

"Darn you Andy Grissom, will you get serious." Kimberly sat down behind her desk and tapped her finger on the now red 18th day of February. "Today I decided to make the Army my career."

"Hot damn, Ah always wanted the mother of my children to be a general."

"One more comment like that and you'll be going to the symphony alone tonight."

"O.K., O.K. But that's great news."

"It's not news. And I'll thank you to keep it to your self."

"One last thing before I go. Doesn't this qualify as an occasion for a kiss?"

"Are you in uniform?"

"Damn, yes."

"See you tonight."

"Ah'll be in civies."

Kimberly picked up a plaque with a small replica of "Iron Mike," the quintessential airborne soldier on it and took aim at Andy's head.

"Peace, Ah'm leavin'. See y'all at 7:00 tonight."

Andy was gone as quickly as he had arrived. Kimberly stared at the now red square on her calendar. "I wonder," she said to herself out loud. "I wonder."

<u>Boston, AWE Headquarters. 11:30 a.m.</u>
McGillicuddy stood quietly in Fulton's office watching two men in headphones pass what looked like a Geiger counter over every square inch of the place.

"Excuse me," Mrs. Tierney interrupted. "Have you found Mr. Fulton yet?"

"No."

"Well, please let me know as soon as you do. He'll need some updated production information for his meeting with Mr. Greer." She held up a computer disk.

"He has a computer with him?" McGillicuddy asked.

"Yes, his laptop."

"When did he leave for San Francisco?"

"The Friday before Mr. Johnston died."

"That was the eleventh?"

"Yes."

"Where was his laptop?"

"Wait a minute." Mrs. Tierney walked quickly over to Fulton's desk and pushed the intercom button.

"Mary, it's me."

"Hi, Mrs. Tierney, what do you need?"

"Some information. Do you know if Mr. Fulton took his laptop with him when he went to San Francisco last Friday?"

A short pause.

"I know he didn't."

"What do you mean?"

"I worked overtime Friday night loading it with last-minute production details on the Jet Age acquisition. I was out sick Monday. Then with Mr. Johnston's death and all, I didn't ship it out to Mr. Fulton until late on the fifteenth . . . sent it overnight on one of our planes."

McGillicuddy moved closer to the intercom.

"Where did he keep it?"

"Right on his desk."

"When you finished loading it, where did you leave it?"

"Back on his desk . . . did I do something wrong?"

"No Mary, thanks." McGillicuddy made a fist and slammed it on the desk. "Damn it all, that would be a perfect booby trap," he said, looking toward the two technicians for confirmation.

"One of the best. Programmable, some empty space in the console, doesn't take much to kill you from close range," said the shorter man.

The tall guy nodded in the affirmative. "Hey, tell him to leave that thing alone and call the local bomb squad."

"But I don't know where he is," McGillicuddy said.

"Oh, dear," said Mrs. Tierney, "what can we do?" She became obviously distraught.

"This is all just speculation, Mrs. Tierney," McGillicuddy said in an effort to assuage her fear. He left the room, with Mrs. Tierney following closely. Within seconds, he was in Baxton's office. "Sorry to interrupt," he said.

"So why in hell did you?" Baxton shot back. "Dammit, can't you see I'm busy?"

"I have bad news, Mr. Baxton. Time is of the essence."

"Jesus, I don't need bad news."

"It's about Fulton."

"What about him?"

"He has a laptop computer with him that might have been armed and programmed by Johnston's killer."

"Whose bright idea is that?" Baxton raised his right index finger to his temple, feigning deep thought. "Don't tell me. You've been talking to Coine again."

"No sir. But it's really his idea about a long-range hit that got me thinking."

"What good is your thinking when Fulton's put himself out of reach?"

"Well, I can understand why Fulton thinks he's safe by being out of reach," McGillicuddy said confidently. Baxton frowned. McGillicuddy ignored it and continued. "But he's oblivious to the real danger he's in. He could be carrying the damn thing with him or using it as we speak."

"So what can we do?" asked Baxton angrily.

"Everything we can. We call local radio and television stations and ask if they can just mention the name and ask him to call the company."

Baxton jumped to his feet. "Now, I know you've lost your mind," he yelled. "Mrs. Tierney, please leave us alone. And absolutely no calls."

"Yes sir, Mr. Baxton."

When the door closed, Baxton went into one of his tirades. "How fucking foolish do you want us to look? Jesus God Almighty, someone on the fucking *Today Show* is going to look into every living room and say, 'Will Mr. Sid Fulton please telephone his mother?' No way we're gonna do that. He made his goddamn bed, so let him lie in it."

"Damn it, Mr. Baxton, at least let's call Greer immediately. Fulton's supposed to meet him at 10 a.m. their time. If he's spooked, he may call earlier, to change their meeting place or time. We tell Greer briefly about the urgency of the message and let him tell Fulton personally either on the phone or in person."

"No," shouted Baxton. "We leave Greer out of this. My plans for him do not include asking him for favors or crying on his shoulder. Just tell Greer to tell the idiot to call us at once."

"Mr. Baxton, I was a good cop for 30 years. I know what I'm talking about. You ordered me to not let one more man get killed. Well, right now you're my biggest obstacle. If Fulton's laptop is boo-by-trapped and he dies, you and you alone will be responsible for his murder." Mc Gillicuddy took a deep breath as he faced Baxton's icy stare. "Either you make the calls to Greer and the TV studios, or I'll do it myself."

"Joseph, you are insubordinate. But your words make sense." Baxton picked up his phone and spoke to Mrs. Tierney. "Please place two calls for me. First, call Jason Phillbrook at Station WSFT in San Francisco. Then get me Arthur Greer. Try his office first, he's an early starter. Thank you."

<u>San Francisco, 8:50 a.m. Pacific Time.</u>
Jessica Everett sipped from her third cup of coffee and was quite happy she had three new house guests so soon after placing her sign in the window. Odd bunch, she thought as she turned on the TV in the guest lounge. No luggage, somewhat bedraggled, but they paid in advance and seemed like nice gentlemen. At 87 years of age, she hardly ever met anyone whom she thought was not nice. After her husband died somewhere in the Pacific when his fishing trawler sank in '69, she turned their sprawling home into a homey bed and breakfast.

A familiar face slowly appeared on the screen. The announcement was a bit unusual.

Downsized

". . . and so, Mr. Fulton, wherever you are, please contact your office. Hopefully, it's about a pay raise. Hey, maybe you won the lottery. But we're told it is important -- so do it. Now back to our morning weather report. It's going to be cool and damp in the Bay Area today, with temperatures . . ."

Jessica heard footsteps coming down the stairs. She turned without getting out of the chair.

"Good morning, Mr. Jones. Sleep well, I hope? But for heaven's sake, it certainly wasn't long."

"Yes . . . and you're right about how short it was. Hey, do you have any more of that great-smelling coffee?"

"You betcha," Jessica said, slowly rising from her chair. "We keep a bottomless pot here. And do you want one of my famous cranberry muffins? I'm originally from Massachusetts. Love cranberries."

"By all means. I wouldn't miss it for the world. By the way," he added, holding up his laptop, "do you have someplace with a phone and an outlet where I can plug this in? I need to make an important call."

"Certainly Mr. Jones. Come right along with me and I'll fix you up."

Fulton cleared a space on Jessica's desk in a small pantry-turned office. He opened the computer, plugged in the cord and inserted a disk. Fulton picked up the phone and dialed Greer's number awkwardly with his left hand.

"Hello, Jet Age Aircraft Co. How may I direct your call?"

Fulton cradled the phone snugly between his neck and left shoulder as he maneuvered the mouse. The screen came to life.

"Arthur Greer, please."

"Whom shall I say is calling?"

"Sid Fulton."

"Mr. Fulton, I'm connecting you, but I've been instructed to tell you . . ."

Fulton pressed "Enter."

". . . do not use your computer."

The receptionist's message was strange. What suddenly appeared on the screen before him was even stranger -- and ominous. It froze him in place, muscles tensed.

THE TROUBLE WITH DOWNSIZING
IS IT OFTEN
HAPPENS WHEN YOU LEAST EXPECT IT.

The phone fell from his shoulder. Fulton tried desperately to push away from the desk and the dreadful words on his laptop.

"Sid, are you there? Sid, what's wrong?" Greer cried.

Greer and Jessica heard the awful sound at the same time. An explosion followed by the sound of Jessica screaming.

"Sid, are you there?" Greer yelled into the phone.

Greer was accustomed to emergencies -- usually at 40,000 feet and mach 2. He was calm. He called for his secretary.

"Yes, Mr. Greer?"

"Call the police immediately and tell them to stand by."

A female voice came on the line.

"Oh, God, Mr. Jones has been terribly wounded. Oh dear Lord."

"Who's been wounded?"

"Mr. Jones. He . . ."

That voice was suddenly replaced by a deep, masculine one.

"This is Tony, Fulton;s body guard. Who's this?"

"Arthur Greer. What's happened?"

"Look, no time to waste. Fulton's laptop was booby trapped. Don't know how; I've been stickin' to him like glue. We're at the Captain Josiah Everett Inn on Telegraph Hill. Get an ambulance to meet me at the bottom of the stairs. I'm gonna carry Fulton down to save time. He's bleedin' bad."

"It's done . . . by the way, the lady said 'Jones.' Who the hell is Jones?"

"Long story. This is terrible."

The blast from the computer had knocked Fulton out of his chair. He was lying on his back, legs still draped over the seat, and his eyes were wide with shock. He was fighting to breathe.

"Gimme a plastic bag and a towel," Tony yelled to Jessica. "And a roll of any kind of tape you got."

Tony opened Fulton's shirt and winced at a very bad wound under his heart. Jessica returned with a towel, a white plastic trash bag and a roll of masking tape. Tony folded the towel and placed it gently over Fulton's profusely bleeding wound. He folded the plastic bag so that it was slightly larger than the towel and taped it tightly, creating an air-tight seal. Tony picked the badly injured man up like a baby. Fulton tried to speak.

"Don't say nothin'," Tony commanded. "Now I gotta run down all these damn steps. I told you we shoulda gone somewhere else." Fulton mouthed the words "Thanks" and "I'm sorry."

"Hey, buddy, I ain't ever lost a client, ever. We'll have you up and around in no time. You'll see."

Fulton closed his eyes as Tony lumbered down the long flight of stairs. The sound of a siren was closer, and Tony shouted through clenched teeth, "We're almost there. You hear me? We're almost there."

<u>Boston, AWE Headquarters. 12:03 p.m.</u>
"What the hell does Greer want?" Baxton shouted to Tierney.

"I don't know. He said it was urgent."

Downsized

"Alright, put him in. Fulton's probably too scared to call him."

"Bradford . . .?"

"Yes. What is it, Arthur. I've got an important luncheon meeting and I'm late."

"Fulton's been wounded . . . I think his laptop was booby trapped. Damn thing went off as we were warning him."

Baxton slumped in his chair, the color draining from his face.

"Baxton . . . Baxton, you there?"

"Yes. How bad is Fulton?"

"Don't know. I just got off the phone. It happened only a few minutes ago."

"Where in hell was he?"

"Telegraph Hill."

"Where?"

"That's not important. Look, you've a lot to deal with. You'll get the details from the police. Let me know if there's anything I can do."

"Thanks."

Baxton called McGillicuddy. "Fulton's been wounded. His laptop . . ."

"No! Damn it all, we were so close," McGillicuddy yelled. "Bradford, I want you to leave your office immediately," he added.

"Don't start in," said Baxton angrily. "I'm not changing my lifestyle."

"Listen Baxton," McGillicuddy said sternly. "You're my last chance to get it right. If you're not gonna listen to me, you'll have to get a new chief of security."

"Where should I go?"

"Get down to my office and we'll figure it out."

"Listen," Baxton said apologetically. "This Coine fellow was absolutely correct. I want him on the team. Get him for us, whatever it takes."

"I'll do my best."

"Thanks."

McGillicuddy was unaccustomed to gratitude coming from Baxton. "You're welcome," he said and promptly dialed Coine's telephone number.

<u>Allston, 12:05 p.m.</u>

Jeanie answered the phone and yelled to Coine who was making adjustments to his burgeoning wall chart.

"It's for you Bill. It's McGillicuddy and he says it's important."

Coine walked slowly into the living room and took the phone from Jeanie. "Well, Joe, whatever it is, make it quick. Jeanie's got lunch ready, and she hates it when I keep her waiting."

"You were right, Bill."

"About what?"

"The booby trap idea . . . Fulton's laptop exploded in San Francisco."

"Bingo," Coine said. "Where and when?"

"A few minutes ago in San Francisco. Dammit Bill, we almost saved the guy. I know we would have prevented this if you were on the case from the gitgo."

"Hey, I can't save the world. Never could."

"I don't need world-saving. There's just one man now . . . Baxton."

"He ain't worth savin'."

"He is to a lot of people . . . he's got a nice family."

"Bullshit. You know I'm right."

McGillicuddy changed the subject. "Bill, there's a killer out there who must be stopped. Help me catch the bastard."

"You've got the Boston police, the state police and the FBI. What more do you need?"

"You dammit. Will you and Jeanie meet with me and Baxton for an early dinner."

"Where?"

"The Boston Harbor Hotel."

Bill called to Jeanie in the kitchen. "Honey, want to have supper with Baxton at the Boston Harbor Hotel?"

Jeanie walked into the living room, drying her hands on a paper towel. "I've never been there."

"Jeanie says yes."

"I did not."

"Good," McGillicuddy said.

"Yes, you did," said Coine.

"You talkin' to me," a puzzled McGillicuddy said.

"No, to Jeanie. What time?"

"You tell me . . . what's good for you?"

"Six o'clock."

"See you then. Bring your appetite."

Coine returned the phone to its cradle. "Look," he said. "You've never been there. When would we be goin' to the Boston Harbor Hotel on my retirement income? I can't resist a freebie. We eat, we listen, what's the harm?"

"No harm," said Jeanie sadly. "But I can see the handwriting on the wall. . . and I don't mean your darn ole wall chart."

"And what does the handwriting say?"

"Your insights are desperately needed and you're too good to stay out of this horrific murder case. Am I right?"

"Yes and no. Let's eat lunch."

However, the ringing phone stopped Coine and Jeanie in their tracks. She turned to answer it. Coine held out his arm, gently blocking the way.

"Let the machine get it," he said.

"But what if it's important?"

"They'll call back."

"But . . ."

"For heaven's sake, will it kill ya to ignore the phone just once in your life?"

"Yes."

Coine playfully held Jeanie around her waist. He placed his lips close to her ear and whispered, "Just once, let it go unanswered."

"Bill Coine, you let me go this minute," she said, wiggling her way free.

"I hope it's a wrong number," Coine said, as he walked into the kitchen.

"Hello, John. We saw you on television. You looked wonderful. Yes, Bill's right here." Jeanie waved to Coine. "Please be nice to him this time," she said as she handed him the phone.

"Don't tell me," Coine said, "you're callin' about the hit on Sid Fulton in San Francisco."

"What hit?" Neiberg said, not certain he had heard Coine correctly.

"Sid Fulton. You know, the second name on our killer's downsizing list."

"Bill, this is too serious to joke about. You're joking, right?"

"Hell no. Are you tryin' to kid me? You guys don't know?"

Coine looked at Jeanie with raised eyebrows. "Neiberg doesn't know about Fulton yet." Neiberg had been sitting at a vacant desk immediately outside Warner's office. He dropped the phone and ran in. "Gus," he yelled excitedly. "Call San Francisco P.D. right away. Fulton's been hit. His lap top computer was booby trapped. It happened somewhere in San Francisco just minutes ago."

Warner dialed quickly. "Have you guys heard any reports about someone being injured by . . ." he looked at Neiberg for confirmation. Neiberg shook his head, "yes" . . ." by an exploding laptop?" "You did?" Warner held his hand over the telephone. "Jesus, a cruiser just arrived on the scene," he yelled. "This information is just arriving at their headquarters now." He removed his hand from the phone. "By the way, is the victim's name Fulton?" Warner pushed the mute button and gave Neiberg a menacing look. "Jesus Christ Neiberg, some poor son-of-a-bitch in San Francisco was wounded by an exploding lap top but his name is Jones, not Fulton."

Neiberg ran back to Coine's line. "Shit Bill, San Francisco says the guy's name is Jones."

"Look," said Coine in complete frustration. "I can't speak for San Francisco. It was Fulton dammit. The poor guy went into hiding, probably used a phony name. But it was Fulton. Check the hospital where they took him. When you find out, call me back and let me know."

"Let you know? Jesus, I thought you knew."

"Goddammit, Neiberg, all I really know for sure is I'm retired and I shouldn't be involved in this asinine conversation. Call me back when you guys get your act together." Coine hung up. Jeanie gave him a disapproving glance. "What do you want from me?" he asked sincerely. "I was as nice as I could be to him."

Neiberg rushed back into Warner's office. "Coine says Fulton was using an alias."

"Coine?" Warner yelled as he flopped into his chair, muting the phone again. "You've got me calling San Francisco about some guy named Jones because Bill Coine told you it was Fulton?" Warner released the mute button. ". . . er, Captain, I appreciate all the info . . . well don't ask how I knew, it's a long story."

Neiberg leaned on Warner's desk with both fists. "Please, don't hang up," he urged. "Ask him if they've made a positive I.D. on this Jones fellow."

"One last thing, has there been a positive I.D. on Jones?" Warner looked at Neiberg encouragingly. "No? How do they know his name is Jones?" Warner put his hand over the phone. "Some landlady who runs a bed and breakfast told them," he said excitedly. "She doesn't know him," he repeated as the Captain filled him in. "What about his I.D., his wallet, any luggage?" Warner couldn't contain his excitement. "One suitcase. I.D., if any, is on his person. He's on the way to a hospital in an ambulance with the two men he was with," he told Sandra and Neiberg. "Jesus, that could be Fulton and his two bodyguards," he added in astonishment. Warner spoke to the Captain. "Listen, what's the name of that bed and breakfast. Yes, I can wait."

Warner jotted down the information. "Thanks. I've got it." Warner stood up and shook his head. "How the hell did Coine pull this one off?"

Neiberg smiled.

"Neiberg, I want a full report as soon as you can get back to him. This is beginning to look like Coine may be right." Neiberg left the office with a sense of urgency, excitement and dread.

San Francisco, 9:08 a.m., Pacific Time.

It was approximately fifty yards from the bottom of the stairs to where the ambulance was parked. Tony's endurance surprised him. With medical assistance in sight, he felt a surge of adrenalin. "Hang on, buddy. Help's right over there."

Tony turned his body slightly to the left as he ran so Fulton might see the welcomed sight, but he couldn't. His eyes were closed and breaths were coming in short gasps. As soon as the stretcher was secured in the ambulance, Tony jumped in.

"You really shouldn't be back here," the paramedic insisted.

"No fuckin' way I'm not. Me and Fulton here are like two sides of a coin. We go together."

The paramedic was impressed with Tony's size and determination. "Let's get rolling," he yelled to the driver. The ambulance lurched forward and entered the stream of light rush hour traffic on Battery Street. Within seconds, monitoring devices were attached and the very slow beep, beep of the heart monitor confirmed that Fulton was alive. However, his face was the color of death.

The paramedic shouted loudly into a microphone. "This is Harris's Ambulance Service on route to St. Francis Hospital. We've got a Caucasian male, looks like mid- to- late 40s; he's unconscious due to an open chest wound. Estimated blood loss is approximately one liter, over."

A quick look at the cardiac monitor prompted another stream of data to the hospital ER. "Pulse is thready at 50; BP is 60 palp. He's crashing."

"Shit," said Tony, "don't let him crash."

The paramedic continued in a practiced monotone. "Airway established with a number 8 ET tube. IV's infusing normal saline, wide open, over."

"You're gonna be OK, Fulton. You hang on guy," Tony said.

"Damn," the paramedic yelled.

"What," Tony shouted.

"Ventricular fibrillation," he shouted as he grabbed the defibrillator paddles.

"Charging 360 . . . clear," he yelled as he placed the paddles on either side of Fulton's chest. A bump in the road caused the paramedic to lose the twenty-five pounds of pressure required for the procedure resulting in a bright flash and the smell of burning flesh. Tony gagged. He closed his eyes and placed both hands over his mouth. Two more jolts of the defibrillator and the paramedic shouted the good news. "We've got a rhythm, his sinus brady is in the 50s, and we've got him back."

"Thank God," Tony said.

"What happened to this guy?" the paramedic asked without taking his eyes off Fulton and the monitors. "It looks like he took a blast in his chest. There are smaller wounds over most of his upper body."

"His computer," said Tony.

The paramedic shot a glance at Tony. "His what?"

"Don't know how, but there was some kind'a explosive in his laptop. I know it sounds crazy, but that's what happened."

The paramedic shook his head in disbelief. He replaced a pressure bandage on Fulton's chest. "ETA approximately five minutes, over," said the paramedic confidently.

"Roger that," said the ER nurse. We'll be waitin' on ya."

The ambulance pulled into the ER loading area, backed up to the entrance bay as the rear doors flew open. In seconds, Fulton was in the ER. A nurse spoke on the run, "Where's he at?"

Downsized

"He's been shocked times three," said the paramedic as Fulton was rushed to an operating room. "Sinus brady in the 50s," he added.

Tony ran with the group but was stopped abruptly outside the OR. "This is where you and Fulton part company," the paramedic said. "Sorry."

A tall man, six foot three or four, young -- mid-thirties, blonde wavy hair and dressed in blue scrubs, towered over Fulton's gurney. He removed the pressure bandage covering the wound. "Bad location," he said matter-of-factly to a nurse standing beside him.

Tony shouted to Fulton. "You've made it, fella. You're gonna be OK," he added as the gurney moved out of sight. Tony heard the doctor shouting orders. "Call x-ray, get respiratory therapy, get ABG's now . . . and call thoracics." The slow beeps of the heart monitor changed into a high pitched steady tone. "He's asystolic," the doctor yelled. "Atropine, 1 milligram, now!" The defibrillator zapped Fulton's chest in sets of three. Minutes seemed like an eternity.

"He's gone," said the attending. "Let's call this, 9:35," he said calmly. The OR doors swung open. The doctor walked quickly away from Fulton's lifeless body, snapping off his gloves and removing his surgical mask. "What other mess you got out here," he said to the nurse running behind him through the busy, crowded ER. "God, could I use a cup of coffee," he added. Tony cried.

Boston, 12:40 p.m.
Gus Warner sat on the edge of his conference room table, close to the speaker phone. Sandra Jones, Neiberg and Walsh congregated on the other side of the room. Warner punched in the number he received from San Francisco PD.

"It's ringing," Warner said. The others took their places around the table. Neiberg opened his trusty notebook.

An answering machine responded, "You have reached the Josiah Everett Inn. This is Jessica. It's another beautiful day on Telegraph Hill overlooking the Bay. I'm baking, cleaning or tending to my guest's needs. Please let me know that you've called, leave your number and I'll get right back to you."

"Damn it," Warner said, "a goddamn answering machine."

"Hey," Walsh joked, "the lady needs a new message, like 'sorry, there's been a murder here, call back later.'"

"Get serious," Warner chastised.

"Impossible," Sandra said.

Warner dialed another number. "Captain Tohara here."

"Hi. Gus Warner. I'm the district attorney for Boston. I have a favor to ask."

"Try me."

"Your guys are investigating an attempted homicide at the Josiah Everett Inn. I need to talk to someone at the inn but I'm getting a voice mail message. Can you ask one of your officers to pick up the phone?"

"I'll go one better. Give me your number and I'll have them call you."

Warner complied, sat down in the nearest chair and waited. Dottie appeared. "Joe McGillicuddy's on line one."

"You know what that call's about," Warner said. "Hello, Joe. Don't tell me. Fulton's been hit"

"Yes," a surprised McGillicuddy said. "How the hell . . ."

"Too long a story. Are you certain of your info?"

"No doubt about it. I heard it from Arty Greer. He's president of Jet Age Aircraft in San Francisco. He was talking to Fulton when he got it."

"Thanks, you've been a big help."

Dottie poked her head in. "A patrolman Sanchez is on line two."

"Gotta go," Warner said as he pushed button number two. "Officer Sanchez?"

"Yes. Captain Tohara said you needed some info?"

"Well, that was two minutes ago. I've got news for you now," Warner said emphasizing the word 'you.' Warner visualized a puzzled expression on Sanchez's face. "The victim is one Sid Fulton."

"We've got an innkeeper here who says his name's Jones."

"Well, we just got the straight scoop from a guy that got it from the horse's mouth. Call an Arty Greer at Jet Age Aircraft in your town. He was talkin' to Fulton when he got hit."

"Will do, but how in hell does a Boston D.A. end up tellin' us about a murder we just started investigating?"

"Hey, it's the electronic age, not to mention we're good."

"Well, if this checks out, I'll be a believer."

"Gotta run." Warner disconnected the call and turned to Walsh, "Get packed." He pushed the intercom. "Dottie, get Walsh out to San Francisco on the earliest possible flight." Warner pointed to Jones and Neiberg. "Come into my office. We've gotta talk." Warner wasted no time. "Neiberg, level with me. Are we, shit, is anybody making any goddamn progress toward solving this bitch of a case?"

"Gus, we're all on the bottom rung of a ladder to the sky."

"So what are we doing to get to rung number two?"

"I just received a complete list from state police headquarters of every passenger that flew out of Logan between 9:30 a.m. and midnight on the 17th."

"Christ," Jones said. "That has to be over five thousand names."

"Try 8,210 to be exact," Neiberg corrected.

"That seems like a waste of time," Warner said frowning.

"Gus, I've done airport duty. Most perpetrators of crimes at Logan use a regularly scheduled flight to make their get-away. It's the cleanest way out. I'll give odds that our killer is one of those passengers," Neiberg said convincingly.

Sandra laughed. "Like the ad says, some people really know how to fly."

"Neiberg, do me a favor." Warner said.

"What?"

"Get off the ladder. Go find an escalator."

Dottie's voice on the intercom interrupted. "It's Joe McGillicuddy."

"Put him in."

"Gus?"

"Yeah. You've got Jones and Neiberg here also."

"Fulton was pronounced dead at 9:35 a.m. Pacific Time."

"Has his family been notified?"

"Yes."

"Thanks, Joe. Hey, there's nothing you could have done."

"Yes, there was, Gus. No disrespect to anyone there, but somebody besides Coine should have figured out this booby trap shit."

The words struck hard in Warner's gut. McGillicuddy was right. Neiberg's face flushed.

"Shit, we needed that like a hole in the head," Sandra said softly.

"Well, let's not lose Baxton, OK? We'll give you all the support you need," Warner said.

"Thanks. Baxton's gonna live if I have to sleep with the ballbuster."

Warner slammed the phone down and turned to Neiberg. "Get over to Amalgamated and see what has to be done to bolster security for Baxton. And dammit, find me that escalator."

Boston, AWE Headquarters. 1:00 p.m.
Baxton sat at his desk and stared at the TV wall. He unlocked the lower right desk drawer and removed a phone. He punched in a local number, waited a few moments, and spoke softly. "Hello, this is Geronimo. The situation is out of control. We need to talk."

Boston, The Boston Harbor Hotel. 5:50 p.m.
Jeanie and Bill entered the luxurious marble floored foyer of the Boston Harbor Hotel and

walked up the stairs leading to the main dining room.

"Bill, I hope you won't embarrass me tonight."

Coine smiled. "Jeanie, if I do, I promise it will only be after Baxton pays the bill."

The hostess greeted them politely and led them to a table by a window overlooking Boston Harbor. Logan Airport and the blinking lights of planes landing and taking off were clearly visible across the harbor. Flags on the World Trade Center roof waved colorfully in the glare of flood lights.

"Here's Baxton now," Coine announced. The hostess, Baxton and McGillicuddy marched in single file. Jeanie turned in her chair. "Where?"she asked. Baxton was hidden by the tall young lady escorting him to the table.

Coine whispered, "he's behind the hostess." Jeanie leaned to the right to get a better view. She looked at Coine, eyes wide in amazement. "I didn't know he was so short."

"Jeanie, he's a giant of industry. So no midget jokes," Coine replied, smiling.

Jeanie patted her hair."How do I look?"

"Beautiful. Baxton's gonna want you," Coine said impishly with a wink.

"Bill, you're incorrigible."

"Wow, meeting with a rich man's brought out your ten dollar vocabulary."

David G. Hanrahan Esq.

The three arrived at the table with a modicum of fanfare. A waiter captain deftly moved the chair on Coine's right and gestured to Baxton with a slight bow. Coine started to rise. "Keep your seat," commanded Baxton, extending his hand. "Bill Coine I presume?"

"In the flesh," Coine said crisply.

"And this lovely lady must be Jeanie."

Jeanie blushed and held out her hand. Baxton gripped it gently. Jeanie was impressed. She did not like men who tried to be macho with a crushing handshake.

"Jeanie," Baxton said, "Let me be blunt. I'm going to ask your husband to come out of retirement. Not tomorrow, not next week or next month. I need him to do it tonight."

Jeanie shot a worried look at Coine. He shrugged and smiled.

"I have in mind an arrangement whereby your husband will be independent . . . not an employee. A specialist hired to perform a very special function. I want him to help us find the person or persons responsible for killing my executives. I know that you, of all people, know that your husband is the man to accomplish that." Jeanie started to speak. Baxton held up his hand. "Please, I'm almost finished." He turned to Coine. "Thank you for your patience and for letting me speak directly and candidly to your wife."

Coine selected a piece of toasted bread, buttered it and took a bite.

Baxton continued. "Jeanie, I believe that your husband will resist my efforts. I also know that you will ultimately support him in whatever decision he reaches."

"Yes," Jeanie said politely.

"So I've made a decision," Baxton continued. "It is not intended to offend. I came here unwilling to take no for an answer. If no it is, I would not wish to use money as a . . ." Baxton briefly searched for the right word. He rejected bribe, ". . . an inducement. Your husband is not a man who has let money motivate him. He would not have been content to spend his life working with the State Police if getting rich was his aim. Am I right?"

"Yes," said Jeanie, shooting another worried glance at Coine. He smiled at Jeanie and nodded encouragement.

"And I presume," Baxton said, "that your life with Bill was based upon love and not money."

Jeanie laughed. "That's for sure," she said, winking at Coine.

"So what's this all about?" Baxton said rhetorically, pulling an envelope out of his left inside jacket pocket. "There's a check in this envelope in the amount of one hundred thousand dollars made payable to your husband."

Jeanie placed her hand nervously on her neck as if she was about to choke.

"When dinner is over," Baxton continued, "and our conversation is completed, if your husband's final answer is no, there'll be no attempt on my part to ask him to change his mind because of a big money offer. You simply return the envelope and the matter is closed."

Coine broke his silence, leaning forward and closer to Jeanie. "Jeanie, now you listen to me carefully. When dinner is over, and I've said no for the last time, you pick up the envelope and run like hell for the door. I'll tackle Joe here, and the money'll be ours."

Baxton smiled an uncomfortable smile. "Mr. Coine, I'm serious. The check is simply a retainer. You'll receive your hourly fee, and I will cover all expenses. The goal is to win – to catch a killer and get a conviction."

The appetizers arrived. Coine placed a napkin on his lap and picked up a fork as he spoke. "You've got my ability a bit overblown here," Coine said.

"Do I?" Baxton replied incredulously.

"Damn it, I'm only one man. Combined, the state, city and federal agencies will have a hundred people on this case." Coine gestured toward McGillicuddy. "For chrissake, Joe, tell your boss I'm right. This ain't a one man job."

McGillicuddy toyed with a salad of exotic greens. "Mr. Baxton, Coine here is absolutely correct." Baxton glowered. "This case is not a one man job. But Bill, my friend, you ain't no ordinary man." Coine started to reply. "No," McGillicuddy interrupted. "You listen to me. We lost Fulton this morning. But," he held his right hand up and squeezed thumb and forefinger together, "we were this close to savin' him."

Baxton jumped in. "Mr. Coine, even if there are a thousand people working on this case, they're all in a deep sleep. Only one man predicted the use of a booby trap . . . you! It's this simple. If you had all the information that the authorities had in this case from the beginning, Sid Fulton would be alive today." Baxton thought for a moment. "Hell, so might Van der Meer."

"Did it ever occur to you," Coine said, "that I just got lucky?"

"Sure," Baxton shot back. "I can relate to that. How do you think I got so goddamn rich? Successful men make their own luck. We gamble all the time, but we hedge our bets and improve the odds." Baxton picked up the envelope that was still lying where he had placed it, near Jeanie's water glass. "This money is my bet. One hundred thousand and perhaps more says you'll win. Go ahead, be lucky. Be silly. Make mistakes. But my money here," he waved the envelope, "says you'll win."

Coine liked Baxton's in-your-face style and agreed with his make mistakes philosophy. "One last point and we'll eat in peace," Baxton said as Coine devoured the last piece of his crab cake. "I've never been truly altruistic. Many rich men are selfish, even when they do good deeds. I'm next on the killer's list and my money will be no good to me if I'm dead. With you on the case, I'm sure I will not be the next downsizing victim. Maybe you don't believe that I'm worth saving . . ."Coine struggled to keep a poker face. ". . . But let's be blunt. I want to stay alive. That's the real reason I'm willing to give you this retainer and an unlimited expense account."

Amid the flurry of waiter activity and the smooth transition from appetizer to main course, Coine tried to absorb everything that Baxton said. More importantly, he had to face his own truth. He wanted one more big case, one more hunt. Would he be unfair to Jeanie, he thought if he answered Baxton's and, indeed, his own call to arms. At this crucial point, Baxton stood up executing a pre-planned maneuver. He nodded to McGillicuddy. "Will you excuse me," Baxton said. "I have to make a phone call." McGillicuddy stood up. "And I have to use the facilities."

It was not a subtle move. Coine knew it was orchestrated to give him and Jeanie an opportunity to discuss the matter. "Well, what do you think?" said Coine.

"Whew! Think about what? This was quite a show."

"Show time's over. What do you think?"

"My goodness, with all that money we'll be able to get a retirement home in Florida or Arizona."

"You want me to say yes?"

"We don't need Baxton's money. He was right. We're not motivated by money." Jeanie leaned forward and reached for Coine's hand. "I love you Bill Coine, and I know you would work on this case for free . . . for heaven's sake, our bedroom wall is a testament to that."

"Yeah, but. . .,"

Jeanie held up her left hand. "I'm feeling guilty that I kept you from helping sooner."

"That's pure baloney. I did all that I could."

"Well, I just can't help thinking that you might have learned about the list of victims sooner if I wasn't being an old poop."

"You're wrong. So just get this guilt nonsense out of your head."

Jeanie smiled. "OK. But be honest with me," she said earnestly. "None of this, 'what does Jeanie want?'" She looked deeply into Coine's eyes. "What do you want. What do you really, deep down in your heart, want to do?"

"Damn it, Jeanie. I want in on this case. But I really don't like Baxton and I'm afraid he'll tick me off in no time flat."

"So set limits. Do it your way. If he goes back on his word, you quit. They'll be back soon. So, what'll it be?" She picked up the envelope and waved it in a tight circle, "Meat loaf or filet mignon?"

Coine smiled. "Neither. Bad for my cholesterol... How about a house on a golf course in central Florida, near Disney World?" he added playfully.

"But you don't play golf," Jeanie said, eyebrows raised.

"So, I'll learn," Coine said, grinning.

She raised her glass of water. "Let's drink to that." They clinked glasses.

Baxton was the first to return. "Well, did you two reach any conclusions in my absence?"

Coine cut into his roast chicken, placed a small piece in his mouth and savored it. "I say we do like you suggested. We eat in peace and talk about my decision over dessert."

McGillicuddy arrived in time to hear Coine's last remark. Baxton was not pleased. He knew when he was checkmated. He shot a stiff smile toward Coine and a worried glance at McGillicuddy. McGillicuddy broke the ice. "Bill," he said, cutting into his filet mignon. "Obviously, you've been doin' some thinkin' about this case. Have you done any profilin' on our killer?" Baxton looked on with an intense interest. Coine deftly removed some skin from his chicken. "I wouldn't call it a profile, but I have a few ideas," he said confidently.

"I'd like to hear them," Baxton said.

"First of all, the killer has a bad case of the hots for you, Mr. Baxton. That's obvious."

"Is it?" asked Baxton. "Then why kill Johnston, Van der Meer and Fulton?"

Coine stabbed a baby carrot with a fork and held it up. "Where do they get such small carrots?"

"Well," Baxton said impatiently, " Why kill them and not me?"

"Power," Coine said.

"Power?" Baxton repeated incredulously. "What the devil does power have to do with this. . . this butchering process?"

"Killer has it, and you don't."

"Preposterous. Sneak attacks don't come from power. Weakness forces one to attack from behind."

Coine was delighted with a chance to debate Baxton now, before he accepted the hundred thousand dollar check. Jeanie looked worried.

"Johnston was a sneak attack," Coine said, holding his hand up for a waiter. "The killer signaled the next murder when he sent the press release.

Van der Meer was in your face, right under your nose; a power play if I ever saw one. The Fulton hit was clever, but still a demonstration of the killer's advantage over you . . ." Coine was briefly interrupted by the arrival of a waiter. "I'll have coffee now, please . . . and bring me milk instead of cream," Coine said, returning his attention to Baxton. ". . . at this moment, on a power scale of one to ten, the killer's a ten." Coine pointed at Baxton for emphasis. "You are a one."

Baxton's face reddened. McGillicuddy saw disaster on the horizon and spoke up quickly. "Bill, what I'm more interested in is your ideas on the killer's personality traits, you know, what should we be looking for?" McGillicuddy did not hide his anxiety.

Coine sipped from his coffee cup. "I was getting to that. Number one, our downsizing killer is dedicated."

"Dedicated?" Baxton repeated the word to be sure he heard it correctly.

"Intensely," Coine replied. "Our assassin announced the killing of Van der Meer and Fulton and they're gone. You're next on the hit list and you'll be gone if we don't prevent it."

"We have a choice, do we?" Baxton said facetiously. "I thought I was powerless," he added mockingly, drawing out the word 'powerless,' emphasizing each of its three syllables.

Downsized

Coine ignored him. He took another sip of coffee. "Second, the killer has special training. We are definitely not looking for your run-of-the-mill killer."

"What kind of training?" McGillicuddy chimed in.

"CIA, Navy seals, Army Special Forces, counter-insurgency forces, you know, guerilla operations," Coine thought for a moment. "After Fulton, you can add computer whiz to the list."

"You think a competitor hired a soldier to decimate the company's leadership?" McGillicuddy inquired.

"Nope."

"You seem quick to dismiss a potential motive. I thought you were more careful than that," said Baxton sarcastically.

"I am, but Joe here's asked me about my thoughts . . ."Coine looked squarely into Baxton's eyes. ". . . just call me silly. In case you don't realize it yet, you're being downsized. A killer hired by a competitor wouldn't waste time with such nonsense. That's where my power analysis comes into play. In a RIF, your run of the mill reduction in force, the employee lives in fear, powerless, reduced to hoping it won't be him who gets fired. He's looking for some sign he's a keeper. When the bad news finally comes, to some it has the impact of a death sentence."

"Hogwash," Baxton said, now staring into Coine's eyes, both men locked in an intellectual tug of war. "You're describing the weak-minded. The strong don't wait. They see the handwriting on the wall and get on with their lives. Only the weak cower and grovel."

"Bingo," said Coine, slamming his hand on the table. Baxton flinched. Jeanie jumped. Baxton looked at McGillicuddy with a puzzled expression that quickly changed to anger.

"All you can say is bingo?" he yelled at Coine. "What in blazes does bingo have to do with anything?"

"Your philosophy makes my point. Don't you get it?"

"Get what?"

"You see people as weak or strong. You gobble up the weak and cripple the strong, or they leave you. You live in a black and white world. But what if a weak person gets some backbone and then some specialized training, and then decides to come back and kick ass."

"Good heavens, someone kills three men because when he was weak, an insignificant nothing, he was fired in one of my downsizing campaigns?"

"No, there's somethin' more here . . . much more. The killer wants not only to get even, but to dethrone you personally." Coine hesitated. "The

Downsized

killer wants a regime change at Amalgamated and then, I'm sorry to say, he'll kill ya."

Baxton leaned forward, pushed his plate away, placed his elbows on the table, and rested his chin in his hands. "OK. I'm listening. What do you suggest?"

"You make the bastard think he's won."

"How?"

"You step down. Make a big announcement."

"Then what?"

"If I'm right, the killer will make a move . . . and, hopefully, we'll be ready."

Baxton sat back in his chair, lifted the napkin off his lap, folded it and placed it on the table. "I'm not ready to step down."

"Do it soon."

"What else?"

"A complete search of your office, plane, home . . . anywhere the killer expects you to be."

"Started," said McGillicuddy. "We've got that going on now as we speak."

"Good. All you have to do Mr. Baxton is stay off the ridge line."

Baxton shot a look at McGillicuddy who explained immediately. "That's military lingo for don't be an easy target."

"Mr. Coine, this conversation has spoiled my appetite."

"Sorry."

David G. Hanrahan Esq.

"No, no," Baxton said. "It was necessary, although not quite what I expected. I'm not in the mood for dessert either. So what is it? Do you accept my offer or not?"

"Do we get dessert regardless of my answer?" Jeanie frowned. "Only kidding," Coine said.

"The answer is yes to the dessert. What's your answer to my question?"

"Yes."

Baxton took a deep breath and let it out slowly. McGillicuddy reached for Coine's hand and shook it briskly.

"Hey," Coine said. "I'm gonna do my best, that's all. That may not be enough. Only time will tell."

"That's all I ever ask for," Baxton said. Coine raised an eyebrow. Baxton noticed. "Well, I do expect a hundred and ten percent, but in your case I believe that's what your best is. Enough said. Will you excuse me, Jeanie, Bill. I have some things to do. Please stay and finish the meal. You too, Joe. I'll be fine with my bodyguards."

Jeanie looked at the envelope still lying near her water glass. "Can I take this now?"

"By all means, Jeanie, by all means," Baxton said as he rose and left quickly.

"There is one small problem to resolve before I can cash that check," Coine said. Jeanie looked puzzled. "I'm not licensed," Coine announced matter-of-factly.

Downsized

"Oh," McGillicuddy said, removing an envelope from his inside jacket pocket. "Baxton is way ahead of you. All the forms are here. Sign at the red X's and we'll file everything first thing Monday."

Coine smiled, removed the papers and signed the documents. "Bill Coine, private eye. Has a nice ring to it."

McGillicuddy wasted no time getting down to business. "What do you need from me."

"Everything," Coine replied. "Start with a list of unusual events in connection with your company's downsizing efforts. Don't leave anything out. If you're uncertain if anything's relevant, put it in. We'll discuss it."

"Already started. We're doin' it for Neiberg."

"What did he ask for?"

"Incidents."

"I want more. Something unusual may or may not be an incident. You understand?"

"Yes."

"Good. Tomorrow we look for the bastard in earnest." Coine raised his hand. "Now, let's get a waiter to bring us some of those outrageous desserts."

Allston, 10:00 p.m.
Jeanie responded to door bells as quickly as she answered telephone calls. Tonight she eagerly awaited Sergeant Neiberg's arrival. In light of

Coine's new role, it was not surprising when he agreed to a late night meeting with his former protégé. There was a special chemistry between these two men that ignited their passion for police work whenever they interacted. Jeanie was surprised that she was beginning to feel and respond to the excitement generated by her husband's return to the crime-solving business. She glanced at herself in the hallway mirror as she walked quickly by, tucked in a few loose strands of hair, centered the diamond pendant on her necklace and opened the door.

"Hello, John," Jeanie said cheerfully. "It's wonderful to see you," she added with a warm embrace and an affectionate kiss on Neiberg's cheek. Familiar with the apartment from years of meeting with Coine, he walked quickly past the kitchen and into the living room. Coine sat in his favorite arm chair and did not get up.

"John, what would you say if I told you that tonight, just a few hours ago, I agreed to work as a private detective for Brad Baxton?"

Neiberg looked at Jeanie incredulously.

"It's true," she said.

"That's great news," Neiberg said, grinning from ear to ear. "I'm gonna tell Warner you're my escalator."

"Your what?"

Downsized

"Private joke. But damn, it'll be great to work with you on another case. When can we start?"

"How about right now?" Coine said as he reached for one of two cups of hot chocolate offered by Jeanie. Neiberg took the other. "What can you tell me that hasn't been in the papers? In fact, what's your gut tellin' ya?"

"We've got an angry woman here. I mean we will be looking for a very angry woman."

"How do you figure the killer's a woman?"

"For openers, Johnston was waiting for Ailida, his cleaning lady lover. He would have noticed a man's build comin' at him. You shoulda seen the poor guy. He was stark naked, except for his socks. Apparently, he couldn't wait to take his clothes off."

"I like that," said Coine. "Next?"

"They found a ballerina and the drum from a small music box; the spring from that music box was the trigger. ATF established that the last song Van der Meer listened to was Lara's Theme from Dr. Zhivago, you know, Somewhere My Love. A dainty ballerina, a love song and a dance of death . . . looks like a feminine touch to me."

"Interesting," said Coine. "OK. So we have a lady killer and she's angry. Angry at who?"

"Whom," said Jeanie softly. Coine shot a disapproving glance her way. Neiberg smiled.

"Bradford Baxton, alias the ballbuster," said Neiberg. "Sorry Jeanie, that's his unofficial nickname at the company. It just happens to go well with his personality and the BB monogram on all his custom made shirts."

"That's alright. Bill says a lot worse. I'm used to it."

"I do not," said Coine defensively. He continued questioning Neiberg. "Why is this gal angry at Baxton?"

"That's where I come up short. I can't make sense out of it. I'm certain it has something to do with Baxton's merger and acquisition policies."

Coine took a sip from his mug. "King of Downsizing he's called."

"Yeah," said Neiberg, "and the killer's downsizing memo makes no bones about it. It's clearly aimed at taunting Baxton. Sort of like, how do you like a taste of your own medicine?"

"I agree. I like what you've done," said Coine. Neiberg enjoyed hearing that. Compliments were few when he was working for Coine. "But what's wrong with this picture," added Coine. "Somebody loses a job and painstakingly kills three executives, brutally, and threatens to kill the president and CEO."

"I know," said Neiberg, "losing a job isn't enough of a motive for killing three men."

Downsized

"Unless you're a postal worker," Coine said in an uncharacteristic attempt at humor.

"That's not funny," Jeanie interrupted.

"One suggestion," said Coine. "It could be industrial espionage, sabotage or something like that."

"Explored and we got nothing but dead ends. I don't see our killer as a hired gun. It's personal, very personal." Both men sat quietly, sipping their hot chocolate and thinking. "One thing does bother me," said Neiberg, breaking the silence. "All the companies gobbled up by Baxton over the years were owned and run by men. That doesn't square with my woman theory."

Coine stood up as a spark of insight flashed in his mind. "Suppose one of these guys in Baxton's food chain had a wife, or a daughter even, who didn't like what Baxton did to hubby or daddy?"

"She'd certainly be angry. But what Baxton did to hubby or daddy has to be pretty bad, bad enough to wanna kill four men."

"Yes," Coine said with a big grin, "and guess what?"

"I'm guessing," said Neiberg. "Don't tell me, I'm still guessing." He stood up suddenly. "The worse it is, the easier it will be to spot hubby or daddy."

"Bingo," yelled Coine, slapping Neiberg on the shoulder. "It also reduces the number of possible suspects from somewhere in the thousands down to the manageable hundreds."

"What if I'm wrong?" Neiberg asked sincerely.

"Don't fret, John, you're on the money. I feel it in my bones, and when my bone marrow starts vibrating you can bank on it." Coine frowned. "There is one catch."

Neiberg looked puzzled. "What?"

"Just make sure you get Warner's permission to work with me."

"Hell, I can't wait to tell him. He'll be nuts to veto our collaboration."

Neiberg finished his hot chocolate and left with a new enthusiasm for the case. With Coine on board, something was bound to break soon, he thought.

<u>Fayetteville, N.C. 2305 hours.</u>
Andy Grissom pulled into his parking space at the Camelia Apartments. Since leaving the symphony, Kimberly had been quiet during the ride home. Andy killed the ignition.

"Don't forget the lights," Kimberly said.

"They're automatic. Kind-a like you."

"Meaning?"

"As soon as Ah start to get close to ya'll, you automatically turn off."

"I'm sorry, honest."

Downsized

The lights blinked out as the couple sat quietly in the dark for a few moments, holding hands.

"You're meeting me at a lousy time in my life," Kimberly said.

"How so? You look like you have your shit together woman; like nobody else Ah've ever seen in this man's army."

Kimberly laughed. "Looks can be deceiving. In my case, they're downright fraudulent."

"Look, it's no secret that Ah've got some pretty dern strong feelin's for yer. Hey, gal, you've got a string around this Texan's heart."

"Andy, that's just plain silly."

"Maybe, but it's the truth."

"I didn't mean to put it there."

"Tell that to a long horned steer in a round-up. When you pull that lasso tight, that steer comes up short wonderin' what the hell happened."

"Timing is everything in life. I wish it were different, really. You're a great guy."

"Just what's troublin' ya'll? Can ya tell me? It'll stay locked up with a coupla hundred other secrets the United States Army has entrusted with me."

"I trust you. It's just, well, too personal."

"Little darlin', you're holdin' that lasso around my heart and Ah know you ain't done it on purpose, but Ah reckon ya owe me some explanation."

Kimberly lowered her head briefly and sighed audibly. When she was ready, she looked into Grissom's eyes, barely visible in the darkened car. "Andy, five years ago almost to the day, my father killed himself."

"Now Ah'm sorry for askin'. Shucks, you don't have to say no more. Ah can understand grievin'."

"It's more than that. I forgive him now and I'm done grieving."

"You forgive him?" Andy asked incredulously.

"Yes. Sounds funny, but I hated him for what he did to me. I took it personally. He was dead but he left me wounded. I was finishing my second year of college in Chicago. He never told me he was depressed. He always laughed with me on the phone. Said he couldn't wait until spring break and my visit. Damn, he never gave me a chance to help him."

"Why? Ah mean why'd he do a thing like that?"

"Well, a few months earlier, he lost his job."

"Shucks," interrupted Andy, "you don't kill yourself over a job."

"It's complicated," Kimberly said. "You see he never got over my mom's death."

"Golly, Ah didn't know your mom was dead. Ya'll been dealin' with a lot more sufferin' than your average folk."

"She was only thirty-four. I was twelve. My dad was busy at work. It was snowing real hard. My mom called and asked him to pick her up at the train station. He told her to take a cab. There was an accident and she died. He blamed himself and never truly got over it. He felt he betrayed her. Then his plant in Maine was closed and everyone was terminated shortly before Christmas. He must have felt that he'd betrayed all those people. But he hadn't." Kimberly started crying. "The only person he ever really betrayed was me."

Andy leaned over so she could bury her head in his shoulder. "Ah'm so sorry little darlin'. Ah had no idea; no idea . . . Hey, ya'll dry those eyes. You've got Captain Andrew Grissom on your side. And don't you worry about lassoin' my heart. Ah'm a big boy. I can take it. When you're ready, Ah'd be pleased if you gave me a chance."

"I can't make any promises. I don't know if I'll ever be ready. That's why I spent a month in Boston. I had to sort things out and find some answers. I did find some. One was to forget about finishing college. Another I discovered today. I'm stayin' in the Army."

Andy lifted her head gently with his two big hands. Her face was barely visible in the darkened car. He saw the tears on her cheeks and brushed them away with his fingers. "Little darlin', if we can't be lovers Ah want to be your best buddy. Ah mean it."

"Of course," said Kimberly. "I would like that very much."

"Good. And now that we've got that resolved, will ya still help me study for my exams?"

"Of course."

"Good. Ah've got one next week on long range target interdiction. We'll have supper tomorrow night and you can ask me questions, a deal?"

"Yes."

"And don't worry. Your secret's in this good ole boy's good hands."

"Thanks, Andy." Kimberly kissed him on the cheek. "Hey, it's late and time for bed."

"Ah know what yer thinkin' right now."

"What?"

"That Ah'm gonna say great, let's get to it."

"Well?"

"Well Ah'm not. You're lookin' at a brand new Andy Grissom. Ah'll keep ya laughin' but Ah'll let ya be. There'll be no more silly flirtin'."

"Just make sure you keep me laughing, promise?"

"Cross my heart. Whoops. Finger just got caught on those heart strings."

Kimberly laughed.

"Let's get outta here before Ah tell you one of my secrets."

<u>Newton, Massachusetts. February 20. 10:30 a.m.</u>
Bill Coine parked several blocks from Brad Baxton's home and walked the rest of the way. The

neighborhood was clearly affluent. Large brick houses in a variety of styles on two acre parcels were the norm. Coine leaned into a cold wind and pressed a turned-up collar against his ears. Two sentries were visible at Baxton's front gate dressed warmly, both holding Dunkin' Donut cups. There were other guards, Coine was certain, but they were not visible. Baxton's property looked like a country club. The large main gate was framed by two brick columns. On one was a coat of arms -- a gold shield with crossed battle axes and the name Baxton in large, highly polished bronze letters above the shield.

A call on the security phone opened the main gate. A golf cart suddenly appeared and Coine jumped in. A few moments later he was standing in a large foyer with a marble tile floor and a collection of large paintings on the walls. Baxton entered the room alone and frowned. "I don't remember making an appointment with you," he said coolly.

"Thanks," Coine replied. "I'd love a cup of coffee."

"You must think I'm an idle rich man with lots of time. Well I'm not idle and I have important plans for this morning."

"OK, we'll skip the coffee," Coine said, annoyed with Baxton's attitude. He removed his coat and looked around the room. "Where can I put this?"

"Mr. Coine, did you hear what I just said?"

"Yep, I ignored you. You noticed."

Baxton was noticeably upset. Coine draped the coat over his left arm. "We'll just have to talk here, standin' up. I don't mind. But let me ask you something. Is what you're planning to do more important than catching your killer?"

Baxton was shocked at Coine's choice of words. "My killer? Preposterous. I'm alive and well."

Coine looked at his watch. "I'm a little fast, but your killer has a plan, is probably ready to execute it and, from recent history, will most likely succeed . . . maybe any minute now."

"I don't like your style, sir."

"I haven't cashed your check yet."

Baxton turned quickly away from Coine and shouted. "Alexander!"

A man appeared. He was fortyish and wore a standard butler uniform: black trousers, a white shirt, a bow tie and a white sport jacket.

"Take Mr. Coine's coat." Baxton looked at Coine. "This better be important."

"It is. I may be retired, but I don't have any time to waste either."

"Get Mr. Coine a cup of coffee," Baxton commanded.

"Milk, no sugar," Coine said with a hand gesture on the "no sugar."

Alexander left as silently as he arrived. Coine followed Baxton up a wide flight of stairs, turned left at the landing and entered a large study. Baxton sat behind his desk. Coine lowered himself into one of the two leather chairs in front of Baxton. Baxton looked at his watch. "You have fifteen minutes."

"Who do you think hates you more than anyone else in the whole wide world?"

Baxton laughed. "For this I gave you fifteen minutes?"

"Well?" insisted Coine. "I'm waiting for an answer. We've only got," he checked his watch, "fourteen minutes."

"How the hell do I know? I've made a lot of enemies."

"Can't single one out for us, like the person or persons with the worst case of the hots for you?"

"Damn it, McGillicuddy asked me the same question. No extra charge I might add."

"Touché," said Coine, "but you insisted on giving me that check."

"Was it a mistake?"

"Time will tell. So how long have you been thinkin' about what Joe asked you?"

"Since Van der Meer's death."

"That's three days and nobody comes to mind?"

"No. There are too many weak, incompetent men out there who can't see their own lack of courage, their own lack of confidence as their downfall. They blame me or someone or something else for their misfortune. They never blame themselves. There's a sea of them out there."

"So now you know what we're up against."

"I'm now losing my patience. Get to your point."

"I think you haven't been working hard enough to come up with answers. It's obvious a major portion of the world's population hates your guts."

"That's your opinion Mr. Coine. It's really not that bad."

"It's bad enough." Coine stood up for emphasis and pointed at Baxton. "Look, you've had to come up with at least a thousand ideas to make your first billion. All I need from you now is three or four. Go back in time, like you were being guided by the ghost of Christmas past, try to see the people you've screwed out of their fortunes."

Baxton stood up defiantly and shouted, "You're overstepping your bounds. I'm no Scrooge. I give millions to charity."

Coine had touched a nerve intentionally. He knew Baxton needed to be shocked out of a monumental complacency about the threat he faced. "That's all well and good," he replied calmly. "But someone out there thinks you're worse than Scrooge. Scrooge got to go to a Christmas dinner. If the killer has <u>her</u> way, you're not gonna be around for the Easter bunny."

Baxton's eyes widened. He leaned forward. In an instant his anger at Coine was replaced by an intense curiosity. "You just said her."

"You were listening."

"I always listen. What are you saying?"

"Johnston, Van der Meer and Fulton were all killed by a woman. As we speak, somewhere out there is a member of the fairer sex ready to pull the plug on you."

Baxton stood up, leaned forward, both fists closed, his knuckles on the desk. "You are joking. Please tell me it's a joke."

"Mr. Baxton, believe me, I'm not a comedian. Besides, I didn't figure that you paid me 100,000 big ones to make jokes."

"Preposterous. That a woman committed these...these assassinations is unfounded speculation. What is your proof? Where's your evidence to support such a . . . wild..." Baxton searched for adjectives..."implausible theory."

Coine returned to the chair, sat down and adopted a conciliatory tone. "Mr. Baxton, I didn't come here for your approval. I need your cooperation. The woman I'm looking for had a father or husband who was ruined . . . or worse . . . by you. What happened had to have been egregious; at least perceived that way by this gal."

Baxton sat down, pressed his head into the back of the chair, eyes closed. He exhaled slowly before he spoke. "Mr. Coine, I made business decisions. I did not keep statistics on how those decisions affected others. I didn't have time for that. I am not a compassionate man. My plans demand that I look forward, never back." Baxton pursed his lips. He clasped his hands, index fingers extended, gently placed under his chin. "You're a strange man, Mr. Coine. I think you're wrong. But until I can be sure of that, I'll do what you ask. But it will take time. Research is needed. Van der Meer would have been helpful. He cared for people. It was his only weakness." Baxton stood up abruptly. "Call me Monday after lunch. Make it one-thirty."

"After lunch it is. Mr. Baxton, as for the female perp, if I'm wrong I'm wrong. I've been wrong before but not often. See ya Monday."

Alexander arrived with the coffee. Coine smiled. "It's the thought that counts," he said as he turned to leave.

Baxton raised his right hand. "One last thing Mr. Coine."

"Yes?"

"Is . . ." Baxton hesitated, unable to say the word without a great deal of effort. ". . . she just out for revenge?"

"Don't think so. If that was all, you'd be dead now. Like I told you at dinner, it's more of a power thing. She wants you to know what it feels like to be powerless. Then she'll kill you." Coine turned and left.

"I'll take that coffee, Alexander," Baxton said, visibly disturbed by Coine's visit. "I don't want to be disturbed, not by anyone."

"Mrs. Baxton, sir?"

"Not even by Mrs. Baxton."

Powerless, Baxton thought. Never!

San Francisco, Police Headquarters 7:30 a.m. Pacific Time.

Lt. Walsh stared long and hard at the instrument of Fulton's death. He tried to imagine the suddenness of the unexpected explosion as Fulton sat before his lap top. There was not much left of the computer. The explosive charge was just enough to kill someone at close range but not enough to destroy much else. Captain Tohara, San Francisco's chief of homicide, interrupted the silence.

"Our bomb guys were able to figure out how this was constructed and it was impressive. It required not only sophisticated training but also time to put it all together." Tohara shook his head as he looked at the mess that was once a harmless computer. "We've been wondering when and where the killer got the time to do this."?

"Had to be the night Johnston was killed." Walsh paused for a moment. "That was last Monday. Fulton was already in San Francisco but unfortunately his computer was still in his Boston office."

"We don't know much about what has been going on in Boston, but it sure looks like your killer spent a lot of time hanging around company headquarters before the Johnston hit."

"That's why we confiscated all the lobby security video tapes for a month prior to Johnston's death. We figure when we find the killer we're gonna see her face in the crowd."

Tohara looked surprised. "Did you say her?"

"Yes. I didn't believe it at first but to make a long story short, Johnston and the cleaning lady were screwing around for some time and it looks like he was expecting her when he got whacked. So it's likely it was a female that stuck him."

Tohara smiled a knowing smile. "I don't think someone with all the talents of this downsizing killer would just walk into the building with her face hanging out. I recommend you be on the lookout for the bag lady in the big fluffy wig, long nose and bushy eyebrows. That'll be your killer."

"I like that. I like that a lot." Walsh looked at his watch. "Hey, it's time to get me to the airport."

<u>Boston, District Attorney's Office. February 21. 8:30 a.m.</u>

Warner sat stiffly at the center of his conference room table. Jones, Neiberg and Walsh were spread out on the other side. Warner looked at each of

Downsized

them in turn and halted his gaze when he reached Walsh. A cold stare coupled with a frown accompanied his words. "For chrissake Patrick, I didn't know San Francisco had a gigantic revolving door."

"What's that supposed to mean?" Walsh said defensively.

"You weren't there long enough to need a change of underwear!" Warner held the *Boston Herald* at arm's length, front page facing Neiberg and Walsh. "Another catchy headline," he said. "Like all the others, it has a ring to it." Warner read aloud what the large block letters at the top of the page proclaimed: "COINE RETURN!"

Warner read the lead paragraph aloud with the inflection of a TV anchorman. "In a press release issued by Amalgamated Worldwide Enterprises, it was announced yesterday that retired State Police Detective Lieutenant William Coine was retained as a private detective to expedite the capture of the self-proclaimed downsizing killer who murdered three top company executives last week. Mr. Coine was for years the leading homicide detective in Massachusetts. Well known for his unique investigatory style, Coine only failed to obtain a conviction once in his long career, and that was his first case."

Warner looked up from the paper. "I love this next part," he continued. "Prompted by a police effort that appears stalled," Warner stood up abruptly. "Jesus Christ," he yelled. "Stalled? Johnston was murdered only one week ago."

Sandra interrupted. "And the Van der Meer hit could have been prevented if that asshole Baxton didn't hold onto the downsizing press release."

Warner slammed the paper hard on his desk. "We're chopped liver. Baxton's hired a one man army and the press is going to eat us up alive." He took a deep breath. "Now, maybe now you can appreciate why I'm so goddamned upset." Warner continued, somewhat more composed, but still unwilling to retreat from sarcasm. "What do you think Coine would have done in San Francisco?"

Walsh folded his arms and stared at Warner. Warner pointed to Neiberg. "Stop me if you disagree." Warner returned Walsh's stare as he spoke. "He would have located the courier who delivered the laptop to the Fairmount. He would have reconstructed the chain of possession to see if anyone interfered with the delivery of the computer. He would have busted his ass until he either found something suspicious or was able to rule out any San Francisco involvement in Fulton's murder."

"Dammit, Gus," countered Walsh. "That's not fair. We already figured the damn thing was booby-trapped the night Johnston got killed."

"We were speculating. You could have nailed it for us." Warner hesitated, prompted to change tactics because of Walsh's growing anger. "You think I'm chewing you out because I get some kind of a kick out of it? I have a point . . . a damned important one. What's my point?" He held up the headline for effect. "Coine Return . . . this guy will make us look silly if we don't get our shit together. We have to be 100% professional . . . no let up." Warner pointed to Sandra. "Sandra, what've you got for me?"

"The knife we took out of Johnston's chest was sold mail order from the U S Cavalry catalogue."

"It's a great country," said Walsh.

"Problem is," Sandra continued, "several thousand were shipped around the country in the last few months alone. We've made some random checks on people in the Boston area but" Sandra looked at Neiberg, ". . . if you're right, John, do you think the queen of downsizing would have the murder weapon mailed to her real address?"

"What about the Van der Meer bomb?" Warner asked.

"ATF says it's unique. It doesn't fit any other MO. They hope they don't see any more like it. However, the explosive is definitely military."

"Are we looking for a goddamn soldier?" Warner asked excitedly.

"Not necessarily," said Sandra. "There are a zillion civilians with access to military hardware. I'm sorry Gus, but this case is not easy," she added, emphasizing the words 'is not'

"Gus," said Neiberg. "I have something to tell you. Hope you won't be upset."

"What now?"

"I met with Coine Friday night, late . . . at his apartment."

"Jesus, why didn't you tell me?"

"I was going to. I never expected Coine would be this morning's *Herald* headline."

"What did he want?"

"It was what I wanted. I hoped to bring him into our confidence and enlist his aid. Baxton beat me to it. Gus he's got great instincts, develops excellent insights. He's willing to work with us but he insisted I get official approval in light of his new position."

Warner stood up and leaned on the table. "Damn, that has possibilities." He walked behind his chair. "Can we trust him, I mean, will he use us and upstage us at the end?"

"The guy's never been out for publicity," said Neiberg.

"Until now," interjected Walsh.

"This crap in the paper's not his doing," said Neiberg defensively. "Gus, Coine would never approve an announcement like that. I trust him. He'll be a big help."

"Let me think about it," said Warner. "It might be worth our while to have him as an ally. I like the theme: old top cop back together with his former protégé."

"A veritable dream team, if you include nightmare," said Walsh sarcastically.

Warner shook his head. "Neiberg, check with me after lunch. Meanwhile, do we understand what I'm expecting from you people?"

"Yes," said Sandra.

Walsh shrugged a half-hearted yes. Neiberg shook his head affirmatively.

"Good. We meet here every morning at 8:30 until further notice."

Sandra, Neiberg and Walsh filed out of the conference room. Warner remained, staring at the *Herald* front page, wondering what the next embarrassment would be.

As soon as Walsh closed the door behind the threesome, he put his hand on Neiberg's left elbow. "Hey John, do you have those surveillance videos from Amalgamated's lobby?"

"Yes."

"Can I have 'em for a few days?"

"Sure. Why?"

"Oh, I just have an idea I wanna test out."

"Can you tell me?"

"Nah, It's only a wild hunch. I'll let you know if it works out."

Sandra laughed. "Walshie, are you getting into Neiberg's crystal ball routine?" she said.

"Don't be a smart ass, and don't call me Walshie."

<u>Boston, AWE Headquarters. 1:30 p.m.</u>
Coine was ushered into Baxton's office by Mrs. Tierney. McGillicuddy greeted him with a big smile and a two-handed hand shake. Baxton was at his desk on the phone, his back to Coine. When he was finished, Baxton swung around quickly and wasted no time. "I expected a call from you this morning," Baxton said coolly.

"Really?" Coine replied. "Whatever for?" he added sarcastically.

Baxton clenched his teeth angrily several times. Coine noticed.

"The press release was my idea and I expected you to give me grief about it," Baxton said.

"Never expect me to do the expected," Coine shot back. "It would be a waste of your valuable time. As for the press release, it was a stupid idea <u>if</u> my efforts were really the most important thing in your life."

Baxton's face reddened. McGillicuddy shifted nervously in his chair.

Downsized

"But you're not stupid," Coine said quickly. McGillicuddy relaxed. "So there's something more important on your agenda. That's your business. Mine is getting to the bottom of a very murky pool. Did you do your homework?"

"Yes. But you may not be satisfied."

"We'll see. What've ya got?"

McGillicuddy handed Coine a large box containing hundreds of letters. "These are the more obvious crank letters we received over the years. We still get a few."

"What else do you have?"

"Mrs. Tierney, please give Mr. Coine the memo we prepared this morning," Baxton said politely.

Coine scanned the two page document. "Interesting," he said.

"The first one is weird," said McGillicuddy. "A middle level manager was laid off four years ago . . . Fred Coe . . . worked in one of our New Hampshire operations. He couldn't get a new job at anywhere near his old salary . . ."

"Proof of his incompetence," Baxton interrupted.

"The guy was about to lose everything. So he got this crazy idea to rob a bank. He couldn't do that well either. He got shot and ended up gettin' 10 to 15 years. His wife blamed us. Several of the letters in that box are from her. She has a son and a daughter. But they're still teenagers. The next guy is Jim Tirrel. He couldn't get a job after his lay-off, so he went back into the army. It seemed like the right thing to do at the time. He was in his early thirties and had five years of service. He was a first sergeant, ended up in Iraq and was killed by an IED."

"What am I missing?" Coine said.

"That guy's wife blames us for his death. She sued. Case got nowhere fast. She's a waitress in some joint in Everett, has a couple of kids and hates Baxton's guts. You'll see some of her letters in the box plus the law suit documents."

"That's it?" Coine said, not hiding his dissatisfaction.

"Dammit Coine, you close plants, lay people off, life goes on," Baxton said impatiently. "I wasn't the only person laying people off. Hell, it has been an epidemic."

Mrs. Tierney left the room quietly and returned with a small envelope. "Mr. Coine, this is probably silly, but there is something that I remembered. It's not much. I've kept this thank you card in my desk for several years."

"Who is it from?" Coine said.

Baxton shot her a warning look. She ignored it. "It's from a young woman. Her name is Kimberly, Kimberly Hale."

"Why did she thank you?"

"Well, sorry to say, I was the only person from the home office to attend her father's funeral."

Baxton interrupted. "Mrs. Tierney, Mr. Coine doesn't need to hear about that. Hale's death had nothing to do with us. He was a weak and troubled man."

Coine ignored Baxton. "How'd he die?"

"He committed suicide, Mr. Coine."

"Did he leave a note?"

"No. Not that I ever heard of."

"Why do you think it's related to the company?" Coine inquired.

"I don't. But I thought you should know about it. Mr. Hale was fired when we closed our plant in Farnham's Landing, Maine."

Coine leaned forward in his chair. "December," Coine said matter-of-factly. "Two weeks before Christmas, three thousand people were terminated, practically the whole town."

Baxton frowned. "So you've done some homework, Mr. Coine. But Hale died," he searched his memory "When was that Mrs. Tierney?"

"The following February."

"When you were getting an award in Chicago, for Man of the Year or some such nonsense," Coine said, relishing the moment.

Baxton stiffened. "If you can learn as much about our killer as you have learned about me,

I'll be pleased," said Baxton, ignoring the obvious insult.

"Where's this Kimberly Hale now?"

"Don't know," Mrs. Tierney said, shaking her head. "After the funeral and that card, I never heard from her again," she added sadly.

Coine opened the envelope. The note on the little card was short. "I will always remember your kindness. Love, Kimberly."

Coine tucked the card into his shirt pocket, doing his best to hide his excitement. "Thanks, Mrs. Tierney. These are the kinds of things I'm looking for. However unrelated they may seem, please let me know if you think of anything else."

Coine glanced briefly at McGillicuddy, nodded and looked at Baxton. "If there's nothing else, I'm all set."

"Good," said Baxton. "Keep us posted. Let McGillicuddy know if you need anything."

"Like it says in the paper, I have unlimited resources?" Coine said in obvious jest.

"Not exactly," Baxton replied firmly. "Good day."

Coine winked at McGillicuddy, nodded to Mrs. Tierney, turned and left quickly.

<u>Allston, 3:00 p.m.</u>
Coine sat on the edge of his bed and stared at the three new additions to his wall chart: Fred Coe,

Downsized

James Tirrel and Kimberly Hale. Under Coe was the word "Walpole." James Tirrel had "deceased" next to him in parenthesis. Kimberly Hale was adorned with a big red question mark. The phone rang. "I'll get it," said Coine, "in case it's some media guy who didn't get the word that I've got nothing to say."

"Hello, Coine here."

"Bill, it's me, John."

"Well, don't keep me waiting, yes or no."

"Yes."

"Great," said Coine. He yelled to Jeanie. "Neiberg's got a green light. You'll be seein' more of him."

"Wonderful," said Jeanie, walking into the living room.

Coine went right to work. "Did somebody have enough smarts to get a list of passengers on all flights out of Logan on the day Van der Meer got killed?

"Yes. I did that right away."

"Good. I've got three names to check out. Coe and Tirrel . . . last names only, and a Kimberly Hale."

"What's the connection?"

"It'd be a waste of time to tell you now. If they pan out, I'll explain. Do you have anything else to tell me?"

"No, except I've got a long list of matching names to be checked. I guess three more won't hurt."

"Do it soon," said Coine. "And call me when you get an answer."

"Good night Bill."

"Yeah. See ya."

Neiberg was not encouraged by the conversation. Three names out of the blue did not seem like much. But he learned early in his apprenticeship with Bill Coine that if you did what he asked, you were frequently pleasantly surprised.

West Roxbury. 4:30 p.m.
Lt. Walsh sighed audibly as he contemplated the hard work facing him. There were video tapes covering twenty-eight days starting with January 18th. Each day was divided into four six-hour segments. Scanning all of them was a monstrous task for which he was not mentally prepared. He selected the 6:00 a.m. to 12:00 noon segments, figuring that the killer would have entered the building at a busy time. Walsh had already watched the tapes for January 18, 19 and 20 with no results. He shook off the urge to quit, slowly lifted himself out of his reclining chair and inserted January 21st into the VCR. As with the other tapes, the picture was not very clear. However, something attracted Walsh's attention. A person entered the lobby wearing a large bicycle helmet, a loose fitting one-piece jumpsuit -- the kind skimobile riders wear -- and

ski goggles. A scarf pulled up around the nose covered the rest of the face. The digital clock indicated 10:40 a.m.

Walsh watched intently as the mysterious figure moved quickly through the lobby and disappeared into an elevator. He pressed search and everyone in the picture jumped into fast forward. The tape ended at 11:58 a.m. The helmet and jumpsuit never reappeared. Walsh quickly leaned over and pulled the next six hour tape out of the box. At 4:30 p.m., the baggy jumpsuit returned. The helmet was still on, but now a large back pack was visible. "Jesus, Mary and Joseph, what bike courier stays in a building for six hours?" he shouted to himself. "Damn, that back pack could be used to store clothes, disguises, lunch and supper. Hell, you name it, anything could be in there. Damn, this could be our killer," he added excitedly. "It isn't a wig and a big nose, but it'll do."

Allston, 9:30 p.m.
The phone rang only once. This time Coine answered it quickly. "Coine here."

"It's me, John. I can't believe it."

"What?"

"You won't believe it either."

"Suppose you just tell me and we'll see if I believe it," said Coine impatiently.

"Kimberly Hale. She flew out of Logan on February 17th at 10:05 a.m. on Delta flight 2001 to Atlanta."

"Bingo," said Coine. "Was that her final destination?"

"No. She made a connecting flight on Atlantic Southeast Airlines to Fayetteville, North Carolina."

"Wow, that's Fort Bragg territory. The lady has some explaining to do."

"Bill, the moment I saw that name on the passenger list, I almost . . ." he hesitated briefly, "crapped my pants. But then I started thinking. This is too easy, Bill. You agree? Like, this has to be the mother of all coincidences, right?"

"Well," said Coine. "That really depends on just how many coincidences Kimberly has to explain away. Time will tell."

"But how can it be so simple. One day we've got nothing -- not a clue. The next there's Kimberly Hale."

Coine felt like he was back on the force teaching a young Neiberg. "John, facts don't lie. Only some interpreters do. Our killer's brazen as brass. The best way out of the airport is on a plane. She knew that. What's the next best thing? Use your own name. Why? Because then she can say, 'if I ever did such a terrible thing, why would I use my own name on the plane ticket.' And the answer

Downsized

is?" Coine waited for Neiberg to fill in the blank. It was the one thing Neiberg hated in the old days. "Well?" Coine insisted.

"It's too complicated to use a false identity," Neiberg answered confidently. "She would need phony documents and that could be her undoing if, later, someone recognized the face with two names."

"Not bad John. So let's not worry about how easy it was. We'll do some old-fashioned police work. We'll send some other people to interview Mrs. Coe and Mrs. Tirrel. I want you and me to visit Mr. Hale's little girl, Kimberly."

"I can't wait to tell Gus Warner about this," Neiberg said excitedly.

Coine thought about that for a moment. "John, do you trust me?"

"Are you kidding? Sure."

"Don't tell Gus just yet."

Neiberg suddenly developed a sinking feeling. Coine was always a renegade. He lived by his own rules in a world of rules made by others. Neiberg didn't think he could get away with that lifestyle and he desired a full and successful career. "For chrissake, Bill, how can I do that?"

"It's not a matter of how," Coine insisted. "You just keep your mouth shut for a short time. The real question is why?"

"OK. So why must I keep such an important discovery from Warner?"

"Right now, Gus is like a man in the desert looking desperately for water. You tell him about Kimberly Hale and, before you know it, there'll be a press conference with him announcing a breakthrough in the case. Listen. Do you have people interviewing the matched names on your computer list?"

"Yes."

"Good. Just tell Gus you're gonna go down to Fayetteville for an interview with someone on your list. Now, that's not lying."

"I guess not," said Neiberg, still uncertain about Coine's suggestion.

"John, we talk to the lady. No need for Miranda rights. Officially she's not a suspect. We see what she says, how she reacts. Bottom line, we get to build a case if there is one. Then you deliver the goods to Gus Warner. Bingo, you're a hero."

Neiberg was silent for several seconds.

"Well?" said Coine. "I'm right and you know it."

"Shit, Bill," said Neiberg, exasperated by Coine's insistence. "If Gus Warner ever finds out I can forget being banished to the Berkshires. I'll be a goddamn civilian."

"Good. You can be my partner. The job really pays well."

"When do we tell him?"

"After we interview Kimberly and check out her story."

"OK," Neiberg said nervously. "When do we go?"

"You locate her and we're there the next day."

"You're on."

Coine was not finished. "One last thing, check with Delta. See if that was a round trip ticket Kimberly was usin'. Let's see how long she was in Boston."

"I'll call you tomorrow," said Neiberg.

"Great. Good night. And listen, we're doing the right thing."

"Easy for you to say," Neiberg said.

Coine laughed. "When we're done, they'll be promoting you to lieutenant."

"I have one last question."

"What?"

"Will our firm be Neiberg and Coine or Coine and Neiberg?"

Coine laughed again. "We'll flip a coin. Now good night."

At six-thirty a.m. the next morning, with a late winter dawn bathing the windows softly in an amber light, Walsh put the last tape back in the box, rubbed his eyes and looked at his notes. The courier in the baggy jumpsuit had entered Amalgamated's office building on January 21st, 28th and 31st and again on February 14th. The 28th was a Monday. On that day, baggy pants arrived at 5:10 p.m. and exited at 9:30 p.m. That's when the bugger found out about Johnston and the cleaning lady, Walsh thought. On the 14th the baggy pants courier entered at 4:30 p.m. and exited at 9:15. He hit the note page with his right index finger. "There's our killer," he shouted, "No doubt about it." After a quick hot shower he headed for the D.A.'s office where he would set a personal record for being early.

Boston, District Attorney's Office. February 22. 8:00 a.m.

When Gus Warner poked his head into the conference room looking for Sandra Jones, the last person he expected to see was Lt. Patrick Walsh. "Insomnia?" Warner asked facetiously.

"Worse," said Walsh. "Work . . . all night."

"Work? That's new."

"Didn't think I was the dedicated type, did you," Walsh said as he placed the January 28th video tape into the office VCR.

"Let's just say I've kept an open mind. What's so interesting . . . or important that it deprived you of a night's sleep?"

Downsized

"Let me just say, modestly if I can, it's the first major break in the case. Hey Neiberg," Walsh shouted as Neiberg joined the group. "Watch closely." Walsh pushed play. The tape was preset to begin when the courier entered the lobby. "Note the time, 5:10 p.m."

Warner straddled one of the chairs, leaning forward, his arms folded on the back, face close to the TV screen. "What am I missing?" he said, as he watched the bizarre looking courier disappear into the elevator.

"Well, it's odd that every square inch of this person's body is covered," noted Neiberg. "Not an inch of flesh visible, even the hands," he added.

"Thank you," said Walsh. He pushed the eject button, pulled one tape out, and slid the other into the VCR. It was preset for the exit shot. "Look at the time …9:30 p.m."

"Wow, whoever it is just signed out at the security desk," said Sandra. "Let's get that book."

"I checked and double checked these two tapes," said Walsh excitedly. "The weirdo came in at 5:10 p.m. and did not leave until 9:30 that night. No bicycle courier I ever saw hung around an office building that long. But here is the clincher," Walsh exclaimed proudly as he ran the tape of the 14th. All watched in shock as the person in the weird outfit left the building at precisely 15 minutes after nine on the night Johnston was killed at precisely 9:01.

"Patrick, I owe you an apology. You found the assassin. Now all we have to do is put the right person in the baggy outfit." said Warner excitedly. "Sandra, I want maximum use of this now. Get it out to the press that we've had our first breakthrough in the case." He turned to Walsh. "I want still shots made from several frames, different angles, front and back." Warner began to pace back and forth as he continued issuing instructions. "Sandra, we distribute the photos to every messenger service in the city." He thought about that briefly. "Hell, within the Route 128 circle. Blow the suckers up . . . 8 x 10's. I want a caption. Keep it simple, like 'have you seen this person?' . . . maybe, 'do you know this person?' Hell," he said as he stopped his pacing and looked at Sandra, "use anything else you think will be helpful."

"I'll get on that immediately."

Neiberg now realized the wisdom of Coine's request not to disclose the Kimberly Hale information. If Warner was going ballistic with the mystery courier, he thought, imagine what he would do with the Kimberly Hale revelation.

"We go to the press," said Warner with finality. He turned back to Neiberg. "John, I'd say you are behind. Walsh just got us to the escalator. Tell me you have something up your sleeve."

"Sorry, still doing the slow, methodical police work. We've scheduled a bunch of interviews as a result of our passenger list."

"Well, the pressure's on. Once we give the press the scent, they're gonna want more," Warner explained.

"I'm doing the best I can," said Neiberg. "In fact, I'm going to North Carolina for one of the interviews tomorrow." Neiberg held his breath. He did not want to lie to a direct question.

"North Carolina?" said Warner with a surprised look.

"Hey," said Neiberg. "This is an airplane passenger list I'm dealing with. People boarded planes and went to places like North Carolina. So North Carolina it is." Warner did not ask for specifics. Neiberg breathed a sigh of relief. He quietly slipped out, closed the door to his office and started the search for Kimberly. It only took three telephone calls to locate First Lieutenant Kimberly Hale, Public Affairs Office, United States Special Forces at Fort Bragg. He called Coine immediately. "Hello Bill, did I wake you?"

"Nope, when I'm working a case I consider this a very reasonable hour. If it's important, you call."

"Great. I've got good news."

"What?"

"Kimberly is a lieutenant in the Special Forces at Fort Bragg. She's a public relations officer."

"I'll bet she knows a few good ways to dispatch a person. Tell me more."

"She was in Boston for a month."

"Bingo," yelled Coine. "Fort Bragg here we come."

Coine went immediately to his bedroom wall chart. He added "ARMY - SPECIAL FORCES" under Kimberly's name. The word "OPPORTUNITY" was placed next to her. Well Lt.Hale, just what have you been up to, he mused. Coine had high hopes for his first meeting with Kimberly. He was more excited than at any time in his thirty years in the sleuthing business.

Fort Bragg, N.C. 1500 hours.

Coine parked his rental car directly in front of the main entrance to the XVIII Airborne Corps headquarters building. The front door was on the second floor, reached by two sets of stairs forming a triangle and bordered by a concrete balustrade. It was an architectural detail not in keeping with the plain, red brick facade of the long, four story structure. However, a touch of the Old South was clearly intended. A rapidly darkening sky foreshadowed an imminent downpour.

Coine and Neiberg jogged quickly up the stairs on the left. At the top, Neiberg, a step or two ahead of Coine, ran headlong into three officers -- two men and a woman -- who had scurried up the other side. Neiberg and the woman collided as they tried to enter the building together. "Whoops," said Neiberg as several books fell from the female officer's left arm. "Sorry," said Neiberg, picking up the books. As he handed them to the young woman, he looked into her eyes for the first time. They were a stunning shade of blue, more like crystals than eyes. She smiled. Neiberg blushed. She's beautiful, he thought. It bothered him that she was so much in control while he was flustered. He also noticed the title on the last manual he retrieved from the floor: "Long Range Target Interdiction".

"Thank you," said the pretty face with the captivating blue eyes.

It did not take long for Coine and Neiberg to be escorted to Lt. Hale's office. The door was slightly ajar. Neiberg knocked as he opened it. A woman with short blonde hair, dressed in camouflage fatigues, was on the far side of a small office, facing the wall. Her right hand held an eight by ten inch photograph against a bulletin board. She placed a pin in the upper left hand corner, turning her head slightly at the sound of the knock, her face not fully visible. A small pin with a red plastic head protruded from between her lips. "One second," she mumbled as she removed the pin and stuck it into the upper right hand corner of the photo. "There," she said as she turned to face her visitors.

Neiberg's lips parted slightly as he looked directly into the crystal blue eyes and pretty face of Kimberly Hale -- the woman at the front door. Coine made the introductions, gesturing toward Neiberg "This is Detective Sergeant John Neiberg, Massachusetts State Police, and I'm William Coine."

Kimberly smiled a warm, friendly smile. It was not the smile of a cold-blooded killer, Neiberg thought. Coine merely took note. "Well," she said as she walked around her desk, hand held out to greet them. Kimberly nodded to Neiberg. "Did I hear Mr. Coine say you were with the Massachusetts State Police?"

"Yes, ma'am," said Neiberg.

"My goodness," said Kimberly. "Did you gentlemen take a wrong turn?"

This is a very confident young woman, Coine thought. "Nope," he said matter-of-factly. "We actually came all the way down here to speak with you."

Kimberly removed a few pamphlets from the solitary chair in front of her desk. She pointed to another chair in the corner, near where Neiberg was standing. "Sergeant, will you please bring that chair with you. Thanks." Neiberg did what he was asked to do, realizing her use of his title set a business-like tone for the meeting. It also tended to put him in his place. Kimberly outranked him. "Have a seat gentlemen," she said, walking to her chair behind the desk. Kimberly sat down, leaned back and placed both hands behind her head. It was a gesture more masculine than ladylike. Her pretty face and piercing blue eyes suggested an inner toughness to Coine. She had a special look. He had seen the look before -- but on men, not women. Kimberly Hale was the quintessential leader. She was calm, relaxed, confident and in control. Neiberg was still having a difficult time getting beyond the beautiful face. Kimberly stared at Neiberg for a few seconds as if to take his measure. As soon as her eyes met Coine's, she spoke. "I'm very curious," she said with the hint of a flirtatious smile softening her countenance. "Why would a state cop and a . . . ," she hesitated and raised her eyebrows slightly.

"A private detective" said Coine.

Kimberly continued, armed with the new information. ". . . and a private detective come all this way just to see me?"

"A homicide investigation," said Coine without hesitation.

"I'm sorry, gentlemen, but you'll have to be more specific," she said, removing her hands from behind her head and leaning forward, arms crossed and resting on her desk. "What does that have to do with me?"

Coine chose his words carefully. To say it had nothing to do with her would be foolish -- and untrue. It would come back to haunt him. "It has to do with Amalgamated Worldwide Enterprises," said Coine without expression. "You know the company, I take it," he added.

"Mr. Coine," Kimberly said, angrily, now sitting up straight in her chair. "I frankly wish to hell I had never heard of it. But yes, I'm familiar with it. And unless this is really important, I'd rather not discuss the subject."

"It is important," said Coine softly, "and I didn't intend to get you upset. But there are some things I'd like to know about the company through your eyes."

Kimberly's jaw set. "On one condition," she said sternly.

"What?"

"When I've had enough, I tell you and this interview is over. You leave and that's that."

Coine looked at Neiberg. They had little choice. "You're on," said Coine. "But before we start, can I get a cup of coffee around here?"

Kimberly picked up her phone. She paused waiting for someone to respond.

"Corporal Jamieson, will you please bring me three coffees, one black . . ." she looked at Coine. "Milk no sugar," he said. "Two black," said Neiberg.

"O.K.," said Kimberly, now more relaxed. "What can I tell you?"

"First," Coine said, "do you mind if Neiberg takes notes?"

"No."

The coffee arrived. Coine sipped from his cup and placed it on Kimberly's desk. "O.K." he said. "Johnston, Van der Meer, and Fulton. Ever hear of them?"

"You must be joking," she said. "I can hardly watch television without seeing more news about their murders than I see commercials. I believe they are referred to as downsizing victims?"

The question was designed to deliver maximum shock, catch Kimberly off guard. Her reaction was not what Coine expected. He shifted gears quickly. "I should have said did you ever know them while your father was working for Amalgamated?"

"Mr. Coine, let me try something. You drink your coffee. Sergeant Neiberg, you take notes. I'll tell you all about Amalgamated through the eyes of a nineteen year old. That's how old I was when my father . . ." Kimberly searched for the appropriate word, ". . . lost his job."

Neiberg and Coine intended to conduct an inquiry. This was a surprising change in direction. They exchanged glances. "Shoot," said Coine, reaching for his coffee cup.

"First of all," Kimberly began, "you should know that although my dad wasn't a very important man, I was very proud of him." Coine signaled that he understood. Kimberly looked up at the ceiling briefly, as if an outline for her story might appear there. "When I was a child," she began, but stopped and changed direction. "My father was born and raised in a small town in Maine . . . Lisbon Falls. He never went beyond high school, but he was a very clever guy. When I was a child, he worked for a big paper company. He ran the pulping operation for years before the trouble started. First, there were major environmental issues. The company closed the pulping facility, switched to recycled paper. My father was a valuable asset and they kept him. Then a bad economy hit the company hard. Bottom line: everyone in town was on the verge of losing their jobs when Irving Goldman came along with an idea to save the plant. He bought the mill and retooled the company. Northern Global came out of the paper company's ashes."

Coine interrupted, trying not to sound impatient, "We are getting to Amalgamated soon, I hope." Kimberly smiled. "Any minute now," she said. "But I think it's important to start at the beginning."

Coine nodded. Neiberg was completely captivated by her smile. She continued. "Northern Global was an early entrant into the GPS market . . . Global Positioning Systems . . . Suddenly the field exploded. From fishermen to the recreational boating market. There were even GPS for cars. Unfortunately Mr. Goldman's little venture got big enough for Brad Baxton to notice. Apparently, Amalgamated..." Kimberly paused and looked at Coine. "Soon enough?"

"Yes," said Coine, gesturing for her to continue.

"Amalgamated was looking for a mid-size GPS company to compliment all of its aerospace ventures." Kimberly shook her head and smiled at the thought. "Imagine, not only did Brad Baxton have to have complete control over everyone and everything, he wanted to own the technology that tells everyone where they are in the world." Anyway," Kimberly continued, "Dad was a big shot at Northern Global. Goldman spotted him early as a leader and made him a V.P. In the long run, it was his downfall."

"How so?" said Coine.

"Soon after Baxton's acquisition, all the employees expected to be laid off. There were several opportunities for them . . . one of the big paper mills was hiring. It was summer time and a good time to make a move."

"With Baxton's track record, they were wise to suspect him," said Neiberg.

"That's where dear old dad came in. They used him to convince everyone to stay," she said, anger appearing on her face as if it was happening now, not five years ago.

"Good grief, how could they pull the wool over your father's eyes?" Coine said. "Every Brad Baxton take-over ends in a blood bath."

"You'd understand if you knew my father. He always trusted everyone. That's how it was in Lisbon Falls." Kimberly smiled at the memory. "Dad always said there's a little bit of good in everyone. That was a big mistake when it came to a Bradford Baxton. But my father told me he received a commitment directly from Mr. Johnston . . ." Kimberly checked the ceiling again. "He was the Comptroller."

"The Chief Financial Officer," said Coine. He remained calm, but his alarm bell sounded at the mention of Johnston in that context.

"Well, anyway, he was up there on the corporate ladder. Dad relied on that promise and he assured everyone their loyalty to the new company would pay off. He made speeches and wrote memos promising job security. Hell, all those good people trusted him. They busted their asses under dad's leadership. What dad learned too late, dammit, is that this guy Van der Meer, Baxton's hit man, had already made arrangements to move the whole operation off-shore."

"Just a minute," said Coine incredulously. "How could something of that magnitude be hidden from your father?"

"Easy," said Kimberly. "The deal was put together in Amalgamated's Hong Kong office. And, best of all. . ." Kimberly's eyes moistened for the first time. "my dad was the first to go. He received no warning." she added sadly.

"Did anyone take your father's place?" Coine inquired.

"Yes. Can you believe it? They sent an Amalgamated lackey to keep everyone from panicking. He lied to them for two more weeks before pulling the plug on them." Kimberly became visibly angry again.

"Do you remember his name?" asked Coine routinely.

"Sid Fulton."

Coine almost went into shock. His sixth sense was in the red zone.

"So," said Kimberly, now in control again, "that's a quick look at a truly bastard of a man who runs a truly dirty operation." She looked at Neiberg who was writing feverishly. "Get all that?"

"Enough."

"I appreciate this info," said Coine. "But I'm curious. How did you end up in the Army?"

"Easy. Dad was not good with his personal finances. When he died . . ."

Coine noted the characterization, no reference to suicide.

". . . I could no longer afford to stay in school. So I joined the Army . . . not only to be all that I could be," she said jokingly but quickly became serious, "but to participate in the college tuition program. That offered up to forty thousand dollars for future college expenses. Then came OCS, jump school and here I am."

Coine finished his coffee with one long tip of the cup. "Your mother?" asked Coine sympathetically.

"Died years ago," said Kimberly, "but let's not get into that," she added firmly.

"Have you been to Boston recently," said Coine, trying to act nonchalant.

"Why do I get the feeling you already know the answer to that question," she said, returning to her semi-flirtatious, steely smile. Coine silently returned her stare. "I just returned from a month's leave. By the way, I returned on Delta Flight 2001 from Logan on February 17th."

"Where were you staying?" said Coine.

Kimberly stood up. "That's personal," she said flatly. "Remember our agreement?"

Coine and Neiberg nodded.

"Time's up," she said crisply. "I hope I've been helpful." Kimberly walked around to the front of her desk and held out her hand. Coine and Neiberg took turns shaking her hand. The clouds had dissipated when they reached the stairway at the front of the building.

"Jesus," said Neiberg.
"Wait'll we get in the car."

Kimberly sat at her desk for several moments, contemplating the significance of Neiberg's and Coine's visit. She reached for her phone and dialed a familiar number. A short wait and Andy Grissom's voice, reassuring as usual, was on the line.

"Captain Grissom here."

"Andy, this is Kimberly."

"You're not callin' to cancel tonight's study session, are ya?"

"No nothing like that." Kimberly paused, searching for the right words. "I think I've got a problem."

"Well, you just tell ole Andy Grissom and that problem will be dead as a doornail before you know it."

"Not over the phone. Can you meet me at my apartment a bit earlier than we planned, say six?"

"Will do. Meanwhile little darlin' don't you go frettin' any. You've called the right guy."

"Thanks Andy. See you at six."

Neiberg slid into the passenger seat and adjusted his seat belt. He did not wait for Coine to get comfortable behind the wheel.

"Jesus, Bill . . ."

"Will you stop sayin' 'Jesus', sounds like you're praying," Coine interjected.

"Damn, you were pretty blunt with Lieutenant Hale."

"You know me John, I sometimes get to the point quickly." Coine looked back, placed the car in gear and slowly pulled away from the curb. "You disapprove of what I did?" he said defensively.

"I don't know, it's just that until yesterday there were a thousand potential killers out there and suddenly there's Kimberly Hale on a silver platter." Neiberg shook his head. "Hell, if it wasn't for Baxton's secretary, we'd be talking to some idiot bank robber's wife. I mean, how lucky can you get. The odds of Hale being a cold-blooded killer have to be a million to one."

Coine laughed.

"What's so funny?"

"You've got a schoolboy crush on our lady Lieutenant!"

"Nonsense," said Neiberg, irritated by the suggestion. "Ridiculous," he added.

"I saw your face when our Lt. Hale turned out to be little miss blue eyes who got you all flustered at the front door."

"I was just surprised, that's all."

"Then what the hell's your problem?"

"I don't have a problem."

"You bet your ass you do," said Coine, pressing the point. "Do you realize we just talked to a person who rattled off the names of Johnston, Van der Meer and Fulton like they were characters in a fuckin' fairy-tale. And what did she call Van der Meer?"

"Baxton's hit man," said Neiberg.

"And Fulton was some Amalgamated lackey who took daddy's place and then pulled the trigger on the whole goddamn plant."

"Damn it, Bill, there are a hundred . . . hell, maybe a thousand people who could tell a story like Kim . . . Lt. Hale just did . . . every one of them would be talking about Johnston, Van der Meer and Fulton. They were the guys that did Baxton's dirty work."

"How many flew out of Logan the day Van der Meer bought the farm?"

Silence.

"How many of them have a goddamn desk calendar with February 18th all shaded in red?"

"What?" said Neiberg, shocked by that news.

"You heard me. February eighteenth was a red letter day for Lt. blue eyes. It also just happens to be the day Fulton turned his computer on for the last time."

"I didn't see that. Are you sure?"

"You were too busy making eyes at her and takin' notes. I saw it plain as day. Almost soiled my pants with her tellin' a story of how dear old dad got screwed and there, right in front of my eyes, is her calendar with a big red box, neatly done I might add. She didn't even go outside the lines. What are those odds?"

"Jesus," said Neiberg.

Coine looked at him for a second, eyebrows raised. "Do you realize the significance of what I'm sayin'?"

"Yes, but . . ."

"No buts about it. The odds are a million to one that those coincidences would occur to one of the thousands who might have a motive to kill Amalgamated executives; and the lady is a trained soldier. When you take those odds and match 'em up against a million to one shot that she is our killer, I say they even out."

"I don't see a clear motive yet," said Neiberg, "and I don't agree with your math."

"O.K.," said Coine in an uncharacteristic show of patience. "We have a difference of opinion. But one last point. You're the hot shot who says we're lookin' for a dame. Well?"

Silence. Neiberg had no answer.

"A quick quiz," said Coine. "I'll beep the horn for every correct answer."

"Are you serious?"

"What is the sex of the downsizing killer?"

"This is ridiculous," said Neiberg, not hiding his irritation at being treated like a child.

"Do it," said Coine, insisting.

"Female."

Coine hit the horn. "What is Kimberly Hale?"

"Female."

Another blast on the horn. "Where was she when Johnston and Van der Meer were killed?"

"Boston."

A long horn toot. "What day did she fly out of Logan?"

"The day Van der Meer was killed there."

A longer blast on the horn.

"You're attracting attention," said Neiberg.

"I hope I'm getting yours," Coine shot back. "I have one last question. No horn. Does she have a goddamn good reason to be more than a little pissed off at Brad Baxton and Company?"

"Yes, but Jesus . . ."

"You're praying again. Face it John, this lady deserves our attention . . . with no apologies. If we're dead wrong we look for other leads. But this minute, Lt. Kimberly Hale is an interesting candidate for killer of the month club."

Neiberg could not think of any more defenses for Kimberly. Perhaps she was in a pickle by sheer happenstance. But far worse was that she was in Coine's sights. "What's next?" asked Neiberg, beaten into submission by the horn quiz.

"We're going to her apartment."

"What?" said Neiberg, voice raised. "You're serious," he added.

"Couldn't be seriouser. I figure I can break in before she gets back, you stand guard at the door and I'll look for evidence."

"Have you lost your mind?" said Neiberg excitedly.

"Nope, I'm only kidding. Gotcha," said Coine laughing. "But we are going to pay her a surprise visit. I'd love to see her apartment."

"We'll miss our plane," said Neiberg.

"Look, we're here. She gave us enough info to warrant a good look at where she lives."

"Which causes me to ask just why in hell was she so cooperative if she's our killer?" said Neiberg, reaching over and sounding the car horn.

"Simple," said Coine. "She didn't tell us anything we couldn't have learned ourselves by conducting an exhaustive investigation. Hell, Mrs. Tierney probably knows the whole story. She's seen more than anyone realizes." Coine tapped Neiberg's shoulder. "As soon as I got personal with Lt. blue eyes what happened to cooperation?"

Neiberg looked at his watch. It was three forty-five. "When do you figure she'll be home?"

"Her duty day ends at four. I'm plannin' on about a quarter to five."

"And if she's a no-show?"

"She'll be there . . . she's gotta come home sometime."

"What are you gonna say?"

"Don't worry, I'll think of something."

"That's what worries me."

It was just getting dark when Kimberly arrived at her apartment at 5:50 p.m. The only illumination in the parking area was provided by two sets of floodlights mounted on each corner of the three story building, just below the eaves. Coine and Neiberg were merely silhouettes sitting on the middle tread of a five step staircase leading to the rear door. Kimberly was not pleased when she finally saw their faces. She was carrying two shopping bags, one in each arm. Car keys were dangling from the fingers of her left hand.

"Gentlemen," she said calmly. "This time I know you must have taken a wrong turn."

Coine stood up slowly, stretching each leg to eliminate the kinks. Neiberg simply rose to his feet.

"Nope," said Coine. "It's you again. We're here to see you. But I can see how you might think we got lost," he added, tongue in cheek.

"I thought we had a deal?" said Kimberly.

"We did. And we honored it," said Coine.

"Good, then you'll excuse me, I've got to get ready for company," Kimberly said with just a slight touch of annoyance in her voice.

Coine stepped aside, creating a clear path to the door. Kimberly took two strides and was about to set foot on the first step when Neiberg spoke.

"Can I help you with your grocery bags, Lieutenant?"

"No thank you, sergeant."

"Ma'am," Neiberg continued, "because of the deal we made with you, there were questions that needed to be asked that didn't get asked and we'd like to take a look at your apartment."

"Am I a suspect?" Kimberly said, not hiding her impatience.

"If you were," said Coine, "Neiberg here would've given you a Miranda warning." Coine could not now retreat. "Me, I'm different. I'm a retired cop. I don't have to worry about rules. Even if you were a suspect, I could have come out here alone and done a job on you."

"Not for long, Mr. Coine, not for long," said Kimberly, now upset by Coine's frankness. The headlights of a car suddenly spotlighted the trio. A car door slammed and within seconds the lights were gone. Within a few more seconds Andy

Downsized

Grissom dominated the scene. At six foot three inches and two hundred twenty pounds, he was an imposing figure in combat fatigues, winter jacket and hat. At five-eleven each, Coine and Neiberg were not necessarily midgets, but there was a striking difference in size and apparent strength of the three men. As Grissom neared the group, he was mindful of Kimberly's message. He figured the two strangers might have something to do with her problem. He approached them cautiously.

"Howdy," he said politely. "Lieutenant Hale, can Ah help you with those bundles?"

"Yes, they're beginning to get heavy."

"Excuse me," he said as he squeezed by Coine and Neiberg and took one of the shopping bags from Kimberly.

"Captain Grissom," said Kimberly, pointing to Neiberg. "I'd like you to meet Sergeant John Neiberg of the Massachusetts State Police." An almost unnoticeable hand gesture in Coine's direction, "and this is Mr. Bill Coine." She looked at Coine. "You are a private detective Mr. Coine?"

"Yes," said Coine with a smile and a nod of the head.

"They're investigating a very interesting homicide case," said Kimberly. "They came all the way down here just to talk to me." The expression on

Grissom's face prompted an explanation. "You've probably seen something about the case. Three executives were murdered, downsized according to the killer." Kimberly spoke in a matter-of-fact tone of voice with no hint of concern. However, it did raise a red flag for Grissom. "My dad worked for that company and wouldn't you know, I was on leave in Boston when two of the guys were killed. One of them was murdered at the airport the same day I flew out of Logan."

Grissom remembered Kimberly's brief story about her father's suicide. He was very concerned about the inference to be drawn by the horrendous coincidence. Standing on the top step, he looked down at Neiberg. "Sergeant, Ah'd say you should be talking to our JAG people if you want info from Lt. Hale here."

"That's not necessary," said Kimberly. "I've already told them what I know about Amalgamated and Dad and . . ."

"Ah wish you hadn't," said Grissom, now reacting to a heightened concern for Kimberly's safety.

"I certainly want to help any way I can," she said. "Now Mr. Coine wants to inspect my apartment."

"Definitely not," said Grissom. "Look here," he said sternly to both men, "if you need any more information, arrange a meeting through JAG."

"Well," said Kimberly, "I appreciate your suggestion, but I've got nothing to hide; nothing at all."

Grissom frowned and looked angrily at Kimberly.

"Perhaps you can join us," Kimberly said to Grissom.

"Ah wish you'd let me call Lt. Colonel Scharth. Ah'd certainly feel better," said Grissom, doing his best to remain calm. With a wave of her hand, Kimberly invited the group to follow her.

Kimberly's one bedroom apartment was tastefully furnished. Grissom followed closely as Coine and Neiberg meandered through the three rooms. It did not take long for Coine to get excited. A collection of little music boxes adorned shelves, a dresser top and several end tables. He picked one up. "You're a collector?"

"Not really. My father started giving me a little music box on special occasions ever since I was twelve. They mean a lot to me," she said softly.

To me also, thought Coine. He tried not to signal his intense interest as he looked for a ballerina gracing the top of one of the little contraptions. There was none, as far as he could see. Suddenly, a five alarm shock jolted his system. On the floor, next to an armchair were two hand grip exercisers. Neiberg also noticed. They exchanged glances. Grissom had lost patience. "Well gentlemen," he said, "you've had your inspection. It looks like it's time to go."

Coine had seen more than enough. He looked at his watch. "Hey, if we hurry, we'll be able to catch the last plane out of here."

Grissom closed the door behind Neiberg and Coine. He turned to Kimberly, a stern look on his face; a side that he had never shown to her before. "Damn it," he said when he could no longer hear footsteps in the hallway. "Why in hell didn't you listen to me? They had no right to come up here. Ya'll need ya head examined."

"I'm sorry it upset you," she said apologetically. "But I thought the best thing to do was cooperate. I've nothing to hide; really."

"Of course you don't. That's not the point. They came over a thousand miles to speak with you. Did they tell ya they were comin'?"

"No."

"Damn," said Grissom, punching his right fist into an open left hand. "Then they wanted to catch ya by surprise. You may not have anything to hide, but you can bet your fanny that they've been hidin' somethin'." Grissom picked up the phone and dialed.

"Who are you calling?"

"Lt. Colonel Scharth."

"Do you really think that's necessary?"

"Necessary?" he yelled. "Necessary?" he said again louder, excitedly. "Woman, it could be the most important damn call in your little ole life."

⇌

"I know what you're thinking," said Neiberg as Coine inserted the key into the ignition.

"What?" said Coine.

"Bingo!" answered Neiberg.

"Try double bingo. Good God Almighty," Coine added excitedly, "did you see all those music boxes . . . and the fuckin' exercise grips."

"I'm not blind," said Neiberg. "But I can't for the life of me figure this gal out."

"Just how many women have you figured out young fella?" said Coine in a mocking tone.

"All that really matters is this one. Damn it, Bill, she let us in knowing we'd see the hand grips and all those music boxes. She must be nuts."

"Not crazy, just very clever John. Clever as hell," added Coine as he stopped for a red light. "Listen. With her face, nobody's gonna believe she's a brutal killer. Now she's got a witness to how cooperative she was. Her pretty blue eyes and I've-got-nothing-to-hide routine will go far."

It was evident to Neiberg that Coine was ready to slap a big number one over Kimberly's name on his wall chart. However, one thing was very clear. If Lt. Kimberly Hale killed Johnston, Van der Meer and Fulton, it would be an uphill battle to convict her on just circumstantial evidence.

"What next?" said Neiberg.

"I'm only a private eye and a brand new one at that. Ball's in your court, my man. I say write it up and give Gus Warner a thrill. But there's a lot more to be done. Closing in on Lieutenant Pretty Face is gonna be hard work, but a lot of fun."

Neiberg agreed with Coine's hard work assessment. However, he did not see any fun in using his best efforts to send a beautiful young woman to prison for life.

Newton, 11:00 p.m.

Alexander walked quietly into Baxton's study. "Would you be in the mood for some tea or hot chocolate, sir," he said, casually, always alert not to startle Baxton who was usually deep in thought. Tonight was no exception. Something Coine had said at the Boston Harbor Hotel was eating at him. Somebody wanted to render him powerless and then kill him. Was it already happening, he wondered. AWE's stock was tumbling, he was losing control of Amalgamated's board and, in the void created by Van der Meer and Fulton's death, Arty Greer would be in firm control of the stratocruiser project for the indefinite future. Could this all have been conceived and carried out by a woman bent on teaching him a lesson? Baxton wracked his brain for answers. He could not think of a single enemy who would dare to take him on and, more importantly, get this far.

Alexander walked over to the large TV built into the bookcase on the wall to the right of Baxton's desk. "It's time for the evening news, would you like me to turn on the TV?" Alexander asked, preempting the answer and picking up the remote control.

"Yes," said Baxton swiveling around in his chair as he spoke. "You can leave now," he added as the TV screen came to life. The scene was the front entrance to police headquarters in Boston. Baxton was now very familiar with it.

The news anchor was wrapping up late breaking news". . . and so we will keep you advised of this developing news. The Commissioner is playing this one close to the vest. All we know is there was a shooting at police headquarters. A policeman has been wounded and has been brought to Mass General for emergency surgery. His identity is being withheld until next of kin have been notified. An unidentified man, posing as a uniformed policeman, was shot and killed. Again, the details have not been provided. We will bring you an update as soon as we receive any information. This is . . ."

Baxton reached for the remote and shut the TV off. Alexander turned to leave. He hesitated. "The violence is deplorable, Mr. Baxton, deplorable. Shall I douse the fire?"

"No thank you, I want to enjoy it awhile longer."

The large marble fireplace was on the far wall across from Baxton's desk. The fire had consumed several logs that had been placed there earlier by Alexander. What remained was a bed of glowing embers out of which a small flame erupted now and then depending upon the vagaries of wind currents. Baxton walked over to the bookcase as soon as Alexander closed the door. He removed several books to the right of the TV console, dialed a combination and opened a small wall safe. A quick shuffling of envelopes produced the one for which he was looking. It was a plain white business size envelope with one word typed on it: "Geronimo". Baxton walked quickly toward the fireplace but stopped. He locked the study door and returned to the fading embers. He held the envelope by one corner and dropped it onto the fire's smoldering remains. Several expanding brown spots on the white paper exploded into flames that devoured the envelope. A computer disk appeared but in a few moments it melted beyond recognition. Baxton removed a poker from its nearby stand and thoroughly mixed whatever was left of the disk with the hot ashes. There was one more thing to do, he thought. But it would have to wait until morning.

Baxton returned to his chair and stared at the diminishing glow in the fireplace. Was it a metaphor for his life, he wondered. Was his fire about to go out? Powerless, he thought. The word consumed him until he said it out loud, more like a question. "Powerless?" he yelled between gritted teeth. "Never," he hissed as he banged his desk with a clenched right fist. "I will never be powerless."

<u>Boston, District Attorney's office. February 23. 8:00 a.m.</u>
Warner sat at the head of his conference table. Sandra and Neiberg sat to Warner's left directly across from Walsh. Warner looked at Neiberg impatiently.

"Well, where's your report?"

Neiberg shifted uncomfortably in his chair. He hated making excuses. "Dottie's got it and she's making copies. She'll be here in a minute," he said, taking a quick look toward the door, expecting her arrival any second. Warner turned to Sandra.

"Make me happy."

Sandra smiled and slid a document toward him. It stopped short of its target. Warner reached out and, with his right index finger, coaxed it closer.

"Is this what I think it is?" he said excitedly.

"If you're thinking it's a copy of Amalgamated's sign-out register for January 28th, you win," Sandra said. "Look at where it's circled."

"I'm lookin'. All I see is a doodle of some kind."

"Well, you should be happy then because that's what our mystery courier scribbled in lieu of a signature at precisely 9:30 p.m. when," she hesitated, giving a quick nod to Walsh, "it signed the book on the way out. Forensics believes whoever did this was making it look like a signature." Sandra stopped and demonstrated. "See," she said as she scribbled on the pad in front of her, "some of the characteristics of my handwriting are built into it."

"So there's hope of comparing a handwriting sample," Warner said excitedly.

"Yep and I hope that makes you happy?"

"Pleased," Warner said. "We're slowly getting somewhere." He looked at Walsh.

"Hey, they don't pay me to make you happy . . . or pleased," Walsh said in his typically sarcastic fashion. "We've covered the metropolitan Boston courier companies with a blanket. But nobody on the face of the earth knows any bona fide courier who delivered messages dressed like our weirdo."

"That's what we were hoping for," Warner said, ignoring Walsh's initial comment.

"There's more," Walsh said. "Our lab crew did some high tech black magic," he added proudly.

Downsized

"Several of the people in the TV picture with the weirdo in the jump suit were located, measured and weighed . . ."

Warner raised his eyebrows in anticipation.

". . . and the answer is," said Walsh, pulling an envelope out of his left inside jacket pocket.

"For chrissake, will you stop your clowning around," Warner said.

"Our killer . . ." Walsh stopped and looked at Neiberg. ". . . and it is our killer . . . is between five foot five and five foot six inches and approximately 125 pounds."

"How tall is our cleaning lady?" said Sandra.

Neiberg leaned forward. "Ailida could wear that outfit comfortably. She's approximately five foot five, maybe 120. We'll nail that down . . . How reliable are those figures?" he asked.

"Dr. Romanoff says you can take 'em to the bank," Walsh said smugly. "I'm tellin' ya, we're gettin' real close to breakin' this case."

Dottie walked into the room with Neiberg's report. Warner practically pulled it from her hand and began reading on the way back to his chair. He never sat down. "Jesus Christ, gimme that FBI computer list," he yelled. Neiberg obliged. Warner ran his finger down the numbered paragraphs until he came to paragraph seventeen. He read the entry loudly, "Kimberly Hale, First Lieutenant, 82d

Airborne, Fort Bragg, Public Affairs Office for the U.S. Special Forces Command." He slammed the folder down hard on the table. "This is who you interviewed yesterday?"

"Yes," said Neiberg.

"Neiberg, the FBI ran a computer cross-check matching names of people who flew out of Logan on the eighteenth with the last names of persons downsized by Amalgamated. How in hell did you get face to face with priority cross-match number seventeen?"

"Bill Coine had a hunch. It short cut the process by weeks."

"Why didn't you tell me?"

"I had not yet read the FBI list." Neiberg replied apologetically. "I was working off the list we compiled."

Warner shook his head from side to side. "That's why I've been telling you guys to coordinate. What does Coine think?"

"He believes Lieutenant Hale is red hot. Coine says Lt. Hale is a good candidate for killer of the month club."

"How tall is she," said Sandra.

"She's about five-feet five . . . and trim. Not more than one-twenty," Neiberg said.

"Did you Mirandize the lady?" Sandra asked, looking at Neiberg with a concerned expression.

"Hell no Sandra," Neiberg said, not hiding his displeasure with the suggestion he should have given a Miranda warning. "She wasn't a suspect when we walked into her office. It was purely an informational meeting."

Sandra shot a worried glance in Warner's direction. "What about at her apartment," she insisted.

"She still wasn't a suspect in my mind," said Neiberg, defensively.

"What about Coine? Did he suspect her?" Warner asked, now sitting on the edge of the conference room table.

"You don't know Coine. He's got a sixth sense," said Neiberg. "But his suspecting her was not influencing me."

Warner looked at Sandra and they exchanged worried expressions.

"Joint enterprise," said Sandra.

"Just one minute," Neiberg said hotly. "We've got a horse and cart thing goin' on and I don't like it. Kimberly . . . Lieutenant Hale fell into my lap."

"Did it hurt?" said Walsh, smiling.

Neiberg ignored the joke and continued excitedly. "She came to me out of the blue in a call from Coine. In all the circumstances, there was no reason for me to spook the lady with a Miranda warning. You guys are now lookin' at a report that sums it all up after the fact. Next time I speak to Hale I'll have to warn her. But there was no reason to do it until after I was through walking around her apartment. Besides, the lady was completely cooperative from the moment we laid eyes on her."

"Finished?" Warner said tersely.

"Yes."

"Well, if she's our gal, some goddam defense lawyer is gonna tuck this up our butt." He returned to his chair at the head of the table and changed the subject. "I have one last item." He looked at Neiberg. "You hear what happened last night at BPD Headquarters?"

"No. Came right here and buried my nose in the computer."

"Your nose gets around," said Walsh with a grin.

"Knock it off will ya," said Warner. "A little excitement," he resumed. "Seems someone thought it was damned important to try to break into the evidence vault."

"What the hell for?" Neiberg said.

"Well, for openers, that's where Johnston's computer is being stored," Sandra said.

"On the off chance it's related to the downsizing murders we've slapped a lid on it. All the press knows is an unidentified man was shot and killed during an aborted break-in attempt at headquarters." Warner pointed his right index finger at

Neiberg. "We don't tell Coine about the possible Johnston computer connection to the shoot-out at headquarters."

Neiberg looked puzzled.

"For Chrissake John," Walsh said, "Coine's on Baxton's payroll. Until we know what we're dealing with the info stays with us."

"All of you," Warner said. "The morning meetings are off until further notice. But be in touch every day. Let's kick some ass." The trio turned around and left without another word being spoken. Warner opened Neiberg's report and studied it line by line. Please let it be, he thought. Let it be Kimberly Hale.

<u>Allston, 8:30 a.m.</u>
Coine fumbled through the manila envelope into which he had placed the many magazine articles he assembled when this case was just a hobby. He finally found the clipping for which he had been searching, held it under a lamp and examined the face of the young woman carrying a sign outside Baxton's award dinner in Chicago. The hair was longer, the face a bit younger, but it was unmistakably Kimberly Hale. "Bingo," Coine yelled. He placed the photo on his wall chart, attached a string from Kimberly to the picture and assigned it a big red one.

Fort Bragg, N.C. 0915 hours.

Lieutenant Colonel William Scharth had been a JAG officer for slightly more than fifteen years. A competent lawyer, he was first and foremost a soldier. Kimberly and Gus Grissom saluted smartly as they entered his office. Scharth half-heartedly returned the salute and waved his hand signaling them to be seated. "Now, what's this nonsense about a murder investigation and nobody bothered to call us? Lieutenant Hale, don't you know that you're entitled by right to have a JAG officer by your side at all stages of a civilian criminal investigation." He did not wait for Kimberly to respond. "Hell, all we usually get is the aftermath of a drunken brawl in Fayetteville, thank goodness. But to be visited by a sergeant in the Massachusetts State Police who just happened to be investigating a murder . . . no, three murders . . . well, that's a happening. I don't like the fact that it happened without my presence. So young lady, tell me about it."

Kimberly recounted the initial visit to her office and the conversation at the rear entrance to her apartment.

"Lieutenant, Captain Grissom gave you damn good advice. I hope you realize that," said Scharth instructionally. He looked at Grissom. "Captain, I know you are concerned, and I appreciate your calling us. But now me and the lady have to get down to attorney-client status. So. . ." Grissom did not wait for the sentence to be finished. He stood up quickly, saluted, turned and left. Grissom stopped at the door and spoke to Kimberly before leaving. "You heed this man's advice darlin', if you know what's good for you."

Kimberly smiled and nodded. Grissom turned and disappeared through the slowly closing door.

"Darlin'?" said Scharth.

"It's just a manner of speech," Kimberly said.

"Well, let me ask you a few questions if I may," said Scharth, standing as he spoke. He walked around to the front of his desk and sat down on it. "I've got the date here from the newspaper when this Sam Adams Johnston was killed. February fourteenth, it was. So where were you young lady between the hours of, let's say, six and ten in the evening?"

"You're not serious!"

"I am dead serious."

"If I may be impolite, sir, where were you that day?"

Scharth stood up, walked behind the desk and resumed his seat. "If a sergeant in the Massachusetts State Police asked me that question . . . and you better believe he will ask you, I'd bust my ass, if you'll pardon me, trying to remember where I was." He paused, looking for a reaction.

"You think he'll be back?"

"You can count on it. There are too many unanswered questions. So let's start with mine."

Kimberly leaned forward, placed her head in both hands, closed her eyes and thought hard. "Damn it," she said in complete frustration, "every day was just about the same. Boring," she said, emphasizing the word. "I was alone in my friend's apartment. She was in Paris the whole time."

"Bad answer, think some more. Think hard."

"I went to a local convenience store . . . quite a lot. Maybe I went on the fourteenth. Did I?"

"Kimberly Hale, did you kill this Johnston character?"

"You can't be serious."

"I'm very serious and I want an answer."

"No. Hell no. Jesus no," said Kimberly defiantly, clenching her fists.

"Good. Then you've got a lot of work to do. You better get started." Scharth handed Kimberly a legal size lined yellow pad. "I want you to prepare a diary for me of each boring, each goddamn boring day."

Kimberly looked astonished.

"I don't have to know how many times you went to the bathroom."

"Thanks for little things," she said jokingly. Then she became quiet, her face set, muscles tensed. "You're really serious?"

"Madam, I have never been more serious." Scharth stood up and walked Kimberly to the door. "Speak to no one, not even Captain darlin'. And you call me as soon as you hear from anyone investigating these . . . whatever the hell the company's name is . . ."

"Amalgamated."

". . . these goddamned Amalgamated murders."

"Yes, sir, I will definitely call"

"There's one last thing and it is critical. Don't touch or change a thing in your apartment. Not a thing."

"Can I make the bed?"

"Only if you're a neat freak and you must." Scharth smiled for the first time since Kimberly met him. Kimberly left quickly. Scharth searched through the middle drawer of his desk, retrieved an old, well-worn address book, flipped pages until he was at the R's, picked up his phone and dialed a number from the past. "I wonder if this number is still good?" he asked out loud. "I wonder if he'll even remember me?"

<u>Boston, AWE Headquarters. 10:00 a.m.</u>
Brad Baxton left orders with Mrs. Tierney that he was not to be disturbed. He looked at the innocuous *Boston Globe* article in the Metropolitan section for the sixth time. Why is it so short, so

insignificant he wondered. He read it aloud this time, softly, "Last night, an unidentified man dressed in a Boston policeman's uniform was shot and killed in an aborted attempt to break into a secured area of Police Headquarters. Sergeant Brett Schultz first encountered the intruder and was shot in an exchange of gunfire. Sergeant Schultz is at the Massachusetts General Hospital and is reported to be in stable condition. Officials declined to speculate why an armed man, disguised as a patrolman, would attempt such an impossible task. Terrorism has been ruled out. An unidentified spokesman for the Police Commissioner said the dead man took an extreme risk and suffered from bad timing. A routine identification process is in progress, said the spokesman, and the incident will be thoroughly investigated. Meanwhile, the Police Commissioner has placed a lid on the matter."

Baxton opened the lower right drawer of his large desk and removed the phone that for so long had been its only contents. He dropped it into a large shopping bag and placed several items of clothing on top, making adjustments until the phone could not be seen by a casual observer. The intercom intruded.

"Mr. Baxton," Tierney said. "I know you didn't want to . . ."

"Who is it?" Baxton interrupted impatiently.

"Mr. Coine."

Baxton put the bag under his desk.

"I'm sorry for the interruption, but he's a persistent man."

"Send him in."

Coine walked quickly into Baxton's office. He held up a large Dunkin Donuts cup and smiled. "I brought my own this time." Coine sat down in front of Baxton's desk and wasted no time. "Do you like to live dangerously?" He said, his inflection suggesting a challenge.

"Well, like is the wrong word. But I've been known to take risks."

"Good, then what say we open the security blinds on the window behind you and let some natural light in here."

He's in an uncharacteristically good mood, Baxton thought as he carried out Coine's suggestion.

"Don't tell McGillicuddy on me," said Coine, "but I did think the blinds were a touch of overkill. Besides, if my hunch is correct, you're safe as long as a certain Lieutenant Kimberly Hale is doing her Army thing at Fort Bragg."

Baxton returned to his seat behind the desk. Coine crossed his legs at the ankles and sipped from his coffee cup. He read Baxton's face. It clearly registered disbelief.

"Rushing to judgment, Mr. Coine?"

"Not really. On the evidence thus far she is unquestionably the top suspect."

"Tell me more."

Coine summarized the facts convincingly. He painted a picture of a beautiful, but deadly, killer out to destroy Baxton personally. Coine linked each piece of circumstantial evidence, building a strong pattern of suspicion. "Bottom line," said Coine, "I think our lady lieutenant fits the bill."

Baxton sat quietly for several seconds before he spoke. "Mr. Coine, I'm naturally suspicious of quick solutions. You've only been on the case for less than a week," he said. "But I'm mindful of the important role of luck." Baxton paused. "No offense, but I think you're operating on purely blind luck."

"And I think you would never admit that a young woman," a brief hesitation, "hell, any woman, could bring you and your powerful company down," Coine said as he stared deeply into Baxton's eyes. Baxton didn't flinch. However, he did smile faintly.

"So you think you know me?" he said, cocking his head slightly to the left, taking Coine's measure.

"Not completely, but enough to bet money on the fact that you would rather see the murders go unsolved than have it turn out that a pretty face screwed you over royally."

Baxton was not happy with Coine's candor. "Don't waste your time evaluating me, Mr. Coine. I'd hate to ruin your batting average for knowing it all. So let's just stick to business."

Coine shrugged, took a long drink from his cup and uncrossed his legs.

"Fair enough," Coine said. "My hunches are usually more right than wrong and that leaves a little room for me to be wrong about Lieutenant Hale."

Baxton raised an eyebrow. "I didn't know humility was one of your traits?" he said sarcastically.

"Not on your life," Coine shot back. "I am relying on statistics."

Baxton visualized an endless conversation, point and counterpoint. Coine had an answer for everything. "All right, Mr. Coine, where do we go from here?"

"I'll be spending a lot of time getting to know Hale's dad. I'm gonna need some help from you."

"I hardly knew the man."

"Somebody in your organization must know something about what went on between him and your company. Find out. Meanwhile, I've gotta figure out what little Miss Muffet was doing here in Boston for thirty days. I'll also be going back to Fort Bragg." Coine turned to leave but stopped. "Hey, on second thought, close the blinds."

"I thought you said I was safe from the big, bad Kimberly Hale?"

"You are, for the time being," said Coine with a big grin on his face. "But you've got so many enemies all this killing might give someone else an idea." Coine lifted his coffee cup and aimed it at Baxton in a mock toast and turned to leave.

"Just a minute," Baxton said, as an afterthought. Coine stopped.

"Did you hear about the shooting at Police Headquarters?"

"Yes."

"Do you think it has anything to do with this case?"

Coine frowned. "What makes you ask?" he said suspiciously. Baxton noticed and chided himself for asking the question. "Do you know something I don't," Coine added, raising his eyebrows.

Baxton felt the sting of that question. ."Just curious," He said, "It's certainly an unusual event at a time when unusual things were happening to my company. Curious about the timing, that's all. Good day, Mr. Coine."

Baxton watched the door close slowly behind Coine. He stood motionless for awhile pondering the circumstantial evidence he heard linking Lieutenant Hale to the murders. Then he remembered Coine's little joke about a danger from others, turned, walked to the window and closed the blinds.

Boston Police Headquarters, 11:15 a.m.
Walsh looked carefully at the mug shot produced by the fingerprint identification unit. The face he had seen in the flesh had been distorted by the trauma of a nine millimeter bullet ripping the man's skull apart. Nevertheless, the dead man and the emotionless face in the police photo were one and the same. "Thaddeus Korensky, a/k/a the Professor," was the name beneath the face. Walsh, a homicide cop for most of his career, had never heard of him. The report was short, but the attached list of computer crimes was long. Korensky was a Russian immigrant who taught computer science for awhile at one of Boston's many college level trade schools that offer evening courses and great post-graduate placement services. Unfortunately, Korensky was not satisfied with his paltry earnings from teaching. He expected much more from capitalism. After all, there was so much opportunity here. Ultimately, Korensky found his little niche in the field of computer larceny. A world of illegal electronic money transfers opened before his eyes. He knew more about corporate computer security than anyone in the world, and thus, was able to penetrate any computer network in the world. Corporate secrets were

the Professor's for the taking. All he needed were customers and soon there were many.

Walsh looked up from the report and tried to recall the dead man, sprawled across the stairs, head down, in a police uniform. It was not easy to figure what a dead man's personality was like when he was among the living. But he had a soft appearance. Walsh remembered the carefully manicured fingernails. This guy Korensky was a computer genius. A white collar freak, Walsh thought. What in hell was he thinking? What in hell was he doing in a cowboy role, and who in hell, Walsh wondered, was he doing it for?

Walsh returned the picture and the report to its folder, but not before he jotted down the Professor's last known address. "20 Rowe's Wharf, Boston, Unit 605."

Fort Bragg, N.C. 1530 hours.
Andy Grissom could not believe his eyes. With everything that was going on in Kimberly's life, it was the last thing he expected to see. He had dropped in to her office to see how she was doing after her talk with Lt. Colonel Scharth and to schedule another study session.

"Just what in tarnation do you think you're doin'?" said Grissom, in a tone more scolding than inquisitive.

"What does it look like?" Kimberly answered as she finished buttoning up her civilian topcoat and extended the handle on her standard flight attendant style suitcase on wheels.

"Well darlin', it looks like ya'll decided to go somewhere. By the looks of it, you will be stayin' somewhere for a spell."

"Andy, can I make a suggestion?" Grissom looked puzzled. Kimberly did not wait for an answer. "See if you can call me Kim, or even Kimberly or, last but not least, Lieutenant Hale, but darlin' is getting to be an embarrassing habit."

"Shucks,". . . He didn't get to finish the thought.

"Honestly," said Kimberly, placing an envelope in her pocket, "Colonel Scharth referred to you as Captain darlin'!"

"Great," said Grissom, flashing a big smile. "Ah'll call you Kim and you can call me Captain darlin'!"

"You're absolutely impossible," Kimberly said, trying to maintain a serious attitude. "Now if you'll just step aside," she added impatiently, "I'll be on my way."

"Good grief, where in blazes are ya'll goin'?"

"I will be at a secluded place where I will not be disturbed and where I can think."

"Why?"

"Scharth gave me an impossible homework assignment. I'll never be able to concentrate around here. I just need some time alone. Don't worry, I'll be returning Monday."

Grissom did look worried. "Seems to me bein' alone's what got ya'll on somebody's shit list in Boston." He looked at his watch. "Give me twenty minutes and Ah'll go with you."

Kimberly sighed audibly. "Andy please, I really appreciate all you do and want to do for me . . . but alone means alone. Besides, you've got an exam tomorrow."

"Ah'll cancel it. They'll let me make it up. Ya'll should not be doin' this alone. Damn, you're a stubborn gal."

"Look, I'll make sure I'm noticed. I'll leave a trail that will be easy to follow."

Grissom's eyes widened. "But not by you," she quickly added.

"Shouldn't you check with Scharth?"

"He's the reason I'm doing this. Trust me. I'll be OK. Hey, I'm the Army's new secret weapon. Killer Hale, remember?"

"Don't joke around about that," Grissom admonished.

"Now look who's serious," Kimberly said, with one of her half smiles. She reached up to give Grissom a kiss on the cheek and stopped. "You're just too damn tall," she said.

"Ah'll bend down."

"Too late," she said as she walked out the door, stopped and blew him a kiss with a free hand. "See you Monday."

Grissom did not follow. Instead he looked on her desk for some clue as to where she might be going. He stopped short of searching her desk drawers. For a split second, he was almost afraid of what he might find. Then he reminded himself, Kimberly was the last person he'd ever believe went on some brutal killing spree. He decided ultimately to respect her desire for privacy and hope for the best.

<u>Boston, 20 Rowes Wharf. 3:35 p.m.</u>
Walsh stood outside unit 605 in the luxurious Rose Wharf residential building. A forensics team was on the way but he was impatient. Walsh inserted the key that was removed from Korensky's body. It fit. But the door was not locked. It opened slowly, effortlessly, when Walsh pushed on it. His heart rate increased noticeably. "What the fuck," he said to himself in a whisper, drawing his nine millimeter police issue Smith and Wesson. He had not done so in a long time. He hesitated for a moment. I'll wait, he thought. No, I'm going in, he decided. He held his gun close to his hip, not extended. Walsh walked through a large living room, richly decorated. It was a waterfront unit with a breath-taking

view of Boston Harbor. He stopped and listened intently. Not a sound could be heard except his own breathing. There was an eerie silence, not even the sound of a clock ticking.

Walsh stood in the center of the room and turned slowly, counterclockwise. A long corridor separated the living room from the rest of the apartment. Several closed doors led from the corridor to some great hiding places for an intruder, if there was one. The apartment was enormous. Walsh figured it had to be at least two thousand square feet and worth more than a million bucks. The Professor's business was goddamned good, Walsh thought. He looked at his watch. "Where the fuck is everybody," he whispered. "Come on, damn it, get here," he added.

Walsh decided to look in one more room. He slowly opened the first door on his right. Curtains were closed, the light was dim. Walsh could discern several computer consoles and an assembly of electronic gadgets along the far wall. He took two steps beyond the door and turned to his right, slowly. A blinding pain to the back of his head caused his knees to buckle. He stumbled forward, trying to turn to face his attacker. A well-placed kick to the small of his back drove Walsh across the room and into a wall, head first. He felt a sharp pain in his neck as he crumpled to the rug. Somewhere, from the moment he was first struck until he hit his head on the wall, he dropped his gun. He groped for it, blinded by pain and panic. A big shoe came down hard on Walsh's forearm. He felt his arm break. "Fuck," he yelled, and stifled a scream. The shoe smashed into his face and Walsh lost consciousness.

Boston, AWE Headquarters. 3:55 p.m.
Glenn Franklin once had high hopes of being a senior partner in a prestigious Boston law firm. Although he did not place very high in his law school class, he did have that all important Harvard law degree. When he failed to make the cut at the prestigious law firm of Palmer, Davis and Wyeth his dreams of making the big time in private practice vanished. Douglas Rawlings, the senior partner in charge of transactional law, broke the news to him with a practiced look of solemnity and sorrow. After a brief discussion about how everyone was not cut out to be one of the great lawyers presumably like him and, hence, a partner at PD&W, Rawlings fat, wrinkled face broke into a big grin that caused his eyes partially to close. The good news, it seemed, was PD&W did not abandon their failed fledglings and Franklin's "good fortune" was his immediate acceptance by Amalgamated Worldwide Enterprises as an associate general counsel. The apparent gift from PD&W

was illusory. It was a clever way for the firm to lock in a corporate client's business. Franklin saw only the opportunities and grabbed for it twenty years ago. He soon regretted his decision as he watched many of his contemporaries reach the legal heights to which he once aspired.

Now, with Amalgamated's fortunes fading quickly, Franklin decided it was time to inspect a section in Johnston's private file room that had always been off limits to him. To his surprise, it wasn't locked or guarded. He soon learned why. There were 120 files with an assigned number marked "Special Project." The only reference contained in each folder was a terse note: "See Johnston Special File."

A special project file that sent you to another special file spelled trouble. Amalgamated was a public company. Stockholders had rights to information and the SEC frowned on secret operations that dealt with corporate finance. So did the IRS and other agencies. He was now convinced that Baxton's initial keen interest in Johnston's computer had to do with the special projects. The information was protected by an electronic security scheme, passwords, encoding and the like. He also knew that, although he had no knowledge, his saying so would not be believed. When a man like Baxton fell, his general counsel usually toppled with him. If Johnston and Baxton were engaged in illegal activities, it was time for Franklin to distance himself. He smiled as he returned the last folder to its numerical resting place. It was payback time for PD&W. If Baxton's ship was going to sink, how fitting it would be for PD&W to be at the helm. Rawlings was long dead, but some other pompous senior partner was about to earn his keep. The trick was getting Baxton to buy into the scheme.

Baxton kept Franklin waiting for ten minutes. At approximately 4:30, Mrs. Tierney said he could go in. Franklin walked into the big office with a new air of confidence. The blinds were still drawn.

"… it's still too early to tell," Baxton was saying to someone on the other end of the telephone. "Just be patient. I'll keep you posted and don't call me again." Baxton hung up the phone and shot a disapproving glance at Franklin. "What bad news do you have now?" he said curtly.

"The worst imaginable," said Franklin, enjoying every word that came out of his mouth. He did not wait for Baxton to tell him to be seated. "You're about to be held in contempt of court," he said as he lowered himself into the chair on Baxton's left.

A lamp partially blocked the view. Baxton had to lean over to see Franklin fully.

"Bullshit," Baxton said.

"No, sir," said Franklin. "The judge wants <u>you</u> to sign an affidavit, certifying that neither you nor anyone alive knows the password into Johnston's confidential computer file. My guess is you won't do that. Am I correct?"

"My God, I have never seen such a colossal failure to perform up to standards in my life," Baxton yelled, his face getting redder by the word. "Damn you Franklin, I thought you had some modicum of competence."

"Hell, you know damn well that I'm not a trial lawyer."

Baxton was astonished at Franklin's response. His jaw dropped. He said nothing as Franklin continued. "We pay PD&W a million dollars a year to pull our chestnuts out of the fire in litigation matters. You wanted this kept in-house. Well, it is and it shouldn't have been in the first place."

Baxton stood up. "You are bordering on insubordination, damn you," Baxton yelled. "Christ Almighty, have you lost your mind?"

"No. I just lost a case, a motion. And, while we're pinpointing the blame, try this on for size. The judge doesn't believe for one minute that no one here knows the password. So he's set a nifty trap. If you do know it and lie, you perjure yourself. If you don't know the password honestly, then everyone in Johnston's department must sign an affidavit. Someone will tell the truth. Game, set, match," said Franklin, staring into Baxton's keenly focused eyes.

"Appeal!"

"Useless."

"I don't admit defeat."

"Then bring in PD&W like I suggested. Their senior litigator serves on the same bar association committee with Judge Franey who entered this order." Baxton thought about that suggestion for a moment. "Knows him well?" Baxton asked, suddenly interested.

"Yes. And he does a lot of bragging about how wired he is in the Superior Court. Bring him in now so he'll have time to prepare for Monday."

"What's Monday?"

"The deadline for the affidavits."

"Get an extension!"

"Not in the cards." Franklin paused, rubbed his chin as if the thought just occurred to him. "I'll bet you Rod Halloway can get one," he added.

"Who's he?"

"PD&W's senior litigator."

"Get him, brief him, and goddammit, don't paint a bleak picture. Meanwhile Glenn, I'm not going to forget this, this colossal fuck up on your part."

Franklin feigned a worried look. Neither will I, asshole, he thought, wishing he had the courage to speak the words. Just thinking them made him feel better. He stood up and returned to a more familiar role. "Yes, Mr. Baxton. I'll get on it right away."

Franklin left the office feeling better about himself than he had in a long time. Meanwhile, Rodney Halloway was in for the shock of his life.

<u>Massachusetts General Hospital, 7:30 p.m.</u>
Lieutenant Patrick Walsh awakened to a headache that rivaled his biggest hangover. When the haze cleared, he saw Gus Warner standing at the foot of his bed. Sandra Jones was sitting in the chair near his head. He was heavily sedated but he felt pressure from a cast on his right arm that went from just above his elbow to below the wrist.

"What the fuck happened," he said thickly, slurring his speech through swollen lips.

"Lieutenant Walsh," Warner said, "you got the shit kicked out of you."

Walsh tried to remember but couldn't. "Well, if that's the case, you should see the other guy." he said from past practice.

"Walshie," Sandra said, "I'll bet his shoes are really scuffed."

Downsized

Walsh's face was too swollen and his speech too difficult to protest the Walshie. He closed his eyes and tried to remember. "Ouch," he said suddenly.

"What?" Warner said. "You need a nurse or something?"

"No. I just remembered what happened. Did you catch the bastard?"

"No, but you were lucky forensics and security people showed when they did. Doctors said if there was any longer delay, you might have suffered brain damage."

Sandra smiled. "And I told them that if you had, we wouldn't have noticed it."

"Very funny," Walsh said, wincing with each word.

"Don't talk," Warner cautioned.

"Impossible," Sandra said.

"Try me," Walsh replied.

"We've got great news," Warner said. "You must have interrupted the intruder before he could do any damage. All of Korensky's files seem to be intact. We have about forty code names used by his customers. Dr. Veith is whacking away at those now. He's gonna call us if he hits pay dirt."

Walsh held up the thumb on his left hand. He could not force a smile through the swollen tissue of his badly battered face.

"This guy saved a lot of his phone messages," Warner continued. "Every caller had a phone attachment that camouflaged the voice. Hell, one of the code names is 'Geronimo.'"

Walsh could barely muster a puzzled raise of his eyebrows, slowly.

"It was the airborne soldiers' battle cry in World War II, and our pretty lieutenant is airborne," Warner added excitedly.

Walsh shook his head from side to side. "Just a coincidence," he mumbled.

Warner looked at Sandra. She nodded agreement with Walsh.

"When will I get out of here?" Walsh asked.

"Three days," said Warner. "But you'll need a couple of weeks to mend after that. Walshie, you did a great job."

"Who's workin' the case?" Walsh asked.

"Neiberg."

"I'll be ready in a week."

Sandra laughed. "There's nothing like competition to shorten healing time."

Walsh closed his eyes and returned to the peace of sleep.

Allston, February 24. 9:30 a.m.
Bill Coine was glued to his TV, remote in hand, studying the comings and goings of the so-called

mystery courier. He tried to visualize Kimberly Hale's face behind the ski mask and goggles, her trim body beneath the baggy jumpsuit. It was not an easy thing to do. His meeting with Kimberly left him with the uneasy feeling that she would be embraced by all as the girl next door, or at least the girl you'd love to have next door; not a vengeful killer. Jeanie walked into the living room drying her hands on a paper towel and announced the call.

"Bill, John's on the phone. He says it may be important."

Coine pushed the pause button, freezing the courier in mid-stride entering the lobby. "If it might be important, I'd say it is," said Coine into the phone as he brought it up to his ear.

"Well," Neiberg said, "I'm mindful how hot to trot you are with our lady lieutenant." Neiberg waited for Coine's snide retort. There was none. "So," he continued, "I thought you'd like to know, she's disappeared."

"When did that happen?"

"Wednesday evening."

"Are you sure?"

"I checked it out with Captain big foot. You know, the guy that lives in Kimberly's apartment complex. His name is Grissom. At first he told me her whereabouts were none of my business. Then when I told him I was going to persist until I found her, on or off the base, he relented, and said she left for parts unknown. Said we were wasting our time and should let the lady be. I'll keep you posted."

"You do that." Coine quickly dialed Baxton's number. It only took a few seconds for Mrs. Tierney to answer and tell him Baxton could not be disturbed, not even by Coine, no matter how important it seemed to Coine. He requested Joe McGillicuddy. A short pause, a few beeps and an answer. "McGillicuddy here."

"Joe, Coine. You've got to convince Baxton to lay low for the next couple of days."

"Give me something easy to do, like eat a glass sandwich. The asshole is giving a speech tonight."

"Shit, where?"

"The Westin Hotel."

"Has his appearance been publicized?"

"Take your pick. *Globe*, page 12, *Herald*, page 7."

"Joe, he's got to cancel."

"Hey, Gus Warner just hung up on him in disgust. If he won't listen to the D.A., why in hell do you think he'll listen to me?"

Coine knew when to fold his cards. He also knew his suspicion alone would not impress Baxton nor encourage law enforcement agencies to treat the matter with the urgency it deserved. "Make sure he has bodyguards stickin' to him like glue."

What's got you and the D.A. spooked?"

"I'll tell you but it has to be kept in strict confidence, Joe, and only for your ears. OK?"

"Yes, absolutely."

"We have a suspect."

"Damn, that's good news."

"It's not for publication yet, so stay calm. The bad news for Baxton is that she's missing right now."

"She?" McGillicuddy said incredulously.

"In confidence, Joe. Promise?"

"Yes . . . but it's a she?"

"Don't let the thought keep you up nights. The important thing is to make sure you cover your boss' ass."

"Gotcha. Damn, a she," McGillicuddy said, not hiding his excitement. "I gotta hear more as soon as you can tell me."

<u>Boston, AWE Headquarters. 10:00 a.m.</u>
Rodney Halloway was Columbia undergrad and Yale Law School. He knew Baxton controlled millions of dollars per year in outside legal fees. He also knew that one wrong word could send all that money to any one of several equally large and prestigious firms in town.

"Mr. Baxton," he said politely, "let me see if I can sum up what you, Mr. Franklin here," gesturing, "and I have been talking about."

Baxton shifted impatiently in his chair. Halloway noticed, but remained calm, and spoke confidently. "Mr. Johnston was brutally murdered and the police confiscated his computer. A few skirmishes before Judge Franey, a trip to the Appeals Court, and now you face criminal contempt because you failed . . . actually, refused . . ."

"Failed," Baxton insisted. "We've tried to cooperate with the goddamn authorities, haven't we, Franklin?"

"As best we could under the circumstances."

Halloway read something into Franklin's use of the phrase 'under the circumstances' and changed course. "The point is there is a password blocking access to information on the computer and the D.A. wants it. And you, Mr. Baxton, don't know what it is. And nobody else in the company does either."

"Correct."

"Well, I'm glad you called me. This should be easy. But first, let me get to something quite basic." Halloway looked into Baxton's eyes, keeping his expression friendly, non-threatening. "Now, the D.A. wants the password only as a means to an end. He really wants the information that's in there." Baxton frowned impatiently. "What do you suppose is in that computer in the first place, at least the stuff that Johnston has so carefully protected?"

"If we know, Mr. Baxton, we really should let Mr. Halloway know," Franklin said, relishing the opportunity to watch both men squirm. Baxton shot a warning glance at Franklin. Halloway noticed.

"We don't know," said Baxton crisply. "End of issue."

Halloway could not let this moment pass without making an important point, even at the risk of alienating Baxton. "Mr. Johnston was the Chief Financial Officer. Did he have complete autonomy?" Amalgamated was a publicly traded company. The CEO and Chairman of the Board could not let a CFO operate outside corporate policy. Baxton was now being skillfully squeezed into a tight space.

"No," said Baxton. "But I relied on him a great deal. I didn't look over his shoulder."

"Are you worried about what the police might find on Johnston's computer?"

"No, damn it. No," Baxton said angrily, folding his arms tightly across his chest and setting his jaw as if for a fight.

"Well," Halloway said, looking at the sheaf of papers on his lap, "Why didn't you just accept the D.A.'s offer to get a copy of the data and agree to a confidentiality stipulation?"

"Are you accusing me?" Baxton replied, ominously.

"It's not my place to accuse you, Mr. Baxton. But when I enter my appearance on Monday, and file a large number of affidavits saying nobody knows the password, well, the judge may, with or without a request from the DA ask me the next question. 'What's in the computer that is buried beneath the password?' And you . . .," Halloway tried to get less personal, ". . . the company certainly acted as if it knew what it was and did not want anyone to ever see it."

"We stopped our efforts," Baxton said, with a wave of his hand.

"That's true, but only recently."

Franklin decided it was time to turn up the heat. Halloway was skirting the issue carefully, tactfully, but with great skill. A little push should do the trick, Franklin thought. "Mr. Baxton, I think we should tell Mr. Halloway about Johnston's special projects." Baxton's face reddened noticeably. Halloway sensed trouble. Franklin was thrilled that he was about to have a great burden lifted from his shoulders and strapped to the back of Rodney Halloway.

"Mr. Baxton, you don't want me to get involved in a serious court matter and not give me all the information I need to protect you," Halloway said smoothly, ". . . and me," he added for effect.

"Listen," Baxton replied angrily, "Johnston was always working on this or that special project.

The world of high finance was a game to him." Baxton tried desperately to minimize the impact of Franklin's disclosure.

"Well, going to court, for me, might look like a game, but I assure you it's not." Halloway shot a glance at Franklin and returned his intent gaze on Baxton. "Well, what were these special projects?" he said, in a tone that made it very clear he wanted an answer. "Certainly you must have some general idea."

"Don't know," said Baxton curtly.

Halloway looked at Franklin with a look that said, "do you know?"

"I was a mushroom general counsel when it came to these special projects of Johnston's," Franklin said impishly. "You know, he kept me in the dark and fed me a lot of shit."

Baxton sent another menacing stare at Franklin. Halloway noticed and was visibly unhappy with the turn of events. PD&W's involvement was now clearly going to suck the firm into a black hole of corporate malfeasance at best. Halloway pressed on. "So Johnston did have complete autonomy to involve himself with so-called special projects that were unknown to you and the company's legal department."

Baxton was now impaled on the horns of a deadly dilemma. A yes was an admission to conduct that would violate SEC regulations. A no would be perceived as an outright lie. He stood up and stared at his big firm trial lawyer, speaking through tight lips. "I'm paying you," he looked at Franklin for help.

"Nine hundred an hour," Franklin confirmed.

"And now I'm going to tell you what I want for my money," Baxton said sternly. Halloway's face reddened. "You will craft the appropriate affidavits, you will represent me in court, and you will deflect any questions from the judge as one, something about which you know nothing, and two, a matter that is none of the D.A.'s or the court's business." Baxton paused. "Do we have an understanding?"

Losing millions of dollars-a-year in cash flow would put a major dent in Halloway's personal income based upon the established formula for partner compensation at PD&W. If there was to be trouble ahead, Halloway decided to deal with it one step at a time. For now, he would lay the foundation for protecting his butt. "Mr. Baxton, I'll do what you ask. But I must warn you, if you know anything about Johnston's special projects you'd be well advised to tell me so I can help you if help is needed."

Franklin shook his head up and down in agreement.

Downsized

"We are finished Mr. Halloway. Good day," said Baxton, turning and leaving his office through the private entrance into the boardroom.

Halloway and Franklin exchanged glances. Franklin shrugged. "Hey, it's good money. Sometimes we just have to earn it the hard way. Ain't easy takin' shit from the big money guys, is it?" he added, relishing the role Halloway, the big shot, big firm partner now shared with him. Meanwhile, Halloway realized something dark and sinister was lurking in Johnston's computer and Baxton knew what it was.

<u>Boston, The Westin Hotel. 7:00 p.m.</u>
Brad Baxton felt extremely secure in his Rolls Royce. Relaxed and confident, he was deep in thought and oblivious to any potential danger as his vehicle slowly turned left and joined a long line of vehicles vying for a space to unload luggage and guests at the front of the Westin Hotel. He looked up when he sensed the limo had stopped moving. A van suddenly slipped in between the Rolls and an unmarked police car that had been assigned for extra security. Traffic was log-jammed and the limo was still on Huntington Avenue just short of the hotel entrance. One of two SWAT team men jumped out of the cruiser and took a position that gave him full view of Baxton's limo. Making

matters worse, the van driver jumped out and ran ahead to deliver a package to the hotel door man. The private bodyguard in the right front limo seat slowly withdrew a .357 magnum, and held it on his lap.

"Let's back out of here while we can," Baxton yelled to his driver. "We can go in at the side entrance." Baxton turned to see if the way was clear for the driver to move the car in reverse. The bodyguard opened his window and informed the cop what they were doing. Suddenly, Baxton screamed. "Jesus God Almighty!" A vision from hell turned from Dartmouth onto Huntington. Baxton's words froze in his mouth. The jumpsuit, helmet, goggles and backpack which had been plastered on the front page of the *Herald* were now on a motorcycle barreling toward Baxton at high speed.

"Down," shouted the bodyguard in the rear seat, throwing Baxton hard to the floor and jumping on top of him. "Everyone get down."

A full clip from an M-16 was emptied into the rear and right side of the Rolls in a matter of seconds as the motorcycle sped by. Several high-powered rounds harmlessly entered the front seat before the driver managed to raise the passenger side bullet proof window. The two SWAT men moved quickly into position behind a parked car and tried to get a clear shot at the attacker. There was none. Heavy traffic on Huntington Avenue and in front of the hotel made a clean shot impossible.

Baxton held his hands over his ears as bullets crashed deafeningly into the lexan bullet-proof windows and steel sides of the vehicle. He could still hear the roar of the motorcycle above the screams of panic-stricken pedestrians. Shards of plastic and glass pelted Baxton's head as the rear window gave way to the relentless pounding from the assault weapon. Suddenly, the bike skidded into a tight turn and headed back, now moving rapidly, directly into oncoming traffic.

"Christ, do something," commanded Baxton.

"We're doin' it," said the bodyguard, still lying astride Baxton. "Stay down and shut up. The best place for our asses to be is right here."

Baxton could not see it, but a black and white turned onto Huntington and, in a blocking move, stopped beside Baxton's Rolls. The cop on the passenger side had a clear shot at the approaching cyclist and took it. The rider absorbed the bullet in the area of his right shoulder, jerking his body to the right. But he leaned forward and kept coming.

"Fuck it! The bastard's wearing a flack jacket," the cop yelled. The attacker reached over with his right hand and grabbed an object he was holding between his left hand and the handle bar and tugged. He made a quick throwing gesture with his left hand as an approaching vehicle caused the rider to veer suddenly to the left.

"Jesus," yelled the cop, "A grenade."

"Take cover," yelled a SWAT cop as he watched the deadly object drop short of Baxton's limo and slam into the front of the blocking cruiser, falling to the ground a few inches away.

The men in the black and white jumped into the street and ran, diving over a car hood in the process. The explosion lifted the front end of the police car slightly and, in a split second, the entire cruiser was in flames. The burning cruiser was just feet from the Rolls Royce. Baxton could feel the intense heat being conducted through the steel of his limo.

"Dammit, we're gonna burn to death," Baxton cried. "Let me out of here, damn you," he screamed, reaching up to grab the handle on his side. "Shit," he yelled, recoiling from the red hot metal.

"Where's the fuckin' asshole on the motorcycle?" the guard shouted.

"Turnin' left onto Dartmouth," said the man in the front seat.

"Jesus, we're gonna blow up," Baxton whimpered. "Please let me out," he implored.

"When I say now," the man on top of Baxton said, jamming his knee into Baxton's back to push himself into an upright position, "Gun the fucker and shove that goddamn van out of our way." The driver complied. Wheels spun, tires screeched and the big, four thousand pound Rolls hit the van and careened slightly to the right as the van jumped the curb and slammed into the wall of the hotel.

"Now," yelled the bodyguard.

Baxton's legs were too weak from fear. He stumbled out of the limo and fell to the pavement, face down. The bodyguard, built like a linebacker, grabbed Baxton's left hand and dragged him another twenty-five feet to the safety of the hotel lobby.

Hotel security personnel quickly attacked the blazing patrol car with hand-held extinguishers. People dressed in tuxes and evening gowns rose slowly from hugging the cold ground, brushed themselves off, and wondered how anyone had survived the attack. Soon, Boston fire trucks crowded the intersection of Huntington and Dartmouth and Baxton was in an ambulance heading to the Massachusetts General Hospital complaining of chest pains.

Meanwhile, Baxton's attacker reached the Longfellow Bridge which was under repair and raced toward Cambridge with the police in hot pursuit. Three MIT Campus police cruisers moved into place and blocked the northerly end of the bridge. Trapped, the motorcyclist stopped in a sliding turn, almost toppling the bike. Several revs of the motorcycle's loud engine preceded a dash to the westerly side of the bridge. The figure in the black jumpsuit pulled a wheelie at the last second. Bike and rider hurtled over the railing, plunging into the icy waters of the Charles River some forty feet below. Barely visible in dim light, rider and machine separated in mid-air. The motorcycle hit first, bobbed to the surface briefly, and spiraled out of sight. The mysterious courier splashed into the black water a few feet away and disappeared into the murky depths. Ripples lapping on the edges of small ice flows were all that remained. Flood lights mounted on the front of police cruisers crisscrossed the waters of the Charles for twenty minutes. There was no sign of life.

<u>Boston, Massachusetts General Hospital.</u>
<u>7:30 p.m.</u>
Neiberg notified Coine about the attack on Baxton before the news hit the airwaves. Baxton only suffered a broken rib and a serious blow to his dignity. A doctor and a team of nurses were taping his rib cage when Coine barged into the room.

"Sir," said the older nurse politely, "you can't come in here."

"Yes, I can," said Coine. "I'm his father." The nurse looked puzzled and then annoyed.

"You're not old enough to be his father."

"Hormones," Coine replied. "Baxton, for chrissake, tell the lady you want me here."

"Let him stay," Baxton said, begrudgingly, cracking a thin-lipped smile at Coine's audacity. When the last bandage was in place, the doctor told Baxton he would prescribe a pain killer. "Now, I want you to take it easy for a few days," the Doctor instructed. "No heavy lifting." As soon as Baxton and Coine were alone, Coine couldn't resist a golden opportunity. "When the hell's the last time you did any heavy lifting?" he said good-naturedly.

"For heaven's sake Mr. Coine, you obviously thought it was important to speak to me, so get on with it."

"Big or small?" said Coine.

"What?"

"The person on the motorcycle. Did you get a good look at the bugger?"

"Yes, briefly, I'll never forget it. Awful," Baxton said with his eyes closed as if to block out the memory.

"Well, tell me about it. Describe your assailant."

"For chrissake Coine, it was the person in the jumpsuit, helmet and goggles . . . just like in the picture."

"No," Coine insisted, "It was just a pile of clothing. You don't know who was in there. So, please think. Could you judge the size of the motorcyclist?"

"No. When I saw the gun hanging from a shoulder strap that's all I focused on until my own bodyguard threw me to the ground and . . .," Baxton pointed to the fresh bandages, "did this to me."

"Shit happens," Coine said, unsympathetically.

Baxton frowned. "Did you come here to abuse the hell out of me?"

"No. But I did want to get to you before you jump to any conclusions and start issuing press releases."

"You're my private detective, not my P.R. man," Baxton said, annoyed at Coine's impudence. He knew Coine was on target, but Baxton was contemplating the favorable impact on his company's stock that would result from an announcement that his executives' killer drowned in the Charles River.

"Listen," Coine insisted, "Please think of the long term."

"Where did you receive your M.B.A.?" Baxton replied arrogantly.

Coine ignored him. "The yo-yo that played Rambo tonight is not the downsizing killer."

"After practically predicting the event, how can you say that with such authority?"

"Easy. If it was our killer, you'd be dead now."

"Bullshit! If it is her . . . her luck ran out."

Coine looked at his watch. "Any minute now, the police will be here and the press will be all over the place. Don't blow it. Give it time. Just give some no comments and a statement how you're grateful to be alive. That's all."

Baxton listened and did not reply. Coine turned to leave, walked several steps, stopped and faced Baxton. "If you want my advice, and you sure paid a lot of money for it, you are still in danger. Your would-be assassin is out there. Tonight you got hit by a copycat weirdo nutjob." Coine threw a two-finger salute to Baxton and walked away quickly. As he passed the nurse with whom he spoke earlier, he smiled, "It's hormones, honest!"

<u>Boston, Longfellow Bridge. 9:00 p.m.</u>
Gus Warner hunched his shoulders and shoved both hands deeply into the pockets of his fashionable Brooks Brothers topcoat, collar raised in a futile attempt to block the frigid air. The night breeze blew out of the northwest and slammed into his face with a wind chill of ten degrees above zero. It felt like a hundred razor blades cutting into his cheeks. The formal garb and black tie he donned for Baxton's charity ball were under his coat. He wished it was long underwear instead. Neiberg and Sandra Jones wore hooded parkas that were more appropriate for the occasion as the trio stood

mid-bridge, peering over the railing where the motorcycle and its rider tumbled into the Charles.

"Lieutenant Kimberly Hale is definitely not down there," Sandra said confidently.

Warner looked at Neiberg for a comment. Neiberg shrugged and looked puzzled.

"She's too smart," Sandra said. "She spent a great deal of time and effort planning to kill Johnston, Van der Meer and Fulton. Nope," she said, convincingly, "our gal would have had a small air tank in the backpack, a diver's dry suit on under the baggy jumpsuit and I figure she'd be drinking a cup of hot chocolate right now in front of a cozy fire." Sandra paused. "That's if the beautiful blue eyed Kimberly Hale was here tonight in the first place."

"Well, there goes the easy case scenario," Neiberg said, wistfully.

"What easy case scenario," Warner wanted to know.

"Lieutenant Hale never shows up, the body is never found and we call it case closed."

"Yeah," Sandra said. "Try this scenario on for size. She shows up at Fort Bragg and we never find a body in the river. We're back to square one and no proof she went scuba diving."

"So let's get a body out of that goddamn river," Warner demanded, looking down at the blackness.

"And if it's not Kimberly Hale?" Neiberg said, rhetorically.

"I don't need that shit," Warner said. "One last thing," he added, grabbing Neiberg by the left arm as they walked the quarter mile back to the Boston side of the bridge. "Get me some twenty-four hour surveillance at Hale's apartment. I wanna know the minute she surfaces, no pun intended."

<u>Cohasset Harbor, Massachusetts 11:06 p.m.</u>
Ashley Riley followed her husband Dan from their tastefully decorated living room into the richly wood-paneled den. One minute they were cuddled on the rug before a cozy fire watching the news, the next Dan was on his feet mumbling something about where he put a phone number.

"What's come over you?" Ashley asked as Dan rifled through a pile of papers.

"The attack on Baxton," he said, not looking up from his search.

"What's that got to do with you?"

"Nothing yet, but Bill Scharth, a law school classmate called me the other night and asked if I would help a young lieutenant at Fort Bragg. I wrote his number someplace…here it is," he said, holding up a blank sheet of legal size paper. Barely visible on the bottom line were a series of scribbled numbers.

"Are you going to call someone at this hour? It's late," said Ashley.

"It's Friday night," Dan said. "Besides, it's too important to wait until tomorrow."

Dan dialed the number. Ashley sat in one of two chairs in front of and slightly to the left of the desk. Dan placed his hand over the phone. "Remember Bill Scharth?"

Ashley obviously did not and shook her head.

"He was in my evidence class some years back when . . ." Dan removed his hand from over the phone and swiveled slightly in his chair as he spoke. "Bill, Dan Riley. Hope I'm not disturbing you, but your young lieutenant just got a lucky break."

"A lucky brake, I don't understand."

"Someone tried to kill Brad Baxton a few hours ago here in Boston. Just saw it on the news."

A long silence.

"Bill, what's the matter?"

"Kimberly disappeared two days ago."

"That's bad timing . . . again."

"It's my fault. I gave her a homework assignment. I told her to diary her stay in Boston. Apparently she needed to hole up somewhere to do it."

"Well, with any luck, the police will find the attacker's body."

"What body?"

"Whoever attacked Baxton took a plunge off one of our scenic bridges into the Charles River. He hasn't surfaced yet."

"Damn, what if it's her?"

"Then her troubles are over. But what's with this doubting? You told me you believed she was innocent."

"I do," Scharth said. "I do," he said again to reassure himself.

"Good, then keep the faith."

"You'll take the case if the police stay on her ass?"

"After tonight, there may not be any case."

"But if, for any reason, there is?"

"Then we'll have to talk money. This is definitely not your run-of-the-mill murder case."

"Dan, please see what you can do."

"Call me as soon as you hear from Lieutenant Hale. Goodnight."

Fort Bragg. 2315 hours.
"Glad you're at home," Scharth said to a disappointed Andy Grissom who had hoped the call was from Kimberly. "Brad Baxton had an attempt on his life tonight."

"Where?"

"Boston."

"Great news," Grissom said excitedly.

"I don't know about that. It's great news only if she's got a goddamn good alibi."

"Don't worry about Kimberly. She's got her butt covered, you can bet on it."

"Well, whoever tried to kill Baxton is at the bottom of the Charles River."

"Good news again, 'cause when Kimberly gets her ass back here that'll be that. Case closed. Ya'll stay calm. She'll be home Monday night at the latest and her troubles will be over."

"Well Captain," Scharth said in an official tone, "you bring her to me as soon as she gets back."

"Yes sir, can't wait. But I'm not the only one waitin'. There's an unmarked police car parked across the street sitting quietly without lights."

That's not good. Get her to me as soon as she gets back. Good night."

Grissom looked at his phone longingly, tensing his face muscles. "Damn it all Kimberly," he said as if she was in the room with him, "a simple little ole call would be awfully good for my morale right now." He turned and walked slowly into his bedroom, shaking his head from side to side as he spoke. "You are a stubborn woman. No doubt about it."

Boston, District Attorney's Office. February 26. 11:30 a.m.

"Damn it all," barked Warner uncharacteristically into the phone, "how far can a corpse drift all weighted down with body armor and a big, baggy jumpsuit? I know your dive team is doin' its best, but for chrissake, it hasn't been good enough. Please get me a body, will ya?" He slammed the phone down hard and took aim at Neiberg. "Where the hell do we go from here?"

Before he could answer, Sandra walked in smiling. "I say we start building a case against Kimberly Hale and see what it looks like," she said confidently. "Let's not waste time waiting for a body."

"I think Sandra's right," Walsh chimed in. He returned to work early, defying doctor's orders.

"Is anyone the slightest bit concerned that Hale kind of just fell into our lap?" Neiberg replied cautiously.

"Not me," Sandra said.

"Hell," said Warner, "she was in Boston during the killing spree. That's opportunity."

"And the last family member she had in the world was pushed to the wall by Baxton and company and the poor bastard broke. That's motive," Sandra added.

"Thin," said Neiberg.

"We don't measure motive by the pound," Sandra shot back.

"And for the frosting on the cake, she's a paratrooper in the Special Forces. How's that for means?" said Warner excitedly.

"I'd say the ball is in her court," Sandra said. "Let's close in on the lady and if she has no alibi, we nail her."

<u>Georgetown, Maine. 12:45 p.m.</u>
Coine pulled into an unpaved driveway leading to a big yellow house. It was perched high on a hill overlooking Harmon's Harbor on the island of Georgetown, Maine. Wisps of steam rose from the harbor, attesting to the frigid air. Lobster traps were stacked neatly behind the house waiting for warmer weather. A thin column of smoke rose from Andrew "Scottie" MacPherson's chimney, filling the air with the wonderful fragrance of burning birch and oak.

MacPherson was a big man, six feet two or three inches, three hundred pounds or more. His face was still showing a summer tan, with leathery cheeks surrounded by an old salt style gray beard. Buttons on a black and white flannel shirt struggled against a barrel chest. Gray corduroy trousers held up by bright red suspenders were tucked into brown and tan L.L. Bean hunting boots. MacPherson held out a large, calloused right hand. "You must be Bill Coine," he said in a deep voice.

Coine turned, gestured. "And this is my wife, Jeanie," he said as he gingerly placed his hand in the big man's grasp.

Downsized

"Better come in quickly," MacPherson said, "before we freeze right here where we stand." He spoke with a slight Maine accent, converting the word "here" into two syllables.

"Let's talk in the living room," said MacPherson, leading the way. A fire in the small Franklin stove at the far end of the room sizzled and held the cold Maine air at bay.

"I love your house Mr. MacPherson," said Jeanie as she and Coine sat down on a couch which seemed like the logical choice -- far enough from the hot Franklin stove to avoid being slow roasted.

"Call me Scottie," he said smiling. "Now, what's this investigation you're doin' that brings you all the way up here?"

"I'm trying to learn as much as I can about John Hale," said Coine.

"Why?"

Coine explained his role as Baxton's private detective and the possibility that Hale's death might be connected to the murders of Johnston, Van der Meer and Fulton. He decided it would be unwise to mention that Kimberly Hale was a suspect.

"Where would you like me to begin?" MacPherson asked. "It's a long story. Me and Hale go back twenty years and I considered him a close friend."

"Well, I'd like to focus on Hale's," Coine hesitated briefly, "suicide."

"I like a man who get's right to the point." MacPherson leaned forward as if to share a secret. "There's somethin' I never told anyone before," MacPherson said quietly. "That's because my theory sounds a bit far fetched."

"I'd like to hear it," Coine said eagerly..

"I never completely bought the idea that Hale killed himself . . . Nope. Don't know all the details, but Hale went back to Amalgamated's headquarters in Boston after he was fired. It was late January, early February. Seems he ended up in Johnston's office when no one was around and got caught trying to get information off Johnston's computer." MacPherson shook his head. "Can't imagine what he was thinkin'. It's risky business snoopin' around in Johnston's office. Baxton had him arrested for trespassin' and got a restrainin' order against him."

"Do you have any idea why Hale was snooping around in Johnston's office?"

"Well," said MacPherson, still softly, "I think Hale had hopes of bringin' a big lawsuit. He had this idea if he could prove Baxton and his men were up to no good, maybe he could sue Baxton for big bucks and bring Baxton down. Could he have seen something he shouldn't have when he was in Johnston's office tryin' to get into his computer?" MacPherson hesitated and took a deep breath. "You know, Mr. Coine, I wouldn't put it past Baxton to have someone killed if he thought he was a threat to the evil empire." He sat back in his chair and paused for a few seconds. "Hale is…was a strong man and I don't see him takin' his own life."

Coine and Jeanie exchanged glances.

"Silly thought," said MacPherson. "But that's my take on Hale's suicide."

"Thanks," Coine said. "You have really been a big help." Bigger than you know, he thought. He and Jeanie exchanged pleasantries with MacPherson and walked quickly to their car. Coine waited until they were both buckled up and the engine running before he spoke. "Jesus," he exclaimed, "how in hell could Baxton and McGillicuddy not tell me about Hale snooping around in Johnston's computer?"

"They didn't?" Jeanie said, surprised by Coine's statement.

"No, dammit, and more importantly, Baxton asked me whether the shooting at police headquarters the other day could be related to the recent killings at his company."

"What shooting?"

"Hey, you better start reading the papers."

"Why? It's all bad news anyway."

"Well, Baxton has some explaining to do."

"Do you think Baxton had Hale killed?"

"What I think's not important. But if Kimberly came to the same conclusion that Scottie arrived at, that would explain things more clearly. Up 'til now, Kimberly's motive is a little thin. Daddy gets fired, kills himself and Baxton and his henchmen are responsible. Add the possibility that Daddy learned something bad about Baxton and was killed for the knowin', well that's a much better motive."

"I have a problem," Jeanie said, eyes glued to the curving, icy road ahead.

"What?"

"Well, Baxton just paid you a lot of money to find the killer. Are you telling me you'd have a better case against Kimberly if you prove Baxton had Hale killed?"

"Yep, ironic, isn't it?"

"Wow! Baxton never bargained for that."

"Hey, you pays your money and you takes your chances."

"My, my, this case is turning out to be more exciting than I thought. What's next?"

"We stop at The Cabin in Bath for some pizza. Scottie says it's the best pizza in Maine. It's time for a break."

"Good idea. I could use one too."

Coine smiled but did not respond as he contemplated his next meeting with Baxton.

Fayetteville, N.C. 6:10 p.m.
Andy Grissom was in the kitchen when the first ring jolted him to attention. Don't be anxious, he instructed himself as he walked quickly into the living room and fell into his favorite armchair. Three rings were all he could stand.

"Grissom here," he said cautiously, holding his breath.

"Miss me?" said the familiar, almost teasing voice.

"Miss ya? Hell woman, Ah've been walkin' around all bent over, practicin' so the next time you try to give me a goodbye kiss you'll be able to reach my kisser."

"If I believed that one I'll bet you'll tell me another one, silly."

"Girl, where in blazes are you? Where in hell have you been?"

"Same answer to both questions, but if I tell you, what assurance do I have that you won't be showing up here tomorrow morning?"

"None."

"That's what I thought. It's nice to know you're truthful. Look, I knew you were upset that I went somewhere alone, so I just called to ease your mind."

"Lil' darlin', Ah'm grateful, truly grateful. But Jesus, do you have any idea how much trouble you seem to be in?"

"If you're talking about those two guys from Massachusetts …?"

"Hell no! Ah'm referin' to the two cops that are stationed in the parkin' lot waitin' for ya'll to get back to the corral. Hell, do you have any idea what's been goin' on in Boston while you've been hidin' out?"

"First of all, I wasn't hiding out. And I don't have any idea about what's been going on in Boston."

"Somebody tried to kill that Baxton fella. Shot the shit outta his limo with an M-16 in a drive-by on a motorcycle."

"Fortunately, I don't like motorcycles. They're too dangerous. But apparently Baxton survived?"

"Yes."

"Too bad, it looks like the downsizing killer's slipping."

"You shouldn't kid around like that."

"I'm not kidding. Baxton's a no good bastard. He deserves whatever he gets so long as it's bad."

"Well, some folks are thinkin' you did it and now you're at the bottom of the Charles River in Boston."

"Well, my demise has been greatly exaggerated. I'm sitting here, high and dry, sipping a glass of Merlot and, thanks to Colonel Scharth, getting writer's cramp."

"Kimberly, if yer not gonna tell me where ya'll are, at least answer me this. Are you at least makin' your presence known wherever the hell you are?"

"If you mean do I have an air tight alibi, the answer's yes."

"Good."

"This whole thing is getting silly," Kimberly said impatiently.

"If you ask me, it's gettin' scary. When are y'all gettin' back?"

"Tomorrow, about 1700 hours."

"Well, like I said, you've got a reception committee waitin' for ya."

"Are they from Massachusetts?"

"Don't know. Ah think they're local guys."

"Andy, I don't like what's going on here. I don't like it at all," she said angrily.

"Well, that's good. Maybe now you'll listen to me. Please don't talk to anyone until you've checked in with Scharth. Promise me," he insisted.

"I pomise. But after this weekend, they'll have to find someone else to bug. As good as I am it's damn certain I can't be in two places at the same time."

"Well, thank goodness for that . . .," Grissom paused. "Are you sure Ah can't come get ya."

"Positive. See ya tomorrow. I'll let you buy me supper at the O Club."

"After the way ya'll been aggravatin' me, Ah think ya'll oughta be buyin' me supper."

"We'll flip for it. Good night Andy and thanks for caring."

Grissom cursed the dial tone. He quickly dialed Scharth's number. "Colonel? Captain Grissom."

"You've heard from Lieutenant Hale?"

"Yes sir. She did tell me she's been visible and has a great alibi if anyone thinks about blamin' that Baxton nonsense on her."

"Captain, that's great news. Don't forget, I want to see her as soon as she gets back. Call me."

"Will do. Tomorrow about," he left time for a leisurely dinner, "2000 hours."

"I'll be waiting." Scharth called Riley. "Dan? Bill here. Lieutenant Hale surfaced . . . I mean she called a friend, a guy named Andy Grissom. She's got an air tight alibi for the fireworks in Boston."

"Call that guy Grissom back. Tell him not to ask her where she was . . . better yet, make sure he tells her not to tell him anything."

"That's easy. What's up your sleeve?"

"Her location is a convenient ace in the hole. We'll know where she was and the D.A. won't until I say when. Our lady lieutenant has spoken her last word to the authorities."

"You'll represent her?"

"We still have to work a few things out. But I'm interested. Meanwhile, the ball's in the D.A.'s court. We're going to keep it there for the time being."

"Great, I'll call Grissom immediately."

Downsized

Kimberly Hale stared at the blank page for several minutes after her brief conversation with Andy Grissom. It was the first sheet on a legal size, yellow-lined pad. Two other tablets filled to capacity lay at her feet. She stood up, stretched her arms high above her head and arched her back. Trying to remember every detail of every day in Boston from January 19th to February 18th was not easy. Worse, writing it long hand made it extremely arduous. Kimberly was upset with herself for not bringing a laptop. She walked over to a sliding glass door that opened onto a spacious porch. A brief scuffle with an uncooperative lock, a hard pull on the handle and a cool breeze brushed her cheeks. Kimberly breathed deeply of the night air, scented heavily with the fragrance of juniper. The pounding surf, visible just beyond sand dunes beneath her balcony sounded like distant thunder. Stars in the early evening eastern sky seemed more numerous, larger, brighter, closer. It was a moment Kimberly wished could be locked in a box, preserved for difficult days ahead. So the police are keeping my apartment under surveillance, she thought, happy that Andy forewarned her. She took comfort from the emotional support provided by her big Texan guardian angel and Colonel Scharth's legal shield.

Kimberly returned to the table in the small alcove overlooking the beach. The page was still blank, the pad angled to the right to accommodate

Kimberly's left handedness. She wrote on the top left, slowly, in large letters: FEBRUARY 14. Where shall I begin, she thought. "Breakfast," she answered as the pen began its journey across the page.

Fort Bragg, N.C. February 27. 2000 hours.
Kimberly Hale sat in a comfortable colonial style wing chair in Lieutenant Colonel Scharth's living room. Mementos of a lifetime in the army crowded shelf space and table tops in his field grade quarters on the base. An eight by ten photograph of a young Lieutenant Scharth, proudly wearing the cavalryman's yellow scarf, occupied center stage on the mantle. Scharth sat on the edge of a matching couch and spoke softly. He did not mince words.

"At this moment young lady, you are at the center of a firestorm of suspicion in Boston." He gestured toward a tea pot on a silver tray directly in front of him.

"No, thanks," Kimberly said.

Scharth poured a cup for himself. He held the pot over the table briefly.

"Are you sure?" he asked before returning the pot to the tray.

"Yes, thank you."

"So where were you this weekend?"

"A lovely place on the outer banks, right here in sunny North Carolina. Sanderling Inn Resort," Kimberly said with a half smile. "A very comfortable distance from Boston, wouldn't you say?"

"Did people see you?"

"Now and then . . . definitely not in the shower."

Scharth smiled briefly then became serious.

"Friday night, six to ten. Where were you? Who saw you? What did you do?"

Kimberly gave the questions careful thought. "O.K.", she said, as she recreated the evening. "I had supper in the dining room until six-fifteen . . . Sally was my waitress."

"That's perfect. Excellent," he added. He sipped from the tea cup. "Continue."

"I was in the East Wing in room 305. I walked up the three flights from the dining room, but did not go into my room right away." Kimberly closed her eyes briefly. "There was a common area just outside my room. It had a fireplace, TV, comfortable chairs, a couple of tables with newspapers and magazines."

"Anybody see you there?"

"Yes, the couple staying in Room 307." Kimberly smiled at the recollection. "The guy couldn't take his eyes off me, you know, he's with his gal but he still has an eye for the ladies."

"Dan Riley will be happy to hear this," Scharth said. "Are you sure you don't want any tea?"

"Positive. Who's this Riley person?"

"Riley is a top flight Boston trial lawyer. I called him. You definitely need his help."

Kimberly was not happy with that news. "Colonel, I appreciate everything you're doing for me, but with all due respect . . . are we overreacting here? I mean, I wasn't in Boston Friday night. The killer was. End of case."

"End of the Friday night attack on Baxton case. But there's still the problem of two murders while you <u>were</u> in Bean Town."

Kimberly frowned. "Ridiculous."

"I know how you must feel. But until the police start looking elsewhere, you need the best advice money can buy and that's Dan Riley."

"Well, I don't have any money, so I guess the dream team is just a bit out of reach."

"You've got a college fund. Hell, I'll bet you have twenty or thirty thou in there."

"Not for a lawyer, sir. No offense." Kimberly stood up. As far as she was concerned, it was time to leave. "It's over, Colonel. Friday night cinches it."

"Don't be so sure, young lady" Scharth said, holding out his hand. "Your homework assignment, do you have it?"

Kimberly reached into a large canvas bag and pulled out four legal size yellow pads. "Here it is," she said with a shrug.

Scharth took the pads and thumbed through the one on top. "Good job. This'll be important if things get worse." Kimberly frowned. Scharth noticed and paused. "I don't mean to be pessimistic. Lawyers spend much of their lives planning for the worst case scenario. It's great when it doesn't happen. But if it does, you're ready for it. So if you don't mind, let me be ready for the worst." He smiled. "Think of me as your reserve chute."

"I can relate to that," Kimberly said as she started to leave.

"There's one more thing. After what happened last Friday evening, don't be surprised if the police show up tomorrow. Call me immediately if they do. No more interviews alone. You'll have a lawyer with you from here on out."

Kimberly shook her head. "Tomorrow, you think the cops'll be here tomorrow?" She smiled. "Don't tell me, worst case?"

"Yep."

"Good night, Colonel. I do appreciate your help. Honest."

"I know," Scharth said with a smile. "Good night."

Scharth watched Kimberly walk away from his house and get into a waiting car. It slowly pulled away. Kimberly waved. He returned to his living room, poured another cup of tea and started reading Kimberly's journal.

Newton. 8:35 p.m.
Glenn Franklin had many late evening meetings in Baxton's study. Usually Johnston, Van der Meer and Fulton were with him. They were now dead and Baxton's world was imploding. This time was certainly different. Baxton leaned forward, reached for a folder on his desk and came up short as pain registered on his face. "Damn fucking ribs," he said angrily. He moved slowly and retrieved the folder. "Our Hong Kong operation needs a personal visit. I've been looking at the numbers," he said, opening the folder. "Let me ask you this. Suppose I leave the country."

Franklin looked surprised. "When? You can't leave until after you prepare and sign the affidavit for Judge Franey."

"What's the penalty for contempt?"

"A big goddamn fine."

"Bigger than I can afford?"

"Nothing's that big."

"So fuck Judge Franey." Baxton leaned back and swivelled his chair, first left, then right. It was a habit to which he resorted when under stress. "I'm going to leave for Hong Kong as soon as I can arrange it. . . on business of course. I need you to swear to me that you will not tell anyone about my trip."

Franklin was now certain that Johnston's computer was toxic. "Yes, of course. Absolutely," assured Franklin. But your ass is grass if I have to protect mine, he thought. One thing was definite. Franklin would not tell Rod Halloway.

"Glenn . . ." Baxton rarely called him Glenn, so Franklin knew whatever he was about to say had to be insincere. "I want to thank you for everything."

"My pleasure," said Franklin, wanting to vomit. "Good night. I'll see you tomorrow after court."

"Good night."

Franklin walked out of Baxton's house desperately needing a plan of his own. Something was about to hit the fan and he did not want to be in range of the fallout.

Boston, AWE Headquarters. February 28. 10:30 a.m.
Mrs. Tierney stood in front of Baxton's desk, shaking her head in frustration. "Mr. Coine is here, sir. He insists on seeing you," she said. "He's quite demanding. What should I tell him?"

"Send him in. I've learned it's easier to let him speak his mind than to tell him you won't see him."

Coine walked directly to the chair on Baxton's right and sat down without waiting for an invitation.

He pulled an envelope from his left outside jacket pocket and slid it across the desk. It over-shot the mark and landed on Baxton's lap. "How're your ribs?" Coine said as Baxton fumbled for the wayward envelope.

"Do you really care?" Baxton replied, placing the envelope on the desk.

"Yes and no."

Baxton frowned. "I shouldn't have asked, but I did. So explain."

"Yes I care, because if you're still in a lot of pain, you'll be harder to deal with." Coine looked at Baxton closely before he continued. The frown seemed permanent. "No, I don't care because for a guy that had an M-16 clip emptied at him and a hand grenade nearly go off in his lap, well, a little pain in the ribs is a blessing."

Baxton's frown disappeared. He picked up the envelope with his right hand and waved it up and down as if he was weighing it. "What's in it?" he said curtly.

"My final report, a bill and a check for the balance of the one hundred thou retainer."

Baxton looked surprised. He was not ready for Coine to stop working on the case. Coine's decision had to be reversed. Baxton started with the obvious. "You're quitting?"

"No. I'm finished," Coine replied with an air of finality.

Baxton casually let the envelope fall to the desk. "Mr. Coine, I know we did not have a contract in writing, but I distinctly recall that you agreed to find and help convict the killer. Am I correct?"

"Yes, that's what I agreed to do."

"So you are quitting. Admit it."

"Semantics."

"Bullshit," said Baxton, shooting a stainless steel look right between Coine's eyes. "You're supposed to be a pit bull. I was told that once you set your teeth into flesh, you hang on." Baxton leaned forward, the stare continued. "So what did I do so wrong . . ." Baxton searched for the right words. ". . . so wrong that you disapprove of me. It's personal, isn't it?"

"You're not going to be happy with my answer. Are you sure you really want to know?"

"Hell, it can't be worse than your attitude about my ribs. I'm a man. I can take it."

"You knew about John Hale, knew he had a daughter, yet you purposely hid him and her from me."

Baxton started to speak.

"Not yet. I'm not finished," Coine said, holding up his left hand like a traffic cop. "And I know why you tried to deceive me. It's whatever is on your damn computer. I know it's Johnston's, but the shit that's on there is yours."

Baxton became visibly angry. Coine noticed but he continued.

"Hale got too close for comfort, so you had him arrested and you obtained a restraining order against him. You did not want me to find out about Hale and his daughtert so you kept him off the list I asked for. That was irresponsible. It's also the sign of a guilty conscience."

"You're now impertinent," Baxton said angrily.

"You said you were a man," Coine shot back. Baxton's face reddened. "I'll stop if you say so."

"You have a wild imagination. This is really entertaining. Continue."

Coine continued with his experienced eyes sharply focused on Baxton's face. "When Johnston's computer was grabbed by the police, you knew that his killer had unwittingly, hell, maybe intentionally, caused you more harm than the loss of your CFO."

No change in Baxton's facial expression.

Coine paused, leaned forward and smiled, "Now for the good part. You, or someone on your behalf, sent some simpleton to police headquarters to tamper with the computer." That produced a reaction, and not so subtle. Baxton stood up quickly, slightly bent at the waist. He held his side, grimacing in pain. "You are really crazy. Your imagination is running wild. I've heard enough."

Bingo, thought Coine. He knew he had struck a chord. Baxton picked up the envelope and held it out toward Coine. "Take this back. I want a conviction. I want what I paid for. I won't settle for less. If this, this woman . . ."

"Kimberly Hale."

"Yes, if this Kimberly Hale is the killer, I want her convicted. The police are bunglers. So is the D.A. Her conviction is imperative."

Coine did not take the envelope. Baxton struggled briefly, but succeeded in tearing it in half. He threw the pieces into the waste basket under his desk.

"With all the shit that's about to hit the fan when the police learn what's on Johnston's computer, there may not be a conviction," Coine said, somewhat relieved that he still had a sizeable bank account.

"Then get her indicted anyway. Make sure she's tried. At least see the damn thing through to whatever the fucking conclusion is." Baxton waited a few seconds. "Tell me you don't want to see it through, with or without the money." Coine remained silent. "I knew it," Baxton said boastfully.

Coine stood up. "O.K., I'll keep an oar in, win, lose or draw."

"You can leave now," Baxton said, tight-lipped.

"Before I go there is one last thing."

"What?"

"What's really in the goddamn computer?"

"None of your business," Baxton said, now red-faced. "Good day."

As soon as Coine left the room, Baxton called Mrs. Tierney.

"Get my limo driver. Cancel my appointments. I'm going home early. And please don't tell anyone where I am."

Fort Bragg, N.C. 1630 hours.

As soon as Sandra and Neiberg left Colonel Scharth's office, he motioned Kimberly to be seated. He dialed and waited. "Dan, Bill Scharth. The snowball is rolling. We had a visit from an assistant D.A., a Sandra Jones and this state police sergeant Neiberg. We're gonna need you. What do you say?"

Kimberly frowned. Scharth held up his hand in a "be patient" signal. "They Mirandized her and we refused to answer any questions. If you ask me, they'll be seeking an indictment." Scharth listened to Riley and smiled broadly. He put his hand over the speaker and mouthed to Kimberly, "He's in." He continued. "Thanks Dan, I feel better already." Scharth hung up and turned to Kimberly. "Young lady, this is your lucky day. There are none better than Dan. He will need a twenty-five thousand dollar retainer."

"You call that good news?" said Kimberly, shocked by the size of the retainer. Scharth did not hide his impatience with Kimberly's attitude. "Damn it all, that young woman you met today is gonna come after you hammer and tong. In case you hadn't noticed, she's black. You're lily white. There'll be no love lost there."

Kimberly looked astonished.

"I know it sounds racist, but goddammit, it's inherent in the mix. She's a tough prosecutor and she's out to win. Your blue eyes and pretty white face are not going to have any effect on her."

"I'd prefer to think of it as a woman's thing and not racial. What happens after my knight in shining armor uses up the twenty-five thousand?"

"Worry about that when the time comes. Right now, you need Dan Riley."

"My God! Twenty-five thousand! That's about all I've got to my name. Is this guy really worth it?" Kimberly said sadly, looking poverty squarely in the face.

"Let's put it this way. Riley's doing you a favor with that size retainer. What's important is you're worth it."

Kimberly questioned that premise with a raised eyebrow.

"Murder one is life in prison without parole. What's your freedom worth to you?" said Scharth pointing his right index finger at her.

"A guarantee comes with this retainer?"

"Now you're being facetious," Scharth said with a frown. "Get the money ready. I'll send your diary to Riley. There's a great deal to do and very little time in which to do it."

<u>Boston, 44 School Street. March 1. 11:00 a.m.</u>
Dan Riley had a full plate of complex cases. His list of things to do always grew larger. Riley's secretary jokingly referred to his plight as her job security. He did not relish the thought of reading Kimberly Hale's incredibly detailed journal; particularly where he had not yet been paid a retainer. But the speed with which the D.A. was moving gave him a sense of urgency. Thank goodness her handwriting is legible, he thought as he glanced superficially at each page until he arrived at a crucial date -- February 14th. Riley moved quickly through the text until he came to an entry captioned, "7:30 to 9:30 p.m.". He was a veteran of fifteen first degree murder trials and not easily excited by a client's story. Yet, his pulse quickened as he read Kimberly's account of her whereabouts during the critical time when Sam Johnston's killer was performing open heart surgery on him.

". . . walked alone to Charles River, near Hatch Shell. Cold evening. Spoke to no one. Walked back to Newbury Street. Did window shopping. Needed hot coffee. Walked to Tricia's convenience store on Exeter Street. Freddie was there as usual. We chatted at counter for several minutes. I browsed through magazines. Bought coffee, three scratch tickets and a Mademoiselle magazine. This should be on surveillance tape. Best guess is left Tricia's between 9:10 and 9:20 p.m. Arrived back at apartment at 9:45 p.m. Read Mademoiselle magazine, made warm chocolate milk; went to bed at approximately 10:30. Nothing eventful this day."

"Maybe not for you," Riley said under his breath. He dialed 411 immediately. Riley dialed the number provided by the information operator and waited. The message hit him hard. "617-422-8817 has been disconnected." He hung up and redialed. Same message. No new listing. "Dammit," he yelled into the phone. "This can't be." He dialed 411 again frantically, waited for the familiar recorded messages to end and asked to speak to a supervisor.

"May I help you?" said a friendly female voice.

"Yes. 617-422-8817, when was it disconnected?"

"One moment, please."

"I'm showing February 16th," said the pleasant voice.

"What address do you have for that number?"

"We don't usually give that information."

"Look, this is an emergency. A life may be hanging in the balance."

"My. I hope things work out. One twenty-four Exeter Street."

Riley dropped the phone into its cradle and ran past his secretary. He knew most stores only kept a surveillance video recording for a few days, at most a week, and then recycled. If Tricia's went out of business on the sixteenth, the recording might not have been destroyed. "Have a cab waiting for me downstairs. Goin' to Exeter Street," he yelled over his shoulder. Riley did not appreciate this sudden turn of events. Kimberly's alibi for the Johnston murder hinged on the now doubtful existence of a surveillance tape or the memory of a counterman named Freddie.

———

At that time of day, it only took twenty minutes for the Top Cab Taxi to deposit Riley in front of Tricia's. Remnants of discount posters hung sloppily in the window. Tricia's convenience store, once proudly living up to its promise of being open from 6:00 a.m. to midnight, was now dead. Riley peered through the glass store front. Retail rigor mortis had already set in. Shelves were gone and the counter was partially dismantled. Wires hung from holes in the walls and ceiling where fixtures had been. Riley tapped on the window with the back of his left hand, using his wedding ring to make an audible clicking sound. Success! A man in his mid-fifties appeared from behind a far wall. He walked slowly to where Riley was standing. He pointed to the sign. "Store Closed."

Riley yelled, "I need to talk to you."

The man shrugged and walked over to the front door. A temporary fumble with the lock and it opened. "What do you want," the man said with an accent Riley couldn't place.

"The video camera, what happened to it?"

The man looked puzzled. "I don't know from video camera, I just clean up mess." He walked over to what was left of the counter and retrieved a business card and handed it to Riley. Tricia's was owned by a Charlotte Fleming. He called the number on the card but that was also disconnected. Riley left Tricia's with an empty feeling for which Tricia's bare interior was a fitting metaphor.

Boston, Suffolk Superior Court. 1:00 p.m.
Gus Warner was a master at obtaining indictments. Only once did a runaway grand jury deprive him of victory. That was not likely to happen today. The 23 jurors -- 14 men and 9 women -- had been together for almost five months. Warner knew their mood and had his finger on their pulse. They respected his professionalism and attention to detail.

Nevertheless, there was cause for concern. The decision to pull the trigger and seek an indictment against Kimberly Hale immediately did not come easy. Warner pushed the start button shortly after eight in the morning when Sandra and Neiberg reported their confrontation with Scharth and Kimberly's unwillingness to cooperate on advice of counsel. Neiberg continued to press for a more cautious approach. Sandra Jones supported Neiberg's go slow approach and suggested waiting until the Charles River gave up its secret. Meanwhile, Walsh relished the opportunity to join with Warner in pulling the plug on Kimberly, particularly since it was against Neiberg's wishes. Bill Coine, in a rare consultation between D.A. and private eye, tipped the scales in favor of a full scale attack. Warner agreed with Coine that it now appeared the lady lieutenant was in the hands of professionals and there would be no further breaks in the case. By striking quickly, he hoped to use the element of surprise to his advantage. On the strong circumstantial evidence skillfully presented by Warner the Grand Jury had no trouble indicting Lieutenant Kimberly Hale for three counts of murder in the first degree.

Boston, District Attorney's Office. March 2. 6:59 a.m.

Slowly, inexorably, nine 8½ by 11 inch pages slid onto the receiving tray of Warner's fax machine.

Without fanfare or celebration, the plain English version of the top secret information in Sam Johnston's infamous computer arrived in an empty office.

Boston, Logan Airport, General Aviation.
7:35 a.m.
Brad Baxton paced back and forth impatiently as he watched his sleek corporate jet being fueled and serviced for the long trip to Hong Kong. He turned to look at the downtown Boston skyline, his blue glass headquarters building sparkled in the distance like a crown jewel. It was not a feeling of nostalgia that compelled him to look. Boston was the seat of his power base. The roar of a jumbo jet leaping into the sky drowned out his thoughts. A sudden gust of cold wind sent a chill through his body. He turned and, contemplating a lengthy exile, walked quickly toward his plane, jogged up the steps and entered the Gulfstream's luxurious cabin. The big corporate jet rolled down the runway at precisely 8:08 a.m., climbed quickly in a graceful banking turn and headed west.

Boston, District Attorney's Office. 8:15 a.m.
Dottie ran into Gus Warner's office out of breath and hardly able to speak. Warner was in the process of placing his topcoat on a hanger and stopped,

holding coat and hanger awkwardly in his right hand.

"Johnston's computer . . . the info on Johnston's computer . . . they did it," she said excitedly, waving the nine unstapled pages held loosely in her left hand. They were soon scattered on the floor as she stumbled unexpectedly. Warner dropped coat and hanger into the chair behind his desk and helped Dottie pick up the mess of loose papers. He read as he gathered. "Good Lord, if this is what I think it is . . .," Warner said, standing up quickly. "Dottie, where's Sandra?"

"She's getting a cup of coffee."

"Get her in here right away," Warner said, scanning all nine pages rapidly. "Wow!" he exclaimed as Dottie ran out of the office. "Bradford Baxton's been a naughty boy."

Boston, Dan Riley's office. 9:10 a.m.
The call from the Suffolk County first assistant clerk for the Criminal Division was not a complete surprise to Dan Riley, but it was shocking nonetheless. Dan had casually mentioned to him just a few days earlier that it probably would not happen, but if a Kimberly Hale indictment should ever be docketed, and if it wasn't too much trouble, would the clerk give him a call. "Mr. Riley," the cooperative clerk said, "I'm looking at a fresh-off-the-press

indictment against one Kimberly Hale, First Lieutenant, United States Army for three counts of murder one." A slight pause. "Looks like you were wrong, but you are the first to know." Another pause. "I mean after the D.A. and Grand Jurors."

"Thanks Chester, I appreciate it." Dan checked the time. Always prepared, he already knew the Delta flight schedule to Fayetteville. If he left immediately, Delta flight 2001 at 10:05 was barely doable. Ironic, he thought, that's the flight Kimberly took the day Van der Meer died. Two quick cellular phone calls on the way to Logan: one to Lieutenant Colonel Scharth instructing him to get Kimberly out of sight immediately, the other to Ashley with the familiar change-in-dinner-plans message. Kimberly Hale, he wondered as he fastened his seat belt and waited for take-off, what the devil are you really all about?

Boston, AWE Headquarters. 11:00 a.m.
Mrs. Tierney's face drained of all color when the significance of the federal search warrant that she held nervously in her hands became apparent. The United States Marshall who delivered it introduced the five FBI agents standing behind him simply as the men who would be conducting the search. "Where is Mr. Baxton?" said the taller of the FBI agents, flashing his identification. Mrs. Tierney

answered nervously. "I don't exactly know," she said slowly. A deep breath gave her time to think. She knew she had to be truthful, not merely give half-truths. "I mean he's traveling. I don't exactly know his destination." The agent stared into her eyes and frowned. "All I know is that he's in our corporate jet . . ." She was about to say "on business" but decided not to characterize the nature of his trip. The agent noticed her hesitation.

"Ma'm, is it unusual for Mr. Baxton to be off somewhere on business and you not know about it?"

Mrs. Tierney's mouth went dry. She could hardly speak. She was only able to muster a very soft, "Yes."

The agent pointed to the two large doors on his left.

"Is that Mr. Baxton's office?"

Another quiet "Yes."

The agents filed into Baxton's office and closed the door.

Washington, D.C. 11:15 a.m.
Teams of FBI agents and government C.P.A.'s descended on offices of the Republican and Democratic National Committees, at least a dozen senators and more than thirty congressmen. One team of investigators focused their attention on the Federal Aviation Authority. The largest

dragnet ever launched to uncover major campaign finance fraud and government corruption had begun. For the officers, directors and stockholders of Brad Baxton's mighty aerospace conglomerate, the day would forever be known as Black Wednesday!

<u>Boston, District Attorney's Office. 11:30 a.m.</u>
Gus Warner was up to his ears in paperwork when the news arrived that the Charles River had disgorged its secret. An unidentified white male bobbed to the surface near the southern shore, just a few hundred yards from the Hatch Shell. The body was badly bloated but the jumpsuit and back pack marked him as the copy cat attacker at the Westin. His six-foot frame ruled him out as Johnston's killer.

"Sandra, get me a press release in an hour. Keep it simple," Warner said, looking for something in the pile of papers on his desk. "Here," he said when he found what he was looking for. "Circulate this picture of sweet Kimberly Hale demanding that Baxton be tarred and feathered." He thought for a moment, looking up at the ceiling briefly when an idea caught his fancy. "From tar and feathers to murder," he said. "Yes, I like that."

Sandra took the picture, looked at it for several seconds and said, "a bit tacky but what the hell, it'll sell newspapers."

"You'll be busy getting ready for trial. Get someone to start the procedure for bringing Hale back to Boston. If we work quickly, we should be able to have her pretty little butt in a Boston jail cell by Friday."

By one o'clock that afternoon Gus Warner sat at the head of his conference table, sleeves rolled up, tie loosened, collar unbuttoned, and a large Dunkin' Donuts cup in his left hand. His team of Jones, Neiberg, Walsh and Coine were present. "All right," said Warner, "I don't have to tell you people we've got our work cut out for us." He paused. "But I can't think of a better group to get it done."

Coine interrupted. "Excuse me," he said, holding an enlargement of a picture of Johnston's dead body draped over the desk, a knife handle protruding from his chest. Coine placed a pocket-sized magnifying glass over the knife handle and examined it closely.

"Do we know if our lady lieutenant is left handed?" Coine asked.

"No. Not yet," said Neiberg, looking around the table for confirmation. "What's up?"

"Well, this is the first time I've seen these pictures and if you ask me, a southpaw stuck this guy."

Walsh could not contain himself. "Just how do you figure that?"

Coine held the photograph so Warner, Sandra and Neiberg could see it. Walsh remained where he was, only moderately curious.

"You can't see it, it's too small, but this knife was not thrust vertically. I mean the knife blade isn't parallel to the axis of Johnston's body."

"What is this, a geometry class," Walsh interrupted. Coine smiled. "It was inserted powerfully with the blade positioned horizontally," Coine stood up and used his hand, fingers outstretched to demonstrate. "See," he said, "my thumb's up and the edge of my hand is down. Picture my hand as the knife. This is the vertical position." Coine rotated his hand a quarter turn to the left, palm down. "Now the knife blade is horizontal."

"So what?" said Walsh.

"The hilt on the knife sticking out of Johnston's chest is uneven. The longer portion is at the top of the blade. There's only a short piece of the hilt at the bottom." Coine glanced around the table, saw a letter opener on the table and retrieved it. "This doesn't have a hilt, but use your imagination. The Army is pretty careful when it comes to teaching you how to use a bayonette, or a knife, in hand-to-hand combat. Sticking a knife between bone and cartilage is not always easy." Coine demonstrated.

He stabbed the back of a legal pad and, as the point of the opener struck hard, his hand slid down over the blade. "There's no time for a whoops if you're tryin' to kill somebody who's tryin' to kill you. So the Army teaches you to hold the knife horizontally, placing your thumb firmly against the long portion of the hilt." Coine did that with the letter opener. "Now, if you hit bone or cartilage, your hand won't slip and the thumb drives the blade in."

"Jesus," Warner said. "How come nobody else saw that?" Neiberg shifted uncomfortably in his chair. Walsh looked disgusted.

Coine continued. "The top of the hilt on this knife is to the right. The person that stuck Johnston was, one, trained in the military and, two, left-handed."

Warner jumped to his feet. "Damn that's important. That could be the clincher. Sandy, we put a lid on this. I want Hale's defense team to choke on it when we unveil this jewel. Neiberg, get me the facts. Is she or isn't she. And, please," Warner looked skyward, "let her be left-handed."

Los Angeles, 12:10 p.m. Pacific Time.
Brad Baxton's ears signalled a change in altitude. The plane's descending, he thought. Why? He pushed a button on the intercom that connected

him to the cockpit. "Hank, can you hear me?" he shouted into the intercom. Hank was too busy to answer. Baxton heard Hank's professional monotone and did not like what he was hearing.

". . . Gulfstream 2042 bravo descending to eight thousand feet, heading 240, roger."

"Hank damn it, answer me!"

"Boss, I'm busy up here. What's the problem?"

"You're descending?"

"That's the basic idea when you're landin'."

"I told you we were going to Hong Kong nonstop. Where are we?"

"L.A.," said Hank curtly as he continued reporting to the tower. "Descending to six thousand, heading two niner five."

"Do not land this plane," Baxton ordered angrily.

"Have to. This is where I pick up my reserve crew and refuel."

"Why didn't you tell me that before we took off, damn it?"

"Boss, I'll be honest. It got me six hours of peace and quiet. Sorry, but up here, I'm the boss."

Red-faced with anger, Baxton knew there was nothing he could say or do. Firing his head pilot now would be meaningless. The odds are still in my favor, he thought.

"How long before we continue our journey?"

". . . Gulfstream 2042 Bravo cleared for final, roger. Boss, I figure forty-five minutes. Stay on the plane, relax. We'll be up in the air again before you know it. Hey, how do you like the ride?"

"It's an airplane, and we are not finished discussing your insolence and insubordination." Hank did not respond.

The landing was perfect. In pilot's vernacular, Hank greased the plane onto the runway. When it stopped rolling and the engines fell silent, Hank walked into the cabin area and opened the door. Three men in dark blue suits entered the plane, flashing I.D.'s. They approached Baxton. "Sir, are you Bradford Baxton the third?" Baxton had stopped using the third years ago and was surprised to hear it now.

"What's the meaning of this," Baxton said in typically arrogant fashion.

"Are you Baxton," said the blue suit impatiently.

"Yes."

"You are under arrest, charged with violating the United States Campaign Finance laws. You have the right to remain silent . . . ."

The FBI agent's words were no longer audible to Baxton. Nothing made sense. He was supposed to be in Hong Kong. Coine's words echoed in his mind. "She wants to take away your power and then she'll kill you."

"Please stand sir, we have to place handcuffs on you."

"That is not necessary," said Baxton. "Not necessary at all. Do you realize who you're dealing with?"

"Yes sir and that's why we're here. Handcuffs are required. It's nothing personal."

"Will there be photographers?"

"Not unless they are mind readers," the agent quipped. "Look, we'll let you place a jacket over the cuffs. Best we can do."

Hank suddenly appeared. "Boss, this is a bad time, but I just received a memo from headquarters. It's for you. Shall I read it?"

"Yes,"

"I'll skip the intro. Says here by unanimous vote of the Board of Directors, with formal notice having been waived in accordance with section 14.2 of the by-laws, you have been removed as President, CEO and Chairman of the Board, effective immediately." Hank folded the document and tucked it into Baxton's shirt pocket. "Sorry boss," he added with a shrug of the shoulders.

"The bitch knew," Baxton mumbled softly, making a connection between Johnston's murder and the confiscation of his computer. "The fucking bitch knew."

"What?" said the blue suit as he adjusted the handcuffs on Baxton's wrists.

"Nothing," Baxton said. "I have powerful connections. I have competent lawyers. You are making a big mistake, a very big mistake, do you hear me?"

Baxton was hustled into a waiting car and, with the suddenness of a gunshot, life as he knew it, an incredibly rich life with unlimited power, was over.

<u>Fort Bragg, North Carolina 5:30 p.m.</u>
Lieutenant Colonel Scharth brought Riley into his home office. Kimberly had been there all day, ever since Riley's phone call. He made quick work of the introduction. "Dan, I've already told Kimberly all about you so let's not waste any time." Scharth handed Riley an envelope. "Here's your retainer."

Riley stared into Kimberly's eyes. They took each other's measure, silently. Scharth coughed once to get their attention. "There are some things I want you two to discuss without me. Dan, if there's anything you want just ask." He looked at Kimberly. "You're in good hands, lieutenant, the best."

Dan was struck by Kimberly's beauty. A touch of toughness did surface on an otherwise angelic face. Kimberly was impressed with Dan's youthful appearance. He had energy deep within, she could feel it when she looked at him. They both sat down in the chairs in front of Scharth's desk. "So where do we start?" she asked.

"With your alibi for February fourteenth," Dan said, not hiding his frustration. "Tricia's is out of business. Wednesday the 16th was their last day and . . ."

"There's Freddie the counterman. He'll remember me. He liked me. He'll tell you I was there." Kimberly said confidently.

"I'm positive he liked you," Dan said stating the obvious. "But he's disappeared. Apparently he's a free spirit and the spirit moved him to plink his guitar and sing folk songs in L.A. We're looking for him."

"What about the surveillance video?" Kimberly asked with a touch of concern in her voice.

"That's missing too."

Kimberly sat back, raised her hands in mock surrender and laughed.

"What's so funny?" Dan said incredulously.

"So what you're telling me is I should save the twenty-five thou, use a court-appointed lawyer to stumble through a hopeless case and accept my fate."

Now it was Dan's turn to laugh. "Kimberly, I dropped everything to fly out here and take on your case. Do you think I would do that just to tell you to surrender? Freddie and the surveillance video are momentary set backs. We have a lot to do and, by the way, I never admit defeat. We've got a ton of discovery to get from the D.A. Besides, the dead man they dragged out of the Charles River is gonna be one of your best witnesses."

Kimberly smiled, briefly, but captivatingly. "Scharth didn't tell me you specialized in cross-examining dead men," Kimberly said facetiously.

"I don't have to. That yo-yo's presence will be felt throughout the trial. And the D.A. knows that whoever defends you will be running that guy up the flag pole at every opportunity."

"So you're not discouraged?"

"Let's just say I'm concerned; discouraged, no."

Kimberly liked Dan's no nonsense style and confidence. "Like I said a few minutes ago, where do we start?"

"There's no set rule. Do you have any questions?"

"Do you believe me when I tell you I'm innocent?"

"Is my believing in your innocence important to you?"

Kimberly became pensive. After a lengthy pause, she said, "No."

"That's good, because I haven't the slightest clue whether you killed anyone or not. I just met you a few minutes ago. I deal in evidence. The evidence will either convict you or exonerate you. If there's enough to convict you, I want to be the first to know it. Getting caught up in personal feelings for you and a misguided belief in your innocence will take away the edge that only complete objectivity gives me."

This guy doesn't mince words, she thought. "So what's next?"

"As we speak, the District Attorney is probably forwarding the application for your extradition to local authorities in Fayetteville. I figure by this time tomorrow you'll be on your way back to Boston in handcuffs."

Kimberly winced. "What do you suggest?"

"We go back tonight. Tomorrow we show up at the D.A.'s office and shock the living daylights out of him."

"I like it. Let's do it," she said, eyes bright with excitement.

"Are you sure?"

"Couldn't be more certain," she said happily. "Besides, it's a good military solution.

Sneak attack," she explained.

"You're right. But promise me something."

"What?"

"No more military analogies." After giving Scharth a brief explanation of his plan, Dan turned to Kimberly. "Let's get started. You need to pack?"

Kimberly smiled. "I did that already." She quickly added, "Damn, there is something I must do back at the apartment."

"Captain darlin'?" Scharth said with an understanding nod of the head. Kimberly looked at Riley.

"Look," Dan said, "we're a step, maybe half a step ahead of the D.A. I'll bet ten to one there are cops waiting for you in your parking lot right now. Hell, they'll be at the airport and broadcasting an all-points bulletin on your car as soon as someone realizes you're not here."

Scharth stood up and left the room. Kimberly and Riley exchanged glances. He returned quickly with a set of keys on a thirty caliber bullet fashioned into a key ring. He removed one. "Here, use my car," he said, handing the key to Riley, "they won't be looking for it."

"Sir," said Kimberly, "that's very nice of you, but will this get you in trouble?"

Scharth laughed. "If you end up in Mexico with my car I'll be in all kinds of deep shit. But," he looked at Riley for agreement, "I'm lending you my car so you can surrender yourself to authorities in Boston."

"A technicality," said Dan, "but a very important one." Riley took the key. "Thanks," he said. "We'll ship the car back to you tomorrow."

"But I'm not leaving until I say good-bye to Andy," she added firmly.

"That's Captain darlin'," said Scharth.

Riley would have liked to accommodate her, but there was a very important reason he could not. "Look Kimberly, Scharth and I are within the attorney client privilege. If this Captain..." Kimberly interjected quickly before Dan could say darlin', "Grissom!" Dan smiled and continued, "If Captain Grissom is questioned I want him to be able to answer honestly that he does not know where you went, why or even when you left." He looked at Kimberly compassionately. "I don't mean to sound harsh, but we're about to make our first move in a very dangerous game. I want us to start off on the right foot."

"I understand," said Kimberly sadly. She looked at Scharth, "Colonel, you will tell him I wanted to say goodbye won't you?"

"Of course."

"Good." Riley looked at Kimberly from head to toe. "The uniform is not a good idea. Do you have civilian clothes handy?"

"Yes."

"Change into something casual for the trip and let's get going."

<u>Boston, Harbor Towers. 7:00 p.m.</u>
Gus Warner sat in his favorite lounge chair, legs outstretched, seat angled back almost to the point of reclining. The phone by his side rang only once before he snatched it from the cradle and practically slammed it into the side of his head. "Warner here," he said anxiously.

"Gus, Sandra. I have bad news."

"Shit," Warner said. "I don't need bad news."

"Kimberly Hale," Sandra said excitedly. "She's disappeared again."

"How can that be," Warner shouted, "Who screwed up?"

"Nobody."

"Bullshit. She should have been arrested before the ink was dry on the indictment."

"Gus, I personally contacted the Fayetteville police and the military police before ten this morning."

"Then <u>they</u> fucked up," Warner shouted angrily.

"The lady just disappeared, Gus. Nobody screwed up."

"Jesus, the press will have a field day with this."

"Gus, nobody knows yet," said Sandra reassuringly. "Besides, they've got enough to keep them busy with Baxton's arrest and all the speculation about the asshole in the Charles River. And when we find her, her attempt to flee will spell guilty in capital letters."

"If we find her," Warner lamented as he contemplated the next Herald headline.

<u>March 3. 8:05 a.m.</u>
Gus Warner closed his eyes and adjusted the shower head. Needles of steaming hot water stung his

face. He turned the dial one click to the right. A fine spray was instantly transformed into pulsating bursts of water. He spun around and positioned himself to receive a massage on his chronically sore back, now acting up when he could ill afford it. The hot water and steam were comforting. His thoughts were not. The soft ring of his cell phone, strategically placed on the edge of the tub behind the shower curtain, eased him out of his reverie. This is it, he thought as he shoved the curtain aside and grabbed the phone tightly with a slippery right hand. "Warner here."

"It's me, Sandra. In case you are not lookin' at your TV set, turn it on . . . channel five and do it quickly."

Warner's stomach muscles tightened. It had to be about Kimberly, but what could be on TV so soon, he thought. "What the hell is it, damn it," he yelled into the phone as he quickly stepped out of the tub, clumsily wrapped himself in a large bath towel and hurried to the living room.

"You're gonna love this. Our fair lady's giving a press conference in none other than Dan Riley's office . . . have you got the set on yet?"

"Tell me you're joking?" Warner pleaded as he pushed the on button and watched Dan Riley's face slowly fill the screen of a fifty-seven inch high definition television set with surround sound. Warner stumbled backward and fell into a large leather couch as the volume slowly rose. Riley's voice poured out of six speakers strategically aimed at Warner.

"Jesus," Warner yelled incredulously into the phone. "Riley's representing Kimberly Hale?"

"Quiet, listen," Sandra urged.

". . . and so, it's my pleasure to introduce you to the young woman who only yesterday was thrown into the national spotlight when Boston District Attorney Gus Warner announced her indictment as the so-called downsizing killer."

An audible off-camera reaction from a dozen media types punctuated the shocking announcement.

"Damn, that bastard's got a pair of balls," Warner shouted. "Sandra, where's Neiberg?"

"He's at your office."

"Call him. Get his ass over to Riley's office. Tell him to take Walshie and two uniformed guys. Tell him to arrest her ass before this circus is over."

Meanwhile, Riley had pushed an intercom button and within moments a strikingly beautiful young woman entered the conference room. She squinted slightly as she walked into the glare of TV lights, smiled briefly and took a seat next to Riley. She was dressed modestly in a blue skirt and white blouse with a cute ruffled collar. The image was that of the typical girl next store and definitely not a mass murderer.

"The bastard has choreographed this press conference like a ballet," Warner yelled at the TV screen. Warner knew Riley was one of the best criminal defense lawyers in the city. He also knew Riley had enough time to prepare Kimberly Hale for every question the press corps could conceivably ask. Kimberly Hale was ready to put on a show. Warner hoped it would be interrupted by Neiberg before too much damage was done. He sat back, listened and waited for the fireworks.

Riley remained standing next to Kimberly and placed his left hand gently on her right shoulder as he spoke. "Ladies and Gentlemen, this is Kimberly Hale. She's come to Boston voluntarily to surrender to authorities and face the charges leveled against her. We will do our best to answer some questions, but I'm going to have to remind you we may not be able to answer all of them because of the pending trial."

"Bullshit," Warner said loudly. "You'll answer every question that gives your client a chance to look like little Bo Peep and only avoid the hard ones."

Riley pointed to one of the many hands raised in unison. A deep voice spoke, crisply. "Ms. Hale..." "Please call me Kimberly," she interrupted. That sent a column of hot blood pumping into Warner's ears. ". . . Kimberly," the deep voice continued. "Why do you think the D.A. indicted you?"

"Because she's guilty as fucking sin," Warner yelled. Kimberly smiled. "I really don't know how to answer that," she said demurely. "But Riley does, damn it," Warner said in disgust.

"Ed," Riley said softly. "That question is really one that can best be answered by the D. A."

"And I will," said Warner. "You can bet on it.

" . . . But I can only speculate," Riley said pensively, pausing to appear thoughtful. Riley looked directly into the lens of the TV camera as he spoke, making eye contact with the real audience as if they were in his office. "Gus Warner," Riley continued in a personal, conversational tone, "is an elected official. And it's no secret he's got his sights on the governor's office. Brad Baxton, the President and CEO of Amalgamated Worldwide Enterprises, has a great deal of influence even in the custody of the United States Marshall's Office." Baxton's arrest was already chronicled on the evening news and was a developing story in the morning papers. Riley played that card cautiously, no details, just a brief mention. "The pressure brought to bear on the D.A. to indict someone quickly for the murders of his top three executives must have been intense. Hey," Riley said as if the thought had just occurred to him, "the king of downsizing is also the king of politics."

"You bastard," Warner hissed between clenched teeth. "Neiberg, where the hell are you?"

"That kind of pressure can interfere with a person's professional objectivity." Riley was careful not to say it did. "Can you imagine anyone in Gus Warner's position seeking an indictment before the body of Brad Baxton's attacker at the Westin Hotel..." Riley let it sink in briefly, "before that body surfaced in the Charles River."

"Are you saying there was a rush to judgment here?" the deep voice asked. Riley again paused for effect. "That's become a well-worn cliché lately, but Ed, I think you've hit the nail on the head in this case."

A barrage of questions from several persons at once combined to create an unintelligible cacophony. Riley pointed. "Rita. . .,"

"Kimberly, it's no secret you could've fought extradition. Why didn't you?" the female voice asked.

"Jesus, will you stop throwing up soft balls," Warner said with a shake of his head in disgust.

"The short answer," Kimberly said sincerely, softly, "is that I'm innocent." She glanced at Riley briefly. "With Attorney Riley's help," she added confidently, "I can prove I'm not the downsizing killer. The place to do that is here in Boston, in a court of law, in a fair jury trial."

"Bullshit," Warner sneered. "We're gonna fry your ass."

Riley pointed to another raised hand. Another deep voice spoke.

"Kimberly, you're a soldier. You've had training. . ."

"At last," Warner yelled, slapping his knee with his right hand. "Good damn observation."

". . . so didn't that training give you the skills needed to kill people?"

"Hooray," Warner said, grinning.

"Good heavens," said Kimberly, not surprised at all by the question and carefully prepped by Riley to answer it. "It's my job to publicize the army in a favorable light. I'd hate to think my conduct would ever discredit the military or that service to my country was a justification to brand me as a killer. Besides, what combat training I've had was designed to help me defend the United States against its enemies."

"So," said Warner, "if in your warped mind you saw Johnston, Van der Meer and Fulton as enemies, you'd just be doing your fucking job. Please take the stand when the time comes. Sandra will tear you to shreds."

Warner's wife walked into the room. "My God, who the devil are you talking to?"

"The damn television set."

"Well, if you're going to go nuts on me, how about doing it with some clothes on?"

The cell phone rang once. Warner grabbed it and yelled even before it was against his ear. "Where the hell is Neiberg?"

"At your office," Sandra replied.

"Damn it, did you tell him what I wanted?"

"Yes, I did. Are you sitting down?"

"Cut out the crap. What's goin' on?"

"You're looking at a pre-recorded interview. Riley and his innocent-as-hell client just walked into your office."

"Sonofabitch," Warner yelled. His wife returned with clothes. "Here, maybe you'll be more civilized when you're dressed." Warner ignored her. "Tell Neiberg to read her her rights, arrest her ass and bring her to the Suffolk County Jail."

"But I can have her arraigned in an hour," Sandra said, questioning the unnecessary trip to the County jail.

"I want her to get the message she's gonna spend the rest of her life in a jail cell . . . and it starts now. We'll arraign her at two this afternoon. Riley may be clever, but he's run out of running room."

The press conference continued on the big screen. ". . . so this picture that was released yesterday by the District Attorney's office," said an unidentified female voice, "shows you holding a picket sign threatening to tar and feather Bradford Baxton. Will you comment on the caption, 'from tar and feathers to murder'?"

Kimberly reached out and a copy of the picture was placed in her hand. She looked at it and slowly shook her head from side to side. "This is so unfair," she said sadly. "I was twenty years old, in college near Chicago at the time, and I couldn't resist getting a glimpse of my father's boss, a man who destroyed so many hard-working men and women's lives." Kimberly's eyes filled with tears, but she did not cry. "He closed my dad's plant down just two weeks before Christmas, that was only a couple of months before Mr. Baxton got this award." She held up the picture for emphasis. "I was astonished that anyone would consider him a true man-of-the-year. But I guess money can buy anything, even a ridiculous award. When I arrived at the hotel I had no idea there would be men picketing outside. One of them handed me a sign. I thought the words were clever, not a threat at all. This picture was taken just a few seconds after I held it up. I did not stay long. Mr. Baxton went in through a rear entrance. I never did get to see him. I left shortly after this picture was taken. I gave someone else the sign." Kimberly frowned briefly. "Would I do it again if I had the chance?" she asked rhetorically. "Yes. I would. But is holding a picket sign written by someone else a stepping stone to murder? Hardly," she said, pushing the photograph away contemptuously.

That speech hurt. Warner had played hard ball with Kimberly Hale. Now Riley, a major leaguer, was at the plate. Kimberly's trial was not going to be a cake-walk in any event. Now she would have a following. Damn, she is likeable, Warner thought.

"Kimberly," a female voice asked, "do you have an alibi for these murders?"

Warner listened for the answer intently. Riley raised his hand. "That question gets us into the defense of the case and a comment at this time would be inappropriate."

"Bullshit," said Warner. "You don't have one, at least not one you can prove, otherwise you'd be tucking it up my ass right now." Warner was finally encouraged. Riley knew it was a negative note on which to end the press conference, but Kimberly did well overall. He knew she had won a lot of support. Warner watched Kimberly and Riley leave the conference room. Kimberly was the epitome of innocence and she exuded confidence in a humble way. She was an instant celebrity.

<u>Boston, District Attorney's Office. 8:30 a.m.</u>
Kimberly exchanged glances with Riley as Neiberg read her the now familiar Miranda warning in

a practiced monotone. Her expression reflected impatience. Riley's was intended to be reassuring. The arrest process was routine. He had prepared her for it in broad strokes on the walk over from his office. However, Riley was not prepared for what happened next. In a split second move, Neiberg held out a small card from which he had just been reading and a pen. A compliant Kimberly took the card with her right hand, the pen with her left.

"Sign at the bottom, please," Neiberg insisted. Before Riley could speak, Kimberly began signing with her left hand. Neiberg quickly stepped aside and Walsh took a picture with a small instant camera.

"What the hell is this picture taking crap," Riley said angrily.

"Hey," said Walsh with his patented annoying grin, "the lady here is a TV celebrity. Maybe she'll autograph the picture for us."

"Bullshit," Riley shot back. "I demand you give me that picture."

"Fuck you," Walsh said with disdain. He turned to the female cop. "Cuff her."

"That's not necessary," Riley said. "She travelled a great distance to be here voluntarily."

"Now that's bullshit if I ever heard it," Walsh replied with a sneer.

Downsized

Kimberly stood up, hands in front of her abdomen.

"Not that way. Turn around and put 'em behind your back," Walsh commanded. Kimberly obliged. "Fairy tale's over," said Walsh smugly. "This is reality," Walsh added for effect as the handcuffs were locked shut.

"Are the cuffs too tight?" Riley asked.

"They're fine," Kimberly replied. She turned, looked directly at Neiberg and smiled. "I know you're just doing your job." Neiberg watched without expression as Kimberly was led out of the office by three uniformed cops. Christ, Neiberg thought, why in hell do I feel like I just arrested Saint Joan of Arc?

<u>Los Angeles, 6:00 p.m. Pacific Time.</u>
Stanley Grzwynsky specialized in locating missing persons. A short, chubby man, Stan was affable; nothing like the nasty personality suggested by his nickname, Grizzly. It was simply a function of a lifetime of explaining how to pronounce a name with nine consonants and not one, single vowel. "What's that," the first-time hearer would say. "Griz," Stan would answer. "GRIZwynsky," he would add. "You know, like grizzly bear . . . GRIZwinsky." Grizzly stuck.

Stan was excited by the opportunity to work for a prominent east coast attorney and he accomplished his assignment quickly. Locating Tricia's former counterman, Freddie, was not difficult. Flyers announcing his folk singing gig at Sophia's Coffee House in Marina del Rey littered streets all over town. Stan waited patiently outside Freddie's third floor apartment in a rundown section of L.A. not far from Sophia's. The smell of Mexican cooking in the apartments below made him hungry. Hurried footsteps coming up the stairs announced Freddie's arrival. A tall, thin, bushy-haired man in his late twenties ran up the last flight two steps at a time. Stan, lurking in the shadows, watched as Freddie fumbled with a key ring. He tapped him on his right shoulder as the door opened. Freddie jumped.

"Shit man! Who the hell are you?"

"My name's Stan. Stan Grzwynsky."

"What?"

"Not important. Call me Stan. I'm a private detective."

"Hey man, no need to scare the shit outta me."

"Can I come in?"

Freddie looked him up and down. "No," he said defensively. "Waddaya want?"

"Do you remember a young woman by the name of Kimberly Hale?"

"No, and if she says I made her pregnant man, then she's lyin'!"

"Nothing like that," Stan said, smiling. He took a picture out of his jacket pocket and handed it to Freddie.

"Hey, this is miss blue eyes . . . I'm bad with names."

"So you know her?"

"Yeah, man. Like she was one beautiful babe . . . too high class for me, but . . . well, she's been the star in some of my greatest fantasies." Freddie winked. "Like, know what I mean?"

"Sure, sure, now can I come in?"

"Not yet. One more question. What about miss blue eyes . . . this Kimberly person?"

"She's in trouble and may need your help."

"I'm there, man. Like my right arm for her . . . any time she wants it."

"Now can I come in?"

"Yes," Freddie said, swinging the door wide. Stan followed him into a messy one bedroom apartment. Empty frozen dinner trays were strewn around the room. Empty beer cans were not far away. Freddie removed sheet music from an oversized bean chair and pointed. Stan lowered himself into it awkwardly. Freddie sat in front of him, cross-legged on the floor. "So what kinda trouble is miss blue eyes in?"

"She's been indicted for murder in Boston."

"Wow, heavy."

"Yeah, it's very serious."

"So how can I help?"

"You worked at Tricia's convenience store?"

"Yeah, I did. That's where I saw miss blue eyes. It made my day every time she came in."

"Do you remember how often Kimberly came into the store while you were on duty?"

"A lot . . . like I wish I knew when she'd be comin', I woulda signed up for that shift. But I did see her alot."

"Can you remember any particular days when she came into the store?"

Freddie thought hard. He frowned. "Shit man, what month was it, like at least gimme a hint."

Stan looked into Freddie's eyes. Too much dope had slowed his cognitive function. How the hell does this guy remember lyrics, he thought. "I'd like you to answer the question. It's better if you can tell me without hints."

"Yeah, I see what you mean." Freddie got up and walked over to a backpack lying in the corner. He retrieved a check stub. "This is my last paycheck from Tricia's." Freddie examined it closely. "Place closed," he shut his eyes and frowned until a spark of recollection ignited his memory. "Hell, she was comin' in right up until we closed. So it was February." Freddie smiled proudly.

"Good. Now can you remember if she came into your store on the evening of February 14th?"

Freddie shook his head from side to side. "This is real heavy," he said. "That was St. Valentine's Day."

"Yes."

"What does miss blue eyes say?"

Stan did not like leading him, but there was little choice.

"She says she was there about 9:00 p.m."

Freddie looked at her picture again, "Well, she was there then."

"Are you absolutely certain? Do you have an independent memory?"

"Shit man, yeah. I'll never forget it."

"So how is it you can remember February 14th as a day Kimberly was in your store?"

"It was St. Valentine's Day, man. Like it was special, like Christmas or somethin'."

"What was she wearing?"

"Who the fuck knows?"

"What did she buy?"

"Hey man, ain't it enough I remember. Like how can I remember all the other shit?"

"She said she purchased a People's magazine," Stan said with conviction.

"Yeah," said Freddie eagerly. "Yeah, that's right."

"Bullshit," said Stan, raising his voice for the first time. "I just made that up."

"Don't yell at me, man. I'm just tryin' to help."

"Don't lie," said Stan. "That will never help. If you take the stand to testify that you remember

David G. Hanrahan Esq.

that Kimberly Hale, miss blue eyes, came into your store, the D.A. will be all over your ass. So you have to start thinking. Can you do that?"

"Sure. I understand, man. But, like this is heavy. You just caught me by surprise. Sure. I'll start thinkin' about it."

Stan gave Freddie a business card. "Call me if you leave this place. I'll get back to you soon." Stan struggled out of the bean bag, retrieved the photo and turned to leave. "Keep the pay stub."

"Yeah, I will."

"I'll call you in a couple of days."

"Come down to Sophia's, any time. I'll buy you a cappuccino."

"I just might do that." Stan paused before leaving. "Think about the fourteenth."

"I will. Honest. I wanna help."

Dan Riley answered the phone in his study. He looked at his watch. It was 9:30 p.m. "Dan Riley here."

"Hello, this is Stan Grzwynsky. I found your boy, this Freddie fellow."

"Great job and fast. Is he any help?"

"Well, yes and no."

"The yes?"

"He wants to help. He says he remembers her comin' in on the evening of the fourteenth."

"Fantastic," Riley yelled excitedly.

"Not so fast. Do you want the no?"

"Hell yeah, but how bad can it be if he remembers?"

"Unfortunately, he's a loose cannon. Once he realized Kimberly needed help he was ready to say anything." Stan described the interview.

"Damn," said Riley, not hiding his disappointment.

"I'll arrange a TV conference call. You can see for yourself."

"Please do that and soon. Call me at my office tomorrow."

"Sure. Goodnight."

Riley dropped the phone into its cradle and buried his head in his hands. He turned to the April page on his desk calendar and circled April 18, the day he would be starting Kimberly's trial. "Impossible," he said to himself. "Goddamn impossible."

ONE WEEK LATER

<u>Newton, March 10. 9:20 a.m.</u>
Rod Halloway stood outside the door to Baxton's study. He was about to face a Bradford Baxton stripped of all political and corporate power, his wealth reduced to something slightly below a billion dollars. In all the circumstances, neither he nor his firm was happy about defending him, despite the big money involved. Halloway did succeed in getting Baxton out on a very large bail but he came to tell Baxton his firm wanted to withdraw from the case. He took a deep breath, opened the door and walked into the study, topcoat on and still buttoned. He nodded a polite gesture of greeting and, without uttering a word, took a seat in front of Baxton's desk.

"Dammit. Where the hell have you been," Baxton yelled. "I learn more about what's going on from the papers and television than I do from . . . from my own attorneys. What's going on? What have you been doing and when are you going to get these ridiculous charges dismissed?"

Halloway placed a stack of documents on the desk and pushed them toward Baxton. Baxton shoved them aside contemptuously. "I don't need to read that . . . that . . . crap. Just tell me," he shouted.

"I will, but you should read that . . . crap," Halloway insisted.

"Don't tell me what to do."

Halloway bit his lip, looked Baxton in the eye and spoke firmly. "You've been charged with federal campaign finance fraud, money laundering and income tax evasion."

Baxton shot up from his chair, his face red with rage. "I've paid more taxes than any human being on the face of this earth . . . how can anyone accuse me of tax evasion?"

"Easily on all the evidence they have against you."

Baxton made a fist, leaned across the desk and shook it in Halloway's face. "Don't you dare tell me it's easy, or I'll . . . I'll . . ."

Halloway was now emboldened by that threat and the fact he would soon be out of Baxton's life. "Or you'll what, Mr. Baxton? You'll fire me?"

Baxton put his two fists on the desk and shot Halloway a red hot stare. "You bastard," he said with a hiss. "That's what you really want. You . . . you came here to tell me you and your . . . your stuffy partners don't want to soil your hands." Baxton sneered. "That's why you haven't unbuttoned your coat. You ungrateful bastards, I paid you a fortune over the years. I made your firm what it is today. You are a bunch of fucking cowards."

Halloway did not reply immediately. He knew Baxton was speaking the truth. The partners at PD&W had concluded that the case against him could embarrass the firm. The information in Johnston's computer revealed an aggressive campaign fraud scheme. Baxton wanted to buy high voltage political power while spending very little of his own after-tax dollars. Phony corporations were formed to perform phantom services for Amalgamated. Bogus invoices were paid and, in a foolish case of greed, deducted as legitimate business expenses. Meanwhile, the phantom companies made campaign contributions for which Baxton received full credit from the grateful candidates for being a prodigious fund raiser. The operation required transferring large sums, always in excess of ten thousand dollars, through banks and labor unions. As a result, many United States Congressmen and federal judges had attained their positions thanks to Baxton's now tainted power base.

"Well?" Baxton yelled. "I'm right, aren't I?"

"Mr. Baxton, you're free to think whatever you want but . . ."

"Goddamn right I am," Baxton shouted with his enraged stare locked on Halloway.

"But if you'll calm down and think about your situation . . ."

"You're nuts if you think I'll calm down."

"O.K., don't. But the crimes with which you have been charged are not what my firm is experienced in handling. We specialize in securities fraud . . ."

Baxton laughed out loud. "Yale," he shouted. "Harvard, Columbia . . . you've got some of the best legal minds in the country. Whatever you may think of me, I'm not stupid." Baxton sat down. He took a deep breath. "O.K., you want out. Damn, have the balls at least to tell me that honestly."

Halloway's face reddened, in part from anger but primarily from embarrassment. He remained silent.

Baxton looked disdainfully at Halloway who was now shifting nervously in his chair. "I don't need a team of cowards and that's precisely what you are. All of you," Baxton added as he gathered the papers Halloway had placed on his desk. "I will read these. I presume you came with a recommendation for replacement counsel?"

Halloway almost breathed an audible sigh of relief. "Yes."

"Who is the lucky cousellor?"

"His name is Louis Frascone."

Baxton looked astonished. "Jesus, I've read about him. He's a . . . a mob lawyer." His face reddened again. "You bastards expect me to walk into federal court arm-in-arm with a well known Mafioso lawyer?"

"Damn it, Baxton. The guy's wired in all the right places. He's got guts. He's not afraid of anyone or anything. He knows how to tie the legal system in knots, even when he represents some guilty bastard."

Baxton frowned.

"I don't mean you," said Halloway defensively. "You've got defenses. If you think about it objectively for a minute, you'd realize he's the man."

Baxton reflected for a moment. "This fellow, Riley, he's the man I need, isn't he?"

"He's one of a few, including Frascone, who could tie the system up in knots. But Frascone's available. I've talked to him and he's eager. But it's your call, Mr. Baxton."

"I'm thinking my call is to sue your ass," said Baxton angrily. "When can I meet my mob lawyer?"

"Anytime you say."

"Get him here this afternoon, after lunch. Two o'clock."

"We'll be here."

"Not you," Baxton said, dismissing Halloway with an insulting wave of his hand. "I just want him. I don't ever want to see your ungrateful, cowardly face again."

Halloway turned and walked away quickly. "Fuck you, Bradford Baxton, sir. Fuck you," he said under his breath. It was not intended for Baxton's ears, but it made Halloway feel better.

<u>Boston, Suffolk County Jail. 11:00 a.m.</u>
The tantalizing aroma of coffee greeted Kimberly as she entered the small conference room where Riley was waiting. "French vanilla?" she asked.

Riley nodded. "Yes. Consider it a peace offering."

Kimberly gave him a puzzled look.

"I haven't had time to visit you. I've been busy," Riley said as he handed her a medium size Dunkin Donuts coffee cup and a packet of sugar. Kimberly waited a few seconds until her prison escort left the room and the door lock clicked shut. "Dan, I'm paying you my life savings to defend me, not for being my companion," she said sincerely.

Riley smiled. "I don't hear that very often. My clients are usually so upset at being in jail they want me to be in the bunk next to them." Riley reached into a small paper bag. "I'll be seeing you more often soon." he added, handing her a jelly donut and several napkins.

"This is wonderful," she said, smiling, lifting the donut as if it were a cherished prize. "I've been feeling sorry for myself in here." She took a bite out of the donut and wiped jelly off her chin with one of the napkins. "How are we doing so far?" Kimberly asked eagerly.

"We," Riley said emphasizing we, "have not yet begun to fight," he added facetiously. "Right now, we are simply circling the wagons. I'm still in the process of getting discovery from the D.A. We attack only when we're ready." Riley waited for a response. Kimberly merely nodded her approval.

"Cynthia Pogue," Riley said suddenly.

"She is my former college roommate. She let me use her apartment during my leave."

"I know," said Riley. "That wasn't a question. She says she called you only once from Europe and has the hotel bill to confirm that. Says it was February 14 at 10 p.m. your time. Problem is, you were supposed to be there according to your diary but you didn't answer." Riley stared directly into Kimberly's eyes. He had great intuitive skills. Eyes were the windows through which he could see the inner workings of a person's mind. "Can you explain that?"

Kimberly thought for a moment. "Yes, I can," she said emphatically.

"I'm listening."

"I never picked up the phone. I wasn't expecting any calls so I didn't want to interrupt Cynthia's voice mail. The phone rang frequently. Dan, if I started answering that damn phone I'd be taking messages all day and into the night. I honestly felt it was best to let the machine get the calls."

"I like it."

"It's the truth."

"Andrew . . . my friends call me Scottie . . . MacPherson, Georgetown, Maine," Riley said, trying unsuccessfully to mimic a Maine accent.

Kimberly's face registered surprise. "What's he got to do with me?"

"Maybe nothing, but then again, maybe a lot. Scottie says your dad was snooping around Johnston's computer and Baxton caught him." Riley waited for Kimberly's reaction. Her shoulder shrug clearly signaled "so what?" Riley made sure he took full measure of her eyes when he gave her the next piece of information. "Scottie says he thinks Baxton had your father killed." Kimberly's expression did not change. "What do you think of that idea?"

"Fanciful."

"Fanciful?" Riley repeated, signaling surprise at her response.

"What can I say . . . I mean, what did you expect me to say?"

"I have no expectations." Riley again quickly changed the subject. "Kimberly, did your father ever tell you he was caught snooping around in Johnston's office and that he was actually trying to get info from his computer?"

"Is that important?"

"Yes. Very."

"Yes," Kimberly replied without hesitation.

"Yes?"

"That surprises you?" Kimberly asked, a worried expression settling uncomfortably on her face.

"Well, yes it does. Why didn't you tell me about this before? This guy MacPherson calls from Maine, out of the blue, and hits me with what I find to be a real shocker. I don't like shocks when I'm preparing a defense. What really hurts is that he was visited by none other than Bill Coine who now knows this little detail."

"I'm sorry," Kimberly said contritely. "I didn't think that kind of detail was important, honest."

"It goes to motive," Riley said. "Maybe you figured like MacPherson did. Maybe you believed your father didn't kill himself. Maybe you believed Baxton ordered him killed because of what he learned about Johnston's computer. That's a good reason for a vendetta against Baxton and his company."

Kimberly frowned. "Now that is truly fanciful," she said. "Do you believe for one minute that that's what happened?" she added, looking as if her feelings were hurt.

"I'm neither a believer nor a non-believer. I'm a trial lawyer. That means I'm a natural born skeptic. You take something like you knowing about your dad's curiosity, and add to it the inference that it got him killed, at least in your mind, it could be an important factor in deciding whether you can take the stand in your own defense. Unless you tell them you knew about the snooping, they'll have no evidence to prove you did."

Kimberly stood up abruptly. "No way," she said loudly, lips tight and trembling. "I will take the stand when the time comes. Don't ever deprive me of that opportunity."

"Kimberly," Riley said in a fatherly tone, "when this case is over, I'm praying you walk out of the courtroom a free woman. Don't tie my hands in the effort to accomplish that objective by asking me to make a promise to you that I might not be able to keep. Please don't do that."

Kimberly sat down. "All right for now. But I don't ever want to look like I've anything to hide."

"O.K., I'll keep that in mind. Meanwhile, I spoke with Freddie the counterman and the news isn't good." Kimberly's worried look returned. "He's anxious to help you, but for now he doesn't remember any details to bolster his testimony. The D.A. will eat him for lunch."

"But at least he'll say I was there?"

"Oh, yeah, and if he thought it would help, he'd tell the jury the Queen of England came in right after you left. Let's face it, Freddie's bias is so obvious it glows in the dark."

"Can you use him?"

"I have no choice ... and while we're on the subject of problems, finding Tricia's surveillance video is worse than the proverbial needle in the haystack. It may never be found."

Riley watched Kimberly's expression change from worried to scared. Good, he thought. At least she's in touch with reality. Riley stood up and leaned on the back of his chair as he spoke. "Finding the video tape is certainly crucial. But I want to level with you. My concerns run much deeper."

Kimberly stiffened at that remark. "Just what does that mean?"

"So long as you're asking, I'll tell you," he said as if he had been challenged. "If you're the killer, then you were at Johnston's office at 9:00 p.m. and, therefore, not the star attraction on Tricia's surveillance video. You'd know that, the D.A. is betting on that being the case, and in the meantime, I'm running around like a fool looking for something that proves your guilt. But if you level with me, tell me you're not in it if it does show up, I stop looking, hopefully nobody finds it and I put my energy into creating reasonable doubt."

Kimberly laughed. "Is this where your murder clients usually break down with remorse and confess?"

"Not often. They usually threaten to fire me for doubting their innocence."

Kimberly looked hard into Riley's eyes. "There is a video and I am on it. So please keep looking."

Riley was surprised by her confidence. However, he decided to leave well enough alone and end on a positive note. "Good, then we'll find it."

Boston, District Attorney's Office. 11:30 a.m.
Gus Warner walked into Lieutenant Walsh's office without knocking. Walsh was sorting through a pile of documents with his free hand while dictating into a cassette recorder held gingerly by the finger tips sticking out of his full length arm cast. He did not look happy or comfortable.

"Hey Walshie," Warner said excitedly, pointing at the cast. "How would you like to meet the guy that broke your arm?"

Walsh ignored the "Walshie" and dropped the recorder. "Are you kidding? . . . You're joking."

"I wouldn't joke about that. Sergeant Donaldson, you know, over at vice says one of his informants told him there's a guy in Southie bragging about how he kicked the crap out of some cop."

Walsh's face reddened at the painful memory.

"And guess what?" Warner said facetiously. "You're the only policeman that's been beat up in Boston in the last few weeks."

"It was a damn sneak attack," Walsh said, red hot with anger. "And if that is our guy, please let me have two minutes alone with him."

"We have to get him first. Guy's name is Billy O'Toole. His brother owns Three Shamrocks Pub on A Street. The snitch says he's a regular at his brother's place every Friday at 10:30 in the morning for a cup of coffee. The joint doesn't open until 11:30. I say we pay the guy a visit tomorrow."

"Why not find out where the fucker lives and bust him there now?"

"Don't like that idea. All we have is a snitch's word and the guy will tell us to go to hell. No, I like surprising him in a place he'll never expect us to find him. I wanna see his reaction with no time to think."

"Can't wait," Walsh said, making a fist.

"Good. Let me tell you what I've got in mind."

<u>Newton. 2:00 p.m.</u>
Brad Baxton waited for Louis Frascone in the sun room. Frascone arrived on time. Baxton liked that.

Frascone had a pony tail. Baxton did not like that. But for the pony tail, the two men shared common traits. Both were short, with dark hair framing stern features.

Frascone took a seat opposite Baxton on the other side of a large, round glass-topped table.

"I know what you are thinking right now," Frascone said with a knowing grin.

It was an odd beginning to what would prove to be an odd relationship. "Do you really think you can read my mind?" Baxton said with a frown.

"Yeah, you're thinking I'm a low class wop lawyer from the North End and not good enough for you."

Baxton shot Frascone an angry stare. "You're way out of line Mr. Frascone and you're dead wrong."

"Am I?" Frascone shot back. "Well let me tell you something I'm dead right on. You, sir, are as guilty as sin. Who besides you benefited from all the illegal campaign contributions?"

Baxton stood up, face beet red. "I don't have to listen to this . . . this . . ."

"No, you don't, but you better hear it from me 'cause you're sure as hell gonna hear it in court, and see it on television, and read it in the papers."

"You, sir, are insolent."

"Thank you, I've been called worse." Baxton started to leave. Frascone stood up and blocked him with his body. "Listen. I'm here because I like your case. I've got the balls to do what's gotta be done to beat the rap."

Baxton could not believe what he was hearing. "How can you be any help to me when you're convinced of my guilt?"

"Easy. Winning a case for an innocent man is like eating plain oatmeal for breakfast. Beating the system for a guilty guy, now that's eggs Benedict."

"What chance do I have?"

"A damn good one. The case against you is all circumstantial. Johnston was the bad guy here. If nobody fingers you directly, I figure you walk." Frascone pulled a document from his attaché case. He handed it to Baxton who took it and returned to his seat. "A motion to dismiss," Frascone said, pointing. "I think it's a winner."

"And if it isn't?"

"Then the U. S. Attorney will have played all her cards at the motion hearing, we'll see exactly what her case is and we beat her ass at the trial."

Baxton was encouraged by Frascone's confidence. "How much does it cost me to give you this great opportunity for . . . eggs Benedict," Baxton said, smiling for the first time since Frascone's arrival.

"Steep. How much is your freedom worth?"

Baxton did not hesitate. He was in the fight of his life and Frascone seemed to be the right mix of brains and sleaze to do battle with the feds. He removed a checkbook from his jacket pocket. "One thing," he said as he wrote a check for two hundred and fifty thousand dollars.

"What?"

"You were not exactly correct when you were reading my mind."

"What'd I miss?"

"I don't like men with pony tails."

Frascone laughed. "Well, my hair style levels the playing field."

"How so?"

"Toni Williams, the U.S. Attorney who'll be prosecuting you, wears a pony tail." Frascone pocketed the check without looking at it and turned to leave.

"Just a minute, there's something you should know."

"What's that?"

"I'm really innocent . . . not guilty."

Frascone winked a knowing wink. "If it makes you feel better, great. I'll see you in court."

South Boston, March 11. 10:45 a.m.
Lieutenant Walsh walked slowly up A Street toward the Three Shamrocks Pub. An unmarked Crown Vic slowly turned into the alley just beyond the pub. Warner waited in a van across the street with

Neiberg and four S.W.A.T. team members. Walsh stopped in front of the two big front doors, each adorned with three Kelly green shamrocks, and pulled firmly on the handle. The door opened and Walsh stepped in. Sunlight, streaming through two small windows just to the right of the entrance, carved a bright swath of dust-filled air, making it difficult to see the two men sitting in a booth at the far end of a long mahogany bar. Walsh walked through the haze and his eyes quickly adjusted. "Great," he said softly into the mike under his lapel as he made eye contact with the large necked, curly red haired man facing the entrance, "the bugger looks just like his mug shot."

Billy O'Toole pointed casually at Walsh. His brother, Patrick, spoke without turning around. "We're not open until 11:30."

"I know," Walsh answered. "I'm not here for lunch," he added as he approached the booth.

Patrick turned to face Walsh who was now standing directly in front of the booth. "Then beat it."

"Not 'til I talk to Billy boy here," Walsh said, gesturing.

"Who the fuck are you," Billy said with a snarl.

"Billy boy, Billy boy," Walsh said in sing-song fashion, shaking his head from side to side. "When you jump a man from behind, kick him when he's down and break his fuckin' arm, well, you should at least remember him. You hurt my feelings," Walsh added mockingly.

Billy's eyes widened with the shock of recognition.

"Oh, you do remember. Well, you cocksucker, I'm here to arrest your ass," Walsh said with a wide grin.

Billy grabbed the beer bottle near his right hand and, with one continuous motion, lunged at Walsh, swinging the bottle directly at his head. Walsh grunted as he raised his right arm to absorb the blow with his cast. The bottle broke harmlessly. Billy pushed past Walsh and ran into the kitchen.

"He's headin' out the back," Walsh yelled into the mike.

Patrick started to move toward Walsh menacingly.

"I'm a cop," Walsh yelled. "Move one more fuckin' inch and you'll be goin' to jail with Billy."

The big man froze. Just then, two detectives barged through the front door and Billy, all six feet two inches of him, reappeared at the kitchen entrance, brandishing a cleaver.

"Billy boy, you're not too smart. Now it's gonna be attempted murder," Walsh said with relish.

Billy raised the cleaver for a split second, but decided to throw it down. He made a desperate dash for a nearby window. Walsh, with another grunt, swung his right arm up into the big guy's face as he ran by. The cast, weakened by the beer bottle, cracked. Billy crashed to the floor hard as Walsh let out a muffled scream. The pain was intense but the blood flowing from Billy's nose made up for it.

"Hey, you bastard," Patrick yelled, "that's police brutality."

"You like runnin' this place?" Walsh hissed through clenched teeth, holding his arm at the point of fracture. "You keep talkin' like that and you and your roach infested shit shamrock kitchen'll be outta business." Walsh watched as one of the detectives rolled Billy onto his stomach, cuffed him, read him his rights and called for an ambulance. Walsh turned and walked out of the pub into the bright sunlight. He breathed deeply and suddenly felt like vomiting. "Shit," he yelled as he surveyed his broken cast and reinjured arm, "sometimes this job really sucks."

<u>Newton. March 16. 12:30 p.m.</u>
Alexander ushered Frascone into Baxton's study. Baxton sat stiffly behind a large desk. It was a desperate effort to hang onto some last vestige of power over someone. It did not work. Frascone remained standing and pointed at him accusatorily. "Did you do business with this Korensky asshole,

the guy that got killed trying to break into the evidence vault at police headquarters? And while we're at it, are you this fuckin' Geronimo ass hole mentioned in an affidavit signed by some third-rate creep named Billy O'Toole?"

Baxton jumped to his feet, fists clenched, eyes wide with rage.

"On second thought, don't answer. If I can't make some deal to save your ass from a lifetime in prison, I may have to try this crazy cuckoomunga case. And you may have to deny all this shit under oath."

Baxton banged both fists on the desk. "You insolent bastard," he shouted.

"Good, bang the desk, yell. Go ahead. And while you're at it, try comin' up with some answer to how a fuckin' phone number linked to your office is in Korensky's little black computer disk."

"You're fired," Baxton yelled.

"Good. Then I won't be responsible when you get convicted in state court for that stupid break-in at police headquarters, get sent to Walpole and end up as some big bubba's bitch takin' it up your ass or anywhere else the fucker wants to put it."

Baxton's face went from red to white when that thought settled heavily into his consciousness. He fell back into his chair. "They can't convict me. They can't," he said as if saying it would make it so.

"Mr. Baxton, you're between the proverbial rock and a hard place. There's so much shit comin' down on you that sooner or later, people who conspired with you on the campaign fraud shit will start comin' outta the woodwork to make their own deals. If you don't make one first, you're dead meat." Frascone waited for his message to sink in. "I mean it," he added. "And I've represented the best of the worst in the criminal world. I can look a bunch of jurors right in the eye and tell 'em a bunch of bullshit without one ounce of shame." Frascone turned as if to look at an invisible jury, gesturing as he spoke. "The janitor put the phone in the desk drawer, he was Geronimo. Johnston must have gone nuts and put all that stuff on the computer. All those people who are pointing fingers of guilt at innocent Mr. Baxton are lyin'!" Frascone returned his gaze toward Baxton who by now was sitting limply behind his big power desk. "And I look the jury foreman right in the eye when he says, 'Guilty,' and for effect, I look hurt, like how could you not believe me?"

"Enough! What must I do. I can't go to Walpole . . . or any jail."

"I'll keep you outta Walpole but, Mr. Baxton, you will spend some time as a guest of the United States Government in a nice limited security facility. "Here's what we're gonna do . . ."

Downsized

<u>Boston, Suffolk County Jail. 3:30 p.m.</u>
Riley's jelly donuts and coffee had become a welcome relief from Kimberly's drab jailhouse fare. Already seated at the small table in the conference room, she greeted Riley with a wide-eyed, eager expression. Kimberly was tough, fragile, sexy and childlike all at the same time. It usually took Riley a few minutes to get past the sexy part whenever he met with her. Even in prison garb, she evoked a sensual response in Riley. He shook it off and readied himself for work. He took his usual seat in the uncomfortable wooden chair opposite Kimberly. "There's some very good news," he said, handing her a cup of coffee and pushing the box of donuts toward her. Kimberly fumbled briefly with the small tab and then removed the entire lid from the cup. "Don't keep me in suspense," she said, sipping from the cup as Riley gave her the news.

"Freddie's shaping up as a more credible witness. He's been doing his homework . . . dates, times, conversations with you. I'm encouraged . . . but nervous. He'll be here for the trial."

"Wonderful news," Kimberly said with a big smile. "But have you made progress on the search for the surveillance video?"

"I'm afraid not. We may be trying this case without it."

Kimberly frowned.

"But I'm encouraged by the ton of discovery I've obtained, which leads me to an important question." Kimberly leaned forward. "I know you were in public relations and not in the Special Forces as a combat soldier. So what the hell were you doing with a training manual dealing with long range target interdiction?"

Kimberly smiled. "That book was Andy's . . . Captain Grissom's," she said as if she did not grasp the title's significance to her case.

"What were you doing with it?" Riley said, standing up. Kimberly was now accustomed to Riley's style. She leaned back in her chair and got ready for a cross-examination.

"I helped him study for exams," she said demurely.

"How long had you been doin' that?"

"For about a year... maybe a little longer."

"I thought his training was classified. What were you doin' helping him study?"

"Is this going to get Andy in trouble?" Kimberly asked, now looking worried.

"To hell with the trouble Andy might be in, answer my question."

"It's not really allowed, but a lot of the guys do it when they have military girlfriends kinda like we're all in the same army so there's no real harm."

"But you were not Captain Grissom's girlfriend."

"He wanted me to be . . . helping him study was about as intimate as I would let him get."

"Suppose you tell me what other subjects you helped him with."

Kimberly shook her head slowly. "You're not going to like this. Explosives, use of computer technology in obtaining military intelligence and a few more highly technical subjects." She bit her lip nervously.

Riley turned and walked slowly away, stopped and drove the next question right down her throat. "Lieutenant Hale, did you plan on killing Amalgamated's officers before you started studying with Grissom or did the idea pop into your head after you read Grissom's training manuals?"

Kimberly gasped. "What kind of question is that," she said in shock.

"Oh," said Riley sarcastically, "just the kind the D.A.'s gonna ask you in front of the jury."

Kimberly's shoulders sagged. "But that's an unfair question."

"And I'll object strenuously . . . and the Court will sustain my objection. But the jury will have heard it and you are suddenly a lady with a motive and one helluva lot of sinister book learning."

"Does the D.A. know any of this now?"

"He knows about the long-range target manual."

"They'll learn the rest if I take the stand?"

"Definitely."

"And about my knowledge of my father's poking around Johnston's computer?"

"Yes, they'll learn that from you also."

Kimberly pushed the jelly donuts away. She held the coffee cup in both hands and pondered her dilemma. "When do we have to decide, I mean if I should take the witness stand."

"The day before I'm ready to rest my case."

"So we've got time."

"Yes."

"Good," Kimberly said with a shrug. "Let's not worry about it now. What else do you have for me," she added calmly.

Riley outlined some of his ideas, but as he spoke with her at length, he realized he could not read her at all. She could step into a bell jar at will and escape reality. Before he left, he gave Kimberly one last piece of information. "The trial is set definitely for April 18th."

Kimberly smiled. "Oh good. It should be a nice spring day."

Riley smiled. "Perhaps," he said. Back in the bell jar, he thought as he turned and left the room, wondering who Kimberly Hale really was.

THREE WEEKS LATER

<u>Allenwood Federal Prison Camp, Pennsylvania. April 15. 1:30 a.m.</u>
Brad Baxton was wide awake in the upper bunk of his prison dormitory cubicle. He stared at the ceiling, eyes filled with tears, unable to focus. He wished he was dead. He cursed Kimberly Hale over and over again for not making quick work of him, for allowing him to live to face a hell for which he was completely unprepared. Death was preferable to what he now faced. He arrived at the camp in a bus with twelve other prisoners. Baxton had forfeited the right to surrender himself to this minimum security prison when he gambled on a flight to China. Stripped of all possessions, he was given a navy blue, one-piece jumpsuit and assigned to housing

dormitory "A". His dormitory area was windowless and housed eighty men in separate, but completely open cubicles. The cubicle walls were only four feet high. All of the top bunks were visible. From what he could see, more than two-thirds of the inmates were black or Hispanic. His bunk mate was a six foot, two hundred and fifty pound black man named Reshawn Morehouse. The sight of him and the thought of what Frascone had said about Walpole made Baxton sick to his stomach. Now, in the semi-darkness of his new universe, the once powerful Brad Baxton tried to drown out the sounds of eighty loudly snoring men. Reshawn farted loudly several times. Baxton gagged and stifled a scream. He buried his head under the pillow. I won't survive this, he thought. How can I possibly live another day, let alone for four years. He never slept that first night. With no windows, Baxton could not see the sun rise over the Allenwood camp. The tennis courts, baseball diamonds and walking paths gave the place the look of a pleasant summer camp. They would bring no solace to Baxton. In prison lexicon, he was a rat. His prison life was going to be miserable.

<u>Boston, Suffolk County Jail. 11:30 a.m.</u>
Dan Riley was already seated in the small attorney's conference room when Kimberly arrived. The front page of the Boston Globe was on the

table so Kimberly could see it as soon as she entered the room. A short, punchy headline and subtext told it all:

BAXTON BEGINS SENTENCE
Amalgamated CEO to Serve 4 years
In Federal Penitentiary

Kimberly casually glanced at the paper and smiled at Riley.

"How does that make you feel?" he asked as she sat down. She reached for one of the two coffees on the table. "How should it make me feel?" Kimberly replied, looking slightly puzzled and wondering why Riley asked such a question.

"I asked you first," Riley insisted, sitting back in the chair and folding arms across his chest.

"Look, I dislike the man," Kimberly said, not hiding her annoyance with the question. She sipped from the cardboard cup before completing her answer. "He deserves a longer sentence for what he did to . . ."

Riley cut her off abruptly. "To?" he said loudly. Kimberly frowned. "You were going to say to all those people he downsized . . . and your dad . . . weren't you?"

"So what? That's how I feel . . . you asked me, dammit," Kimberly shot back angrily.

"So what?" Riley said mockingly. "Downsizing isn't a crime, last time I checked," he added, intentionally baiting Kimberly. She rose to the bait.

"It's a crime against humanity. Baxton is no different than Hitler."

"Is that so? So you see Baxton's downsizing policies as rivaling the holocaust?"

"He killed people's hopes, dreams and for some he extinguished their very souls," Kimberly shouted, clenching both fists and slamming them on the table, her right fist coming to rest on the Baxton headline.

"Wonderful," Riley said, throwing up his hands. "Just wonderful," he added, looking deeply into her eyes beyond the ice cold stare. "The downsizing killer couldn't have said it better himself."

"Him and a thousand others," Kimberly shot back.

"But you, not him and not a thousand others are on trial for murder."

Riley let that message sink in. Kimberly sipped from the cup. "Look," she said calmly, "you're good at setting mind traps, catching people off guard."

"So's the D.A., and he wants to win this case in the worst way."

"O.K., I've got it out of my system. I'll be more careful . . . I'll be ready for mind games."

Riley stood up suddenly.

"Oh, no, here we go again," Kimberly said, getting ready for another blistering cross examination.

"Are you aware that Baxton's undoing began with Johnston's murder?"

"Never gave it a thought."

"It would have been easier to kill Johnston at home, on the way to work or in a hundred other places . . . you agree?"

"So what?" Kimberly replied with a shoulder shrug.

"Kill him in his office, just a few feet from his computer and maybe the cops just might grab the damn thing, looking for evidence. Do you agree with that statement?"

"Ridiculous. It would be easier to just call the police and . . ."

". . . and tell them what? The illegal information was encoded."

"I don't know," Kimberly said, looking frustrated.

Riley stared intently at Kimberly. His voice assumed a hostile, inquisitorial tone. "You majored in computer science, didn't you?"

"Yes," she answered, her cold-as-ice stare aimed at Riley.

"And your father was practically computer illiterate, wasn't he?"

"How in hell do you know that?"

"Easy. And what's more important, if I know, you can bet your bottom dollar the D.A. knows."

Riley returned to his chair, sat down and stared at Kimberly for several seconds. They exchanged intently focused eye contact. Riley pointed an accusing finger as he spoke slowly, deliberately. "You, Kimberly Hale, the young, angry college girl, you told your father to fight back at Baxton."

Kimberly's lips tightened. Her eyes told Riley his educated hunch was on-the-money. He bore in for the kill. "You coached him, and you told him how to get into Johnston's computer, didn't you?"

Riley exposed a raw nerve. Kimberly's eyes began to water. Her lips quivered. Riley continued. "And when he got caught, that wasn't the first time he went snooping into Johnston's computer, was it?"

"No," she yelled. "No." She began sobbing. "He didn't want to do it."

"And you learned from one of his forays that Johnston had a secret project hidden behind a code word you didn't get a chance to crack."

Tears streamed down Kimberly's cheeks. "How did you know?" she said, shaking her head and sobbing. Riley reached out to touch her hand. She withdrew, angry that Riley had so easily uncovered such a buried secret.

"I didn't," Riley said apologetically. "I learned enough from talking with your roommate and your dad's co-workers to take a wild guess."

Kimberly wiped her eyes with a Dunkin' Donuts napkin. "What are the chances the D.A. has drawn the same inferences . . . that he's guessed the same thing?"

"I have to assume he has. If you take the stand and he's done his homework, you can be blown out of the water on this point. It's a risk I'm unwilling to take. But if you maintain your silence, the jury never hears this damaging testimony. What you and your dad did and what you knew about Johnston's computer is a real croaker."

Kimberly slowly regained her composure. Riley observed that she was back in that compartment of her brain that ignored reality.

"Dan, I hear you. But we'll still wait until the last minute to make our decision."

"Well, I've made mine. We'll just have to await yours."

"Thanks," she said, the warm smile returning. "Will I see you again before the trial starts?"

"No. I'll be as busy as any human being can possibly be."

"Still no video?"

"I'm sorry. No," Riley said disappointedly.

Kimberly stood up, turned and walked toward the door, stopping just before leaving.

"I'll see you Monday," she said calmly. "Be sure to get plenty of rest."

When the door closed behind Kimberly, Riley looked up, hands outstretched, "Lord, that stuff about daddy and the computer was not what I wanted to hear."

Suffolk Superior Court, April 18th 2:00 p.m.

Kimberly's jury was empaneled quickly and opening arguments began after lunch. The hunting knife, its hilt and most of the blade grotesquely encrusted with Sam Johnston's dried blood, twisted slowly at the end of a string. Gus Warner held the string in his left hand, just below the large yellow exhibit tag. He held the knife high, arm fully extended so that it dangled only a few feet in front of the jury box. All twelve jurors and four alternates sat mesmerized by the sight of the ghastly weapon. One hundred and twenty spectators crowding courtroom 1017 strained to glimpse the instrument of death. Warner stood silently for several seconds, heightening the drama. When he spoke, his voice was solemn, confident.

"This is the knife that was used to brutally murder Samuel Adams Johnston."

Warner lowered the knife, turned and walked over to an easel on his left and slightly behind him.

He quickly removed the cover from a twenty-by-thirty inch color enlargement depicting a close-up of the same knife imbedded up to the hilt in Johnston's naked, bloody chest. Several jurors gasped; a few covered their eyes. Spectators in the rear of the courtroom stood up to get a better look, like fans at a sporting event.

"I'm not showing this picture to shock you," Warner said. "And I apologize if it offends anyone. But this photograph is a key piece of evidence. It establishes a very important point," he said as he tapped his right index finger on the hilt, clearly visible in the rivulet of blood flowing from Johnston's chest wound. "As you can see, one side is longer than the other."

Warner held the weapon high again so the jurors could see the same detail on the real knife. He described the left-handed assassin theory suggested by Coine and summarized the anticipated expert testimony that would establish that hypothesis. Warner turned slowly to his right, extending his right arm, index finger pointed dramatically at Kimberly. He spoke a bit more loudly, with greater intensity. "That testimony and all the evidence will prove, beyond a reasonable doubt, that Lieutenant Kimberly Hale is the downsizing killer and solely responsible for the murders of Johnston, van der Meer and Fulton."

Warner carefully outlined the circumstantial case against Kimberly. Piece by piece, the weight of the evidence against Kimberly took its toll. When Warner finished, Riley placed his hand on top of Kimberly's, a gesture not lost on the jurors, gave it a reassuring squeeze and stood up. He took a deep breath and steeled himself for the task at hand. He knew his opening had to accomplish more than merely neutralize Warner's words. He had to demolish the State's case utterly and convincingly. Riley felt an adrenalin rush as he walked over to the table on which Warner had placed the bloodstained knife. He grabbed it with his right hand deliberately, by the handle. He held it tightly in his fist, the blade and hilt oriented in the same direction as shown in the photograph. He held it high and walked the length of the jury box so everyone could plainly see that a right-handed person could jamb it into a man's chest with the long part of the hilt on the wrong side.

"Ladies and gentlemen," Riley began. "You are looking at the one thing in this entire case about which Mr. Warner and I agree." He turned to look at Warner briefly, holding the knife in front of him, making certain it was always visible to the jury. "This is the knife that was used to murder Samuel Johnston." He paused to let that sink in. "But the hand that held it was not," Riley's voice became noticeably louder, more intense, "is not and could not have been the hand of Kimberly Hale."

Riley returned the knife to the evidence table and dropped it with a bang. He returned to the center of the jury box and spoke in a more relaxed tone. "The judge will tell you at the conclusion of this case that Kimberly Hale's innocence is presumed throughout this trial." Riley gestured in Warner's direction as he continued. "Mr. Warner alone has the burden of proving guilt beyond a reasonable doubt. Despite that," Riley continued in a serious tone, "I want to make you a promise, a promise the law does not require me to make . . ."

Warner jotted a note on his legal pad and angled it toward Sandra: "A promise I'm gonna tuck up his butt."

"When the evidence is concluded," Riley intoned confidently, "not only will it not prove guilt beyond a reasonable doubt, it will convince all of you that Kimberly Hale is innocent and that she has been unjustly charged with these crimes."

Another note to Sandra: "IS HE NUTS!?"

A quickly scribbled reply: "He's making it personal, and he's nuts."

Riley walked back to counsel table and retrieved a document. "My client has an alibi witness that Mr. Warner has completely ignored." Riley gestured with the document in his right hand. "Sam Johnston was killed at 9:00 p.m. on February 14th . . . St. Valentine's Day. Warner says the killer also spent time earlier that day booby-trapping Fulton's computer." Riley held the paper high in the air. "This is an affidavit of Freddie James, a counter man at Tricia's convenience store on Exeter Street. You will all get a chance to hear him in person. But here's what he said in an affidavit, under oath," Riley pointed to Warner, "and he has a copy of this affidavit." Riley held the affidavit comfortably in front of him so he could read it and still keep eye contact with the jurors. "I did not know Kimberly Hale's name at the time," Riley paused briefly, "I knew her as Miss Blue Eyes. She was in my store at approximately 8:30 p.m. on Monday evening, February 14th, and left at approximately 9:15 p.m. I spoke with her. I could never forget her pretty face and blue eyes." Sixteen pairs of eyes glanced at Kimberly. Riley knew the jurors would relate to Freddie's assessment of Kimberly's beauty. He lowered the document and pointed to the empty witness chair. "You'll hear Freddie repeat these words in this courtroom," Riley said confidently.

"And I'll tear the little S.O.B. a new asshole," Warner scribbled to Sandra. She waited a few seconds, kept a poker face and nonchalantly jotted an urgent reply: "Dammit, stop writing notes to me. You're not invisible!"

"Freddie's testimony is strike one for Mr. Warner." He unfolded a Boston Globe front page with the headline heralding the shoot out at the Westin Hotel. "This is strike two. A man dressed like the downsizing killer tries to assassinate Bradford Baxton, dives into the icy Charles River, and what does Mr. Warner do? He doesn't wait for the body to be recovered. He doesn't wait for an investigation into the attacker's background." Riley points at Warner. "This man decides to indict Kimberly Hale. Ladies and gentlemen," he continued confidently. "It's not a rush to judgment just because I say it is. It is the <u>evidence</u> that will enable you to reach that conclusion; clear and convincing evidence that District Attorney Augustus Warner completely ignored when he indicted my client." This time, the personal attack was subtle. Riley knew Warner detested "Augustus." It sounded imperial.

Riley summarized the rise and fall of Baxton's empire and his recent incarceration in federal prison. "But once upon a time, Baxton was a very important man with very important and influential friends in government, friends that he bought with illegal campaign contributions and outright bribes."

Warner exploded to his feet. "Objection," he yelled, fists clenched, knuckles pressed hard against the table.

"I'll see counsel at side bar," Judge Waters insisted sternly, rising from his big chair and walking to the far corner of his bench.

"This is an outrage," Warner whispered loudly through clenched teeth. "I've been patient with Riley's opening, Your Honor, but he's gone too far." Warner pointed at Riley. "He's . . . he's linked me to Brad Baxton's corrupt practices. It's outrageous, judge."

"Keep your voice down," Waters admonished.

"But, judge," Warner hissed, "he's left this jury with an inference that I'm one of the bribed government officials. Damn, that's what he just did, judge."

Judge Waters leaned out over the bench. "Stay calm, Gus, He's not gone there yet. But Gus has a point Riley. You're too darn close to suggesting that. Just where in blazes are you going with this line of argument? You've been getting too personal here."

"A murder indictment is personal, Your Honor," Riley quipped.

"Don't get smart with me, Dan. Answer my question. Where are you going?"

"Two points, judge." Riley moved closer to the bench. "First, the stock in Baxton's company was being trashed on Wall Street. Baxton put tremendous pressure on the Mayor and the Governor to get the case resolved quickly and they, in turn, put the heat on Warner. Judge," Riley added persuasively, "Kimberly Hale was indicted in a pressure cooker atmosphere."

Warner rolled his eyes and held out both hands in a suppliant gesture. "Pul-leeese, judge, now he's suggesting that the Governor and the Mayor were on the take."

"Mr. Riley," Judge Waters said with a frown, "you didn't have to wave allegations of illegal contributions and bribes in the face of the jury in order to make point one. Consider yourself on a short leash from now on. I will not permit you to move us into a mistrial. Now, I'll hear your last point."

Judge, may I address your comments and tell you why I referred to Baxton's illegal campaign activities," Riley asked cautiously.

"No," Waters insisted emphatically. "Your last point, now!"

"Bill Coine," Riley answered quickly. "Former state police Detective Lieutenant Bill Coine, your Honor. Baxton gave him one hundred thousand dollars to get a quick solution to this case. Coine used his influence to infiltrate the D.A.'s office and turn this case into a witch hunt for an imaginary left-handed female killer."

"Judge," said Warner angrily. A quickly raised judicial stop sign ended Warner's comments abruptly.

"When my client came into Warner's sights," Riley continued, "he seized upon the opportunity to save Amalgamated's corporate butt. And, because it also got the Mayor and the Governor off his back, Gus Warner bought into Coine's nonsense hook, line and sinker."

"Outrageous judge," Warner sputtered uncontrollably. "If Riley utters one word of that . . . that unsubstantiated nonsense to this jury, I'm moving for a mistrial. That's what he wants, judge, a mistrial. He's gonna push all our buttons judge until he gets it. Don't let him."

"No one's pushing any mistrial buttons in my courtroom. As for you, Riley, if you have any evidence of infiltration and bad faith on William Coine's part, you prove it first. Same thing with this corruption connection thing. If you prove it, you can argue it in your closing." The judge looked Riley squarely in the eyes. "And there will be a closing. I'll not let anyone cause a mistrial. You may explain your pressure cooker theory but unhinge it from any suggestion of bribery or the like. You may comment on Mr. Coine's likely bias as a result of his employment by Baxton . . . but . . . and this is a very important but. You will not accuse him of any wrongdoing until after you prove it in this courtroom with a proper evidentiary foundation. Am I clear?"

"Yes, Your Honor." Riley said politely. "Will you note my objection?"

"Of course," the judge replied, just as politely. "Now let's get on with this case."

The remainder of Riley's opening was factual and avoided further trouble with Judge Waters. His rush to judgment theory, bolstered by key points in the chain of evidence, most striking of which was the raid on Police Headquarters on February 23rd and Baxton's weird connection to Korensky, had succeeded in leveling the playing field. Kimberly's conviction was not going to be a sure thing.

"Ladies and gentlemen," Riley said very seriously. "I want to make one final promise to you."

"Now what?" Warner scribbled on his pad.

"This District Attorney will be introducing a witness, a man who will tell you he is a man of science." Riley intentionally avoided referring to him either by title or name. "A man who will tell you his science can prove that the image on a grainy surveillance video tape of a person dressed in a large, floppy jumpsuit, face and head completely covered was one, a female and two, was approximately the same height and weight as Kimberly Hale. My promise to you is that I will debunk that man and his science right here in this courtroom."

Warner struggled to remain calm. However, his body language telegraphed his anger to the jury. Sandra simply smiled a sarcastic smile and slowly shook her head from side to side, ever so slightly.

"One final point," Riley told the jurors as he walked briskly toward the tripod containing a fifteen by twenty-inch board covered by a blank sheet of paper. Riley tore the paper from the chart, revealing an enlargement of a handwritten note. Riley spoke reverently. "This is the note left for us by Howard van der Meer. He was the second victim and the only person who spent some time in the killer's presence. He was the only victim who had an opportunity to tell us something very important about his assailant. The note is poignant. It was obviously meant to be his last loving thoughts for his wife and children. But in those last moments, he did tell us something about the killer. Although he writes that he can't give us a description, read with me what Howard van der Meer says next." Riley tapped the words with his right index finger. "He," Riley gave a slight emphasis to that word, "just drives. Damn guy," again a slight emphasis on guy, "hasn't said word one."

Sixteen heads turned quickly from Riley, to Kimberly, to Warner and back to Riley. Riley saw that his point was made. He gave it a little shove in the right direction. "Ladies and gentlemen, when the evidence closes, you will all realize that the silent assassin in Van der Meer's note . . . that damn guy . . .," Riley pointed to one of the windows, "is still out there somewhere."

Riley turned and walked slowly past Warner's table, ignoring him. Kimberly greeted Riley with a warm smile. "You were fabulous," she said softly into his ear when he returned to his chair. Only after the judge dismissed the jury for the evening and Riley watched the last juror file out of the courtroom did he notice the trickle of perspiration running down the small of his back. He had declared all out war against Warner and there would be no prisoners. Despite the apparent success of his opening, the awful issue of whether Kimberly could ever take the stand in her defense hung over him like a black cloud.

Suffolk Superior Court, Second Day 9:00 a.m.
The jurors looked rested and eager as they filed into the jury box. Several looked directly at Riley and smiled politely. A good sign, he thought. Judge Waters stormed onto his bench in typical gangbuster fashion, open robe flying. The court officer intoned his familiar, "Cooort." Judge Waters swivelled his high-backed leather chair a quarter turn clockwise and dropped into it unceremoniously. "The court will come to order," he said gruffly with a loud bang of his gavel. "Mr. Warner," he added quickly with a nod in the D.A.'s direction, "Your first witness."

Warner stood up quickly, smiled a "good morning" to the jurors, tugged on his jacket until it hugged his shoulders comfortably and said,

"Doctor Romanoff." Blood ran hot into Riley's ears. He strained with all of his might not to show his anxiety. Dr. Romanoff walked briskly to the witness stand. Riley spoke politely as he rose slowly from his chair. "May we approach the bench, Your Honor," he asked calmly, successfully masking his shock at Warner's surprise.

"Good heavens, we're just getting started," Judge Waters responded with a frown aimed squarely at Riley. When the group assembled on the far side of the bench and the stenographer signaled she was ready, Judge Waters spoke first in a loud whisper. "Riley, what in blazes do you need a side bar for?"

Riley leaned closer to the judge and replied softly, "Your Honor, we went to the trouble of exchanging witness lists. Romanoff was supposed to be sixth, at least not until the third or fourth day of trial."

"So what?" Judge Waters said sarcastically.

"I object to the order being changed without notice. Gus is obviously using the element of surprise to . . ."

"Judge," Warner interrupted, hissing loudly, "Dan told this jury in his opening argument that he was going to demolish Dr. Romanoff. I figure he can do it sooner than later," he added with a nasty grin aimed at Riley.

"Riley, you did make a big thing about turning this trial into a demolition derby," Judge Waters admonished, still frowning. "Do you have anything else to say?" he added, signaling he was ready to rule on Riley's objection.

"No, Your Honor, nothing further, but I have been prejudiced and I press my objection,"

"Overruled," Judge Waters grumbled, shooting a frown at Riley for what seemed like an unnecessary delay. Waters turned abruptly and pointed to the trial clerk. "Swear in the witness," he ordered as he fell heavily into his big chair.

Riley slowly walked back to his table. Kimberly was waiting with a one word message scribbled on Riley's legal pad. "Bad?"

"Maybe," Riley whispered.

Meanwhile, Warner wasted no time. "Dr. Romanoff, will you please tell us about your education, training and academic achievements?" Warner began confidently. Normally, Riley would agree to Romanoff's qualifications to testify as an expert, but a lengthy direct examination was now a much-welcomed ally. He gave Kimberly his cell phone, cupped both hands over her right ear and whispered instructions. Ten minutes into a boring recitation about a Yale undergraduate degree and a Harvard Ph.D., Kimberly jotted a note to Riley. "I got through. Your staff knows. They'll be ready by noon!"

Riley breathed a sigh of relief and glanced at his watch. Keep talking, you pompous ass, he thought, please keep talking.

Warner's direct exam was tedious, but Romanoff was making points with the jury. Riley checked the time: 11:45.

" . . . and so, Dr. Romanoff," Warner asked firmly, "based upon your background, training and the tests you've described here, do you have an opinion based upon reasonable scientific certainty as to the size, weight and gender of the so-called downsizing killer?" Warner turned toward the jury as Romanoff replied.

"Yes, I do," the witness answered confidently.

The jurors stared intently at Dr. Romanoff. Warner turned to face the witness. "Will you please tell us your opinion, Doctor?"

Riley shot to his feet. An objection was certainly in order to preserve the record if an appeal was ever needed. But Riley needed the valuable time another side bar would give him.

"Objection, side bar your Honor," he said firmly.

Judge Waters spoke first. "Dan, you seem intent on wasting time. We've been over this at your pre-trial motion hearing the other day and I've ruled Dr. Romanoff's testimony can go to the jury," he whispered, shaking his head.

"Judge," Riley said earnestly, "this witness might as well be testifying that the killer is, in fact, Kimberly Hale. Please, Judge, consider the facts. Romanoff was given the weight and measurements of the cleaning lady at AWE headquarters, Johnston's mistress, Ailida Estrella."

Warner glowered at Riley. Riley ignored him.

"State Police Sergeant Neiberg speculated the killer was the same height and weight as Ms. Estrella. Romanoff had this information before he started all his mumbo jumbo that he calls testing. It's clear he backed into his opinions, Judge."

Warner started to speak, but Judge Waters held up a hand to stop him.

"You can argue all that to the jury, Dan, and I'm sure you will. Is there anything else?" Judge Waters said, anxious to resume testimony.

"No," said Riley.

"Your Honor," Warner spoke hurriedly, "I'm sorry to ask but I'm gonna need several TV monitors set up for the court and jury. We have some video presentations that'll be helpful when Dr. Romanoff testifies about his opinions."

"For heaven's sake Gus, I've just given you the green light and you want a delay?" Judge Waters said, shaking his head in disbelief. Warner's face reddened. Because of his sudden change in plans, his staff didn't have time to set up the video equipment earlier. Riley was thrilled.

Well, Riley, what do you say?" Waters asked.

Riley smiled broadly. "He doesn't deserve it, Judge, but I have no objection. You owe me one,

David G. Hanrahan Esq.

Gus," he whispered to Warner facetiously as the two men returned to their respective tables.

Waters looked at his watch. It was noon. He banged his gavel. "Well take an early lunch recess. We resume at one sharp."

Sandra wrote a brief note to Warner, "Well, you've succeeded in taking the magic out of the magic moment."

"Thank you God," Riley said softly, "and Gus Warner, Amen."

―――

Dr. Romanoff stepped gingerly over the cables snaking across the floor and resumed his place on the witness stand. Riley cupped both hands over Kimberly's ear and whispered, "Stay calm. This is gonna hurt. But," he added reassuringly, patting the large envelope in front of him, "here are the nails for this guy's coffin." Kimberly sat back in the chair, placed her clasped hands on the edge of the table and focused her attention on Romanoff.

Warner rose quickly and moved confidently to a spot close to the witness stand. "Doctor Romanoff, before we broke for lunch I asked if you had an opinion about the size, weight and gender of the person in the jump suit on the surveillance tape and you said you did." Warner glanced at the jury briefly. "Will you please give us your opinion now." Fourteen heads moved in unison from Warner to Romanoff like spectators at a tennis match.

"Certainly," Doctor Romanoff said as he turned to face the jury. "In my opinion, the person in the infamous jump suit is one, a female, two, five feet five inches and three, one hundred twenty-five pounds."

Fourteen pairs of eyes now shifted to Kimberly. She calmly looked at each juror as each sized up her height and weight. The rest of his testimony was tedious. However, the combination of video and science was very effective. Doctor Romanoff explained how he selected a single frame from the surveillance video in which the suspect was visible from head to toe. He then learned the identity of the seven persons appearing in that same frame. Each was brought to his office, given a number, measured extensively and weighed. Everyone was located precisely on a scale drawing of AWE's lobby and the distance each was from the suspect was measured and recorded on the plan. Using perspective and mathematics, Doctor Romanoff estimated the height and weight of the suspect. Finally he used standard anatomical differences such as hip and shoulder width to determine gender. Bottom line: Doctor Romanoff established what appeared to be a foolproof scientific basis for his opinion. Warner turned toward Riley and, with a touch of smugness, said, "Your witness counsellor."

Riley quickly surveyed the jury. The mood change was palpable. Most of them intentionally avoided making eye contact with him. Dr. Romanoff had delivered a mortal blow and now Riley had to demolish him as he had promised. The number seven juror looked Riley squarely in the eye challenging him to deliver on that promise.

"With the court's permission," Riley said, rising quickly out of his chair and walking toward the VCR on Warner's table, "may I use Mr. Warner's television set-up for a video of my own?" He retrieved a videotape from the large envelope he was holding as he waited for Judge Waters' permission.

Warner jumped to his feet with an objection.

"Grounds?" Waters asked.

"I've no idea what's in it?" Warner said, hands extended, shoulders hunched.

"This is cross. We'll find out together," the Judge answered. "Objection overruled. Permission granted."

All of the TV monitors came to life again. The scene was the now familiar lobby at AWE headquarters. Seven persons, three men and four women, stood in the same place as the seven in Doctor Romanoff's test frame. One at a time, three jumpsuited persons, their faces completely covered, entered the lobby through the revolving door and, in turn, walked directly to the spot where the suspect stood in Doctor Romanoff's test frame. Each had a large number one, two or three on their chest..

Warner scribbled a note to Sandy, "How in hell???"

"He's a resourceful bastard and probably a big pay-off to some idiot night watchman."

"Doctor, I can give you all of the physical measurements and the weight of each of the seven people in the photos." Riley paused for a dramatic effect. "Can you replicate your test here, for the judge and jury, and tell us the height, weight and gender of subjects one, two and three?"

Doctor Romanoff's eyes widened with fear. He looked to Warner for help.

"Objection," Warner yelled. "Side bar."

Judge Waters walked quickly to the far side of the bench.

"What's your problem?" he asked Warner.

"For God's sake, Judge, this is ... this is ... highly unusual," Warner began, nervously.

"Is it?" Judge Waters inquired. "One of the tests of a proven scientific method is its ability to be replicated by others. Heck," said the Judge, with a gesture toward Doctor Romanoff, "if he can't replicate it, then it sure as blazes isn't a reliable scientific method."

Judge Waters looked at Riley and frowned. "You haven't lost your flair for the dramatic, Riley, but do you realize if this guy can do it, your lady is a," the Judge drew his index finger across his throat, "gonner."

Riley nodded affirmatively, exuding confidence. Judge Waters shrugged. "O.K.," he said with finality. "The good doctor gets to do the test. But not here in front of everybody."

"And I want the seven people in that tape to be weighed and measured by Romanoff," Warner said angrily.

"Done," the Judge said.

"They'll go anywhere you say, Gus," Riley said with a grin. "But I'm hurt you don't trust me," he added facetiously.

When the courtroom cleared, Warner looked at Doctor Romanoff intently. "Can you do it?"

"I think so."

"Dammit, you better do it. You better damn well do it."

Boston, Harbor Towers, April 20. 5:00 a.m.
Gus Warner fumbled for the phone in his darkened bedroom and was barely awake when he answered it. "Who the hell is this?" he asked angrily.

"It's me, Fred Romanoff."

"Do you know what time it is?"

"Of course I do. But this is important."

Warner was now wide awake and his instincts told him a call from Romanoff at five o'clock in the morning could not be good news. He maneuvered his free hand until it came in contact with the switch on the night lamp next to the phone. He squinted briefly when the bright light hit his eyes. "Something tells me I'm not gonna like this," Warner said, now sitting on the edge of the bed.

"My method is sound and the math really works," Romanoff said nervously, "but . . ."

"Jesus, what do you mean but?"

"Well," Romanoff began haltingly, his uncertainty clearly evident.

"Dammit, will you just spit it out!"

"I will if you'll let me," Romanoff insisted, upset with Warner's interruption. "Riley can manipulate size, weight and gender," he added dejectedly.

Warner thought about that for a few seconds. "So let's outsmart him, dammit."

"Gus, it's not a matter of outsmarting Riley. The point is if Riley can manipulate weight and body size under that loose jumpsuit . . ."

"Then the killer could've done the same thing," Warner said angrily. "Dammit, you should've known," he added, raising his voice. "You should have told me you were playing a ... a damn guessing game."

"That's not fair. I told you I used standard, average tables. All the circumstantial evidence clearly points to Kimberly Hale. I just wanted to demonstrate it could have been her in the jumpsuit. You pushed for more and it was your big idea to put me on first."

"Shit, we've got no time for finger-pointing. Be in my office in an hour." Warner disconnected Romanoff and dialed quickly. "Sandy, sorry to wake you but Romanoff just called. We're in deep shit. Get to my office in an hour. We've got a lot of work to do. I'll explain when you get there." Warner slammed the phone down hard.

"Bad?" said his wife.

"Devastating," Warner yelled as he hurried toward the bathroom.

Suffolk Superior Court, 9:00a.m.
Judge Waters wasted no time. "Good morning," he said politely, a half smile aimed at the jurors. "You're on, Doctor Romanoff," he added, the smile quickly erased.

A very tired looking man stood in the witness box. Riley noticed and smiled. It was apparent that Romanoff had been up all night. Worse, Warner's eyes were red and his attempt to put on a happy face was not working.

"Attorney Riley, your witness," the judge said matter-of-factly.

Riley sensed there was trouble in the D.A.'s camp so he wasted no time going in for the kill. He began his cross-exam as soon as he rose from his chair, trying not to sound too smug. "Well, Doctor, did you complete your assignment?"

"Yes and no," Romanoff answered softly, no longer appearing as confident as he did on direct examination by Warner.

"Well, suppose you give us the no," Riley asked as he walked to the far end of the jury box, as far away from Romanoff as possible. All fourteen jurors followed Riley's progress across the courtroom. The air was thick with anticipation.

"Well," Romanoff began, as he cleared his throat with a nervous cough, "my math was accurate."

Riley cut him off quickly. "That sounds like the yes part of your answer," Riley said with a hint of sarcasm. "Please, Doctor, just give us the no."

Romanoff blushed slightly. "I started the assignment but stopped when I, er, realized you would not have gone to the trouble of using three fully costumed subjects unless you had planned a trap for me."

The jurors' heads turned in unison from Romanoff to Riley. "You suspected that I planned a trap for you?" Riley asked facetiously, a quick glance at the jury. "Now what kind of trap could I possibly have planned for you?" he added, enjoying the pained expression on Romanoff's face. Fourteen heads snapped back toward Romanoff.

"By adjusting sole and heel thickness with inserts in the combat boots and, or, adding padding on their heads under the helmet, you could and probably did obtain a two to three-inch variance in the subjects' height."

Warner sat stiffly, staring at Romanoff and avoiding eye contact with the jurors. However, he could feel their eyes on him.

"Good thinking, Doctor," Riley said as he moved quickly to the center of the jury box. "And did it occur to you, Doctor," Riley continued, emphasizing the word doctor with a hint of contempt, "that someone else could have done the very same thing."

Romanoff stood silently. He looked briefly at Warner and pursed his lips.

"Well, Doctor?" Riley insisted, staring intently into Romanoff's eyes.

"Yes," he answered softly.

"Please don't keep us in suspense, who, Doctor . . . who?" Riley demanded.

"Johnston's assassin."

Riley knew he had scored a major point. More importantly, it was written all over Warner's face and the jurors got the message. Now there was just one last nail to hammer firmly into Romanoff's coffin. "Is it fair to say you and Attorney Warner stayed up all night trying to figure out how to salvage your questionable testimony," Riley said, pointing at Warner for effect.

"Objection," Warner said loudly.

"Argumentative, Mr. Riley, "Judge Waters admonished Riley, "but overruled anyway."

Romanoff remained silent but that silence spoke volumes and was not lost on the jury.

"So do you want to change your testimony," Riley asked rhetorically.

"Yes," Romanoff replied sheepishly.

"Well, don't let me stop you," Riley said with a smile, "What is it now?"

Romanoff looked at the jury as he tried desperately to regain what was left of his dignity. "Accounting for possible adjustments, the height of the person in the subject video, in the AWE headquarters lobby, is in a range of from five feet, four inches to five feet, seven inches."

Riley was happy with the change in testimony, but Kimberly was in that range. He pressed Romanoff on one last point. "Would you like to guess the gender of my three volunteers?" Riley was now taunting Romanoff.

"No," he replied emphatically.

"Are you afraid of another trap?" Riley smiled. Several jurors laughed softly.

"Your honor," Riley said, not waiting for Romanoff's reply, "the three persons who participated in my little test are here in the courtroom. May they stand up so they can identify themselves?"

"Objection," Warner said.

"What grounds?" Waters insisted.

"They haven't been sworn," Warner replied, now sorry he objected in the first place.

"For heaven's sake," Judge Waters replied. "Riley, do you represent that the persons who stand up were in fact your subjects?"

"Of course, your Honor," Riley answered with a look of disdain aimed at Warner.

"Stand up, wherever you are," Judge Waters commanded whimsically. Three men in the front row stood up. It was clear their ages varied greatly and they were not the same height. "You may sit down," the Judge instructed.

"No further questions, your Honor," Riley said as he returned to counsel table.

Judge Waters banged his gavel. "We'll take a twenty-minute recess."

As the jurors filed out of the courtroom, they all glanced at Kimberly. She smiled politely. Warner jotted a note for Sandra, "The bitch is still in Romanoff's range!" Sandra scribbled back, "So are half the people in the courtroom; we've been torpedoed right in the wheelhouse."

Downsized

"You were wonderful," Kimberly said as she gave Riley a congratulatory hug. The brief celebration was interrupted by a commotion in the rear of the courtroom. It was Riley's assistant trying to muscle his way past two court officers who were about to eject him forcefully. Riley gave a signal to the officers to let him in. "We know where the surveillance video is," he said excitedly.

Riley was shocked by the news. "How the hell did you find it and who has it?"

"The IRS was auditing Tricia's for not declaring all cash purchases. The surveillance video showed people paying by cash for a variety of items and Tricia's accounting fell far short of what it should have been. Meanwhile, the video for February fourteenth was impounded and held for evidence until one of the agents finally woke up that it might have some importance to this case."

Kimberly was ecstatic. "My God that's wonderful news. When will we get it?"

"The agent informed Warner's office also and is delivering it to court tomorrow morning."

Riley looked worried and Kimberly noticed. "Dan, this is it, this means the case is over."

"Kimberly we have the case practically won. God forbid there is a glitch and they find that the video was tampered with."

"Dan, I'm going to try real hard to forget that you seem to doubt me. Just make sure the original is delivered, not a copy. That's very important."

Riley did not question her request and called his office for a subpoena to be served on the IRS requesting the original to be delivered. Things were now out of his hands which is not where a good trial lawyer wants to be.

Judge Waters sat behind a desk cluttered with legal papers from other cases. He was in his shirtsleeves, tie loosened, shirt collar open when Warner entered his lobby followed by Riley and Sandra. Warner was about to sit in one of the two chairs in front of the Judge's desk but stopped abruptly when Waters held up his hand. "Don't get comfortable, Gus," the Judge said. "This won't take long," he added, as he stood up and donned his robe. "Dan, I understand we'll be getting the missing surveillance tape for the night in question?"

"Yes Your Honor, and a subpoena has been served on the IRS keeper of records to make certain the original video is delivered." Riley replied confidently.

"And Gus, you want to suspend until we've reviewed the tapes?"

"Yes, Judge, because . . . "

Waters held up his hand. "Your request is denied."

"Gus, any redirect on Romanoff?"

"No Judge," Warner said, trying to look confident. However, Warner knew Riley had saved a few additional killer questions for Romanoff in case he tried to rehabilitate him. Riley smiled.

"Put on your next witness, Gus," Waters said, as he ushered everyone out.

The jury was already seated when the legal trio entered the courtroom. Kimberly greeted Riley with a bright smile. Riley answered her unspoken question.

"We've subpoenaed the original video tape," he said, standing as Judge Waters entered the room.

"Thank God," Kimberly replied, squeezing Riley's hand. "It'll be over soon."

.Warner stood, adjusted his jacket with the customary tug and called his next witness.

"Prosecution calls William Coine," he intoned.

Riley jumped to his feet. "Objection Judge," he said, not hiding his frustration with Warner's second surprise.

"I know," Judge Waters replied. "Coine is supposed to be Thursday. Objection Overruled. You may proceed with Mr. Coine, Mr. Warner," he added with a wave of his hand. Warner's face reddened slightly. Now the jurors knew he was putting Coine on out-of-order, a sign of desperation for the prosecution.

Bill Coine took the stand, looking every bit like the hard-boiled, experienced cop he had been for thirty years. When Warner was finished with Coine, the roller coaster which had taken a dive with Romanoff's testimony was on the way up again for the prosecution. Warner's sigh of relief was almost audible. Meanwhile, a court officer handed Riley a message slip: "The IRS keeper is here now with the video tape." Riley smiled, thankful that the IRS did not wait until the morning and signalled Judge Waters with a raised right hand.

"I'll see counsel in chambers," Waters said as he stood to leave. He stopped mid-stride and dismissed the jury for lunch.

Riley, Warner and Sandra sat in a tight semi-circle in front of a twenty-one inch television screen in Judge Waters' chambers. The keeper-of-the-records had just confirmed the chain of custody from Tricia's directly to the IRS Boston office. Judge Waters remained standing, behind Warner and slightly to the right.

"Show time," he said abruptly. A court officer closed the blinds, aimed the remote at the TV and Tricia's was back in business. Warner leaned forward in his chair as a female figure appeared in the upper left corner of the screen. He almost fell out of it when the face on the figure was Kimberly Hale's. The picture was grainy, but the beautiful young woman who entered the counter area at five minutes before nine p.m. on February 14th was definitely Kimberly. She appeared relaxed and nonchalant as she browsed through magazines, poured a cup of coffee, purchased three lottery scratch cards and a magazine. After a brief conversation with Freddie, Kimberly slowly walked out of the picture at thirteen minutes after nine.

Riley was amazed. It's exactly what she had written in her diary, he thought. He briefly wondered how she could have remembered so vividly a seemingly routine moment in her life. He stopped wondering and jumped to his feet, looking squarely at Judge Waters. "I move for an immediate dismissal of all counts," he said with a clenched fist, signalling victory. "My client was at Tricia's from 8:55 p.m. on the fourteenth until 9:13 p.m. She could not have been at AWE headquarters during the time of Johnston's murder," he added confidently with an angry glance at Warner.

"Hold your water, Dan," Waters admonished. "What do you say, Gus?"

Warner stood up, red faced. "I say, this is . . . is pure . . . God Almighty, Judge, this is pure bull crap."

"Gus, I can see how this tape is a shocker to you, but I'd prefer a more legal sounding argument if you don't mind," Judge Waters said as he returned to the chair behind his desk.

Sandra put her hand on Warner's shoulder and spoke calmly, slowly. "Your honor, the downsizing killer was highly skilled. We're talking clever disguises, a music box bomb and a sophisticated lap top booby trap. It would not be difficult for someone with these skills to doctor a video tape. The technology is available Judge and let's not forget that Kimberly Hale is in public relations with the Special Forces and . . ."

"Pure speculation," Riley said, interrupting.

"O.K.," Judge Waters said, hands in the air. "Everybody sit down and let's sort this out."

"Your honor," Riley began. Judge Waters stopped him. "Look, Dan," he said, gesturing toward Sandra.. "She's got a point. And you'd be arguing the same thing if you were in her shoes."

"Judge," Sandra urged confidently, "let's suspend and give us forty-eight hours to examine the tape."

Judge Waters gave that request a very brief consideration. "Yes to the request for a suspension but I'll only give you until ten tomorrow morning to analyze the video." Waters turned to Riley. "You better hope your client didn't mess around with that tape. If she did, she's a dead duck."

Riley now had time to prepare his cross examination of Coine, but he knew the video was going to be game, set and match one way or another. He returned to the courtroom and looked at Kimberly for several seconds before he spoke. He explained the judge's order and spoke as he closed his attache case. "Should I have to worry tonight about what Warner's team will find on that video?"

Kimberly frowned and then smiled her steel-like half smile. "Is it customary for all defense counsel to keep hinting that their clients are guilty or is it just a specialty of yours?"

Riley did not answer. Kimberly looked around to be certain her guards were not yet nearby. "Look at it this way, Dan," she began beguilingly. "If I'm innocent, the tape will prove it. And if I'm who Coine thinks I am, and I'm as good as they say . . . well, you'll have nothing to worry about." She gave Dan a wink.

The guards came and as Kimberly started to leave, she stopped and turned. "Dan, you were truly wonderful . . . and thanks for everything."

Dan Riley left the courtroom as bewildered about her guilt or innocence as he was when he first met Kimberly Hale.

<u>Suffolk Superior Court, April 21,10:00 a.m.</u>
"Well," Waters aimed his question at Warner, "did you have a productive night?"

"We did indeed, your Honor," he answered confidently, "and Sandra will do the honors."

That is not what Riley expected to hear. He figured even if Kimberly was the killer, she would never have pushed for the alibi video if it was flawed. "May it please Your Honor," he interrupted, "some electronics wizard apparently spent the night analyzing my client's alibi video to death and he's glaringly absent."

"He probably needs some sleep," Waters quipped with a brief smile.

"I'll bet he does, Judge," Riley said returning the smile but quickly erasing it, "but if Sandra is about to summarize that expert report, I should have been given a copy."

"True. Give him a copy, Gus," Waters said casually.

"We only have the original," Warner replied, trying to ignore the implication of a shoddy trial tactic. "We'll get him a copy as soon as Sandra's finished."

"Wrong," Waters said sternly. "Let's put the horse back in front of the cart. Give Dan the original . . . now," he insisted.

Sandra shook her head in disgust as she handed Riley a two and a half page report, typewritten and single-spaced. She had told Warner to make copies for Riley and the judge and Warner said no. Now Riley had them both on the defensive. Edits hastily made, some in blue ink and some in red, evidenced a rush job. Riley scanned the document quickly, expert eyes separating wheat from chaff. The scanning stopped abruptly at the first sentence in the last paragraph on page three. He jumped to his feet.

"Your Honor, I move for a dismissal of all charges and a dismissal of this case and for sanctions against the D.A.'s office," Riley exclaimed excitedly.

"Sit down and stay calm," Waters ordered.

"Preposterous," Warner shouted, jumping up like a shot, glaring angrily at Riley.

"Like hell," Riley yelled back, rising from his chair confrontationally.

Waters stood up, leaning forward on both hands, knuckles on his desk. "Both of you . . . sit down . . . now," he ordered. When both men sat down, Waters returned to his chair. In a calmer tone he inquired, "Now what in blazes has you so all fired up Dan?" Riley moved forward, sitting on the edge of his chair and handed the report to Waters. "Your Honor, look at the last page, last paragraph."

Waters complied. Riley quoted the key sentence as Waters read from the document. "The video tape tendered for inspection and analysis is authentic. Judge that's the bottom line in that report, and Warner just lied to you."

"How dare you," Warner sputtered angrily.

Waters frowned. "Gus, you told me point blank you had a productive night. What Riley just showed us is more destructive for your case than helpful."

"I press my motion," Riley insisted, more calmly now that Waters understood the issue.

"This is a hearing, Dan . . . and it will remain a hearing," Waters replied. "I don't knee-jerk dismissals, particularly in murder cases."

"I didn't lie, Judge, and I resent Riley's accusation," Warner said, unable to hide his anger.

"Well, instead of resentment, I'd like some explanation," Waters said, sitting back in his chair, arms folded across his chest. Warner leaned forward as he spoke, as if body English would buttress his argument. "Judge," he began softly, "last night our experts came to a dead end. The video brought into court yesterday is authentic. No doubt about it." Warner's mouth went dry as he spoke those words. His tongue felt like it was made of cotton. "What the rest of that report says," he pointed to the document in front of Waters, "is that it was very easy for Kimberly Hale to have made that tape and with equipment you can buy at Radio Shack." Waters raised both eyebrows. Riley squelched the urge to object and listened intently. "We traced her steps," Warner continued, ignoring the raised eyebrows, "starting at exactly 9:00 p.m. in Johnston's office. Remember, Judge, the killer stopped Johnston's grandfather clock at precisely that time. Then there's the fire in the wastebasket an hour later. That got the fire department to the building and the discovery of Johnston's body. We believe the killer knew that if the body wasn't discovered until eight or nine the next morning, the medical examiner's estimate of the time of death would not be precise."

"Have you noticed, Judge, this is sounding an awful lot like a fairy tale," Riley interrupted sarcastically.

"No interruptions, Dan, and I mean it," Waters admonished.

Warner shot a red hot look at Riley and continued. "Kimberly Hale needed precision, Judge. An autopsy performed only a couple of hours after the murder allows the M.E. to establish a time of death within a thirty-minute window. After twelve hours, there would be a two-to-three-hour spread and Tricia's video tape would just be some evidence of innocence, not an iron-clad alibi."

Judge Waters nodded agreement with that hypothesis. Riley shook his head in disbelief.

Warner continued confidently. "Cary Forte did the report, Judge, and he established that it was only a 25-minute walk from Johnston's office to Tricia's. That would put Kimberly Hale at Tricia's somewhere between nine twenty-five and nine-forty. All she had to do is spend eighteen minutes on camera with no one else in the store . . ."

"A bit risky, I would say," Waters chimed in.

"Kimberly Hale is a risk taker. Everything she did in this case ran a risk, but not this time Judge. It was Valentine's night. The next day was the store's last. The shelves were already depleted." Warner hesitated briefly as he checked his notes. "So now our killer has to know a few things about the surveillance system. That was easy. It was actually sold over-the-counter at Radio Shack. Tricia's was open from 6:00 a.m. until midnight . . . that's eighteen hours, Judge . . . ."

"I can add," Waters said with a smirk. Warner gave an apologetic nod and continued. "The system was limited to eight-hour tapes. Tricia's used three tapes per day for six hours each. There were twenty-one tapes in all for a seven-day period and then they were recycled. So Kimberly Hale knew she only had one tape to be concerned with, the one from six to midnight. With her skills, Judge, she would have no problem getting into Tricia's after hours through the service door in the alley behind the store. She removes the video tape from the VCR, replaces it with one of the others, carefully marking it so she could return it to the right place later, and then she goes home. Once back at the apartment, she simply puts the video tape into her own VCR, plugs it into a digital video camera and can go to bed while the six-hour VHS tape gets converted to digital."

"Why does she do that?" Waters inquired.

"Good question, Judge," Warner responded, bouyed by the fact he had Waters' full attention. "Any editing of the VHS tape would be visible. Once she has the alibi sequence on digital, she can make seamless edits on a personal computer with an Adobie Preview software package. In this case, all she had to do was transpose her segment with the one corresponding to her alibi time and change the date and time stamp. There was only one thing left to do Judge. Go back to Tricia's, attach her digital video camera into Tricia's VCR input and make a brand new six-hour tape showing her in the store from eight fifty-five to nine-thirteen. .

"I don't get it . . . completely," asked a slightly confused judge. "How come all those manipulations don't show up?"

"Because Judge, that's the beauty of digital. The edits are seamless. And the really clever part is putting it all back on the same tape as Tricia's VCR. It is Tricia's VCR that puts the final image on the tape and when it's tested, it has the same wave band as Tricia's VCR . . . simple, but ingenious, Judge."

"Can I speak now?" Riley asked, utterly frustrated at having to have kept silent for so long. "A major part of Gus's case has the killer hiding out in the trunk of Baxton's limo during the early morning hours on the seventeenth. Tricia's closed at midnight on the sixteenth. That means the killer had to sit and wait for six hours for the digital camera to input the new tape onto the VHS tape. There would be no time to get from Tricia's to Baxton's in time to pull off Van der Meer's murder."

"Good question, Gus. What about that?" Waters asked. Warner smiled. "I'm glad he asked Judge. We've established that Freddie, the counterman, did not wait until midnight on the last day. He closed the store at eleven on the night in question . . . and we have that on video tape," Warner added with a gotch-a look at Riley. "So Judge, Kimberly Hale had time to get to Baxton's and prepare for Van der Meer's execution by limo."

"Are you finished?" Riley asked. "I don't want to interrupt this nonsense unless you're really done."

"You want more?" Warner challenged. "I'll give you more . . . ."

"Enough," Waters interrupted. "You guys don't know when to quit, do you?" he added, shaking his head. "Dan, I'll hear you now."

"Judge, none of that speculation can be given to the jury. Every link in the chain of evidence must be proved beyond a reasonable doubt . . . every single one. There is one thing Gus did say that is crucial. He said it clear as a bell. If the medical examiner gets the body within two or three hours, the time of death is within a thirty-minute window and Kimberly Hale has an airtight alibi. Well, he did, and she does. There's no way a jury can find guilt beyond a reasonable doubt given the conclusion in that report," Riley gestured toward the document, still resting on Waters' desk. "The alibi tape is authentic, case closed, Judge."

Waters said nothing in reply and stared past Riley as if deep in thought. "I'll consider what I've just heard, read the report in its entirety and give you my decision at twelve noon."

Riley, Warner and Jones left the Judge's chambers without a clue. Worse, Riley found himself impressed with Forte's hypothesis. It was going to be a painful wait.

※※※

Kimberly greeted Riley with a bright, cheerful smile. "Well, do I get to have lunch a free woman?"

"Not quite," Riley replied. Kimberly looked worried but only briefly. "I can understand yes . . . and no is reasonably clear but explain not quite please."

Riley gave her a blow-by-blow explanation of Warner's presentation. She listened carefully and, when Riley finished, the smile returned. "Heck," Kimberly said with a school girl's enthusiasm, "I can make it from AWE headquarters to Tricia's in fifteen minutes. You can add ten more minutes if I stop at Dynasty in Chinatown for dim-sum take out."

"Just what in hell are you telling me?" Riley exclaimed.

"Just this," Kimberly said, now serious, "Warner's expert has a realistic scenario. If the killer was a cross-country star in high school like I was . . . and ran a seven-to-ten mile course through Boston every other day like I did, well, it would be easy to do what this Forte guy says I did."

"Jesus, that wasn't in your diary," Riley replied, not hiding his concern.

"I didn't think my jogging routine was important. Now it is . . . and I'm telling you because I now see the wisdom in my not testifying in my defense if that time should come."

Riley was shocked. "Don't tell me . . . you also know how to do the VHS-to-digital to VHS thing?"

Kimberly smiled again. "Let's keep some things a mystery. Look on the bright side," she added, holding up the Boston Globe front page. "It says here you demolished Romanoff yesterday. I'm confident you will do the same to Coine. So, if the trial goes forward and the jury sees the video tape, you can't lose."

She reached across the small wooden table separating them and held Riley's hand. "Who knows," she said wistfully, "maybe I'll have supper as a free woman."

<u>Suffolk Superior Court, Twelve Noon.</u>
Warner, Sandra, Riley and Kimberly were at their respective tables in front of a packed courtroom. Judge Waters entered quickly, as usual. "Court, all rise," intoned the court officer. "Be seated," ordered the Judge. He turned to face the jurors. "Thank you all for your patience," he said warmly. "Even though you were waiting, counsel and I were very busy. I spent most of the morning deciding a motion to dismiss made by Mr. Riley. You all have

worked hard and I noticed that you listened to all the evidence intently. That's why I've brought you here for my decision . . . ."

"Just make it," Warner said under his breath. Sandra heard it and gave him a gentle kick under the table. " . . . You heard Mr. Riley mention in his opening remarks that he had a witness that placed the defendant in Tricia's Market at a time of day that precluded her from being at the murder scene on February 14th . . . Mr. Johnston's murder. Now there is a surveillance video tape that was found the other day that clearly shows Ms. Hale in Tricia's from 8:55 to 9:13 p.m. on that day. Mr.Warner's technical experts worked on that tape last night and came to the conclusion that it was authentic."

A collective gasp from the spectators shattered the silence. Judge Waters gave a warning stare and continued. "Ladies and gentlemen, without more, I'd say that's an iron-clad alibi."

Warner cursed himself for conceding that point.

"But there is more, according to the District Attorney. The experts apparently were able to create a video, convert it to digital, move it around seemlessly, reverse the process and produce an authentic tape just like the one in this case"

Riley held his breath. Warner squirmed in his seat. Kimberly just sat there calmly.

"However," the Judge continued, "saying it is possible for the defendant to have manipulated that tape . . . even duplicating that effort . . . without a scintilla of evidence she did so, falls far short of the government's burden."

Riley leaned forward in anticipation, both fists on the table.

"So, I'm dismissing this case, there being no evidence upon which this . . . or any jury . . . could find guilt beyond a reasonable doubt."

Riley banged his fists once in triumph. Andy Grissom who had just arrived after returning from a secret mission to Afganistan, all six feet-two inches of him, stood in the first row with his arms held high.

Warner shrugged. "Shit happens," he added. He pushed his way through the crowd, leaving Sandra to pack up, wondering if the crushing loss would hurt his run for governor.

<u>27 Schooner Drive, Cohasset Harbor. 7:00 p.m.</u>
The view from Dan Riley's balcony was always spectacular. In early spring it was special. A blue-grey ocean reflected the twilight sky. The setting sun painted a few puffy clouds pink. Five lobster boats hugged their moorings in flat calm water while three sea gulls glided effortlessly overhead. A southeasterly breeze off the ocean was chilly,

but nothing that a light sweater couldn't handle. Dan and his wife, Ashley, were busy putting the finishing touches on a New England shore dinner -- lobster, steamers, potato salad and corn-on-the-cob. Kimberly and Andy Grissom stood side-by-side, leaning on a teak railing, gazing at the view. Kimberly watched one of the sea gulls dive into the water and come up with a small fish.

"Penny fer yer thoughts," Andy said softly.

"Make it a dollar and I'll tell you," Kimberly replied with a smile.

"Li'l dar . . .," Andy stopped mid-word about to succumb to an old habit, ". . . Ah mean Kimberly, it sure is great to see ya smilin'."

"Lately, I've had nothing to smile about. As for my thoughts," she pointed to one of the sea gulls as it made a dive. "I was just thinking how I used to wonder what it was like to be as free as that sea gull out there. Now I know what it's truly like to be free as a human being." Kimberly placed her hand on Andy's. "Prison is an awful place," she said, squeezing his hand affectionately. Kimberly rested her head on his chest, succumbing to the warmth and security of this big, gentle man's caring embrace.

"Well, all that bad stuff is behind ya now," Andy said reassuringly. "It is over, gal," he added for emphasis.

"I don't think it will ever truly be over," Kimberly said sadly.

Andy pulled back to get a good look at her. "What in blazes are ya'll sayin?"

"There are a lot of people out there who will always believe that I'm the downsizing killer . . . like Bill Coine."

"To hell with them and him. Besides, they jest don't count."

"Then there's Baxton."

"What in the dickens does he have to do with you?"

"The downsizing killer isn't finished," Kimberly said with a frown that caught Andy by surprise.

"Ya'll need to explain jes what in the devil ya mean by that," he said excitedly.

"Simply this. The killer advertised four murders. Baxton is number four. When he gets out of prison and then gets killed, all this legal nonsense will be resurrected . . . and I'm gonna need another air-tight alibi."

"Jesus, will ya'll remind me never to ask to buy yer thoughts. Scary stuff up there," Andy said, tapping Kimberly on the top of her head. Kimberly laughed. "Listen," Andy said, holding both her hands in his. "Maybe this here killer's clever enough to know when to quit. Heck, if the downsizin' dude is really clever, he'll probably figger somethin' for Baxton that's even better than killin' the bastard."

"You're absolutely right," Kimberly replied, hugging Andy tightly then backing away suddenly, smiling broadly. "You seem to have this downsizing killer dude down pat. Not only that, Captain Grissom, sir," she snapped a smart salute, "you always seem to say what I need to hear." She tapped her right index finger on Andy's big chest. "In fact, you are good medicine for me," she added flirtatiously.

"Well, Li'l . . . darlin'," he replied with a Texas twinkle in his eye and an impish grin, "Ah'll have ya know, Ah'm real good at playin' doctor."

"Soup's on," Riley interrupted, opening the balcony sliding glass door.

"And you, Captain Grissom, have been saved by the dinner bell," Kimberly said, laughing as the couple walked hand-in-hand from the darkening balcony into the bright lights of Riley's kitchen.

TWO YEARS LATER

<u>WALL STREET JOURNAL</u>
Yesterday, Arthur Greer, president of Jet Age Aircraft Co., Inc., again made aviation history when he co-piloted his eagerly awaited Stratocruiser to a trans-Atlantic commercial aircraft record. The sleek, supersonic corporate jet flew from Boston to London in two hours, twenty minutes. Greer is the oldest pilot to fly a plane at supersonic speeds, making the feat a double entry in the record books. Jason Todd, Chairman and CEO of Worldwide Enterprises, was on board for this maiden flight. Since replacing Bradford Baxton, III, Todd dropped Amalgamated from the company's name,

declaring at the time that the enterprise is more of a "WE" operation than AWEsome. Todd noted that Jet Age was the first acquisition since Baxton took the company's helm twenty years ago that was not decimated by downsizing and moved off-shore. As for WE's glowing success in the stock market, Todd says, "It's proof that corporate honesty is not only the best policy, it is the only policy."

TWO MORE YEARS LATER

<u>Fort Benning, Georgia. 7:30 a.m.</u>
Captain Kimberly Hale Grissom stood in front of a full length mirror mounted to the left of her bedroom door. It was a ritual she performed every day she donned a uniform. However, this time two faces stared back. Standing proudly to her right was a blonde, adorable three-year-old. Andrea Hale Grissom looked sharp in army fatigues. A gold star adorned each collar. "Mommy, do I have to wear a hat?" asked the precocious general.

"No, dear," Kimberly replied, brushing Andrea's golden hair back lovingly and kissing her forehead.

"Hey, where ya'll goin' so early on a trainin' holiday?" Andy said as he walked out of the bathroom, still wearing pajamas.

"General, shall we tell Major Grissom or do we keep our little outing a secret?" Kimberly replied whimsically.

Andrea smiled and laughed, "A secret, Mommy. I like secrets."

"There, Major, the General has spoken," Kimberly said, snapping a sharp salute at Andrea.

"When will ya'll be back?" Grissom wanted to know as he returned to bed.

Kimberly looked at her watch. It was seven thirty. "About one o'clock dear. We'll be back for lunch."

"Well that secret's gotta be bigger'n a bread box. Ya'll have fun. Ah'm goin' back to sleep."

<u>Same Day, Boston, District Attorney's office.</u>
<u>11:00 a.m.</u>
Sandra Jones read the e-mail message several times and still found it difficult to believe. She had ordered a trace on the source and was not happy when the report finally arrived. The e-mail was not traceable. She reached for the phone. "Get me the Attorney General, please." A short wait. A shorter ring. She grabbed the phone quickly. "Gus, I'm sorry to bother you, but I've got something that could be dynamite and I thought you'd like to be the first to know."

Downsized

Gus Warner decided to pass on a run for governor. He put his hat in the ring for Attorney General and won by the smallest margin in state history. He figured he would have a better chance to become governor after a successful tenure as the state's top lawyer.

"Sandra, you know I don't like surprises. Just tell me."

"Let me read it to you. One week from today, the man responsible for the so-called downsizing murders at Amalgamated Worldwide Enterprises a few years ago will be meeting with the man he hired to do the killing."

"Jesus, are you joking . . . is this a sick joke?"

"Hell no there's more."

"Well don't stop dammit."

Sandra shook her head and continued. "The place, Bunker Hill Monument, at a bench near the base of the monument with the words paddy whack carved into it. The time will be 10 a.m. Who is the man? Why spoil a surprise. You will recognize him when you see him."

"Is it signed?"

Sandra smiled. "It's an e-mail, Gus."

"You didn't tell me," he answered defensively.

"It ends with, be sure to have an ice cream while you wait. There is always an ice cream truck at the south entrance. Well, Gus, what do you think?"

"Jesus, I'm in a state of shock. Trace the damn thing."

"I Tried. No go. Someone used a highly sophisticated system. Something you'd find at the CIA, FBI and the military, to name a few."

"The military?" Gus Warner yelled. "Is that son-of-a-bitch Kimberly Hale still in the army? Jesus, she's the one who sent this. It's gotta be."

"Gus, calm down. We can't trace it. Who sent it is not important. Besides, you don't want people to think you can't get over losing that damn case. It's water under the bridge."

"Then why the hell did you call me?"

"I'm going to give it to the FBI. If this message is the real McCoy . . . and if the real killer shows up at Bunker Hill next week . . . you and I are gonna look bad for having tried to put a noose around little miss muffet's neck four years ago. I just thought you'd rather not be surprised by it."

"I guess I'm supposed to thank you," Warner said angrily.

"Not necessary. I'll keep you posted."

Sandra reached for the phone. "Get me Jim Pickering at the FBI."

One Week Later, Bunker Hill Monument. 10:00 a.m.

From a command post strategically located in a third floor condominium unit in Monument

Square, Sandra Jones and Jim Pickering had a great view of the park. The large front room windows faced west and put them at eye level with the paddy whack bench identified in the anonymous e-mail. The meeting place was very easily located. The words PADDY WHACK carved into the back of the wooden bench at the base of the monument in capital letters two inches high were still visible, although now covered with a thick coat of park green paint.

The task force, whimsically named The Minutemen, consisted of forty-four men and women. They took full advantage of the terrain on which they might have to fight their own, albeit small, Battle of Bunker Hill. Sandra and Jim were on their second cup of Dunkin' Donuts coffee when their radio crackled to life. "We've got a white male, five ten . . . maybe eleven, 180 to 190 pounds. He stopped to get a good look at the back of the bench and he's pacin' back and forth. He's acting like one of our guys."

Jim grabbed a pair of binoculars and focused on the man by the bench. "Can you I.D. the guy?"

"Nobody I know. He just wiped off the bench with a newspaper and sat down."

Monument Park is a perfect square consisting of several acres. It is circumscribed by Monument Street and bordered on all sides by brownstone apartment buildings and condos. There are only four entrances into the park. All are on street level and each is in the center of one of the sides of the large square. The park gently slopes upward from the base of the square to the top of what is left of the original Bunker Hill. The obelisk, a miniature likeness of the Washington Monument, rises 221 feet from the top of the hill. It is surrounded by large, open grassy areas with very few trees. Most of the "Minutemen" were in the vestibules of the surrounding buildings, two manned the ever present "Jimmy's on Top" ice cream truck at the south entrance and three replaced the attendants in the adjacent museum building. The paddy whack bench was a trap from which there was no escape. Three extremely powerful directional mikes were carefully hidden and aimed at the bench. The receiver and recorder were in the command post with Sandra and Jim. The stage was now set and ready for action. Suddenly, the first words from the bench tested the system, "Fuckin' asshole."

"Who's he talkin' to?" Jim wondered, now getting a better look at the man on the bench.

"Himself," Sandra answered, now looking through a pair of binoculars. "The guy's sitting on a wet bench, uncomfortable as hell, waiting for someone and he's referring to that someone . . . I think. Actually, he must be a good judge of people," she added with a smile.

"We've got company," a radio voice interrupted. "You ain't gonna believe this," the voice said excitedly, "But none other than Bradford Baxton is coming to visit the Bunker Hill Monument . . . south entrance."

Jim aimed his binoculars at the south entrance. From his vantage point, it was just below the crest of the hill. He zoomed in. A few seconds later a head and then shoulders appeared. "I'll be damned. It is Baxton, and he looks like shit."

"Four years in the slammer can do that to you," Sandra replied, adjusting her binoculars. She watched excitedly as Baxton completed his climb up the steps and walked toward the monument. He wore light brown slacks, a dark blue sport jacket and a blue and white striped shirt, opened at the collar. His hair was all white and appeared unkempt when a stiff breeze hit him from behind as he strode up the hill. A tan briefcase was gripped tightly in his left hand. His face was gaunt and he already appeared winded after a short walk up the gentle slope. The man on the bench did not react when he saw Baxton. Neither man showed any sign of recognition.

"Steady," Jim cautioned on the radio. "Don't anybody move until I give the word."

Baxton approached the bench but did not sit down. He looked around nervously.

"Dumb," Baxton said softly, tentatively.

"Dumber," the man on the bench replied sarcastically. "This is fuckin' stupid," he added.

"Jesus, they have a sign and a counter-sign," Jim said, smiling.

"And it fits," Sandra added.

"I've got the money," Baxton said nervously, pointing at the brief case.

"Oh my God," Sandra exclaimed, incredulous at what she was seeing and hearing.

"Just give it to me and let's get the fuck oudda here," the other man said, standing and reaching for the brief case.

Baxton jerked the briefcase out of reach. "I didn't want three people killed," Baxton said, "I just wantd one, dammit."

"Oh, my God," Sandra said again.

"Are you gettin' this shit," Jim yelled. The cop with the headset flashed an O.K. sign with thumb and forefinger. "Loud and clear," he added.

"Close in now," Jim commanded. "Keep'em in sight. No one gets outta here. Assume one or both men are armed." Jim turned to Sandra. "And they pay us for having this much fun," he said, as he resumed watching the task force members begin their move up Bunker Hill.

"I don't know nothin' about murder," the mystery man yelled. He grabbed the briefcase out of Baxton's hand.

"But you said you wanted to be paid," Baxton yelled to the man who was rapidly walking away.

"You asked for this meeting," the man said, as he started jogging toward the south entrance, carrying the briefcase under his arm like a running back carrying a football. The first sign of trouble came when he saw two men jump from the ice cream truck at the bottom of the south stairs. Trouble was certain when they drew their semi-automatic pistols. He turned wildly in every direction. There were at least twenty armed men that he could see running up the hill, forcing him back toward the monument. He dropped the briefcase and ran toward Baxton, pulling a thirty-eight caliber revolver out of a shoulder holster when he got within three feet of him.

"Gun," Jim yelled into his radio.

"You did this to me you sonofabitch," the man shouted, shoving the gun in Baxton's face.

"But you . . . you said you wanted the money," Baxton pleaded.

"I ain't takin' no murder rap on account of you," the man said, grabbing Baxton and shoving the muzzle of the pistol under his chin.

Thirty task force members formed a tight crescent from north to southwest, squeezing Baxton and the man with the gun up against the museum building. The museum doors were shut and locked.

Twelve visitors to the monument were safely in the back of the building, protected by three FBI agents.

"Drop your gun and assume the position," an F.B.I. agent yelled.

"No fuckin' way. I'm gettin' outta here or this bum gets his head blown off."

"You've got the wrong hostage," the agent yelled back. "He's nobody worth savin'."

Baxton began to cry. "Did you record my words with this man?" he asked, tears rolling down his cheeks.

"Yes, sir, we sure did," the agent confirmed.

Bill Coine's words, spoken so long ago, came crashing through Baxton's panic driven thoughts. "First she'll destroy you; then she'll kill you." "She did it," Baxton said softly to himself. That realization in a bizarre way had a calming effect. Baxton quickly assessed his rapidly deteriorating situation. His mind raced. How did this happen? Who was this man with the gun? Why did he write and demand payment for the murders and now deny it? How can I go back to prison? God Almighty, he thought. This time it will be for murder. It will be a state penitentiary. Walpole!

"Never," he yelled. "Never," he repeated even louder as he reached for the gunman's hand, found the man's trigger finger, closed his eyes and squeezed hard.

Sandra first saw Baxton's head jerk; then she heard the shot and watched Baxton's lifeless body fall to the ground. The man with the gun had no time to drop it. As far as the agents could see, he had just killed Baxton as Baxton struggled to break free. The man who almost made a quick and easy five hundred thousand dollars was dead before he hit the concrete walkway in front of the Bunker Hill Museum.

"Well," Jim said, "It took a while, but that little mess down there wraps up the downsizing murder case."

"Does it?" Sandra replied. "I wonder," she added, trying desperately to sort out what she just saw and heard. The yet unidentified dead man denied any murder involvement. Was it just a killer's propensity for denying his crimes? Both men accused the other of arranging the meeting. Sandra stopped wondering. Case closed sounded much better than who the devil knows what's going on here. She turned to Jim, put out her hand and said, "Good job. It's nice to know the Minutemen won <u>this</u> skirmish on Bunker Hill."

"Hey, call us any time," Jim replied with a grin.

Sandra suddenly looked worried.

"What's wrong?"

"Hell, Gus Warner's gonna die when I tell him. It'll be all over the news for days. He so much wanted to be governor."

"Hey, he can always run for school committee."

The two crime fighters left the command post laughing at the thought. Meanwhile, the king of downsizing's reign of corporate terror was finally over.

EPILOGUE

<u>Same Day, Fort Benning, Georgia. 8:00 p.m.</u>
Andrea looked up at Kimberly and smiled a proud smile as she finished her bedtime prayer without any prompting from Mommy.

"Mommy has something for her little angel," Kimberly said softly, lovingly, as she opened a small cardboard box. She placed the little music box on the night stand next to Andrea's bed. The base was square, but the figurine on top was a ballet dancer in a classic pose, arms gracefully lifted over her head. Kimberly wound the key and the music began. It was Lara's theme.

"This was my daddy's favorite song, darling, and now it will be ours."

"Good night, Mommy."

"Good night, dear."

<u>End</u>

Made in the USA
Columbia, SC
01 May 2018